In the Verge, first contact can be your last.

The starship *Nightbird* and her crew smuggles a band of renegade sesheyans to a new life of freedom, but treachery from within may kill them all. . . .

An unscrupulous mining corporation is hellbent on killing Helm Ragnarsson, but the down-on-his-luck mutant finds enemies and allies in unexpected places. . . .

The great negotiator who brought humanity together with the fraal is now old and worn beyond her years, but she has one last mission to complete. . . .

A team of archaeologists exploring ancient ruins discovers that the crumbling site is not so empty after all. . . .

Before he can rescue his friends from a band of murdering space pirates, a lonely mindwalker must come to terms with his own inner demons. . . .

D0816045

THE HARBINGER TRILOGY
Diane Duane

Volume One:
STARRISE AT CORRIVALE

Volume Two:
STORM AT ELDALA

Volume Three:
NIGHTFALL AT ALGEMRON
(April 2000)

STARFALL
Edited by Martin H. Greenberg

ZERO POINT
Richard Baker
(June 1999)

STAR DRIVE™

Starfall

EDITED BY

Martin H. Greenberg

STARFALL
©1999 TSR, Inc.
All Rights Reserved.

Distributed to the hobby, toy, and comic trade in the United States and Canada by regional distributors.

Distributed worldwide by Wizards of the Coast, Inc. and regional distributors.

Cover Art by Brom
First Printing: April 1999
Library of Congress Catalog Card Number: 98-88137

9 8 7 6 5 4 3 2 1

ISBN: 0-7869-1355-X
21355XXX1501

U.S., CANADA, ASIA,
PACIFIC, & LATIN AMERICA
Wizards of the Coast, Inc.
P.O. Box 707
Renton, WA 98057-0707
+1-800-324-6496

EUROPEAN HEADQUARTERS
Wizards of the Coast, Belgium
P.B. 2031
2600 Berchem
Belgium
+32-70-23-32-77

Visit our web-site at **www.tsr.com**

CONTENTS

"Point of Contraction" 1
  Gary A. Braunbeck

"The Scent of Evil" 23
  William H. Keith, Jr.

"Daybreak" 59
  Richard Baker

"Unlikely Allies" 99
  John Helfers

"The Life and Death of a Sleepwalker" 127
  Dean Wesley Smith

"The Great Negotiator" 147
  Kristine Kathryn Rusch

"Mind Over Matter" 167
  Matthew J. Costello

"He's A Good Little Boy" 199
  Michael A. Stackpole

"The Ninth Cylinder" 225
  Philip Athans

"A Killing Light" 249
  Robert Silverberg and Karen Haber

"De Profundiis" 287
  Diane Duane

Glossary 326

"POINT OF CONTRACTION"

GARY A. BRAUNBECK

AUGUST 13, 2502
VOIDCORP SURVEY CRUISER 547
BEYOND THE HAMMER'S STAR SYSTEM

After running from lab to lab, Copeland at last found Dr. Glover leaning against a railing on the observation deck, watching with intense, unblinking eyes as the shuttle bay doors began to open.

Glover looked like a man who knew he was about to meet a ghost.

"Dr. Glover?" said Copeland, trying to catch his breath. "I've been looking all over for you, sir."

"You would seem to have found me," said Glover, "clever fellow that you are."

"Is it . . . is it true?"

Glover tore his gaze away from the bay doors and gave his assistant a prism-glare of impatience, sadness, fear, and cautious elation. "Yes. It's an escape pod from the *Unity Gain*."

"Do we have any idea who's onboard?"

Glover turned his attention back to the docking bay. "The voice on the distress signal was confirmed as Blackmore's."

"Jesus Christ," whispered Copeland. "The *Unity Gain* was destroyed back in 2497."

Blackmore sighed and rubbed his temples. "I'm the one who sent Blackmore to that damned ship. All this time I've thought he was dead and that I was his executioner."

"That's a bit harsh, sir."

Glover shot his assistant a look that could have frozen fire. "Copeland, do you have any idea what happened on the *Unity Gain*?"

"Just that a lot of people died."

"No, not simply 'died,' kiddo. They were *expunged*. There is a great difference between the two. Have you ever read any of the reports or the transcriptions of Blackmore's communications while he was there?"

"I've heard that some of his broadcasts were . . . well, kind of crazy."

"You have no idea. Answer my question. Have you ever researched what happened there?"

"No, sir. I don't have the security clearance to access those records."

Glover laughed, but there was no humor in it. "Do you believe in God, Copeland?"

"I . . . I guess I never much thought about it."

"Neither did I . . . until now."

Glover took a deep breath, waved his assistant closer, and began to share some of the classified information about Thomas Blackmore and the fate of the *Unity Gain*.

* * * * *

OCTOBER 28, 2497
VOIDCORP MINING VESSEL 767, *UNITY GAIN*
NEAR THE LIGHTNING NEBULA

Viewed through the fish-eye lens of the ship's observation room iris, Blackmore thought the landing area of the

Unity Gain looked like a steel diamond peppered with ancient smokestacks, but what else should he have expected from a damn-near ancient mining vessel such as this? The area surrounding the pits and pads and terminal structures was a crazy quilt of rampaging colors—landing lights—to offset the cold blandness of the main terminus attached to it, slate-gray alloys macroscopically homogenized to resemble the space surrounding the massive vessel.

The small transport ship glided down, down, down into its designated pit, and the view from the iris vanished. Blackmore and the two fraal sent along with him exited the ship and stepped into the small receiving area where they were greeted by a heavily-armed man named Gillan, who identified himself as Chief of Security GV429 92SQV. Gillan quickly escorted them into a tram cart that would shuttle them through the labyrinthine underpassages of the ship to the area that had recently been isolated.

Once underway, Gillan leaned toward Blackmore and whispered, "Don't they give you the creeps?"

"Whispering won't do any good," replied Blackmore, perhaps a bit more loudly than was necessary. "Their psionic abilities are quite advanced. They also have names—Broca and Sagan. I call them that because I have trouble pronouncing their actual names—besides they seem to like the names I've given them. Plus they have excellent hearing—isn't that right?"

The fraal nodded their pale, bald heads, their large eyes squinting in what Blackmore had learned was their version of a smile. He'd long ago gotten used to their mythic appearances—the luminous skin and swept-back ears had been the hardest part for him, reminding him of those ancient drawings of elves—and found them to be gentle, remarkable, and ultimately trustworthy assistants.

Gillan looked back at the two fraal and offered a pathetic smile and wave, then turned to face the front of the tram as he continued speaking. "There have been some serious developments since you left. The Company decided it would be best for those Employees onboard who had families to be re-assigned, so we've now lost something like forty-three percent of our workforce and population. Add to that the vendors, entertainment complex workers, company prostitutes, and food staff—not to mention the people we've been forced to isolate—and we're down to about twenty-five percent of what we need to function, just barely a skeleton crew. If you can figure out what the hell is happening and put an end to it, then the Company will send everyone back and we can get back to work. Until then, every man and woman left aboard is at your disposal 'round the clock."

The tram came to an abrupt stop, nearly throwing Blackmore into the small control panel.

"For all intents and purposes, Doc," said Gillan, "you're now in charge of this vessel. Tell me what you need to have done and I'll see to it. Since you departed Aegis, there's been something like a riot on the isolation deck. Hell, they're probably still mopping up the blood."

"Some of them have erupted into actual violence?"

"Correct me if I'm wrong, Doc—I mean, I don't have your education and skill and deep psychological insights—but it seems to me you can't have a riot without violence. But what the hell do I know? Might've been their version of a tea party."

Blackmore nodded his head. Gillan was obviously under an unbelievable amount of stress. What crew remained had to sustain themselves on the supplies left behind, which meant severe rationing. Not only that, but odds were they were all functioning on little or no sleep. As if that weren't enough, the *Unity Gain* was trapped in emergency quarantine, forbidden to approach any system or station, until this crisis was resolved, so here was the crew—trapped, tired, hungry, and frightened.

"I'm sorry to have said something that stupid," said Blackmore. "I have no idea how you and the rest of the crew must be feeling right now."

Gillan waved it away. "Didn't mean to snap like that. I just . . . I had to send a message to my wife and kids explaining why I wasn't coming back."

"They weren't already onboard?"

"For a while. I got 'em the hell out of here after the tenth head-case tried to gouge his eyes out with a spoon."

"Why didn't you leave when the Company gave the okay for men with families to—?"

"Because one of the head-cases *knows* about my family. I mean, none of us knew this guy from Adam, and here he is telling me things about my wife and me and our kids that no one but us has ever known. If whatever is affecting these people gives them some kind of . . . of powers like that, then my leaving this ship ain't gonna make my family any safer. I can only do that here."

He removed a small hand-sized metal box from his pocket. "All of the self-destruct codes have been programmed into the mainframe of the vessel, Doc. We can only hold this orbit for so long.

"Please don't shoot the messenger, but if you can't come up with some answers in the next one-hundred-and-twelve hours, my orders are to evacuate the remaining crew, you and your companions included, and destroy the vessel."

"With the victims onboard?"

"Afraid so. If this is some kind of transmittable disease, we can't take the chance of letting it loose out there in the Verge Colonies."

"And if we refuse to leave?"

Gillan's eyes grew even more weary and sad. "I'm a decent man, Doc—least, I like to think I am. The idea of blowing up those folks along with the *Gain* makes me sick to the soul. To tell you the truth, I'm not even sure I'll be able to do it if and when the time comes. I'm fighting with my conscience enough as it is. Please don't force me to—"

Blackmore gripped Gillan's shoulder. "I'm sorry, truly. You're right; this will do us no good. There are enough uncertainties to deal with as it is."

Gillan faced the two fraal. "Broca, Sagan, I apologize if anything I've said or done has offended you. I got nothing against your race myself. I'm just looking out for everyone's own good."

The fraal understood, and accepted his apology. Silently.

Gillan reached up and rubbed his temples. "Wow. So that's what it feels like."

"Off-putting, isn't it?"

"You can say that again." He reached over and pressed the elevator button as Blackmore and the fraal climbed from the Tram. "Feel a little numb."

"They can induce psionic comas in a subject if necessary, even a great number of subjects. You might communicate that to the Powers That Be."

"Gotcha."

They entered the elevator and began their descent into Hell.

* * * * *

AUGUST 13, 2502
VOIDCORP SURVEY CRUISER 547
BEYOND THE HAMMER'S STAR SYSTEM

Glover seemed to lose some of his famous composure as the escape pod came into closer view.

"Are you sure you're all right, Doctor?" asked Copeland.

"Yes, dammit! Stop asking me that."

"Sorry, sir."

Glover looked at his assistant and briefly squeezed the man's arm. "Sorry. Guess I'm more anxious about this than I first thought."

For a moment, they watched as the severely damaged shell of the pod came closer, closer, closer.

"Why did you send him there, if I may ask?"

Glover turned away from the shuttle bay doors. "Certain crew members aboard the *Gain* started manifesting symptoms similar to those associated with the early stages of drivespace sickness—bouts of disorientation, sleeplessness, short tempers. Then they began to hallucinate, which in and of itself is not unheard of with drivespace sickness; what made it unusual was that all of these individuals—none of whom knew each other—were manifesting exactly the same hallucination. The physician aboard the *Gain* refused to provide specifics about the hallucinations. She was worried about the escalating acts of violence."

"They were attacking crew members?"

"No. Mostly it was self-mutilation: blinding themselves, jamming icepicks into the ears, worse. I agreed to send Blackmore along with his fraal assistants."

"Why fraal?"

"If it was as serious as the reports indicated, then the fraal could induce psionic comas in the more aggressive victims until Blackmore could figure it out. At first Blackmore didn't want the assignment, and I wasn't about to force him, but then the *Gain's* physician sent him a personal communiqué." Glover closed his eyes and took a deep breath. "It said: 'I have seen the source of The End. We are not insane. We are simply unworthy.' A few minutes after sending it, she stepped into a detritus chamber and jettisoned herself into space."

"Lord . . . "

"Blackmore knew her. I guess they'd gone to school together. After her suicide, he couldn't get out of here fast enough."

"Did he ever find out what caused her to do it?"

Glover turned back toward the bay doors. "Hopefully. We'll know soon enough."

* * * * *

OCTOBER 28, 2497
VOIDCORP MINING VESSEL 767, *UNITY GAIN*
NEAR THE LIGHTNING NEBULA

Blackmore heard the shrieks from below even before the elevator stopped.

"My God," he whispered.

Beside him, Broca and Sagan were trembling from the onslaught of violent neurobabble snaking up from below. The two quickly joined hands and raised their psionic shields to quiet the cacophony.

"You think it's bad now," said Gillan, "just wait until you're in there, which reminds me . . ."

He handed Blackmore a packet filled with high-density earplugs. "I strongly suggest you use these."

The elevator stopped and they stepped out onto the deck. Except for a small group of armed guards standing in front of massive steel doors, the area was empty. It felt like the entrance to a tomb. It sounded like the entrance to a torture chamber.

As they approached the doors, the guards stood and readied their weapons.

"You'll have to be accompanied by at least four men at all times," said Gillan. "On that I won't hear any arguments. We've got them all restrained, but there's always the chance that one of 'em might break free and we can't take any chances on your safety."

"Understood," said Blackmore, fumbling the plugs into his ears.

Are your psionic shields still up? he asked the fraal, knowing that they would be able to read his thoughts as easily as if he had spoken aloud.

Yes, we're fine.

Good. Don't let them down unless I tell you to do so.

The guards parted down the center; the four men assigned to Blackmore's team took their places at point, sides, and rear, and Gillan entered the security codes to open the massive doors.

"Welcome to the monkey house."

The doors groaned open and the eight of them entered. The first thing that assaulted Blackmore was the stench: sweat, blood, human waste, and rusting metal.

The second was the loud, hysterical howl of an animal in agony, so powerful that the industrial earplugs Blackmore was using might as well have been wads of cotton.

"Ohgodohgodohgod! It didn't work! I CAN STILL SEE IT!"

Blackmore turned and saw that the man who was shrieking those words was chained to an empty tank off in one corner. Where his eyes had once been were two dark, bloody pits. His hands were twisted into claws, their fingernails covered in viscera. He was trying to get at his eye sockets again, but the chains prevented him from getting his hands any higher than his waist. *"Why can I still see it? Why won't it go away? Oh God, look at it! LOOOOK AT IIIIIIT!"*

Blackmore reached into his bag and took out a hypodermic filled with lithiumerol and injected the man. It took a long time for the drug to do its work—nearly a minute—but then the man was completely unconscious.

Silence was suddenly everywhere, not just the absence of the previous noise. It was as if something had reached down into this pit and stolen away even the *memory* of sound.

Blackmore forced himself to look at the victims. Bleeding, broken, chained, manacled, tied with ropes or steel cables, there had to be at least two hundred, maybe more. The only sources of light came from ancient overhead sodium-vapor lamps and a few scattered barrel-fires.

The combination of the harsh light above and glowing flames below made everyone look like monstrosities from a Bosch painting.

"Sleeping Beauty's awake," said Gillan.

Blackmore took the plugs from out his ears. "What?"

"Sleeping Beauty," Gillan repeated. "She was the first one to get it. Everyone else since seems drawn to her. Come on, have a look."

They walked slowly through the space-trapped bedlam toward her.

She was no more than twelve years old, brown-haired and fair-skinned. She floated weightless in a colloidal suspension tank wearing a specially designed suit with a small opening at the base of her spine from which a shining serpentlike cable led to a primitive electronic terminal on the side of the tank.

"Did you do this?" asked Blackmore.

Gillan shook his head. "Hell, no. *They* did it, though I'm damned if I know where they got their hands on the materials. The tank's constructed of some kind of alloy I've never seen before. Don't even get me started on the suit."

Blackmore leaned closer. "It looks . . . my God . . . it looks *organic*."

"New skin," said Gillan. "That's what I called it, anyway. Now look up."

"What?"

"Look up."

Blackmore did and saw that the cable leading to the tank terminal broke off into dozens of small but no less shiny filaments, each one reaching upwards and out to hundreds of membranous sacks dangling from the ceiling. The sacks expanded and contracted in precise cadence, and that's when Blackmore became aware for the first time that every last one of the victims was breathing in exactly the same rhythm. Then he became aware of the pulsing of the floor; steady, strong, equally rhythmic. A heartbeat. The organic structure of this deck was changing; steel to tissue, wires to veins, fuel to blood.

"It's started spreading to some of the upper decks," said Gillan. "It's organic, all of it. Damnedest Rosetta Stone I ever seen."

"Whatever it is that's afflicting them is sentient—or at least, capable of creating sentience in inanimate matter."

"What you said."

Blackmore looked down and saw the stilled, massive body of a weren nearby, held in place by coils of copper easily three feet thick.

"That's CR727 99TSK," said Gillan. "He did a lot of the heavy work 'round the station. Last week he ran head-first into a wall, split his skull wide open, and destroyed his brain."

Blackmore knelt down and turned the weren's head toward the light. The head trauma was the worst he had ever seen in his entire career, but its brain. God, *its brain.*

* * * * *

October 30, 2497
Notes for transmission
VoidCorp Survey Cruiser 547, Unity Gain

In every single case of head trauma I've thus far encountered, the victims' brains have begun to regenerate themselves into a similar form. When comparing—and sometimes superimposing—the scans taken of each brain, I cannot help but be reminded of fractal patterns.

Whatever it is that's altering the structure of the vessel is also enabling the victims' brains to repair themselves, but to only one design. Weren, human, two mechalus, and four sesheyans—all of them now share a frighteningly similar brain structure.

As far as we can tell at this point, the membranous sacks are controlling the bodily functions of the victims. Everyone has his or her own "outerthought cluster" as they are called by the more lucid victims.

The girl in the tank—"Sleeping Beauty" as Gillan calls her—seems to be at the center of all physical and psionic activity. When she is awake, which is most of the time, the victims are docile, for the most part lucid (those who are still alive or whose brains have not yet fully regenerated) and cooperative. My fraal assistants no longer have to keep their psionic shields raised to squelch the neurobabble.

Sleeping Beauty rests every nine hours for exactly seven minutes. It is during this time that the victims become violent, hysterical, unreasonable and uncontrollable. Broca and Sagan have induced massive coma in them only twice so far, but it's a Herculean effort that drains them. I have instructed them not to induce these mass comas again until it is absolutely necessary. I fear for their health.

It has been a little over thirty minutes since Sleeping Beauty last awakened. I am going to attempt a guided mindwalk with her via Broca. After that, barring any injury, I'll finish the brain-wave readings and compare the results—which, I fear, may give evidence of something utterly fantastic occurring here. I cannot say any more for it would be mere speculation and we haven't time for that.

* * * * *

Blackmore stood at the head of the tank, staring into Sleeping Beauty's hazel eyes.

"Can you hear me?"

Yes, she replied through Broca.

"What's your name?"

Ylem. It is all our names.

"Ylem," whispered Blackmore.

"What the hell does that mean?" asked Gillan.

"It's an old physicist's term given to all theoretical matter that existed in the universe prior to the Big Bang." He turned back toward Ylem. "Can you tell me what is happening here?"

We are approaching the Meeting.

"Which Meeting?"

Between us and the Last Ones. The source of The End.

Blackmore decided to let that one go for now. "Why is this happening now?"

Because we have reached too far. We are about to touch the point of contraction.

"The point of contraction, you say? What does that mean?"

This time the answer did not come from Beauty but from the other victims chained throughout the chamber.

"Contraction . . ."

". . . the end of expansion . . ."

". . . snap-snap, the band snaps back . . ."

". . . trapped inside this darkness . . ."

". . . withering in pain . . ."

". . . and loneliness . . ."

". . . lonely . . ."

". . . lonely . . ."

". . . lonely blackboard sky of eternity."

Gillan shook his head and called for the rest of the guards.

Blackmore continued. "Who tells you these things?"

"The Last Ones . . ."

". . . who were the First Ones . . ."

". . . before the Life of Darkness became the Death in Light."

"They tell us . . ."

". . . sing us their songs . . ."

". . . give us things . . ."

". . . comfort us in sickness . . ."

". . . all this sickness . . ."

". . . make us well again after Seeing, after Becoming . . ."

"Becoming what?" asked Blackmore.

"What we should have been all along . . ."

". . . what we should be now . . ."

". . . if only we had been worthy . . ."

". . . if only we had not reached too far . . ."

". . . too far . . ."

". . . .so far . . ."

". . . so far into loneliness . . ."

". . . lonely, lonely, lonely . . ."

"They have been protecting us until now, but we're too close . . ."

". . . trapped inside this darkness . . ."

". . . withering in pain."

"They have touched some of us . . ."

". . . a warning . . ."

". . . turn back, turn back now . . ."

". . . even the Verge reaches an end . . ."

". . . maybe a long time coming, maybe very soon."

"They won't tell us . . ."

". . . because . . ."

". . . because it would frighten us too much . . ."

". . . so They show us . . ."

". . . reveal Themselves to us . . ."

". . . peekaboo . . ."

". . . say hello . . ."

". . . hello to Mommy and Daddy . . ."

". . . look up . . ."

". . . say hello . . .

". . . hello to Mommy and Daddy . . ."

Broca broke the mindwalk trail with Beauty and stumbled away. Gillan and Blackmore quickly followed.

"What's wrong?" asked Blackmore, taking gentle hold of Broca's arm.

Broca and Sagan joined hands. Blackmore understood the meaning under the sea of words and images the fraal had perceived while he used only puny words.

* * * * *

Gillan sat across from Blackmore at the desk in the medical lab as Blackmore explained.

"Point of contraction. It took me a moment to fully understand that."

"Mind sharing it with me or is it just your little secret?"

Blackmore grinned. He liked Gillan quite a lot. "Okay, look." He picked up a rubber surgical glove and slipped it over his hand. "Say my gloved hand represents the universe as we know it. See how tightly it fits? If you look close you can even see tiny strains in the material."

"With you so far."

"Good." Blackmore grabbed the bottom of the glove and began to stretch it even farther down his arm. "Any body of mass, be it this glove or the forces that hold the universe together, can take only so much stress. The universe has been expanding for millennia, and we've known that someday, somewhere, it is going to begin to contract, the Big Implosion. Now, the universe didn't expand as far as it did overnight, so it won't implode instantaneously either, but somewhere out there in the darkness the

universe *does come to its end*. That end, that final edge is
still connected to its point of origin because it's composed
of the same stuff—like the material in this glove. See the
end of it down here near my elbow? Imagine that to be the
end of the physical universe. Now see here where my
knuckles are starting to show through the material? Grab
hold of one of the fingers and pull it toward you."

"This isn't a big build-up to a fart joke, is it?"

"I'm not that clever. Go on, pull the material of the
finger as far as you can and hold it."

Gillan did so, until the middle finger of the glove was
the same distance from Blackmore's knuckles as was the
edge of the glove near his elbow.

"Your knuckles are almost tearing through the
material."

"Right. *That* is the Point of Contraction, the area of
maximum stress that draws all other factors back toward
it. Now let go."

Gillan did so at the same time as Blackmore, and the
glove nearly snapped completely from Blackmore's hand.

"That had to hurt," said Gillan.

"As a matter of fact, it did." Blackmore pulled the glove
off and threw it in a heap onto the table. "Do you see what
I'm getting at?"

"Not sure."

"This vessel, the *Unity Gain*, is orbiting at the precise
point of contraction of the physical universe. Old sailors
would call it the point of no return. There is now less of
the universe before us than behind us. Beyond where we
are at this moment, the universe has begun to implode."

"What's all this got to do with what's happening to
those people?"

Blackmore looked at the fraal for moral support, got it,
then took a deep breath and spoke in a rapid, deadly
cadence. "Do you know the old legend about the city of
Atlantis? That it saw its own destruction and so sent out

various chosen ones to the corners of the Earth to keep its culture alive? The poets, the physicians, the artists, the singers, the philosophers, et cetera.

"These people, these victims, have been contacted by a race that we never knew existed. Perhaps they call themselves the Ylem because they were here before the universe came into existence, I don't know. The Big Bang scattered these beings—maybe they're nothing more than pure consciousness—but scattered they were, all the way to the end of the physical universe. For eons they've been out there, far beyond any race's reach, watching us expand toward them, coming closer, and they know our fate; they're trapped in it. Writhing in pain for the weight of the knowledge they carry. Maybe they've been protecting us all along, keeping the end at bay because they suspected we'd never get that physically close, but we have. We've expanded out into the universe farther than we'd ever dreamed we'd go, and they can't protect us any longer. We've become too curious, too adventurous in our exploring. So all that's left to them is to somehow *frighten* us into turning back—or at least calling an end to the expansion. They have somehow managed to traverse the space between the End and the Point of Contraction to contact us. The contactees cannot deal with what they've been told and been shown, so they mutilate themselves. But these beings, whoever or whatever they are, want us to know just how powerful they are, so they are forcing a kind of accelerated evolution onto those who harmed themselves, bringing them closer to the state which they themselves existed in before the universe came into being, a preview of coming attractions, a warning of what will happen to us if we don't stop."

Gillan took a swig of liquor from the silver flask he'd been holding. "God."

"Quite possibly."

"Come again?"

"All of this is going to be seen as just so much smoke unless I can back it up with hard evidence. That's where the brain-wave readings come in. Let's go. I want to finish them before Sleeping Beauty takes another cat-nap."

* * * * *

OCTOBER 31, 2497
NOTES FOR TRANSMISSION
VOIDCORP SURVEY CRUISER 547, UNITY GAIN

This is absolutely incredible.
The brainwave patterns of all the victims match almost exactly. It's as if some kind of invisible traffic cop is directing their perceptions and thought processes to view reality as it wishes them to perceive it.
"We are all Ylem," said Sleeping Beauty.
God, I'm suddenly so scared.

* * * * *

OCTOBER 31, 2497
VOIDCORP MINING VESSEL 767, UNITY GAIN
NEAR THE LIGHTNING NEBULA

"What do you see?" Blackmore asked Beauty.
You'll see soon enough.

* * * * *

Blackmore said, "I think you and the rest of the crew should get off this vessel as soon as possible."
"I'll be damned if I'll leave the three of you here," said Gillan.
"Leave one emergency escape pod and give me the self-destruct mechanism. I'm not an idiot, my friend. My life is the most important thing to me."

"I'll evacuate the rest of the crew, but I'm staying with you."

"Fine. I don't have time to argue."

* * * * *

Alone now with the victims, the Children of Ylem, Blackmore, Gillan, and the fraal began their last session.

"Can you let me talk to them?" asked Blackmore.

Who? Mommy and Daddy?

"Yes."

Look up. Say hello.

Blackmore looked up into the forest of membranous sacks and saw them expand and contract at a dangerously rapid rate. The victims began to chant in unison, a song of sorts, and the atmosphere above their heads began to ripple and whirl until it created a spatial rip, a hole from which reached the hand of a Thing beyond all Things. It took hold of Gillan and pulled him to its bosom—

—but not before showing something very, very special to Blackmore and the fraal.

Time to go, said Beauty.

* * * * *

AUGUST 13, 2502
VOIDCORP SURVEY CRUISER 547
BEYOND THE HAMMER'S STAR SYSTEM

The emergency pod was now fully docked. Glover stood with Copeland at his side, both of them just staring at it.

"What do you expect to find?" Copeland asked.

"I expect to find an empty Trojan Horse." Glover turned a weary face toward the younger scientist. "If there is anything in there, it's not going to be in very good shape. Care to tell me why, my oh-so-astute assistant?"

Copeland looked quickly at the craft, then back towards his mentor. "I don't believe that model is equipped with either stardrive or cryo-units?"

"Nice to see that what I mistook for a coma in class was actually you being awestruck. You're right, so even if any survivors did manage to get on board, the life support system would have failed years ago."

Both scientists looked once more at the pod; it was an even more pathetic sight this close.

"Come on," said Glover.

They went down onto the deck and entered the pod.

They found the two fraal, their skin darkened and charred, huddled together in the corner, some areas of their flesh burnt so badly they were actually fused together.

Blackmore, pale, his hair pure white, sat staring at the controls with empty, bloody eye sockets, muttering, "Lonely, lonely, lonely . . ."

Glover reached out to touch his friend's shoulder when a small figure stepped from the shadows.

"Look up," said the girl known as Sleeping Beauty.

She clutched a breathing, membranous sack to her bosom.

"Look up," she repeated as the atmosphere began to ripple.

"Say hello to Mommy and Daddy."

About the Author

Gary A. Braunbeck writes poetically dark suspense and horror fiction, rich in detail and scope. Recent stories have appeared in *Robert Bloch's Psychos*, *Once Upon a Crime*, and *The Conspiracy Files*. His occasional foray into the mystery genre is no less accomplished, having appeared in anthologies such as *Danger in D.C.* and *Cat Crimes Takes a Vacation*. His recent short story collections, *Things Left Behind*, received excellent critical notice. He lives in Columbus, Ohio.

"The Scent of Evil"

WILLIAM H. KEITH, JR.

TA SHAA TA crouched on the hilltop above the tortured, eons-old ruins, the age-hoary words of the *Klimaar vach* rising to the star-rimmed glitter of the Great Wheel as he chanted the ancient litany. *We are one with this universe, one with the Great Wheel. We, this universe, are one. . . .*

The world's suns had set hours before, and numberless stars gleamed now within the Deep. The Great Wheel—the river of pale, star-dusted light humans called the Milky Way—arched high, touching the zenith of the Dolthan sky. Ta Shaa Ta raised his gangly arms, long fingers splayed against starlight. *Cast in beauty, lords of eternal night, we are in this universe, of this universe, one with this universe, as this universe is in us, of us, one with us across time unending. . . .*

He used no spoken words, of course. The litany was silent, projected on thoughts taking wing upon the night. Like most fraal, Ta Shaa Ta did not believe in God . . . not in the sense accepted by so many humans. The *Klimaar vach* was not a prayer, but there was undeniable comfort in the logic of the unfolding cadences that served as a kind of spiritual road map allowing individual fraal to find their place in a universe grown vast, strange, and at times indifferent.

He desperately needed to know who and what he was, but this night the universe held no answers.

He squatted on a flat slab of rock on the hilltop, his large head tipped far back as he stared into the uncaring sky. At his back, beyond the intrusive lights of the expedition's primary base, Dolthan VI was a vast dome-shadow against the stars, its ring system an edge-on, nearly vertical slash of pale-lit dust. This world, which the humans had named Lilith, was actually Dothan VI's fifth major moon—Dothan VIe according to the Survey Ephemeris—a chill and barren place balanced on the uncertain edge of habitability by the tidal stresses of its orbit about its gas giant primary.

Before him, at the bottom of the hill, the ruins rose in black towers and strange geometries, broken stone illuminated by starlight and the sharp glare of work lights from the excavation camp in the city's central plaza. Overhead, aurorae flared, blue-green and red. Dolthan VI's radiation fields were less energetic than those of many gas giants, but powerful enough still to energize the moon's ionosphere.

Lilith was not exactly prime real estate by either human or fraal standards. Without the tidal forces that warmed this moon, Lilith would have been locked in ice fields kilometers deep. As it was, an eons-old war between fire and ice continued here among the tortured crags and glaciers and rivers of sullen, molten rock as it had for two billion years. The air, though breathable by both fraal and humans, was thin and cold, made bitter by volcanic sulfur and the sharp, dead-egg tang of hydrogen sulfide, like the scent of evil. He pushed the thought away. Nonsense!

His reverie broken, Ta Shaa Ta rose to his feet. He was tired and confused. If only there were others of his kind here, others he could commune with, mindwalk with, but he was alone. As he'd been alone for much of the past twelve years he'd lived and worked among the humans.

"Ta-Ta!" a voice called from the slope below. The beam from a flashlight flicked and jittered against the night, sweeping here, then there in random sweeps. He could hear the clink and rasp of gravel as the heavy-footed man shuffled up the hillside. "Hey, Ta-Ta! You up there, boy?"

He didn't reply at once. Jeffrey Brody was one of those humans Ta Shaa Ta could take only in small doses. The man's grating voice, his abrasively familiar personality, and his mind closed to ways and thoughts other than his own made him painful to be near for more than brief periods of time.

Ta Shaa Ta didn't like the crude mangling of his public name, either, which Brody and some others had concocted for reasons he could only guess at. Without the all-important *shaa* component of the name, which referred to order, perfected control of body and mind, and discipline, the condescending "Ta-Ta" took on the meaning of an aimless or frustrated searching or thrashing about, what he had heard some humans call "spinning their wheels," though Ta Shaa Ta had never understood that particular phrase.

At last, though, he spoke, the Galactic Standard phrasing harsh to his ears. "I am here."

The light swept up the slope, pinning Ta Shaa Ta to the rock, dazzling large eyes adapted to levels of illumination dimmer than humans preferred. "Ta-Ta! Is that you? Boy, ya could've said somethin' and saved me a hike up this mountain! Whatcha doin' up here, all alone at night, huh?"

His eyes narrowed to slits, Ta Shaa Ta kept his voice calm. "I doubt that you would understand."

"Ahh, more of that Jiz Viddie stuff, I'll bet. Knowing the whichness of the why and the sound of one hand clappin'! Heh! Well, you can contemplate all the peace and universal oneness you like, but you'd better do it later. Prof. Radlevich is lookin' for ya. She wants t'know about those, ah, impressions you got today."

"All is in my report."

"Yeah, well, she has some questions, I guess. Y'know, the impressions you get from your, uh, *talents* aren't exactly the sort of thing you can put in a daily log. You're the expedition's expert on fraal and the fraal culture. That find you made this afternoon, well, I guess it's kind of important . . . like maybe it'll answer some of the big questions we have about this place. You'd best make yourself available to the expedition's leaders, y'know? Maybe they just won't pick up your contract, and then where'll you be, huh?"

Away from you, and away from vile, clumsy humans and the stink of their thoughts. This would not be a bad thing at all.

"I will come."

Vis Jiridiv—the phrase Brody persistently called "Jiz Viddie"—was not a religious order or brotherhood, though that was how the Fraal term *vis* was usually translated; the fraal were distinctly skeptical on matters of faith. It *was* a kind of philosophical association or school of thought, however, one that taught pacifistic acceptance of the things that could not be changed within a universe in which all were one. One did not fight the storm; one rode with it, and in the riding, one survived.

Picking his way through clinking shards of stone smashed from a long-forgotten tower's basalt facade eight hundred centuries before, Ta Shaa Ta followed the human back down the slope.

* * * * *

The frieze had been painstakingly carved from a three-meter sheet of white-smoke quartz. Once it had been part of an elaborate entablature adorning the structure the expedition had named "The Great Temple." Now it was in pieces, some shards no larger than her little finger, but

Diane Radlevich had laid the recovered fragments out on the top of her folding worktable beneath the plastic awning of the shelter the expedition was using as their excavation site HQ. She was well on her way to reassembling the central figure.

She looked up as Brody and Ta Shaa Ta approached.

"Here he is, Dr. Radlevich. Took some findin', but I did it!"

"Thanks, Jeff." She brushed her hair—unkempt, red, with a pale blond streak—back from her eyes. "Ta Shaa Ta! Please! Come and see what we've found!"

The fraal glided closer, his face, as always, revealing nothing of the thoughts behind those wrinkle-wreathed eyes. Barely a meter and a half tall and skeletally thin, his frame was partly concealed by the brown and red cloak he wore, which left his chest and torso bare. His skin, so pale it was nearly luminous in the night, seemed so translucently delicate that a breeze could have torn it. His grace made even Radlevich, slender as she was, feel as awkward as a newborn Tarshadi gangleleap. She found fraal beautiful, especially their eyes, dark windows opening into a very old wisdom . . . and perhaps some sadness as well.

"We're trying to reconstruct the central frieze," she told him. "I was wondering if you could tell us anything about these symbols."

Ta Shaa Ta reached out with one long finger and brushed across the crystalline surface. Instantly, characters incised within the stone glowed with a deep orange light, pulsed brightly, then faded. A smell, the faintest whiff of something like cinnamon and vinegar, lingered in the air.

Radlevich's eyes opened wide and her breath caught in her throat. "It's alive!"

"No, but it can draw energy from a touch, a *fraal's* touch."

"Those symbols, can you read them?"

"Can you read proto-Sumerian," the fraal replied, "or Egyptian hieroglyphics?"

"No."

"This is perhaps twelve to fourteen times older than the oldest language known to you on your world. The fraal who used these characters vanished a *very* long time ago." The wrinkles around his long and sharp-canted eyes deepened. "There is a *feeling*, however."

"Yes?"

"The same thoughts I have been receiving ever since you brought me to this place, a sense of . . . of gathering, of oneness, but also of isolation. These people felt very much alone."

She shook her head. Radlevich had worked with fraal before, but the insights possible through their mindwalking always surprised her. Many humans used extrasensory powers, but the fraal had taken those abilities to depths that seemed like pure magic.

"You know, I still don't understand how you can pick up so much. I thought postcognition could only reach back a short time into the past."

"This is not what you call postcognition," the fraal said. He hesitated, as though trying to put words to a wordless concept. "When an intelligent entity dies," he said after a moment, "there is an . . . an explosion of thought, of mind, of emotion . . . especially if the death was sudden or violent. These . . . call them psionic residues . . . can adhere to material in the vicinity for a very long time, to clothing or jewelry, to stones, especially large and massive ones, or to certain crystalline formations. A mindwalker with a certain sensitivity can read those residues, feel them as though the person who imprinted the area in the first place were still here."

"Psychometry," she said. Providing a name for the magic helped make it manageable, even if it did nothing for her understanding.

"As you say. We call it *et ghaj ic*. It means . . . well, the idea of an object's unique scent probably comes closest to the concept."

"Its scent? You can *smell* things like loneliness?"

"Of all the senses," Ta Shaa Ta replied, "the sense of smell is the oldest, the most basic, the most tightly bound with emotion, with thought itself."

She nodded, trying to understand. "I've heard that, for humans, at least, smell is the only one of the senses that works directly on the brain. Molecules in the air are actually interacting with receptors on a part of the brain itself instead of the extended nervous system."

Ta Shaa Ta cocked his head to the side, a gesture Radlevich had learned to associate with polite disagreement. "To an extent that is true, though the various psionic senses directly touch the brain as well."

"Oh. Of course."

She felt mildly embarrassed at the slip. Diane Radlevich tended to be a touch-it/see-it kind of person. She knew psionic skills existed in humans as well as fraal, but since she'd never experienced them for herself, if she thought of them at all, it was as a kind of murky and third-hand hearsay, something not usually taken into account.

He touched the crystal surface again, evoking once more the faint, mingled scents of spice and acid. "Can you smell it?" he asked. *"Gha,* cloves of *mirithid*, *fra* and *hyast*, with the faintest lingering trace of flowering *dril*. A hint of reddish-brown *kalamav*. A kind of golden *rhu'ev*, shading to yellow-green."

Ta Shaa Ta obviously had a sense of smell far more discerning, far more sensitive and finely tuned than Radlevich's.

"You smell things in color?"

"It's . . . difficult to explain. Unlike the human brain, the fraal olfactory cortex is closely associated with our visual cortex."

This suggested, too, that the emanations from the crystal affected his brain in markedly different ways than they did hers.

"What you are sensing," Ta Shaa Ta continued, "is not actual molecules adrift in the air, of course, but the stimulation of certain parts of your brain by the psionic residues implanted within this crystal."

"*Deliberately* planted?"

"Yes."

"But you're also sensing . . . things, scents, left here accidentally by whatever happened here thousands of years ago?"

"Yes." His large eyes closed, as though shutting out pain, then opened again. "Though I cannot tell you what the writing says, I can tell you that the thoughts deliberately associated with the writing speak of a terrible, empty, aching loneliness."

"And the . . . the accidental imprints?"

The fraal's head lifted, twin slits in the almost noseless face flaring wide. She could see the protective flaps inside the nostrils curling back, as though to admit more of the chill night breeze.

"Fear," he said. "Death. More loneliness . . . and an agonized sense of having taken the wrong path. Of loss. And . . ." He stopped, eyes closing again.

"And what?"

"Over all, the scent of evil."

"Oh, and what color does evil smell?" a man's voice demanded.

Radlevich started at the intrusion. How long had Vince Cathcart been standing there in the dark, listening?

Interesting, she thought. Ta Shaa Ta hadn't reacted to the voice at all; she suspected the fraal had known all along that the expedition's co-leader was there.

Cathcart walked up to the table and dropped a screen pad in front of Radlevich. He brushed against Ta Shaa Ta

as he reached across the crystal entablature and said,
"Oops. Watch it, frail."

"*Don't*," Radlevich flared, "call him that!" She had to
fight to contain the sharp upwelling of anger. She was sure
that the bump had been deliberate.

"Eh? Oh, sure." For Cathcart, it seemed a matter of
complete indifference. "Whatever. Listen, babe, I need
your print on this requisition."

"If you need me no longer," Ta Shaa Ta said, "I will
return to the main camp."

"Okay," she told him. "Thank you for coming. You've
been a tremendous help."

The fraal's hand appeared briefly from beneath his
robes, long fingers moving in a gesture of assent, then he
was gone.

Radlevich felt distressed at the interruption . . . and
impatient with Cathcart because of it. Ta Shaa Ta's discussion of thoughts and scents had been on the verge, she
thought, of opening for her a whole new way of looking at
things. She valued that cast of mind, valued it as much as
she hated the kind of mind that closed itself off from the
new or the strange. To her way of thinking, of all the tools,
character traits, and requirements of any scientist, the most
vital was an open mind.

"Jeez," Cathcart said. "What a crock!"

"What the hell do you mean?"

"All that stuff about smells, describing smells with
colors. I'm beginning to think frails go out of their way to
appear wise and mystical."

"I'm beginning to think you go out of your way to act
like a jerk." Picking up the screen pad, she glanced at the
column of supply requests, then rolled her thumb across
the "accept" box at the bottom. She handed it back without further comment.

"Thanks," he said. "By the way, it looks like we may be
getting visitors."

"What are you talking about?"

"Our portable deepscan's just picked up a ship entering the system. IFF registers as the *Tauran Vortana*, a 15,000 ton transport out of Tendril."

Radlevich's brow furrowed. "That doesn't make sense. The *Concordiat* can't even have gotten back to Tendril yet. Why would they send another transport out so soon?"

He gave a careless shrug. "Could be the Institute's decided our dig here is important enough to send out some more people, like we kept telling them before we left. Anyway, I thought you'd want to know, maybe do something about your hair."

She scowled at that, not that Cathcart was capable of taking notice. When she was in the field, she rarely paid attention to her hair . . . and having the time, facilities, or water to wash it was a luxury rarely enjoyed. Cathcart often found ways both subtle and not-so-subtle to hint that she should pay more attention to her appearance. The feeling that he cared less about her professional expertise than what she looked like infuriated her.

Maybe that was why she liked Ta Shaa Ta's company so much, she thought. There could never be anything even remotely sexual between them. When the fraal looked at her, he saw a *human*, not a woman with unwashed red hair or dirt caked under her nails or a sweat-soaked jumper. That kind of perception, she'd learned in the past few days, could be tremendously refreshing.

The man turned and started to go. "Cathcart?" she called.

"Yeah?"

"Just what is your problem with Ta Shaa Ta?"

"The frail? No problem."

"He's *fraal,* not 'frail.' You've got one hell of an attitude around him, and it's got to stop. We need him."

"Need him! " Cathcart laughed, a bark startlingly loud in the night. "For what?"

"For his insight into fraal thought and culture."

"Bull. You heard what he said. Him and his kind are eighty thousand years removed from the beings who built this place. He's got about as much insight into their thought and culture as you or I have into . . . I don't know . . . *homo neanderthalensis*. I do *not* buy all of that mystic crap. Smelling colors. Smelling evil, for chrissake! Why didn't you bring along a fortuneteller as well? He could tell us where to dig!"

"Ta Shaa Ta can tell us where to dig. His psychometric sense is quite strong."

"Yeah? What other magic tricks does the little creep do?"

She cocked her head to the side. "You're psiphobic, aren't you?"

"Huh? Nonsense!"

"People . . . beings with psionic powers scare you. That's why you ignore them, make fun of them, or run roughshod over them."

"I don't like fraal," he said, "because they're parasites. They're small, they're weak, they're decadent, and the only things they've accomplished in the past three hundred years have been with our help. Sycophantic belly-button gazers, all of 'em."

"I think you feel threatened by their psionic talents. Is it some kind of male power thing, Cathcart? You don't have it, so you have to run it down or pretend it doesn't exist?"

"I don't have to listen to this garbage. If I need instant analysis, I'll go talk to a psych AI." Abruptly, he turned and stalked out into the night.

"Just remember, Cathcart!" she called after him. "Right now we need our fraal mindwalker a hell of a lot more than we need you!"

She wasn't sure whether he'd heard her or not. Radle-vich sighed. Most humans she knew actually liked the fraal. Of all of the sapient species encountered thus far in humanity's outreach to the stars, the fraal had been with them the longest, even before humans had left the bounds of their own planet.

All of the known fraal were descendants of the *fraal-na kilach*, the People of the Crossing. They'd arrived in the Sol system more than ten thousand years ago aboard three immense sublight colony ships, city-vessels adrift on the sea of night for centuries, all records of their homeworld, their origins, lost. Their earliest encounters with primitive humans had not been happy ones; some of Earth's religions and ancient myths still showed traces of those unfortunate early contacts. Horrified at being mistaken for gods, the fraal had retreated, first to the remote, wilderness regions of the planet, then to Earth's moon, and later to more remote and well-hidden outposts in the outer solar system. Open contact hadn't been made until 2124.

Since then, collaboration with the fraal had led to spectacular advances in both the psychological and the physical sciences . . . not least of which had been the stardrive that opened a myriad of worlds to fraal and humanity alike. Radlevich found it hard to understand Cathcart's attitude.

Sometimes, she found it hard to understand any of them. The expedition consisted of forty-eight scientists— mostly xenoarchaeologists and xenotechnologists and a small army of assistants—plus a security detail of twenty mercs under the command of Major Saunders. Organized under the auspices of the Tauran Concord Institute of Applied Xenoarchaeology on Kendai, they'd received Concord funding to investigate a report—sold to the Institute by a freelance explorer—of spectacular alien ruins on Dothan VIe in the Strome system of the Verge. Together with their equipment and supplies for two months, the sixty-eight humans and one fraal of the expedition had boarded the free trader *Concordiat*, which had made the long passage to Dothan.

They'd arrived at the gas giant's moon five days earlier, and after depositing them at their base camp, the *Concordiat* had departed for Tendril once more, leaving them on their own for the next six weeks. They were now, perhaps, as isolated as any party of humans had ever been before, alone on a dead world, several light-years from the nearest known human settlement.

Her thoughts returned to the incoming ship Cathcart had mentioned, the *Tauran Vortana*. What was she doing here?

Something wasn't right. Only Dr. Borgan and the other board members and associates even knew the expedition was here; except for the officers and crew of the *Concordiat* and the tramp that had made the original discovery, only they knew that there was anything here worth examining.

The *Tauran Vortana* *must* have been sent by the Institute, must have launched within a week of the *Concordiat*'s departure, but why?

If they were sending more personnel, she thought wryly, it would be nice if they replaced Vince Cathcart as co-leader. The man was getting on her nerves with his self-absorption and conceit, and she didn't care for his attitude either. She meant what she'd yelled after Cathcart. She wished she had a dozen fraal mindwalkers of Ta Shaa Ta's caliber, or one less like Cathcart's.

She wondered what Ta Shaa Ta thought of him . . . or of her, for that matter. His opinion of humans in general, she imagined, probably wasn't very flattering. All things considered, it was probably good that fraal didn't express much in the way of emotions, at least, not in the way that humans did.

It would be nice, she thought, if emotions were something that could be switched off when they were no longer convenient.

* * * * *

It would be pleasant, Ta Shaa Ta thought as he walked up the hill above the ruined city, if emotions could simply be switched off. Most humans, he knew, thought that fraal had no emotions, but that was far from the truth. The fraal emotional range was somewhat narrower than in humans, true, and the feelings they had were not nearly so mercurial or changing, but Ta Shaa Ta could feel . . . and feel deeply.

What he was feeling now was an almost inconsolable sense of isolation and loneliness. It had been . . . what? Twelve years since he'd turned his back on his *vis* comrades and taken up this mercenary existence with the humans, choosing the Path of the Builder above the Path of the Wanderer. He'd made the choice deliberately, for reasons sound at the time.

He'd never guessed how lonely that decision would leave him. He was beginning to think that he had nothing whatsoever in common with the hulking, slow-thinking, clumsy, half-savage barbarians.

Ever since he'd entered this ancient fraal city and first inhaled the bittersweet miasma left hanging above the ruins, he'd been feeling the loneliness of the city's builders, an echo, no . . . a spur to his own emotions. He'd not expected to miss his own kind so much, so deeply.

It was said that fraal and humanity had much in common. Maybe that was why, Ta Shaa Ta reasoned, the humans were so infuriating at times. Similarities of body and thought could breed deep respect and affection . . . or deadly hatred. A slender difference of thought or attitude could seem far more threatening than the completely alien.

There were fraal, those who called themselves the Wanderers, who insisted that the People would be better off distancing themselves from humankind, even severing their ties and leaving human space entirely, before the ancient ways and thoughts were lost forever in the barbarian sea. Ta Shaa Ta had never completely agreed with that philosophy, even before he'd decided to become a Builder . . . but he was beginning to reconsider his position.

The fraal were not a melancholy people, but Ta Shaa Ta was finding the loneliness and the separation from the comrades of his *vis* unendurable.

"Evening, Ta-Ta. Out for a stroll?"

It was Saunders, the leader of the mercenary detachment assigned to the expedition as security. The man, big, hard, and blond, was seated on a boulder at the edge of the main camp, so silent in the darkness that Ta Shaa Ta, absorbed in his own thoughts, hadn't noticed him. He could smell the man, of course, and sense the turmoil of his thoughts . . . but the human camp was filled with smells and thoughts that the fraal had learned to block out in pure self-defense.

"I am returning from the dig," he replied. He kept walking. Military personnel—even rent-a-guards like Saunders's people—made Ta Shaa Ta nervous. Popular belief held that the fraal were pacifists. That was not true—save for the members of a few of the more introspective of the *vis*—but Ta Shaa Ta did believe that violence was the very *last* option open to any rational, civilized being. The human tendency toward violence as a first resort was one of the traits that made him despair at times. He was not at all comfortable around people like Saunders, who went about packing pistols on their hips.

"Working late at the office, huh?" the mercenary said, showing his teeth in the expression that Ta Shaa Ta knew meant friendliness, even though it really looked like something else entirely.

Human ways were so inexplicable. Was there *anything* the two species genuinely held in common?

Thunder rolled in the distance and continued to roll, growing louder. Ta Shaa Ta stopped and turned, looking toward the west. He'd thought at first that one of the several volcanoes near the base was erupting or that a storm was approaching, but he saw nothing but the stars and the black crags above the city. He looked up.

Lights, a tightly linked constellation of them, were descending from the night. In another moment, he could see the shape behind those lights, long, lean, and angular, the arrowhead-shape of a military corvette riding on thundering, precariously balanced induction fields. Settling toward the city, it raised clouds of dust that turned dazzling colors in the vessel's ventral lights. A fresh wind arose, bringing to Ta Shaa Ta the mingled scents of disturbed earth, ozone, and hot metal.

"That," Saunders said at the fraal's side, "is no damned transport!"

Laser fire and the plasma trail from charge weapons licked from turrets on the corvette's belly, and flame boiled skyward, dazzling against the night. The beams flickered again, and explosions wracked the main camp. Saunders was gone, running back to the sudden ants' nest of turmoil at the base, shouting for his men.

Ta Shaa Ta knew already that the mercs would never be able to defend against an attack from *that*. Tiny shadows darted against the glare of the landing lights—skycycles descending from the corvette's gaping hold.

Emotionless now and cold, he watched the troops land in the heart of the ruined city, followed by the slow-drifting warship. He wondered who the invaders were . . . and why, of all the places to visit in this vast galaxy, they had decided to come *here*.

*   *   *   *   *

Thunder howled as lightning strokes fell from a sky gone mad in whirlwinds of dust, smoke, and darkness. Her hands clamped down over her ears, her hair whipping

about her face, Radlevich looked up into the glare of spotlights and the flash and stab of turret-mounted lasers. An
explosion cracked nearby. She could hear people screaming now, even above the rumble of the ship's engines.

Twenty meters away, Lonnie Myers threw up his hands
and tumbled to the ground in a detonation of white flame,
half of his face burned away. "No!" she screamed, and
started toward him . . . but then a thunderclap of sound
slammed at her from behind, sending her sprawling.

At first, she though the laser bolts were being fired randomly into the camp. It took her a moment or two to realize that the attackers in fact were dropping a curtain of fire
between the archeologists' camp and the distant, hilltop
base, cutting off their panicked escape. Their shots seemed
designed to *herd* rather than kill, though in the next few
moments, several more scientists and assistants were
burned down as she watched in helpless, paralyzed horror.

Something whined low overhead and she glanced up.
Skycycles were spilling from the attacking vessel's open
hold, and armed men were descending on the camp from
every direction.

There was no place left to run, even when the laser barrage had ceased.

*   *   *   *   *

Fifteen minutes later, laughing men in mismatched
pieces of battle-scarred armor yanked Diane Radlevich out
from behind the stack of supply crates where she'd been
hiding, roughly tied her hands behind her, then dragged
her, kicking and struggling, across the dig camp. Fires
were burning against the night, filling the cold air with
thick, acrid smoke and silhouetting the black forms of several more armed and armored invaders.

They passed the sprawled and broken bodies of several
of her colleagues lying on the ground. Pete Haskell, Sue

Karrelton . . . God, *no!* Tears burned her eyes. How many of her people were dead? *Murderers!*

Two of the invaders dragged her to the awning where a tall, blond man was standing in a pool of light cast by a portable lamp. He was leaning on the worktable, studying the crystal entablature she'd been piecing together that evening.

She was unceremoniously tossed to the ground. "Here's another one, Cap'n!"

"Ha! A pretty one, too!"

"Who the hell are you people?" she demanded. Rolling onto her side, she elbowed herself into a sitting position. "You have no right—"

"You're in no position to talk about rights, darling," the blond man said.

Radlevich felt her breath catch in her throat as she looked up at the man towering over her. He was big—close to two meters tall—powerfully muscled beneath a heavy, molded durasteel and leather cuirass, and possessing the curiously vacant good looks of genetic manipulation. A bulky hand laser rode in a holster strapped low on his thigh. The pyramid logo of the Thuldan Empire was molded into the upper left breast of the cuirass.

Her eyes widened. "You're a Thuldan!"

She'd heard some pretty nasty stories about the Thuldans—how they were militaristic gene-manipulating imperialists, how they were out to conquer the universe, how they wanted to "enlighten" the rest of humanity under their benevolent rule.

All nonsense, of course, the Thuldans were no more stereotypical military imperialists than the Rigunmor Collective were all conniving traders, or the Hatire were all antitechnological religious fanatics. They *were* a martial people, however—every male was by right and duty a member of the Thuldan armed forces—and they had some rather distasteful attitudes, at least by the standards of most other governments within the Stellar Ring. They tended to be hard, aggressive, ruthless, and used to getting their way. The rest of the Stellar Ring feared them, and from what Radlevich knew of history, she thought it was with good reason.

The others in the attacking band weren't Thuldans, not recognizably so, at least. She'd seen eight or ten invaders so far, and they seemed a pretty mixed bag, from tall and pale to short and dark, with none of them particularly clean, well-groomed, or well-disciplined.

The big man chuckled, a sound like ice crackling, and his two associates joined in. "A Thuldan? Yeah. Maybe . . . *once,*" he said, "but all those parades and flags and speeches about honor and duty get on your nerves after a while, y'know?"

Her gaze shifted to the ship that had descended out of the night sky in glaring landing lights and flashing laser fire, and then she understood. The vessel didn't have the Thuldan insignia on its fuselage or stubby, delta wings, either. A crude cartoon of a naked woman was painted on the prow, with Standard letters spelling out *Bushwhacker* in flowing red script beneath. Streaks of rust and corrosion marred the hull in places and the black and red paint was chipped and patchy, unthinkable on a Thuldan corvette.

The ship looked more like a private rig than any government or military job, and one operated on a shoestring at that.

"Pirates," she said, and the word soured on her tongue. "Marauders."

"Right you are, sweetcakes," the Thuldan said, "though I prefer to think of myself as a businessman with an aggressive work ethic. Let's get to the point. Tell me what I want to know, and my friends here won't hurt you. Fight me, lie to me, do *anything* except answer my questions fully and truthfully, and you'll die. Instantly. Do we understand one another?"

"Hey," one of the men who'd dragged her here said, leering. He scratched a bristly cheek with the muzzle of an old charge pistol. "Let's not be *too* hasty with killin' her, Cap'n Narvis!"

"Agreed," a tall, almost cadaverous gray man with an eerie, gold-and-black prosthetic left eye said. "I see no problem with mixing business and pleasure here, especially in this case."

"Shaddup, Binny," said Captain Narvis. "You too, Kale. Nobody asked either of you. Well, sweetcakes? You understand me?"

She jerked her head up and down, a reluctant agreement. The pirate's eyes, pale blue and empty of emotion, were as cold as the voice despite the banter.

"Good. What's your name?"

"Radlevich. D-Diane Radlevich."

"What do you do here, Ms. Radlevich?"

"I'm . . . I'm the expedition's co-leader."

The Thuldan's face split in a broad grin filled with perfect teeth. "Bingo! Boys, I think we've found what we wanted!"

"Ask her where the cache is!" the cadaverous man said, his perfectly inflected words as cold as the man he served.

"My friend, Mr. Kale, seems anxious, Ms. Radlevich."

"C-cache? What cache?"

"Why are you people here, Ms. Radlevich?"

"We . . . I mean, the institute we work for, got a report of some ancient alien ruins on this world. We came to investigate—"

"Come, come, Ms. Radlevich," Narvis said. "We're all friends here. You can be frank. You were sent to find the Garvey Cache, weren't you?"

She blinked, caught off-guard. "The . . . what? No, that's just a story. A myth!"

"Indeed? On June 25th, 2414, a freelance scout named Garvey showed up at Brallis with an old map and talked about a gas giant's moon with a huge cavern filled with ancient fraal artifacts. Weapons. Ships. Things he couldn't even begin to describe. He outfitted his ship, the *Finders Keepers*, and took off to find the treasure. He was never seen again.

"Twenty-eight years later, Howard Larabee grounded on Alaundril and sold some very interesting artifacts of ancient fraal manufacture. Wouldn't tell anyone where he got them, but one of his crewmen got drunk and burbled away about a treasure cache on the moon of a gas giant in the Verge. His ship went out again and never came back either. Well, it *was* smack in the middle of the Second Galactic War. Ships disappear in war.

"I'm guessing your precious Concord got wind of the discovery, maybe Garvey's map, maybe vids of that crewman. I think they learned where the cache is. They know how valuable a storehouse of ancient fraal technology might be. Why, we can't even begin to imagine what technologies, what insights, what weapons might be hidden there, waiting, after all these years.

"So. You can tell me the truth, my dear. Borgan and Kelly and the others at your precious Institute, they know about the treasure, and they sent you here to find it, right?"

"No!" She shook her head. "I swear. The trader sold the location of this moon, of the ruins, but there wasn't anything in the report about a . . . a treasure! That *Finders Keepers* yarn has been floating around for years, but it's a myth, a spacer's legend, a yarn to swap over a few beers."

Narvis gestured toward the crystal entablature on the table."

"Then what is *this*?"

"A carving from the face of a building. It's fraal—"

"Ah!"

"We *don't* know about any cache!"

Two more of Narvis's men entered, dragging another man between them. Vince Cathcart landed in the dirt next to her, face covered with grime, hands bound at his back. One of the marauders kicked him in the ribs, and he whimpered, "Don't hurt me! Please! I don't know anything!"

" 'Nother one for ya, Cap'n Narvis! Caught 'im tryin' to sneak up the hill to the other camp."

"Well, well," Narvis said, inspecting the new catch, "and who are you?"

"Nobody!" Cathcart cried. "I'm . . . I'm nobody!" He looked around wildly, then stared at Radlevich. Tears were streaming down his face. "I work for *her!*"

Radlevich looked away, ashamed for Cathcart. Suddenly, Narvis reached down, grabbed her hair, and yanked her head around to face him. "One of your assistants, sweetheart? Maybe he *means* something to you? I wonder how long you could watch while my friends here cook him, real, real slow?"

Cathcart shrieked and started kicking at the ground, trying to get up, trying to get away. One of his captors gave him another kick, laying him out full-length in the dirt, and Radlevich caught the sharp stink of urine.

"Captain Narvis," Radlevich said, shaking her head, *"please.* I'm telling you the truth. This is a scientific expedition under the auspices of the Tauran Concord Institute of Applied Xenoarchaeology. We don't know about any cache!"

Narvis's gaze flicked higher, as he stared at someone behind her, someone she couldn't see. "Well?"

"She tells the truth," a new voice said. It was soft, the words precise, but with an odd but familiar inflection that sent a shiver down her spine. It sounded like Ta Shaa Ta.

"This other one," the voice went on, "is lying. His name is Cathcart, and he is co-leader of the expedition, with her."

"Mebee they just ain't found the stuff, yet," Binny said. "Mebee—"

An explosion blossomed, orange and yellow in the distance, briefly illuminating the hill above the city. Several

more blasts, and the hiss-crack of laser fire, sounded in the
night as a trio of skycycles hummed overhead.

"Hey, Cap'n?" a marauder called out, entering the pool
of light. He held up a portable comm unit. "Red's on the
line for ya!"

Narvis snatched the comm unit away from the
marauder, held it up, and stared into the small view screen.
"What the hell is it, Red? I'm busy!"

"Sorry, sir!" a tiny voice crackled back. "But they got
troops up here, and they're fighting back! They nailed
Butch and Oleg!"

"Okay, Red. Pull the boys back and set up a perimeter.
I'll handle it here." He lowered the comm and stared at
Radlevich. "If you're a scientific expedition, what are you
doing with troops?"

"It's a security detail," she said. "The Institute hired
them as protection against pirates."

Nallis and several of the others chuckled at that.

"How many?"

Radlevich's breath was coming faster now. Her heart
was hammering in her chest. There could be no possible
reason to try to hold anything back from these people, no
point to useless heroics, and if the bastards had a *mindwalker* with them . . .

"Twenty."

"How are they armed?"

"I . . . I'm not sure. I don't know much about guns.
They've got lasers, pistols and rifles."

"Jeez, boss. We could get burned real—"

"Quiet, Binny." He made a sharp gesture. "Get them out
of here. Put them with the others." Reaching down, he
lifted Radlevich's chin, caressing her cheek with his
thumb. "We'll talk more later, sweetcakes. I *promise*."

As two of them lifted her to her feet, she saw the fraal
and felt an almost explosive burst of relief. The voice had
sounded so much like Ta Shaa Ta, but this was a different

fraal. She wasn't very familiar with fraal anatomy, but she was pretty sure that this one was female, shorter and even more slender than Ta Shaa Ta, with a fuzz of pale, silver-blue hair at the back of her elongated head. Her gaze met Radlevich's with an impact that was nearly physical. The eyes were old . . . old and as cold as glacial ice.

Diane Radlevich knew then that none of them were going to leave Dothan VIe alive.

* * * * *

Dothan VIe was tidally locked with its huge primary, which meant that its day was as long as the time it took to circle the ringed giant—just over seventy-three hours.

The aurora-gilded sky was paling to deep blue, a prelude to the sunrise, when Ta Shaa Ta approached Major Saunders at the hilltop main base. "I may be able to help," he said. "I wish to offer my services as negotiator."

The man seemed surprised. "You? Why?"

"Because I am a Builder which, among other things, means I build paths between minds. Because fraal tend less toward emotionalism than humans and can better serve as intermediaries. Because it is something I can do."

He did not add that it was because he was worried about one human in particular. Diane Radlevich, of all of the humans with the expedition, had never patronized him, never ignored him, never given in to the prejudices that seemed inevitable between alien species. According to the Thuldan who called himself Captain Narvis, Radlevich was still alive . . . but might not be for much longer.

The pirate leader had raised Saunders by comm hours ago, demanding that the security detail lay down their weapons and give up along with all of the scientists at the main camp, or he would begin executing his prisoners. He claimed to be holding fourteen people, including both of the expedition's leaders, and he had given Saunders until dawn to surrender.

"What would be the point?" Saunders asked. "That Thuldan bastard's told us what he wants. What I don't know is whether surrendering like he's telling us to will save the rest our people . . . or if he intends to kill us all anyway! Dammit, I just don't know what to do!"

"Allowing me to negotiate will buy time," Ta Shaa Ta pointed out. "I might be able to learn what their plans are. I might even be able to signal you at an appropriate moment, allowing you to take action."

"Yeah, but will they even go for the idea?"

"I think they might. If these *are* pirates, then they don't want a fight. They have no ideology to defend, no honor to uphold. If they can get what they want without fighting, they will do so. Besides, I think they want something here, and they need us to help them find it."

He thought now that he knew what they were searching for.

Saunders looked at the fraal curiously. "Why are you doing this? I've been getting the feeling that you're not exactly thrilled working with humans."

"Am I so transparent?"

"Not really." The human smiled. "It's pretty hard to read you people. You don't exactly put your feelings on display, but I've heard Cathcart talking about you . . . heard him talking *to* you. I can imagine what it's like, being the only fraal in the party."

"Can you, Major Saunders?"

"Well . . . maybe not."

"Twelve years ago, I was of the Wanderers."

"That's . . . that's the fraal who don't want anything to do with humans, isn't it?"

"Not a universal sentiment, but essentially, yes. I lived within one of the great ships, the *Lu Harred Kal,* but I changed my path."

"Why?"

"I could not believe that it was best for my people to close themselves off from the Great Wheel of Thought."

Saunders nodded, though his surface thoughts suggested that he did not understand. "Ta-Ta, you're okay! Is there anything we can get for you? Anything you'll need?"

"Only one thing."

"Name it."

"I would appreciate it if you were to call me by my correct name."

Solemnly, the human extended his hand, a gesture the fraal knew but didn't entirely understand. "Ta *Shaa* Ta, you've got yourself a deal."

* * * * *

The pirates accepted the offer of a fraal negotiator, confirming Ta Shaa Ta's guess that they needed the active participation of the expedition's members for something.

"A fraal?" Narvis said, when Saunders told him. "Ha! Great! But no tricks, understand? You tell your fraal that we've got these people at gunpoint, and if he even twitches the wrong way, they're gonna die. He comes down here naked so we know he's not packing a gun or hiding a prosthetic, and you tell him we have a mindwalker of our own down here. If he so much as *thinks* about using his psionic powers on us, he's dead, the hostages are dead, and you people up on the hill will be dead in another few minutes. Get me?"

"We understand, Captain Narvis," Saunders replied. "There will be no tricks."

"Then send him on down here. I want to tell him just *exactly* what you people are going to do for us."

It was growing lighter as Ta Shaa Ta made his way back down the rocky slope and approached the perimeter where men in heavy, military-style body armor lurked among the cracked and fallen columns, walls, and towers of the city. He was prodded and groped by men searching for prosthetics that might conceal weapons, and one passed a small hand scanner over his body before he was led to the city's central plaza.

To his psionic sense, the thoughts of the men around him were a murmuring undercurrent, a rustle against the air, like a fetid breeze. He didn't need to scan to sense them. They made the air heavy with the wet, sour, yellow-green decay of *hulis ic*, the scent of evil.

Narvis and a dozen men were waiting for him there, grinning as he approached. The hostages were there as well, sitting in a long, bedraggled line on the ground with their hands behind their backs.

A pirate in a suit of antiquated, rust-red armor stood behind them, gripping a gleaming black and silver arc rifle. The warning was clear: a slip on Ta Shaa Ta's part and the hostages would be burned down.

He saw Diane Radlevich in the line of prisoners. He could catch the trapped-flutter of her wildly beating thoughts, feel, as she saw him, the unvoiced plea to be careful.

The other marauders clustered around the fraal. "Haw!" one cried, pointing. The yellow-green miasma was closer now, choking and intense. "They're even uglier without their clothes than they are with 'em!"

"Hey!" another shouted. "Are you a little boy fraal, or a little girl fraal? I can't tell!"

"Back off, boys," yelled Narivs. "He's here to help us work out a deal. Aren't you, fraal?"

"That's right," Ta Shaa Ta replied. "We wish to avoid further bloodshed. We assume that you do as well."

"Abso-damn-lutely. We don't want to kill anybody. If you'll help us get what we came for, you can be on your way in no time, no fuss, no problem!"

"Hey, how do we know we can trust him?" a skeletally thin pirate demanded.

"We got nothing to fear, boys." Narvis signaled the figure in the power armor. Instantly, the arc rifle shifted its aim, dropping a bright point of blood-ruby light against Ta Shaa Ta's naked chest. "He knows what happens if he steps out of line. Don't you, fraal?"

"I know."

"Besides, our boy here is a pacifist. Fraal never fight when they can talk instead!"

That statement elicited guffaws.

"I am of the *Vis Jiridiv*," Ta Shaa Ta said, drawing himself up a bit straighter. "Violence is the very last resort for any civilized being."

"How about that?" Narvis asked, looking at someone behind Ta Shaa Ta, out of his line of sight. "He tellin' the truth?"

Ta Shaa Ta felt a prickle of *suvah*, of knowing, even before he heard the other speak. "He tells the truth."

He turned and looked into the large, dark eyes of a female fraal. Her gaze was cold, as remote as the stars. She wore deep blue robes and the *ahu jisha* pendant of an Adept of the *Vis Orishak*.

"Meet Orid Lu Jic," Narvis announced.

Their minds touched. Her thoughts were as cold as her gaze. *You must obey these humans. I will give warning if you attempt to use psionic . . .*

. . . psionic weapons against them, I know, but why do you walk with these . . .

. . . pirates? Brigands? I have no special love for humans, or for their ideas of . . .

. . . of right and wrong. Yes. But why . . .

. . . do I serve them? I serve myself. The fraal have nothing in common . . .

. . . with the humans. I feel that way myself, very often. Yet we hold . . .

. . . some things . . .

. . . in common. The scent . . .

. . . of hulis ic. . .
. . . of hulis ic . . .
. . . is strong . . .
. . . but stronger in these . . .
. . . in these . . .
. . . who walk alone . . .

It seemed there were degrees of evil and loneliness. The scent of evil was something he'd sensed in all humans to one degree or another, but not until he'd entered the pirate camp had he sensed *true* evil, stifling, foul.

"C'mon, you two," Narvis snapped. "Speak out loud. None of that T-P crap!"

The touch of their minds had lasted only a couple of seconds. Narvis appeared unsettled; possibly he was wondering if he could trust one fraal against another.

Ta Shaa Ta had sensed Orid Lu Jic's determination to warn the pirates if he began gathering the energy necessary to launch a psionic assault.

Do you feel the oppression of this place? he asked, his mental voice soft. He took a deep breath, drinking in the sea of psionic impressions left on this dying moon. *Do you feel the loneliness of those who built this place?*

I feel . . . that they were as alone as we . . .
. . . cut off from the Homeworld . . .
. . . as are we. . . .
. . . and from one another . . .
. . . as are we . . .

The fraal who had journeyed to the Sol system ten thousand years ago had lost all record of where they'd come from, of what world, of what sun the fraal had first called home. Theirs could not have been an isolated case. The city on Dolthan VIe had been built by another fraal offshoot, lost wanderers, alone in a galaxy of surpassing depth and vastness. They had lived here . . . built here.

In the end, they had died here, fighting with one another seventy thousand years before Ta Shaa Ta's ancestors had arrived in the Sol system.

The ruined city's death had been a suicide.

Release . . . she thought.

They fought one another.

As . . . as . . . do we . . . Her thought faltered, the link trembling at the verge of breaking down completely. *Among the humans, we are so alone!*

. . . so alone . . .

It was true. Fraal reproduction rates were far lower than those of the humans, a compensation for their longer life spans. Fraal culture, the fraal sense of worth, of adventure, of outreach, all were in danger of being subsumed into the vast tide of burgeoning, warring, barbarian humankind.

By working with the humans, he thought, *by abandoning my vis and becoming a Builder, I hope to find our lost Homeworld, our sundered People. . . .*

. . . but not in a place such as this . . . .

. . . not in a place such as this, no, but I might yet find clues that will put me on the proper path. To find that path, I must work with the humans, and not . . .

. . . and not against them . . .

. . . or even simply in parallel with them. We need their help, or we are lost . . .

. . . we are lost . . .

Ta Shaa Ta gathered his mental energies, like a strong man clenching his fist for a first blow. He knew she sensed it, but her thoughts were spinning, now. Disjointed. She was lost in the terrible loneliness of this place, of loneliness of her own mind.

We have nothing in common with the humans! The thought was a mental shriek.

We do. More than you realize. They are capable of great evil . . . as are we.

. . . as are we!

They are capable of recognizing evil, of fighting against it.

He could sense the mind of the human inside the power armor, a dark green bubbling of surface thoughts. There was greed there and self-centered preening and a vile, frothing lust. When Narvis's people had what they wanted, the men in the archeological expedition would be killed. The women, though, the pretty ones, would be kept alive for a time. The red dot of targeting laser light on Ta Shaa Ta's breast wavered as a succession of wandering, brutally erotic images centered on the expected celebration promised for that night flickered through the barbarian's mind.

What . . . is . . . evil?

Destroying the individual. Mutilating the spirit. Crippling potential. Twisting personality. Hurting others to advance self. Using them as tools. Wasting mind. All bear the hulis ic *for humans, as well as for fraal. . . .*

He felt her struggling against the closing trap of her own thoughts. *Guilt.* She'd walled herself up against her own people, against herself for so long.

You embraced the hulis ic, he told her.

You get used to hulis ic *after a while. Eventually . . .*

. . . you learn. . .

. . . to like it. . . .

. . . to like it. . . .

As she screamed, he struck.

The fraal called it *gorud chah,* deaththrust, a slender, hot, needle of psychic energy riding the arc-gunner's thoughts and exploding deep within his brain. The power armor's hydraulics locked in place as the gunner screamed. Pivoting, Ta Shaa Ta whipped the steel-rigid blade of his outstretched hand into the side of the head of the pirate nearest him, snapping the man's neck before he could draw a single quick gasp of a breath.

"Stop him!" Narvis yelled.

Like flowing water, Ta Shaa Ta moved forward, slipping past the falling body of the marauder, focusing all of his strength into a stiff-fingered stab into another pirate's throat. As the man battled for air through a crushed larynx, the fraal plucked the falling laser rifle from the air in front of him, snapped it around, and loosed a bolt of coherent light that burned through a gunman's skull, just above his prosthetic left eye.

Now! The thought, mustered and hurled with the same power as the mind blast, was directed at Saunders. There would be no time to wait for rescue, however. Ta Shaa Ta killed another pirate standing near the prisoners . . . and then another.

Narvis had his own laser out of its holster now was bringing it up in a two-handed grip. Ta Shaa Ta dropped a fraction of a second before the pirate captain fired, mustering a mind blast in reply that smashed Narvis back a step, with blood spilling from ears, nose, and eyes, and when he screamed the sound was strangled to a harsh burble.

Crouched low, Ta Shaa Ta launched himself in a leap that carried him over the heads of the bound prisoners sitting on the ground. Dropping the laser, he grabbed the arc rifle instead, still clutched in the dead trooper's hands.

The arc gun's targeting laser found a running pirate as the fraal's slender finger closed on the firing switch. A laser bolt seared the air, followed in an instant by a lightning bolt riding the path of ionization, exploding the running man's chest in flame, thunder, and a burst of greasy smoke.

Spinning right, he took aim at the grounded pirate ship, resting at the edge of the city plaza a hundred meters away, targeting the weapons turrets. There would be men aboard that ship still, and some might be panicked enough to open fire, even at the risk of hitting their own people.

Several rounds snapped past his head. Turning back, he loosed several more bolts in a savage *crack-crack-crack* of lightning.

Most of the surviving pirates had already thrown down their weapons and were fleeing wildly. One, however, braver or more lost in battle lust than the others, advanced toward the line of prisoners, firing a laser rifle from his shoulder above the captives' heads, trying to burn down the smoothly shifting, slender form of the fraal who was sheltering behind the still-erect husk of power-suit armor. One round blasted a mist of molten ceramic from the armor's shoulder guard, splattering the side of Ta Shaa Ta's face with white-hot pain. A blur topped by red-blond hair launched itself from the line of prisoners. Diane Radlevich, hands still tied, struck the pirate rifleman hard across the legs, sending them both down in a struggling tangle.

Ta Shaa Ta vaulted the line of prisoners again. He couldn't use the arc gun without the danger of burning Radlevich. Instead, he reached past her, grabbed the pirate's head and snapped his neck.

"Thank you," he said.

"Don't mention it!" Her voice was cracked with thirst, fear, or some other emotion.

He pivoted once again at a metallic clatter of stones, raising the arc rifle for another assault . . . but held his fire when he saw Major Saunders and a number of security troops spilling into the city plaza.

Thunder rolled, and a sudden, stiff wind lashed at them with stinging dust and grit. A hundred meters away, the *Bushwacker*, the marauder corvette, was rising on hard-pressed inductors. Whoever was still alive on board had evidently decided to abandon the field . . . and the world of Lilith. Saunders's people opened fire, a snapping, hissing barrage of lasers and particle gun bolts, but the *Bushwacker* continued to rise, turning slowly, then accelerating toward the east.

The crack of its departing sonic boom lingered for several seconds afterward.

Saunders caught him with a strong arm around his shoulders as he slumped, weapon clattering to the ground at his feet.

He was exhausted, utterly drained by a burst of physical and mental exertion that had lasted all of ten seconds, but there was one thing more he needed to do. . . .

Orid Lu Jic lay on her back in the spill of her blue robes. Narvis's shot had missed him and struck her. He could sense the rapid flutter of her heartbeat within the blood-filled crater in her side.

I am sorry!

Her thoughts, like her heartbeat, were fading already. *After a time, the smell really wasn't that bad.*

The clean air is better. You can breathe deeply again, my sister.

Reaching down, his long fingers touched her head as he focused his final thought for her, granting her Release.

* * * * *

Diane Radlevich found Ta Shaa Ta later, after the bodies had been gathered in careful rows for burial, after the survivors had had time to realize that they were, in fact, alive. The sun hung low in the eastern sky, illuminating the vast crescent of Dolthan VI and gilding the knife-slash rings in gold-white glory. He was clad again in his red-brown robes as he listened to Vince Cathcart.

"Man, that was *something*," the expedition's co-leader was saying, eyes wide. "Never seen anything like it! Where did you learn to *move* like that?"

"The *Vis Jiridiv* is a martial order," the fraal replied. "You might call them a brotherhood of warrior philosophers. The exact martial form is called *du shaa*. The word '*shaa*' denotes perfected control of mind and body."

"But . . . but I thought you guys were pacifists! Violence is the last resort for intelligent beings and all that."

"Indeed, it is, but the brotherhood's adepts are trained to know when *only* the last resort will suffice."

"I guess . . . I guess I should thank you. . . ." His mind betrayed his confusion—a confusion of prejudices exposed. Ta Shaa Ta could feel the man's discomfort as he finally, reluctantly, stuck out a hand. "Thank you, Ta Shaa Ta. I guess . . . I guess you're okay."

Gravely, the fraal accepted the human's hand.

"Ta Shaa Ta," Radlevich said, approaching the two, "are you all right?"

Lightly, he touched the blistered side of his face. "The injury was minor."

"I . . . I meant the other fraal."

"Orid Lu Jic. A terrible waste of mind and thought. She was . . . lonely."

"As are you."

"I was." His long fingers spread in an indecipherable gesture. "The fraal are a social species," Ta Shaa Ta told her. "We enjoy the close company of our own kind and find comfort, solace, and peace in numbers. Those of us who have chosen more lonely paths, isolation, the company of aliens, at times suffer. . . ."

"You could have joined her, I suppose."

"Perhaps. The cost would have been too high. You can be isolated from your own kind. You can also be isolated from yourself. The last is infinitely worse than the first."

"If there's anything we can do . . ." she began.

"I still hope to find some clue to the location of the fraal homeworld," he told her. "I suspect it will be a long and difficult search. The Great Wheel is vast."

"It is that."

"Still, this may help." Reaching into his cloak, he pulled out what looked like a book . . . flat, with a leather cover curled and chipped with age, stained with dirt. "At least, it will help you with your quest. Perhaps that will help me with mine."

"What is it?"

"Something I found last night," he said, "after our talk. It was in the eastern part of the city, near some relics I think our team will want to investigate." *Our* team. He found himself surprised, using that word. He handed her the book.

It was a ship's written log, supplement to the electronic version that was subject to computer failures, crashes, and power loss. The cracked, partly burned cover was embossed with the vessel's name, still legible in gold script:

Finders Keepers.

About the Author

William H. Keith is the author of over fifty novels, divided more or less equally between science fiction and military techno-thrillers. While most of his SF is written under his own name, he writes the military novels under a variety of pseudonyms. His most recent works include *Diplomatic Act*, a science fiction-comedy written with television actor Peter Jurasik, and *Semper Mars*, the first in a planned series of military science fiction novels written under the pseudonym Ian Douglas.

"DAYBREAK"

RICHARD BAKER

CORASON DIAS adjusted the designer glasses on the bridge of her nose and dropped her pack to the thin red dirt of the vehicle lot. Harsh white arc lights carved a hemisphere of unforgiving glare out of the darkness. Nearby, the town's foggy duraplas dome descended from the sky like a curtain of dust, curving down to meet the ground. Beyond the cheerless halo of artificial light the cold desert waited beyond the town's walls, a sea of absolute darkness beneath the stars.

The barren parking lot sat next to the dome's vehicular airlock. One battered and dusty groundcar waited beneath the arc lights. An old survey ATV, its front fenders were worn to gleaming bare metal by years of dust storms, and its windshield was pitted and scored. *Kile Excursions Ltd.* was stenciled across the car's flank.

Beside her, Jerrin scowled. "You've got to be kidding me," he said to no one in particular. *"This* is Kile Excursions?"

Corason shifted to her customary half step behind him, and shrugged uncomfortably. "I guess so, Jerrin. The address is right. This is the south vehicle lock. I don't see how we could have missed it."

Corason was a pretty girl, young like Jerrin, only twenty-four Standard years. Dressed in a tailored pantsuit, she'd added a yellow scarf to her jacket to set off her dark hair.

Jerrin, a tall young man, wasn't used to being disappointed, and what he saw in front of him was certainly not what he'd been expecting. He snorted in disgust. "They told me that Olympus wasn't much of a town, but I never imagined anything like this. This is the planetary capital we're standing in. Can you believe it?"

Corason started to answer, but he cut her off with a rueful grin, running his hands through his hair and sighing dramatically. "Did you keep the comm number? I guess we need to call this guy. Someone's got to keep the natives honest."

While Corason searched her dataslate for the comm address, Jerrin paced over to the car and leaned against the fender, gazing off into the night. Tall and good-looking, Jerrin had already mastered the art of looking like he was in charge of any situation he found himself in.

Corason often wondered what Jerrin saw in xenoarchaeology; he seemed more suited to a career in business, using his easy smile and quick intelligence to win power, prestige, and allies in some kind of abstract corporate environment. The only answer she could muster was that Jerrin was a young man of fierce interests. When something caught his eye, he didn't give up until he got it. Four or five years ago, the mystery of ancient alien civilizations had worked its way under Jerrin's skin. He wouldn't give up on his studies until he mastered the field, then he'd probably find something else to do.

Corason found the number, dialed it on her fashionable comm pad, and handed it to Jerrin. "Here you go."

Jerrin took the comm pad without thanks and waited impatiently for the call to ring through. After seven rings, he finally got an answer. The screen flickered, and a bleary-eyed man with long, unkempt hair stared out of the unit at him.

"Yeah, what is it?"

"Is this Martin Kile?"

"Who's asking?" The man rubbed his eyes, shaking his hair out of his face.

"This is Jerrin mac Alisten. I'm supposed to be renting your groundcar today."

Kile blinked twice. "The transport's in already? Damn, it usually runs eight or ten hours behind schedule. Uh, okay, where you at?"

"We're down at the south vehicle lock, looking at your car," Jerrin said. "We're supposed to be leaving now, remember?"

"Oh, wow . . . okay. I'll be down there in a few minutes. Go ahead and stow your gear or whatever. It's unlocked." Kile killed the connection, but not before Corason caught a glimpse of the guide collapsing back into his bed.

"He's on his way?" Corason asked.

"That's what he says, but I wouldn't hold my breath."

Jerrin shouldered his pack and studied the groundcar. For all its wear and tear, the groundcar had a rugged, solid appearance. It was more than ten meters long and almost three meters high, riding on six huge balloon tires on a heavy-duty suspension that kept its pressurized cabin a meter above the ground. Jerrin skipped the driver's door and went straight to the cabin hatch, struggling with the balky seal for a moment before wrenching it open with a sigh of pressurized air.

"Must not get a lot of car thieves out here," he observed.

Corason smiled gamely, dragging her own kit after him. "If somebody took the car, where would they go? Olympus is twelve hundred kilometers from the next town."

Jerrin let himself into the cramped cabin of the groundcar and started searching for a place to stow their bags. "No wonder they're a little rustic out here." He laughed at his own humor.

Corason looked at him and waited. "I don't know . . . it seems kind of interesting to me," she said thoughtfully.

"No crime, no traffic, no congestion, nothing to do but catch up on your reading and admire the view."

"You'd be climbing the walls in three days," Jerrin predicted. "People aren't built to be isolated like this, not in this day and age, anyway."

Corason frowned, trying to frame her thoughts more accurately, but she eventually gave up. Jerrin was probably right.

While he stowed all of their belongings in the various cabinets and lockers of the groundcar's interior, examining each instrument and shaking his head at the litter and debris Kile had left behind in his cargo compartments, Corason flipped on her dataslate and read more about the planet. She was a physics student, not an archaeologist, but planetology had enough physics in it to catch her interest when she started poking around into orbital characteristics and chemical weathering.

High Mojave was famous for its Glassmaker ruins; that was why Jerrin was here, and she was here because he was. The more she read, the more Corason found herself slipping into the tiny world on her screen, captured by the magnificent desolation. She'd never experienced anything like it. She had lived her whole life on a planet called Anacortes, a world of cool rains and rocky coasts cocooned by a planet-wide metropolis. She couldn't imagine a world so empty, so lonely.

It was an old planet, the oldest humans had settled anywhere. It might have been Earth-like once, but now High Mojave was almost eight billion years old, tired and worn. Of course, people had only been here for maybe two hundred years. The planet had been one of the last ones settled in the wave of colonization that broke across the Verge in the middle of the 2300's. Dead and desolate, its sun was a bloated orange orb. In twenty, maybe thirty, millennia, Mantebron—the planet's sun—would burn the last of its hydrogen and begin to consume its stores of helium, cooling and growing until it engulfed everything she looked at now.

Humankind might grasp briefly at High Mojave, scattering a little bit of cosmic driftwood on the shores of this distant and dying strand, and then it would move on to greater and bolder things. Of the people who settled this planet and built their lonely towns and barren farms, nothing would remain.

Dead seas stretched for thousands of kilometers. Mountains worn down to mere ripples of sand and fractured rock by the march of eighty million centuries littered the landscape. The atmosphere was desiccated and thin, nothing left but a sparse blanket of nitrogen and carbon dioxide. Days and nights were more than a hundred hours long.

Slow, so slow, High Mojave was a broken toy, winding down on its axis, a world crushed by time, terrible and incomprehensible, a march of eons that overwhelmed her. Time had consumed its oceans, time had leveled its mountains, time had stolen its air, and time was going to put out its sun.

From her seat at the groundcar's dining alcove, Corason could look out the window toward the whole of Olympus, a collection of maybe forty or fifty prefab buildings surrounded by a faded dome of duraplas. Like candles floating on a vast, dark pond, its scattered lights and tired signs futilely illuminated the immense night of the endless plains outside. It seemed like she was looking at the last star in creation, a weak flicker of light and life at the end of everything.

Behind her, Jerrin paced impatiently, glancing at his watch constantly. "It's been almost half an hour," he complained. "Where's Kile?"

Corason couldn't understand the importance of the question. She stared at a single image on her screen, the encyclopedia's single holo of the entire planet. It showed an elegant spire of glass silhouetted against a sunset that lasted for thirty-one hours, a gleam of rose against a cold and starless sky.

If you could paint a picture of time, it might look something like that glass tower.

* * * * *

Beneath the endless night, the heavy car hummed and creaked, rumbling across the cold, dry plains. Corason sat in the navigator's seat, an uncomfortable round stool at the back end of the cab. Jerrin lounged in the passenger seat below her and to the right, his handsome features limned by the green glow of the ATV's instrument panel. He stared out at the featureless plains, his eyes fixed on some imaginary distance that Corason couldn't see.

They'd been driving for almost twenty hours now, and she could tell that Jerrin's shallow store of patience was exhausted. Even tired and dull with the fatigue of the ride, he still captivated her. Mutual friends were surprised that they'd taken up with each other. He was mercurial, brilliant, a fire that was always in motion. If his impatience sometimes impinged on petulance or exasperation with the people who couldn't keep up with him, she was willing to forgive him the fault. He was basically a good man, young and cocky, but usually right, and he lavished attention on her like no one she'd ever known before.

She was quiet and shy, the class brain, a girl intimidated by more than two or three people paying attention to her at one time. Like Jerrin, she was a professional student. They'd both been born to affluent families and sent to a school for the children of the well to do. Both were now engaged in finishing their education in fields neither would probably ever make into careers. Jerrin had his father's mercantile empire waiting for him when he tired of the dull and methodical routine that composed the vast bulk of the archaeologist's experience.

No formal arrangements had been made yet, but Corason expected that she'd leave her studies in theoretical
physics to go with him when he decided he was done with
his schooling. After all, she'd used the semester break to
travel two hundred light-years at his side, drawn by his
passion, his vision, and his fascination. The Glassmakers
were Jerrin's challenge, not hers. Sometimes she wasn't
sure if she really loved him or not, but even if she didn't,
Corason had found that she always wanted to see what he
would do next. If Jerrin turned his mind, his heart, to
something, it had to be a goal worth achieving. He didn't
do anything that wasn't worth doing.

In the seat directly in front of her, Martin Kile beat a
staccato rhythm against the steering column with his long-
fingered hands, humming the words of a song he'd been
singing for the last five hundred kilometers. Corason
thought he was a striking character, simply because he was
completely outside her experience. Kile wasn't very old,
probably not more than thirty-five Standard years, but his
long bleached hair and sun-darkened skin spoke of a lifetime out in the open. Short and wiry, he wore an oil-stained
tee shirt and the trousers of a dusty blue jumpsuit; the torso
and sleeves of the overalls were knotted carelessly around
his narrow waist. A good-natured, vaguely scatterbrained
smile permanently marked his face. Even when Jerrin had
harangued Kile for missing the pick-up at the landing pad,
the driver had grinned and bobbed his head like he was
joking with his best friend. That might have made Jerrin
madder than before, but Kile's insincerity was infectious;
he was one of those people you just couldn't get really
mad at, a wide-eyed kid who'd never grow up.

"How much farther is it to the White Temple?" Jerrin
asked abruptly, breaking the droning of the engine and
interrupting Kile's incessant humming.

The driver looked over and shrugged. "Oh, I'd say
another two hours or so. It's about a twenty-two hour drive

from Olympus, and we've been driving twenty hours, right?"

"Don't you have the Temple marked on satnav?" Jerrin leaned back to flip on the car's navigation console. He frowned and poked at the display. "Say, your nav unit's not working. What course are you following?"

"Oh, the nav unit works fine," Kile laughed. "It's the bloody satellite. The last one stopped chirping six or seven years back, smashed into junk by a big meteor—figure the odds on that! But no more satellite navigation for High Mojave, get what I'm saying?"

"No nav signal?" Jerrin shot Kile a sharp look. "How do we know we're not driving around in circles out here?"

Kile pointed out the broad windshield. "See that star? It's Lucullus. I've been keeping it just on the other side of that strut there. That'll point me about thirty degrees south of due east." He thought for a second, squinting comically, and then put the groundcar into a wide, sweeping turn toward the left. " 'Course, we've been driving this way a long time, so Lucullus is a little bit higher in the sky. Better turn a little back toward the north."

"Don't you have a compass?" Corason asked.

"Sorry, the planet's got no magnetic field to speak of— not enough rotation, and the planet's cold all the way through. I had a gyrocompass, but that broke three months ago, and I'm still waiting for parts to fix it."

Jerrin gaped in the darkness of the cab. "You mean you've been driving all this time without any kind of course to follow? Are you insane?"

Kile laughed. "Man, I've driven all over this worn-out planet. I've logged almost five million kilometers in this groundcar. I know every Glassmaker site there is. I'll get you there."

Even in the half-light of the cabin, Corason could see the contentiousness brewing on Jerrin's brow. He was working himself up to a real storm. She decided to create a distraction before he embarrassed himself.

"You seem like you're not worried about getting lost, Mr. Kile."

The guide laughed. "Kile's fine, Miss. The only people who call me Mister are the cops. I'm not worried about getting lost because every place on this planet is pretty much like any other. It's all the same place out here, the middle of nowhere. Besides, if I managed to get myself really lost, I could always tune in on the beacon back at Olympus and drive the radio beam back. Done it before."

"Did you grow up around here?"

"Me? Oh, no." He shifted in his seat so that he could look at both her and Jerrin, absently hooking one arm across the control yoke. "I came here about ten years ago to look for Glassmaker artifacts. I'm originally from Bluefall."

The mention of the Glassmakers caught Jerrin's interest. Despite himself, he asked, "What sites have you checked out?"

"Oh, I checked all the big ones first: the White Temple, Six Spires, Jenner's Arch, the Crazy Cross. They've all been searched and searched again, of course. Then I spent a couple of years searching secondary sites, even the unsecured ones, hoping to find something everyone else had missed."

Jerrin recoiled. "Unsecured? That's illegal!"

Kile shrugged. "Well, I was down on my luck, and I was looking for a big score. I came to High Mojave with a stake of thirty thousand credits and old Jenny"—he thumped on the driver's console—"figuring I'd drive to the nearest Glassmaker site, do a little digging, and walk off this planet as a rich man. When I didn't get anywhere by sticking to the rules, I decided to bend a few and try some of the unsecured areas. Everybody out here does it sooner or later."

"You're lucky to be alive," Jerrin countered. "I've seen the reports, Kile. The Coleman expedition was wiped out to a man only three years ago in an unsecured site, and no one knows what happened to Juryovic and Bryce last year. They left Olympus heading for an unsecured site and were never seen again."

"That might have been the weather," Kile pointed out. "High Mojave isn't a friendly planet, mac Alisten. No oxygen in the air, temperatures dropping to more than a hundred below for fifty or sixty hours a night, an atmosphere so thin you'd die gasping in ten or maybe twenty minutes even if you could breathe it. You don't need to walk into an unsecured site to get killed out here. The planet's happy to do it for you."

Corason looked out the window at the gray, cold landscape sliding past. She couldn't bring herself to look at High Mojave as a place capable of malevolence against something as insignificant as a human. If it had any kind of sentience, of presence, it was an uncaring spirit, something so old and so deeply asleep that no human power could awaken it now. She looked back at Kile's green-lit features.

"Did you ever find anything big? Any real discoveries?"

"If I had, I wouldn't've stayed here for ten years, hiring my rig out to anyone who wanted to see the ruins." Kile changed position again, casually swerving the ATV around a boulder too large to drive over. "No, I never made the big score. Maybe I'm still hoping to. I mean, I'm staying here, right? When I can't line up a supply run to someone's farm or a tourist gig, well, I like to light out for the open desert and just see what I can find. You never know when a little erosion or sand-drift might have revealed something that no one else has ever seen before. Hell, maybe there's a Glassmaker Taj Mahal five meters under us right now, buried under dust and sand." He cackled with mirth. "Oh, there's a thought. Maybe I've driven right over the top of the big one ten or twenty times, and I just never knew to stop there and dig."

"Is there something big still out there, undiscovered?"

Jerrin snorted and answered for Kile. "How would we know that, Corey?"

"You know what I mean. Do you think there's still a piece of the puzzle we haven't found yet? Something"—she frowned and worried at the thought—"well, something that's *missing*, something that ought to be there but isn't. Granted, I'm no archaeologist, but I can name a dozen instances in physics where the evidence at hand indicated a big find that could be out there, if we only knew where to look for it. Dark matter, for instance, or the unified field theory."

Jerrin mulled it over for a time. "Archaeology is the science of missing pieces, Corey. We have to infer everything from fragmentary evidence. Unlike physics, there aren't experiments we can perform to confirm a theory or investigate interesting phenomena. If you want to know what's missing about the Glassmakers, I hardly know where to start.

"We don't know what they looked like. They didn't leave pictures of themselves. Maybe it was a religious issue; maybe they loved self-portraits but rendered them on a medium that didn't stand up to a million years of weathering. All we can do is look at the size of the buildings they made and guess that they were generally humanoid and maybe just a little taller than we are.

"We don't understand the technology we find in their ruins. Everything that lasted until our time is made out of silicon compounds, but somehow the Glassmakers built extremely complex circuitry in the form of molecule chains of different conductivities into the walls and blocks of their buildings. We can't do that.

"Some of their machinery is a kind of organic glass, silicon compounds that seem to alter shape and ductility

when you apply power. No hinges, no joints, no wheels—
if the Glassmakers wanted something that would open, like
a box or cabinet, they just applied a little energy and the
cabinet would somehow know that it needed to open by
changing its shape."

"That's how we get into their buildings," Kile remarked.
"You'll see a big 'X' marked at a spot on a wall, and you
carry a big damned power cell with you to shock the wall
and make it open. Sometimes it takes hundreds of hours of
random searching to find the access for a building."

"We don't know a thing about their language, their culture, or their history," Jerrin continued. "We've got some
guesses, but they didn't leave behind any written records,
and no one's been able to decode any data crystals or storage devices yet. We don't even know what they might look
like."

Corason weighed his words for a moment, thinking in
the darkness. She tried to imagine a Glassmaker, to think
about what he or she might have looked like, whether he
had a family, a homeland, a particular star in the sky he
liked to look for at nightfall.

"So what do we know about them?" she asked finally.

"They were here at least three hundred and thirty million years ago," Jerrin said quietly, "maybe a lot longer
than that. They made buildings, machines, and automatons
that survived more or less intact for that whole span of
time. None of the buildings we've found are less than seventy million years old, and that's about it."

"How do they establish the dates?" Corason asked.

"Weathering simulations, measurements of radioactive
content in the materials, even some mindwalking tech-
niques—although I don't view those as too reliable," Jerrin
said. "The dates are debatable."

"Man, that's an understatement," Kile laughed. "You
know what? I know people who'd swear the Glassmakers
are still living here. Can you believe that?"

Corason didn't answer. Jerrin would laugh, but she almost could believe it. High Mojave was possessed by some kind of *genius loci*, a spirit, a presence in the endlessness. She suddenly longed to be out of the car, in fact to be so far from the car that it wasn't even in sight anymore. She wanted to stand alone on the dusty hills with nothing but the cold, bright stars over her head, to feel like she was the only human in the world, in the universe. Maybe the Glassmakers would speak to her then.

"Hey, there's Steamship Rock," Kile said suddenly. He pointed out across the horizon toward a dark shape looming up above the horizon. Three distinct columns formed the imaginary funnels of some old oceangoing ship, swept back from a blunt prow of crumbling stone. It looked like it was sinking in dust, going down by the stern. The guide turned the groundcar a little to the right of the landmark.

"Good news, boys and girls. The White Temple is only about a hundred kilometers farther."

*   *   *   *   *

It was still dark when they reached the site. The night was only about two-thirds done. According to the almanac, sunrise was still thirty hours away, but Corason decided she was lucky to catch her first glimpse of the White Temple in starlight.

It stood on top of what might have once been a promontory overlooking the sea, before the sea had dried up and the dust had come to fill its bed. Seventeen shining white minarets swept into the sky. They were arranged in a circle, each one higher than the last, so that it looked like a crystalline staircase spiraling up into the sky. In the center stood a curious half-dome the size of a small auditorium. Circular ramparts, glittering pathways and walls sculpted into the face of the old rock surrounded the entire structure.

As they drove up, Corason could see that the complex had once included an outpost or marker at the tip of the promontory. With hundreds of millions of years of weathering, the rock itself had failed, toppling the smaller structure to the dead sea below where its gleaming glass segments lay scattered but unmarred by their fall.

She wondered if the stuff from which the Glassmakers raised their fairy tale towers might be strong enough to endure when the planet itself was engulfed in its swelling sun a few thousand years from now. They'd lasted through the mundane weathering of hundreds of thousands of centuries; could the fires of a star be any worse? When Mantebron exploded in a nova a million or two years later, would the Glassmaker constructs be scattered across the cosmos still intact, gleaming missiles of glass cast upon the stellar winds?

"Here we are," Kile announced unnecessarily. He pulled the ATV up to a flat, sandy patch at the base of the promontory, killing the drive. "This is as far as I can drive. The rock's too weak to stand up to heavy vehicles."

"Good enough," said Jerrin. He pulled himself up out of his seat and stretched. "I'm going to go out and have a look around."

"Slow down," Kile drawled. "Let me suit up, and I'll come with you."

"You don't have to do that," Jerrin snapped.

"Oh, yes I do. What kind of suit experience do you have, Jerrin?"

The student shrugged. "Some. I've taken some zero-atmosphere tours back in my home system."

"That's not enough. Look at the temperature readings, man—it's minus one hundred and twenty C out there. If you don't know exactly what you're doing with a climate suit, cold like that'll kill you before you know you're dead. As long as it's dark out, no one goes out without an EVA buddy, okay?"

Jerrin grimaced, but acquiesced. "All right. Better safe than sorry."

Corason gazed at the glimmering white spires, pale needles of light standing over the cold gray plain. "Can I come too?" she asked.

Jerrin shrugged. "I'm just going out to look around for a few minutes. It's going to take me a while to set up my equipment before I scout the site." He looked over at her and saw something in her face that made him hesitate. He forced a smile. "Well, okay. It was a long ride, I guess we all need to stretch our legs."

Under Kile's supervision, they laboriously donned their climate suits—thick, semi-pressurized garments with oxygen tanks, heated boots and gloves, and sealed helmets crowned by powerful spotlights. It wasn't a true environment suit for zero atmosphere, but it was the closest to such a suit that Corason had ever put on. As she climbed into the baggy trousers and shrugged the tunic over her shoulders, she found her hands starting to shake and her mouth dry with fear. It was a cold, airless, alien night outside their tiny bubble of technology. All her life she'd read stories of explorers and spacers dying through failures of their protective devices.

"Hey, relax," Kile said from beside her. He helped her wrestle the heavy gloves over her hands. "You guys bought top-line gear, I see. The stuff's foolproof. You could lie down in that suit and sleep a solid day right out on the Temple terrace without a worry."

"What about air?" she said nervously. "How long can we stay outside?"

"Oh, you're fine. Look—this is a rebreather system, not real bottled air. These intakes draw in High Mojave's air, which is mostly nitrogen, then you've got a heater to bring it up to a comfortable temperature, and an oxygenator to put the O2 into it. All you really have to carry is the oxygen pack"—he held up a metal canister the size of a paperback book—"and one of these will last ten hours or more. No worries, right?"

She mumbled some half-hearted reply and concentrated on slowing her racing heart and controlling her breathing as the rigid plastic helmet clicked into place over her collar. Jerrin struggled a little with his own gear, but he figured it out fast. He'd worn suits before.

Kile checked them both over and then climbed into his own suit, a battered and dusty wreck that didn't look like it would keep out a hard rain, let alone the cold of High Mojave's night. He dressed fast, humming into the suit radio.

When they were all done, they crowded into the big airlock at the back of the groundcar's cabin. The lock doubled as the car's shower and toilet alcove; the ATV was big, but not so big that it could waste space on a dedicated airlock. They cycled through and stepped outside. Corason followed the two men, hesitant to leave the perceived shelter of the lock.

Sand crunched beneath her feet, covered in a thin layer of sparkling diamond frost. She took a few steps, then raised her eyes to see what was around her.

Nothing but a vast, endless plain marked by a single set of tire tracks greeted her when she looked back the way they had come. The stars, cold and brilliant in the thin atmosphere, burned fiercely in the heavens, so bright that she could see to the horizon by starlight alone.

She turned and faced the White Temple. The tallest minarets, maybe a hundred meters in height, towered over the humans. Silent and majestic, it looked ageless, unmarked by the hand of time. People like Jerrin thought it might be more than one hundred million years old. A thousand thousand centuries.

"It's beautiful," she murmured.

"Yeah, it's something, isn't it?" Kile said. The suit radios carried his voice directly to her ear, giving her the

curious impression that he was standing right behind her
even though she could see him and Jerrin standing ten
meters ahead of her. "I've been here dozens of times, and
it still gets to me."

Jerrin was silent, confronting his own awe. He'd studied images, plans, diagrams of these sites for years, but this
was the first time he'd ever seen one with his own eyes,
standing on the alien soil of a world at the edge of human
civilization. Corason found tears in her own eyes as she
thought of what it must mean to him. It was like she was
seeing a new facet of his personality, a vulnerability he'd
always hidden before.

"I never knew . . ." Jerrin managed before words failed him.

Pacing slowly, Jerrin began to circle the site, following
the white ramps as they spiraled up to the broad colonnade.
Kile followed, whistling tunelessly in the suit radio. Corason brought up the rear, savoring her amazement, her open
wonder. They reached the top and stepped out onto the
gleaming floor beneath the slender needles. From here, she
could clearly see that each of the minarets was no more
than two meters in diameter. A hundred meters high and
only two wide, she thought, and it's stood for millions of
years.

"What is this place, Jerrin?" she asked. "What's it for?"

Jerrin swung around to face her and said, "No one
knows. Unlike the other Glassmaker sites, there's no
machinery here, no devices, no storage units. It doesn't
seem to have any particular function, other than its aes-
thetic value, so we call it a temple."

"But you think differently, don't you?"

Behind the clear visor of his helmet, he smiled. "I do. I
think this is some kind of power station, and that these
columns are a kind of antenna array for broadcast power."

"Broadcast power?" Corason glanced up at the needles.
"You mean, these might have beamed power to other
buildings or vehicles nearby?"

"That's what I think," Jerrin said. "Some of the other sites I'm planning to visit have similar structures, although none as large or well-preserved as the one here at the White Temple."

Kile looked over from a low wall where he stood, admiring the view. "Haven't heard that one before," he said, "but wouldn't you have a major machinery installation at a power plant? There would have been some kind of power generation system."

Jerrin nodded. "That's the real part of my work in the field for the next few weeks. I brought a high-powered transducer along. I'm going to search the foundations and the surrounding area for subterranean structures to see if there's more to the White Temple than meets the eye." He offered a shallow laugh. "Even if I'm wrong about the broadcast power, I might turn up something new."

"That's the part of my job that I really like," Kile said. "You're always meeting new people with interesting ideas." He stretched in his suit, then shambled toward them, kicking up faint puffs of dust with his booted feet. "That sounds like a lot of work, and we're all beat from the drive. I'd suggest we get a few hours of sleep before we start any major projects."

Reluctantly, Jerrin agreed. "I suppose you're right."

The three of them started back toward the car, following the curve of the glass ramps. The ATV was only a hundred meters or so from the Temple, an ugly and ungainly thing next to the smooth perfection of the Glassmaker site. Corason felt almost embarrassed that she'd made the pilgrimage to this place in such a crude device. It seemed irreverent.

"What was that?' Jerrin's voice, strange and tight.

She emerged from her reverie slowly, shaking off the fog of waking dreams and the incessant *swish, swish, swish* of her feet across the sandy ramp. Blinking, she looked around, wondering what he was referring to, then she saw it herself.

An orb of green light danced and flickered out on the open sand, a kilometer or two away. It wasn't bright, not the way a human light would be in the starlight, but instead phosphorescent, a subtle glow that moved easily over the waste. Without saying a word, all three humans slowed their steps and halted, gazing at the distant light.

"Right there," Jerrin said, pointing. "Do you see it?"

"Oh, shit," Kile said absently. "Oh, man. Everybody stay cool. Let's just keep walking toward the car. No sudden moves."

"What? What is it?" Jerrin demanded.

"I think it's a werewisp. Come on, boys and girls. Back to the car." Kile reached out for Corason's arm and urged her to take a step, then two, nodding vigorously behind his frosted visor. "Oh, man."

Surprised but not yet alarmed, Corason hesitated. "Jerrin?"

The young man gazed out over the starlit plain, stiff and ummoving. He didn't reply; she called him again. "Jerrin? What's wrong?"

"I've heard about these things," he said. "They're extremely rare. No one's ever gotten a good look at one of them. They just streak in out of the desert, nose around a camp for a while, and then move on."

"Is it some kind of animal?" she asked.

"I don't think anyone knows for sure. They're associated with Glassmaker sites—might be an artifact or automaton of some kind." Jerrin stared in wonder. "Wow. I can't believe we're actually seeing one."

"Come on, dude," Kile interrupted. He gently pushed Corason toward the groundcar and retreated a couple of steps to take hold of Jerrin's arm. "Don't just stand there. Time to get back in the car. You don't want to be caught outside by one of those things."

"Why? They're not supposed to be dangerous."

Kile laughed nervously. "Yeah, well, neither are cigarettes anymore, but you won't catch me smoking. I've

heard stories, man, talked to people who really know the
Wide Open out here, the Big Nada. They'll tell you about
the 'wisp. You want to watch the pretty light, you can do
it from inside the car."

Reluctantly, Jerrin turned toward the car and allowed
Kile to drag him toward the ATV. Corason followed, working hard to keep up in the unfamiliar pace of the bulky suit
and heavy boots. Her breath rasped in her ears inside the
helmet, now growing muggy with her own perspiration.
She looked down to pick her way across the sandy scree
of rock and rubble at the foot of the plateau. Green light
glimmered on her faceplate.

Startled, she looked up just in time to see the werewisp
streak past the three of them like a missile of emerald
energy, throwing a shifting curtain of pale shadows from
the car and the men around her. It darted past, looping
around in a great sweeping curve that carried it hundreds
of meters across the sandy desert floor. So fast, she thought
in dull amazement. A moment ago it was a couple of kilometers away!

A staccato burst of static filled her ears, crackling over
the suit radio. Through it, she heard Kile's cry of astonishment and Jerrin's urgent calls, all washed out by the
interference. She followed the 'wisp with her eyes as it
arced high, wheeling in a graceful turn. It hovered at the
apogee of its curve, sinking slowly against the dark line of
the horizon, and then it arrowed straight at her.

Corason stood petrified, too startled to be afraid. In the
span of two heartbeats the 'wisp grew from a distant globe
into an express train bearing down on her. She got one
good look at the creature or device before it hit her. The
thing was an orb of pale green glass filled with coruscating fields of brilliant light, a living lantern only a meter or
so across, even though its glowing emanations threw arms
and streamers of jade dozens of meters in each direction.

It was beautiful.

Then she was lying on her back in the cold, cold sand, blinking the light from her eyes as it darted past her and streaked away. Her suit was dark and silent; the radio was dead, the hum and whir of the rebreather had stopped.

Am I dead? she wondered. What happened?

Green witchfire danced and arced on her gloves, fading slowly. She stared at her hands in wonder, afraid to move or look around. The distant stars watched impassively above her, the only thing she could see. Despite her astonishment, her education and training asserted itself. Oddly analytical, she filed away the phenomena she'd observed. Electromagnetic, she thought. The static buzz on the radio was EM interference. When it raced past me, its EM fields charged the metal fastenings of my suit. That's why I'm glowing.

Something fell onto her, a dark suited figure, brilliant white lights shining in her face. She thought she saw Jerrin's face behind the glare. He shook her by the shoulders. His mouth was moving, but she couldn't hear anything. He doesn't realize my radio's out, she thought. Carefully, she sat up and pressed her faceplate against his to hear what he was saying.

"—you okay? Corey! Are you hurt?"

"I'm fine," she managed. "Jerrin, I'm fine. What happened?"

"The 'wisp ran right over you. Corey, are you sure you're okay?"

"My suit's dead," she managed. "EM pulse killed the radio."

Jerrin looked at the control unit and display on her breastplate and frowned. "Damn! Your power cell is dead. You don't have heat or air circulation." He struggled to his feet and pulled her up. "We've got to get you inside fast."

She steadied herself on his shoulder and looked around to get her bearings. Kile stood by the airlock of the ground-car, holding a long weapon. He was looking past them, back at the White Temple. Even as Jerrin half-carried her toward the car, she twisted around to see what he was looking at.

The werewisp hovered a few dozen meters away. It abruptly bounced about thirty meters straight up, dropped down and began to roll toward them.

The air in her helmet was growing stale, humid. Her hands and feet tingled with the first insidious touch of cold, jolts of ice jarring the soles of her feet with each step. Green luminescence threw her shadow out before her, shrinking and disappearing as the cold jade glow engulfed her again. This time she felt an icy touch over her spine, through the fiber of her body, a spreading numbness that staggered her in her steps. Beside her, Jerrin's helmet lights went dark. Ghostly vapors wreathed his body, crawling over him as if he were burning in phosphorescence. He flailed for balance, and both of them went down in the cold dust.

Kile raised his rifle and fired at the 'wisp, blinding flashes at the muzzle stretching out over their heads. Even with her suit's audio pick-ups dead and cold, Corason could still hear the bark of the charge rifle. She looked back over her shoulder; the werewisp hovered there. Bright green flashes marked the impact of the slugs against its energy fields, like the splashes of stones falling into water.

The creature shuddered violently, its whirling lights spinning crazily, then it darkened and suddenly reached out with one narrow, focused lance of icy green energy, spearing Kile high on the torso. Sparks showered from the guide's damaged suit, a puff of gas that condensed like diamond frost on the ground around his feet; he silently went to his knees, clapping one hand over the hole in his suit and dropping the rifle.

A buzzing sound filled her head, and her vision began to swim drunkenly. The werewisp angrily streaked toward Kile and the car, only to veer away at the last moment, darting up and over the ATV. She stared after it until Jerrin seized her arm and dragged her toward the airlock.

Moving like a sleepwalker, she finally found some measure of control over her shaking limbs. Jerrin pushed her up into the open doorway, and she fumbled her way inside. A moment later, Jerrin dragged Kile inside and slammed the door's cycle button.

As the hatch slid shut, Corason saw the 'wisp circling outside, darting and flashing. Heavy and sleepy, she watched it until her sight failed.

* * * * *

"Come on, Corey. You've got to wake up." Jerrin's voice, warm and close.

She opened her eyes. They were inside the car. She was lying on the deck, entangled in her half-opened climate suit, the helmet on the floor next to her head. Groggily, she groped for her glasses and pushed them onto her face, blinking. The air was sweet and cool in her lungs.

"Jerrin," she breathed. "The werewisp?"

"It's still out there, circling the car." He frowned. "Don't worry. It's outside, and we're inside. We're okay."

"What about Kile? I thought I saw—"

"Saw it take me out?" At the other end of the cabin, the guide smiled and laughed weakly. He'd pushed his climate suit down around his waist, and he had a black, singed hole on his thermal undershirt. A first-aid patch gleamed under the shirt. "Nope, not quite. Just a surface burn. The 'wisp torched me once and then buzzed away. I guess I made it mad when I shot it up with the rifle."

She sat up, leaning against a storage cabinet. "Good Lord. That thing could have killed us all."

Seeing that she was okay, Jerrin relaxed and dropped against the bulkhead across from her. His handsome face was tight with concern. "It drained my suit," he said. "Just emptied it of power. If we'd been any farther from the car when it came by . . . "

"You'd have been a popsicle, dude," Kile said sagely. "At least it didn't shock you or Corey. I get the feeling we got off light."

"I thought you said they weren't supposed to be dangerous," Corey said to Jerrin.

"They're not. I've never seen any documented cases of werewisp attacks. Just sightings, a few casual contacts, that's it."

"You live out here a few years, you hear stories," Kile said from across the cabin. "Travelers disappearing without a trace, lonely homesteads that turn up empty when no one had checked up on them in a long time, strange things that happen out here in these long, long nights. The werewisp may look curious and playful, but it's got a mean streak. As long as you're on your guard, it'll just drift on by, keeping an eye on you, but if you're out here by yourself and there's no one else around . . . "

"Come on," Jerrin said. "You make it sound like the damned thing's got it in for us. We must have trespassed on its territory or something, provoked an attack response. Simple programming, right?"

"You know what else they say about the werewisp?" Kile asked. "They say there's only one. That's it—one of 'em on this whole planet. Its home is the Big Nada, all the empty space on this dead old world, thousands of kays in every direction, and it's the only thing out here—the Devil in a green dinner jacket."

"If you're trying to rattle me, you can stop now," Jerrin replied, annoyed. "I'm already shook up. You don't need to make up ghost stories."

"I agree," said Corason. "Let's just—"

Coruscating green light streamed into the cabin, dancing and fluttering. She flinched away; the werewisp was hovering right in front of the car's control cab, its eerie light shining through the windshield and illuminating the interior of the cabin. It slowly rotated, a blind emerald eye staring in at them, and then it drifted up and over the cab.

Faint glimmers of green energy crackled and danced over the metal counters, the cabinet handles, the heavy storage cases and instruments of the car's interior. Then, soundlessly, the interior lights died. Corason gasped in surprise; Jerrin cursed.

"What the hell?" he growled. "Isn't this thing done with us yet?"

Kile muttered to himself and clattered around in the cabin. After a few minutes, he produced a chemlight and snapped it, shaking it to illuminate the cabin. Clambering down to the control cab, he held the lightstick over the console. He whistled. "Wow. I think that son of a bitch just drained the car batteries."

Jerrin got to his feet and moved forward; Corason followed a moment later. They could see the 'wisp, drifting aimlessly a hundred meters away. Kile winced and dropped into his driver's seat, staring out at the creature. Jerrin crouched beside him, double-checking the instruments.

"Looks like it just got the auxiliary power circuits. The main cells are still at seventy percent charge." He glanced out at the 'wisp, then back at Kile. "How much charge did you spend driving out here?"

"About twenty percent." Kile shook his head. "You wouldn't believe the size of the power cells they built into these old Surveyor Kings. I can drive ten thousand kays on full batteries." He flipped a couple of switches and tapped out a set of commands on a board behind the driver's seat. In a moment, the cab lights flickered on, and the air systems purred to life again. "There we go. Lights, air, and heat are back."

Corason gasped. "The 'wisp!"

Arrowing straight toward the car, the green orb rocketed past, its pale rays streaming like a comet's tail. The car radio hissed static, and then the lights failed again. The three humans sat blinking in the ruddy light of Kile's chemstick.

"Oh, *man*," Kile said. "Did you see that? It cleaned us out *again*."

"Don't tell me you weren't expecting that." Jerrin leaned forward to check the instrument panel. "That says fifty-nine percent, right?"

Kile nodded slowly. "Yeah, that's what it says."

"That thing just ate ten percent of our power?"

"Yeah, that's what it did. Wow."

Corason leaned back to look out the side window. "It's still out there."

"Just waiting for us to plug in the free lunch sign again," Jerrin said bitterly. "Don't charge the support batteries again, Kile. It's just like ringing a dinner bell."

"Dude, I'm with you, but we've got a problem. It's a hundred and twenty below zero out there. If we can't heat the cabin, we're going to freeze." The driver paused, then added, "Make that two problems. We'll need air. The recirc fans take power, too."

Kile's words silenced all of them for several minutes. Behind her, Corason heard Jerrin sigh in exasperation and collapse into one of the seats. She kept her eyes on the werewisp, watching the random motions of the flickering orb of light. Somehow it managed to convey a near-human sense of mocking playfulness as it danced and flitted across the darkened plains as if to say. Almost, it seemed to say, *Come on out and play! Don't hide in your car.* Corason wondered if it would kill them.

"Well, we've got three choices," Jerrin said. Strain put an edge in his voice. "We can sit here for a while and try to wait it out, we can call for help, or we can get the hell out of here."

"I think you've only got two choices, Jerrin," she said, watching the 'wisp dart and dance. "The radio won't work.

Remember the static on the suit radios? That thing is broadcasting some serious interference on radio wavelengths."

"Damn. I guess you're right." Jerrin slumped back. He paused, then asked, "Do we try the radio anyway, do we wait it out, or do we move?"

Kile cleared his throat. "We can try to move, dude, but if I activate any of the car's power systems, the 'wisp is going to knock us flat again."

Jerrin didn't reply for a long time. Corason finally tore her eyes away from the glowing apparition outside to look at him; his jaw white and clenched, he was simply staring straight ahead.

"I guess we'll have to wait it out," he finally said.

Kile stood, stretched gingerly, and moved over to a small panel that held most of the car's life-support displays. Equipped with a small independent power supply, it was still working.

"Temperature's eighteen degrees C in here," he said. "Looks like the O2's fine for now. We'll give it an hour, and if we need to, I'll open some bottled oxygen and cycle the airlock. Can't do much about the cold without running the heaters, though."

Jerrin turned to look down at Corason. He smiled and reached down to zip her climate suit up a few centimeters more. "We've got the suits if it gets real cold," he said. "Come on. Let's get something to eat and see how long it takes the 'wisp to get bored."

Moving back to the main cabin, they crowded around the tiny dining alcove and ate a meal of cold rations and water by the ruddy light of Kile's chemsticks, then they settled down to wait. Kile wrapped himself in a shiny thermal blanket, stretching out his lanky legs across the pair of captain's chairs at one side of the cabin. Jerrin and Corason lay down side by side on the folding bed. She could feel his tenseness in the set of his shoulders, the restless shifting of his position. Waiting never agreed with him.

For her own part, she closed her eyes and listened to the low moaning of wind outside the car, the gentle rocking of the groundcar on its high wheels, the faint hiss of dust streaming against the old metal of the hull. She imagined what it would feel like to let that cold dust, the dust of centuries, of millennia, run through her bare fingers, to stand open and unprotected in front of the living face of Time as it existed on this old, old world.

How long has the 'wisp moved across the face of this world? she wondered drowsily. A hundred years? A thousand? Ten thousand? Made of energy, of ether, it might have survived since the time of the Glassmakers themselves. Why not?

She tried to measure their wait by the count of her own heartbeat, by the blinking display of the delicate wristwatch on the back of her hand, by the gusts of wind outside. The chill in the air slowly increased, a pervasive cold that slowly began to reach her through the thick hull, through the blankets, even through the warmth of her lover beside her.

Half-dozing, she didn't even notice when Jerrin wrapped his arms around her, trying to warm her. Sometime later, he stood and moved up to the cab. It seemed like he was gone for a long time before he stamped back into the cabin, arms wrapped around his torso.

"I cycled some oxygen into the cabin," he muttered, white smoking breath streaming from his words. "We're at fifteen below in the cab, and the werewisp is still out there. Time to come up with another plan."

Kile stirred, shaking his head groggily. "Guess it can't hurt. I'll fire up the engine."

Corason shook the cobwebs from her head and sat up, rubbing her arms vigorously. She followed the two men as they moved up to the front of the ATV and clambered stiffly into the seats. White frost coated the inside of the windshield, except for a single bare patch where Jerrin had brushed a clear spot. A dim green glow hovered outside.

Kile brushed frost from the instrument panel, rubbed his hands together, and offered a desperate grin. "Hey, here goes nothing," he said as he powered up the car again, waking it from its icy sleep. Lights flickered to life, pumps and fans began to hum, the radio crackled to life with an abrupt burst of static.

He waited for a minute, then two, triggering the electric defrosters to clear the groundcar's sloping windshield. "All right. The 'wisp is keeping its distance. Maybe he's going to let us drive on out of here now."

Gingerly, he put the car into gear; the heavy wheel-motors growled as the car lurched into motion. Wheeling away from the glittering spikes of the White Temple, he set his course toward the open desert, lurching across the dust and rock.

Corason held her breath, waiting for some interference. They drove a hundred meters, then two hundred, and then the 'wisp streaked by them, overtaking them from behind. Dashing out in advance of the car, it looped three times in glee and then rocketed back at them, filling the windshield with its emerald radiance. She cried out in fright; Jerrin threw his arms over his face. Then the glow was past them, but still near, crowning the car like Saint Elmo's fire, throwing long flickering shadows out in front of the lurching car.

"It's on top of the car!" she cried.

"Son of a *bitch!*" Kile swore. He blinked and rammed the throttle forward, increasing their pace. "I thought the crazy bastard meant to climb in here with us!"

"Forget it! Go, go, go!" Jerrin yelled.

The lights of the car began to brown out, flickering awkwardly. Corason shifted her seat and looked over Kile's shoulder at the control panel. It took her a moment to find what she was looking for, and then she gasped in alarm.

The charge meter was dropping, fading, moment by moment. "Kile! The power cells!"

The guide glanced down, then did a double-take and rapped on the panel. "Oh, man, it's eating us alive!"

"Keep going!" Jerrin said.

Corason shook her head. "No, don't! It'll drain us dry. You've got to kill the motor!"

"Like hell," Kile growled. "We'll freeze to death if we sit here!"

Jerrin looked up over his shoulder at her. Something in her face convinced him. He grimaced and reached out to pull Kile's hand off the throttle. "She's right. Better to save what we have. The 'wisp can't stay out here forever."

His good humor failing him for the first time, Kile slammed his good fist on the controls and pushed the throttle away with a curse. He slashed at the power, killing the motor and cutting power to the life support systems. In a moment, they were sitting in the dark again, watching the frost slowly reclaim the windows. The motors ticked underneath the car's deck, adjusting to the bitter cold.

"Great. What now?" he asked the dark plains in front of him.

Jerrin shook his head. "I don't know. Damn, I don't know."

Corason reached up to rub her temples, shocked at how cold her hands felt. In a heated suit, cocooned in tried and proven technology, the dangers of High Mojave's achingly long night hadn't seemed anything more than scenery. The agelessness of the dry seabed, the brilliant starlight, the old worn dust . . . just a few hours ago it was quaint, romantic. Now it seemed immediate and deadly.

Outside, the 'wisp wheeled and drifted, a malevolent lantern adrift on a dark sea. All three of them watched it for a long moment before Jerrin remarked, "How in the hell does that thing survive out there, anyway? It's cold enough to condense half the damned atmosphere onto the ground, and the werewisp is perfectly at home. Doesn't it get cold?"

"Adapted to the environment," Kile said numbly. "High Mojave's still got plant life, did you know that? Tiny cactus-like stuff, scrub brush, grasses, mostly in the equatorial regions. Not much of it, of course, and if it lives through one or two nights, it's a wonder, but it's still out there."

Something clicked in Corason's mind, a connection she couldn't yet put her finger on. Frowning, she asked, "Does anything else on this planet move around at nighttime?"

"No, anything that wants to stay alive goes to ground when the sun goes down," Kile said. "It's just too cold."

Carefully, she asked, "What about the 'wisp? Does it only come out at night?"

"Jeez, what difference does it make?" Kile snorted.

"It might be important. Have you ever heard of a werewisp being sighted during daylight?"

The guide remained silent for a long moment. "No," he finally admitted. "I've never heard a word about a 'wisp sighting in daylight. Doesn't mean it didn't happen, though."

"All of the accounts I've read were night encounters," Jerrin added. "What are you thinking about, Corey?"

She ignored him, pulling out her notepad computer and turning it on. Protected inside the car, it hadn't been damaged by the 'wisp's attacks. "When we left Olympus, it was about thirty hours until local sunrise. That means that the terminator was"—she performed some quick mental calculations—"about five thousand kilometers east of Olympus. It's been about twenty-six hours since we left, so the terminator's advanced by forty-one hundred kilometers during that time. We were driving northeast for most of the time, so we actually traveled another two hundred kilometers towards the terminator."

"Terminator? What are you talking about?" Jerrin asked.

"You know, the terminator, the dividing line between night and day, the current location of sunrise or sunset on a planet's surface." She leaned forward and pointed toward a discernible lightening along one horizon. "Guys, sunrise is only seven hundred kilometers that way. Four hours and twenty minutes, to be precise."

Kile laughed softly. "So when the sun comes up, we won't have to worry about freezing. Hey, that's the first good news we've had all night, but that won't help us when the O2 runs out and we can't call for help."

She smiled. "Maybe, but I'm betting that the werewisp is going to have to run for cover when the sun comes up. I don't think it can stand warm temperatures."

Jerrin turned his torso, shifting to face her. He couldn't keep the surprise out of his voice. "Corey, how do you know that?"

"I'm guessing now," she warned him, "but here's what I think. The 'wisp uses electromagnetic energy; it leaves a wake of radio noise when it passes close to you. It must fly through some kind of levitation—magnetic, I'd guess, though I can't imagine that High Mojave has much of a magnetic field anymore—and it uses magnetic fields to interfere with the operation of our power cells. All of that says one thing to me: superconductivity. It's not that big, so it can't be making *all* that power continuously, right? It's got to have some extremely efficient way to store and use electricity and make its magnetic fields. Material conductivity is related to temperature. Maybe the werewisp stays out all night because that's when it's cold enough for its tissues or structures to superconduct. If it gets too hot, it dies."

The two men were silent for a long time. Finally Jerrin spoke. "It makes sense."

"Wow," Kile breathed. "All we got to do is hang on until daybreak, and the 'wisp is going to have to bug out."

"It's damned cold in here," Jerrin said. "Three hours is going to be a real long wait. Maybe too long. How much of a charge do we have left in the main cells?"

"Twenty-eight percent. Oh, man. We burned thirty percent of the charge driving away from the Temple."

"We won't get seven hundred kilometers on what's left if the 'wisp was draining us the whole time," Jerrin said. "We'd be lucky to drive ten kays before it killed the car. Think we can hold out in here for four more hours? Cover up with thermal blankets, maybe run the heater a little when we really needed it?"

"The climate suits need power for their heating elements," Kile pointed out. He squinted and rubbed at his stubble-covered jaw. "I'm guessing we'd get down to fifty or sixty below zero in here within a couple of hours."

"Damn. That's pretty rough." Jerrin shivered and blew into his cupped hands. "If we could keep the werewisp off the car for an hour, we could drive towards the sunrise, maybe scare it off, but the minute we move, it'll be on us again."

"Wait," said Corason. "I think I have an idea."

* * * * *

It took them almost an hour to rig the car. One of them would step outside, and the 'wisp would circle in curiosity before darting in to drain the power from a suit. The person with the dead suit would have to quickly duck back into the cab before the suit air and heat ran out, change out the power cells, and then come back outside to go back to work. Corason had to return to the car interior twice while she worked. Jerrin only got chased back once. Kile, on the other hand, was drained five times by the 'wisp. Apparently, it remembered which of them had fired at it.

By the time they finished, the temperature in the cab was sitting at forty-four degrees below zero and dropping faster. Without running the heaters in the climate suits, the groundcar was quickly becoming uninhabitable; a fine frost covered all of the interior surfaces, and when Jerrin tried to break open some rations for a quick snack, they found that the food storage cabinets were frozen shut.

"Corey, I think we'd better try your plan," Jerrin said, blowing onto his hands. "If we wait too much longer, it's going to be too late."

She managed a small nod, holding her arms clamped over her torso to keep the heat in her body. "R-r-right," she managed. "I'll g-g-go outside." She started to clamber to her feet, trying to control her shaking limbs.

Jerrin stopped her, putting his hand on her shoulder. "No. You'd better stay. You're smaller than either Kile or me. I know you've got to be colder. I'll do it."

The driver shook his head and stood. "No way, man. You guys hired me to keep you out of trouble. It's my job."

Jerrin offered Kile a genuine smile. "Dude," he said, mimicking the driver, "the 'wisp can't stand the sight of you. It'll chase you back inside the minute you stick your head out the door. I'll go."

Forestalling any more argument, he pulled the helmet of his suit over his head and sealed it, starting up the life support unit with their last remaining suit cell. He fumbled his way back to the airlock and cycled the mechanism. A moment later he appeared in front of the car, waving at them through the windshield. The werewisp drifted aimlessly past him, perhaps forty or fifty meters away.

Jerrin ignored the alien creature and trudged around to the front left fender. The empty helmet of one of the spare climate suits sat there, secured to the car by duct tape. Standing in front of the helmet, he took a flare from his belt and snapped it in half, igniting the pyrotechnic with a shower of sparks. The magnesium burned brilliantly in the darkness, bright as a small sun.

He let the flare burn for a moment, holding it at arm's length, and then he stuck the end into the helmet. A pile of green pellets had been heaped inside, and the flare ignited them at once. Hot and yellow, they burned fiercely with strange streamers of white smoke spiraling away in the wind outside.

"That's the first one," Kile said, watching anxiously. "Damn, Corey, you were right. It's burning, and there ain't a sniff of free oxygen out there."

"Oxygen c-c-candles," she said. "The s-s-suits use them to replenish the O2. They'd b-b-burn underwater. Self-oxygenating. They've been using them in rebreathers since the t-t-twentieth century."

Jerrin moved stiffly to the right fender and lit the next pile of pellets. They'd spent almost half an hour cracking open the climate suit oxygen canisters, carefully emptying the chemical pellets from the rebreather units. Flickering yellow flames cast a ruddy light over the tall suited form, shades of yellow and red that didn't belong on the cold blue landscape. Behind him, the 'wisp began to dart forward, only to bob and quiver in agitation.

Jerrin worked his way around the side of the car, and the 'wisp followed. "Damn, it's going after him," Kile said. He ducked back and clambered through the cabin to stare out one of the side windows, now limned in eerie green light. A litter of shredded canisters and emptied cabinets clattered and crunched under his feet. "Okay, he's got the third one lit. Ah, jeez—the 'wisp knocked him down."

Corason squeezed her eyes shut, trying to control the shaking that wracked her body. Come on, Jerrin, she prayed silently. I know how stubborn you can be. You can do it.

She could almost hear the fatal radio voice of the werewisp with some unknown sense. It hissed and crackled, it moaned and it roared, it fumed and cackled in a bandwidth beyond human perception. Its voice was legion, the madness and inhumanness of naked time and dead worlds, jealous souls imprisoned in a night that never ended on a world where time itself had ceased to have any meaning.

She bit her knuckles and whimpered in fear.

"He's up again," Kile reported from the back. "Okay, he's got the last one lit. He's coming back inside." The guide scrambled forward and threw himself into the driver's seat. He glanced over his shoulder at the back of the cab. The airlock opened, and Jerrin staggered inside. "He's in! Can I punch it now?"

Mutely, she nodded once. Kile grimaced and ran his hand over the engine panel, activating the safety locks that allowed the motors, the heat, the life support, the lights, the radio, all the systems of the car to draw power from the massive lanthanide cells that held the groundcar's reserve of power. The lights flickered to life, halogen headlamps burning a brilliant path across the dark desert. The fans quietly hummed to life, and the car shook and rumbled as the drive motors began to spin.

"Okay, we're live!" he cried.

The 'wisp darted into view, throwing itself against the massive groundcar like a green missile. Faerie light danced and flickered over the car's surface, seeking to empty the main cells now that they were open to its touch, but as the emerald orb rounded the front of the car, hovering over the burning candles on the fenders, it began to darken and sink.

Kile whooped in glee. "Holy Christ, will you look at that? It can't stand the heat!"

Jerrin stumbled to the front of the cab and dropped into the seat behind Corason. Cold radiated from the suit on his body, but he grinned fiercely. "Take that, you green bastard," he laughed. "Cut in the heaters, Kile!"

Strapped to the outside of the car, four powered space heaters intended for use in Jerrin's camping dome glowed to life, throwing a ruddy light across the bare sand. Long power leads taped the car's hull tethered the portable units to the groundcar's external power jacks. The werewisp rolled away, regaining its color as it moved farther from the car. Agitated, it circled and tried to move in closer, only to be repelled by the warmth flooding from the car.

Kile put the car in gear and started to drive slowly, wheeling in a generous turn toward the east. The 'wisp followed, dancing as close as it could to brush them with its eerie radiance. At each touch, the power gauges wavered dangerously, dipping and then recovering, but always a little less than before. The 'wisp couldn't maintain its ethereal grasp on the car, not against the faint glow of the heaters and the dying heat of the oxygen pellets.

"I think it's going to work," Kile crowed. He slapped Corason's back, rattling her in her suit. "Good thinking! You get a gold star."

"Keep d-d-driving," she said.

She hardly noticed when Jerrin moved up close to her, wrapping a thermal blanket over her shoulders and holding her close to warm her body with his. Lurching and reeling like a ship on fire, the groundcar rumbled toward the lightening in the sky.

The werewisp followed them for almost a hundred kilometers, dancing in their wake, drifting close to siphon their power for a few seconds before the glowing heat-lamps drove it away again. Its touch darkened the lights, slowed the drive motors to a sluggish churn, crackled and snapped on the radio channels . . . but it couldn't slow them with its tenuous hold.

Corason watched the creature drowsily, struggling to keep her eyes open. It streaked and darted, flaring with impotent fury a few dozen meters from the car, whirling and flickering as if it was working itself into a frenzy, but despite its anger, it couldn't come near. Each time the creature attacked the car, the ruddy lights drove it away again.

"I don't believe it's working," Jerrin said quietly. "The space heaters can't be putting out that much heat. The external thermometer still reads fifty below zero."

"Thin atmosphere," Corason said sleepily. "There isn't enough air to soak up the radiant heat. For the 'wisp, it's like standing next to a bonfire."

Jerrin murmured something in reply, but she missed it, slipping into a strange and dreamless sleep. She'd been awake too long, exposed to the cold and the wear of the planet, challenged by extremes she'd never imagined in her previous life. All she knew was that Jerrin held her the whole time, stroking her hair, keeping her warm.

The change in the light woke her up sometime later. Delicate and tentative, faint streamers of rose and gold illuminated Jerrin's features as he looked down at her. Through the skylights of the cab, she could see the cold and proud stars fading in a rusty haze that grew stronger as she watched. She pushed herself upright, looking around. The car was climbing a long, dark slope crowned by a soft light, a subtle rise in the endlessness of the plains. She shifted in her seat, looking left and right.

The werewisp toiled a few hundred meters away, dark and small, still doggedly trailing them.

The car shuddered to a stop. Light now filled the windshield, flooding into the cabin. Kile shook his long hair and sighed. "Here we are," he said. "Sun-up." The desert floor in front of them stretched as far as the eye could see, soft and crimson like a carpet of felt, growing brighter with each passing minute. In silence, the three of them watched High Mojave's tired sun climb slowly, slowly into the sky.

Behind them, the 'wisp wavered, and then turned and fled into the west, a green pearl of light receding on the ebbing tide of darkness. In a moment, it was lost to sight. Jerrin rubbed his face, bathing in the sunlight. When he looked at her, his smile was open and generous.

"I think you saved our lives, Corey," he said.

She leaned her head against his chest. "I didn't," she said. "The daybreak did." Then she fell asleep again, looking at the sunrise.

About the Author

Author of *The Shadow Stone* and *Easy Betrayals*, the eighth book in the DOUBLE DIAMOND TRIANGLE SAGA™, Richard Baker has been writing for TSR, Inc. since 1991. Originally a native of the Jersey shore, Rich graduated from Virginia Tech and received a commission in the United States Navy in May of 1988. He served as a deck officer on board the USS *Tortuga* and qualified as a Surface Warfare Officer before becoming a game designer. Since joining TSR, Rich has worked on most of TSR's product lines, including the ALTERNITY® science fiction role-playing game, the STAR*DRIVE™ campaign setting, and the PLAYER'S OPTION™ series of rules expansions. In 1995 he won an Origins award for Best New Role-playing Supplement for the BIRTHRIGHT® game setting.

So far, Rich has hung his hat in New Jersey, Virginia, Rhode Island, Virginia again, Louisiana, Virginia a third time, and Wisconsin. He now lives in Washington State with his wife Kim, his daughters Alex and Hannah, and a brace o' cats. He's a fan of Golden Age SF and the Philadelphia Phillies, although he hopes he'll recover soon.

Rich's first STAR*DRIVE novel, *Zero Point,* will be published in June 1999.

"Unlikely Allies"

JOHN HELFERS

PLEASE HELP.

They were returning from the mission when Ridyha heard the voice. Instantly she froze, looked all around, and sniffed the air for any trace of an enemy's scent. Her weren mate and partner, Cher'nath, didn't immediately see her stop. He trotted a few steps farther before realizing she wasn't following. He hurried back to her, scanning the surrounding foliage as he did so. The fur on his neck and arms stood up, his nervousness at stopping so close to their enemy apparent.

"Ridyha, what's wrong?" he asked, speaking in the guttural dialect of their clan.

"Didn't you hear it?" she whispered, staring off into the dark jungle, not back the way they had come but to the west. Cher'nath looked as well, tensing in case something came charging out of the thick underbrush at them. Like everywhere else on the planet, animal life was nonexistent on their small part of the Hegelian continent, but that didn't mean something or someone not native to Spes hadn't followed them. The clan they had been spying on would certainly take a dim view of their actions.

"Hear what?' he asked, lowering his voice as he searched the trees. His massive hands tightened on his chuurkhna, the four-bladed weapon that all adult members of his clan carried.

Both Ridyha's and his fur blended with the mottled colors and shadows of the jungle, rendering them practically invisible as long as they stayed still. It would fool most trackers, although other weren knew what to look for and were skilled at picking out their brethren. It was a game all weren participated in as children, blending in with trees and bushes, trying to spot each other, playing "seen and unseen," all in preparation for a time like this, when spotting the tiniest movement could mean the difference between life and death.

"A call for help," Ridyha said, cocking her head to listen again.

Cher'nath frowned. He obviously hadn't heard what she had. Since birth, she had possessed an uncanny intuition, one that was more often right than wrong. The clan shaman had prophesied great things as well as great loss in her future because of this almost supernatural insight. If this was another example of it, she would follow it, and he would follow her.

"From over there?" Cher'nath asked, pointing with the edge of his weapon.

Ridyha nodded.

Please help.

The call hit her again, and she winced and shuddered as if in pain. "It asks again," she gasped. "It sounds as if it's injured, whatever it is."

"Another weren? One of the Rladh clan?" Cher'-nath's lips peeled back from his teeth in a frightening grin.

"No," Ridyha said, shaking again, "it doesn't sound like any voice I've ever heard. I can't describe it. I only know that it needs help."

"You know the Council is waiting for our report," Cher'nath said, "This raid is very important for our village. We need the most accurate data on their population and the surrounding land if we are to strike successfully. For all we know, this could be a trap."

Ridyha looked at him, and the pain on her face was evident. "The Council can wait a few hours, but whoever's out there may not. Besides, the Rladh aren't going anywhere." She shook her head, as if trying to clear it. "I . . . must go to it. You can go back and make our report. I will join you when I'm able."

Cher'nath stretched to his full two meter height in an effort to see over the spindly trees that blocked his vision. He sighed and looked back at her. "No. You know I'm coming with you. We'll find this thing, whatever it is, together."

Ridyha smiled and slipped her smaller hand inside Cher'nath's massive one. "Thank you."

"It'll probably be the death of both of us. Lead the way." Cher'nath grunted, motioning her forward. With hardly a sound, the two weren slipped into the forest.

* * * * *

The pair traveled inland for several minutes toward the edge of the thick forest that shrouded the continent's coastline. The interwoven trees gave way to relatively open plains dotted with clumps of tall bushes covered with spiky, serrated leaves. Here and there, the occasional tree grew, but the rest of the ground was covered by short brown grass that puffed up a cloud of white spores with each step. Ridyha knew these were harmless, it was just the way the grass reproduced. However, the annoyance caused as the spores clung to their fur was considerable. After a few dozen steps, the two looked as if they had been dusted in sugar from the waist down.

Help.

Again the desperate call exploded in her mind. Her subsequent gasp interrupted Cher'nath's latest attempts at brushing the irritating plant life from his legs. She staggered, her long throwing blade slipping from her grasp. Instantly Cher'nath was by her side, holding her. "What? Are we close?"

Ridyha pointed in the direction they had been traveling. "It's huge, whatever it is. Somewhere beyond the next two hills." She started to walk forward again, but Cher'nath restrained her with a thick arm.

"No," he said, "you wait here. I'm going to have a look around. Don't come up until I signal you. Agreed?" Cher'nath waited until Ridyha nodded her head in agreement, then he turned and loped off over the hill.

Ridyha watched him go for a second, then retrieved her blade and sheathed it in the bandolier across her chest. Although there were plenty of energy weapons on Spes, she and Cher'nath preferred to rely on weapons that didn't need any form of energy other than strength. A weren's strength, male or female, was usually more than enough. Although Ridyha was slightly shorter and fifty kilograms lighter than Cher'nath, she was still as strong as any weren in their clan.

Please help us. I know you are close.

The voice caused Ridyha's head to snap up, looking toward the hills again. She took a step, then another, heading in the direction Cher'nath had gone.

*   *   *   *   *

Cher'nath crept through clusters of plants and sprouting brown grass. He crested one hill, trotted quickly down its other side, then climbed the second. Crouching down at the hilltop, his chuurkhna ready to slash or throw, he peeked over the hill.

In the valley below, at the end of a trail of crushed foliage and shredded ground, lay a spacecraft unlike anything Cher'nath had ever seen. It was three times as large as any scout ship and looked as if it could hold a dozen people comfortably. That was where any resemblance to any other spaceship he had ever seen ended. Instead of the blocky, bulging cargo hold of a freighter, this ship's lines were sleek and aerodynamic. There didn't seem to be any weapon ports, ruling out a cruiser, nor did it have the powerful engines of a corvette. It didn't even seem to have any entry portals or view ports. The whole ship seemed to be crafted out of one uniform piece, perfectly seamless. Cher'nath couldn't make out engine housings, a bridge, or any other recognizable starship features, just the smooth, unbroken gray-white fuselage.

Well, almost unbroken. Looking more closely at the ship's bottom, Cher'nath saw several long tears where it had apparently sustained damage during landing. A dark green, viscous liquid was seeping from several of the gashes in the ship's skin. The liquid didn't smell like anything even remotely familiar.

Almost like it's bleeding, Cher'nath thought.

There didn't seem to be any signs of life around the ship. Cher'nath rose to his feet and was about to circle around to the other side to see if anything was lying in ambush, when a rustle from the far end of the clearing caught his attention.

The tall bushes parted, and Ridyha stepped out from the jungle, walking straight for the ship. She didn't appear to be taking any precautions whatsoever but walked as if she was taking a carefree afternoon stroll. Cher'nath couldn't believe his eyes. Cursing under his breath, he broke from cover and ran toward her.

"Ridyha, stop! What are you doing?" Cher'nath asked as he drew near her. His mate didn't respond to his

presence in any way, but kept walking, her blue eyes fixed
on the strange ship in front of them.

"Ridyha, what's happening—"Cher'nath said as he reached
for her shoulder. Those three words were all he got out. As
soon as his fingers touched her, a jagged bolt of pain lanced
through his head. Dropping his chuurkhna, Cher'nath growled
in agony and staggered back, his hands clutching his skull.

Through a haze of pain and tears, he watched helplessly
as Ridyha walked up to the spacecraft. He tried to go to
her, but the closer he got to his mate and the ship, the
worse his head pounded. Even so, he forced himself to
keep going, fighting the increasing pressure. When he was
about one meter away from Ridyha, the pain was so great
that Cher'nath sank to his knees, unable to even think
about taking another step. He forced his eyes open just in
time to see a section of the ship open up, revealing an inky
black hole that Ridyha stepped through. As Cher'nath
watched, the skin of the ship closed again and his mate
vanished as though she had never existed.

*　*　*　*　*

As soon as Ridyha entered the alien craft, a feeling of
immense peace overwhelmed her. The strange compulsion
to come to the ship disappeared immediately. Looking
behind her, she found that the portal she had walked
through was gone, replaced by smooth seamless wall.

She found herself in a small corridor that appeared to
open into a larger, more brightly lit room. Keeping her
hand near her bandolier of blades, she walked slowly down
the corridor. After a few meters, she relaxed a little and
straightened up. If this was an ambush, whoever was
behind it was taking his time. If he did intend her harm, it
probably would have happened by now.

Another few steps brought Ridyha to the end of the corridor and the doorway to the room. She looked in, trying

to spot any possible danger, but saw none. Sniffing the air yielded no results either. Taking a deep breath, Ridyha entered the room.

As soon as she did so, she heard a faint hiss behind her. She knew what had happened but turned to look anyway. The doorway to the corridor was sealed. The walls were the same smooth, slightly lustrous gray-white color as the outside of the ship. The light in the room seemed to come from the walls themselves. Ridyha pushed at the wall experimentally, finding it slightly yielding, but very strong.

I apologize for forcing you to come here, but it seemed like the safest way to communicate. The voice came from everywhere and nowhere all at once, from the walls around her and from inside Ridyha's head at the same time. Who-ever or whatever was communicating with her, he spoke flawless Weren. Ridyha looked around, her hands closing and unclosing in reflexive combat readiness.

"Are you the one who called for help?" she asked.

Yes. I am grateful to see that you have responded, the voice replied. *My companion and I require assistance.*

"Who are you? Where are you?" Ridyha asked.

The weren heard a small noise that sounded like laugh-ter. *I am the ship you are currently standing inside.*

Ridyha looked around at the barren room. "You . . . *are* the starship?"

That is correct.

"How are you able to . . .?" Ridyha started, then trailed off, unable to ask one question out of the dozen that was whirling in her mind.

I will explain everything in a few seconds. I assure you that neither my companion nor I mean you any harm. However, right now we had better let your mate know that you are not in any danger.

"Cher'nath? Is he still outside?"

Look for yourself.

A section of the wall turned transparent, and Ridyha looked out over the valley in which the ship lay.

* * * * *

Once Ridyha disappeared and the hole in the ship's side had closed, the valley was utterly quiet. The constricting pain in Cher'nath's head stopped just as suddenly as it had begun. For a second, Cher'nath was unable to move, barely comprehending what he had just seen, then the rage took him.

A low growl rumbling in his throat, he picked up his chuurkhna and prepared to make his own entrance in the ship's fuselage. Cher'nath had just planted his feet and was about to swing when a voice from behind him startled him so much that he almost dropped his weapon.

"Query:" the voice said in perfect Standard, "why do you prepare to assault/attack/harm my friend?"

Cher'nath spun around so fast he almost missed his questioner, who was standing calmly a few meters away.

The creature was shorter than Cher'nath, the top of his head only coming up to the weren's broad shoulders, a humanoid, but definitely not human. The few articles of clothing he wore did nothing to hide the intricate patterns of circuitry and conduits covering his body, gleaming veins of copper, platinum, and monofilament wire running down his arms and legs just beneath the skin. His hair clicked as it rustled in the slight breeze, and Cher'nath could see bits of what appeared to be thermoplast conductors woven into each follicle. His eyes were pupiless, blank black orbs, but Cher'nath knew the creature could see him with no difficulty.

This was a mechalus, one of a race of machine-men who possessed an amazing rapport with computers. They were a seamlessly evolved combination of creature and machine. Many mechalus were technicians and gridpilots, but the bulky pistol holstered at this one's side suggested he was involved in something a bit more dangerous.

Cher'nath blinked at the mechalus, the heavy chuurkhna in his hand almost forgotten. Whoever this creatures was, Cher'nath hadn't heard him approach, which put the weren's combat senses on alert.

"Repeat query: why do you prepare to assault/attack/harm my friend?"

Although the question made almost no sense to Cher'-nath, he assumed the mech meant the ship. "This thing," he growled, pointing to the curved wall of the starship, "took my mate. I'm going to get her. I'd stand back if I were you, so you don't get hurt."

The mechalus seemed to slip into a vacant trace for a moment then came back. "Statement: ship does not intend harm/damage to her. Conditional statement: cease/stop initial intended action or probability one hundred percent that I will intervene to prevent/stop."

Cher'nath looked at the slim mechalus, whom he outweighed by at least two hundred kilograms. He grinned, a truly fearsome sight. "You're welcome to try. After I finish with you, I'll still take this ship apart." With that he hefted the chuurkhna and looked back at the ship for a likely spot to bury the wicked blades.

"Statement: warning has been given. Statement: active defense/protection beginning," the mech said.

With his back to the mechalus, Cher'nath's sensitive ears heard the faint sound of the laser pistol being drawn. He shifted the chuurkhna and twisted his upper body, swinging the weapon behind him in a vicious arc sure to decapitate anyone standing there. His surprise was nearly total when his blades met no resistance. Overbalanced from his attack, he stumbled and nearly fell.

The mechalus, who had ducked under the melee weapon, now straightened. While Cher'nath fought for balance, the mech rapped the hand holding the chuurkhna with the butt of his pistol, knocking the weapon to the ground.

"Statement: your chance of defeating me in unarmed combat/battle twenty-two percent plus/minus five percent," the mechalus said as he holstered his weapon. "Query: will you surrender/submit?"

Cher'nath's eyes narrowed to slits, evaluating the distance between himself and his opponent. With a low growl building in his chest, he charged, intending to bury the mechalus in an avalanche of angry weren. The sight alone of a snarling, full-grown weren running towards an enemy usually caused them to freeze or flee. This one did neither.

The mechalus took one step to the side, evading Cher'-nath's grasping claws. He grabbed the weren's hand with his own and pivoted, redirecting the force of Cher'nath's movement straight down while his leg shot out and hooked the weren's own. Caught off guard, Cher'nath went sailing through the air, landing flat on his back with a crash. Before the sky and trees above him came back into focus, the mechalus appeared in his vision, standing over him and holding Cher'nath's chuurkhna in his hands.

"No!" Ridyha's voice echoed though the clearing, causing both weren and mechalus to look at the ship. Through a transparent section of the fuselage, they could see Ridyha pressed up against the barrier that held her inside.

"Ridyha!" Cher'nath used the distraction to grab the mechalus's foot and heave him to the ground. Scrambling to his feet, he lumbered to the spacecraft's side. When he got close, he could see that she was smiling at him.

Cher'nath heard Ridyha's voice in his head. *Cher'nath, I'm fine. Everything is all right. It was the ship that was calling to me. It brought me here. It and the mechalus need our help.*

"How is this— How are you speaking to me?" Cher'-nath asked.

With my mind. This ship says that I am psionic and is augmenting my natural abilities. With practice, I will be able to do this on my own. That explains the "intuition" I've always had, and the shaman's prophecy. "Great things," remember? Cher'nath, I feel like a whole new world has been opened up to me! Ridyha could hardly contain herself.

Great change. Cher'nath did remember, but there had been more as well. *And great loss.*

"When will they let you go?" he asked.

That, I'm afraid, is a bit more difficult, a new voice, calm and decidedly feminine, said. *You see, Cher'nath, as your mate has told you, we need your help.*

Cher'nath became aware of another presence beside him. He looked over to see the mechalus standing next to him. As he watched, the mech extended his hand towards the ship. Tiny filaments extended from his fingers and merged with the ship's skin. The mechalus appeared to enter a trance again, although his pupiless eyes remained fixed on Cher'nath.

Ah, I feel that Tau has joined us. Where are my manners? Allow me to introduce ourselves. My companion is Tau Omicron, and I am usually known simply as the ship. We've been debating choosing another name for me, one with a little more individuality to it, but the Negationists came and chose to interrupt the discussion—

"What are you talking about?" Ridyha and Cher'nath both broke in together.

"Negationists?" Cher'nath continued. "Living ships?"

Tau spoke this time. "Introduction: summary follows. Statement: Negationists, definition: a small radical/splinter faction of the mechalus whole. Statement/speculation: they believe that peace can only be attained if all biological life is discarded/removed. Addendum: only one hundred percent artificial/cybernetic life forms acceptable. Statement: considered non-violent to other races, but fanatical to their cause.

"Statement: spacecraft, unknown alien design/manufacture, discovered drifting near our homeworld, Aleer. Addendum: when taken to Aleer and examined, intelligence in spacecraft awakened/manifested, but memory banks damaged; point of origin unknown/forgotten. Speculation, verified: Negationists discovered/learned of ship intelligence capabilities and attempted to acquire/procure/steal for own research. Statement: spacecraft launched from Aleer and attempted to escape pursuing Negationists. Addendum: physicist Tau Omicron accompanied ship.

"Speculation/analysis: malfunction occurred. Statement: spacecraft appeared in the Verge without functional/operational spacefold capability. Statement: spacecraft self-navigated to the nearest habitable planet to attempt repairs. Target: Spes. Statement: orbit had just been achieved when we were discovered/located by Negationists. Statement: attempting escape/evasion in lower atmosphere, we crash-landed on continent/planet, with spacecraft sustaining considerable damage/injury. Statement: probability Negationists still hunting/searching for us: ninety-three percent, plus/minus four percent."

That's why we need to help them, Cher'nath—Ridyha began.

"Help them? This is not a matter that concerns us," Cher'nath growled. "Let these Negationists and the other mechalus squabble over their prize. We have problems of our own without getting involved in offworlders' concerns."

Unfortunately, I realized that there was a high probability of the situation happening almost exactly as it has, the ship said. *Cher'nath, all we'd really like is to repair my drive engines and be on our way. While orbiting the planet, my sensors detected a large deposit of a mineral that will regenerate my engines and allow us to leave this planet and system. When we crash-landed, I tried to put us close*

*to the deposit. Unfortunately, my internal sensor systems
were blanked in the crash, and due to local interference, I
cannot get a fix on the location again. I do know, however,
that it is somewhere to the north of us, near a small village, I believe. I can send a collector with you that will be
able to trace the mineral's exact whereabouts, once it gets
close enough.*

A portal opened and a small, round machine floated out
and took up a position behind the mechalus.

*If you would just act as a guide and take Tau and the
collector to the general area, they will be able to gather
enough to complete my regeneration, and we will leave
you in peace. I will not leave you with nothing, however.
While you are gone, I will train Ridyha in her psionic
powers. That should be a fair trade.*

Cher'nath's lips peeled back from his fangs. "If I
refuse?"

Well, the ship calmly, *then we shall have to attempt to
locate the mineral ourselves. The choice is yours; we will
not force you into anything you do not wish to do.*

Tau's modulated, hollow voice spoke again, this time
incorporating several terms. "Statement: without weren
assistance/help, obtaining element will consume longer
time parameters than originally allocated/planned for.
Speculation: percentage chance Negationist scout ships
will arrive before I locate element: eighty-two percent and
increasing/rising. Corollary statement: Negationists will
forcibly alter/convert anyone who knows of the starship's
existence into complete/total cybernetic entity/lifeform."

Wait, I thought you said they were non-violent? Ridyha
asked.

Oh, they are, replied the ship, *in their own way of looking at things. However, that would not preclude them from
performing experiments on you. They feel their goal of
pure cybernetic consciousness surpasses moral bound-
aries. They told me so when they first contacted me. They*

also cannot afford to have word of my existence get out, for there would be many interested parties who would seek to recover me. The Negationists seek to unlock the final mysteries of total cybernetic intelligence, and they believe I am the key, all of which does not give me a lot of confidence in my continued existence should I fall into their hands.

Cher'nath was about to protest again, but when he looked at Ridyha and saw the pleading look in her eyes, he knew he would help them. *A woman's will is stronger than the tightest fist*, or so the old weren proverb went.

Besides, Cher'nath thought, the way they've outlined it, what choice do I have?

Cher'nath, said Ridyha, *please, don't just do it for me, but for them as well. I can assure you that they mean no harm to either of us.*

"I'm sure you can, but what assurance do I have that this alien ship is not controlling you as well?" Cher'nath said. "I know you are my mate, and we have pledged to be together and share our lives, and as such I should trust you, but after what I've just seen, how can I?"

Perhaps this will help you. Ridyha looked towards the inside of the ship for a second, then turned back to Cher'-nath. *I just told him I would stay with them of my own free will until you returned.*

"What?" Cher'nath bellowed. "Woman, this is black-mail!"

Ridyha placed her clawed hand on the ship's fuselage and looked at Cher'nath.

The huge weren muttered a few dire threats, then reached up and placed his hand over hers, holding it there for a few seconds. He took his hand away, snatched his chuurkhna, and nodded to the mechalus and the collector. "Let's go." With that, he turned and loped into the forest.

* * * * *

Cher'nath set a deliberately grueling pace, wanting to test his companion. While he ran, his hunter's mind constantly alert for danger, he tried to make sense of what had just happened. It all whirled through his mind in a confused jumble . . . living ships . . . Ridyha with psionic abilities . . . Negationists . . .

That last thought caused Cher'nath to scowl, and he looked behind him at the mechalus. The cyber-man was keeping pace with him perfectly, maintaining a precise distance behind him. The collector floated along unobtrusively between them. While it had been silver when it had first exited the ship, now it was colored a dull-gray edging into black, camouflaging itself against the fading light. Cher'nath returned his gaze to the forest ahead and quickened his pace.

The weren and mechalus's long legs covered a lot of distance, and soon the collector chirped repeatedly, stopping at the edge of a large clearing. The three companions looked down at a sizeable village composed of clusters of single-story buildings, most of them built into hillsides. Dozens of hulking weren walked around or worked at various tasks. Cher'nath and Tau crouched in a thick copse of trees about fifty meters away and watched the scattered weren go about their business as night fell.

"Don't tell me. That mineral you want, it's in there, right?" Cher'nath pointed towards the grouped buildings.

The collector chirped softly behind them. Without looking, Tau reached out and placed the communicating tendrils of his hand on the collector.

"Statement: the collector has completed/finished preliminary probe/scan of the area. Speculation/analysis: probability ninety-three percent plus/minus five percent that element deposit/vein located in proximity of water pump in center of town/village. Statement: collector can access element by filtering it from liquid/water," Tau said.

"Great, just great," Cher'nath replied.

"Query: what is problem/difficulty?" Tau asked.
"Query, extended: are these not the same genus/race as
yourself? Query: Why not simply ask/request mineral
from them?"

"This is the Rladh clan. My clan has been skirmishing with
them for several months now. *Ris*, or full war, is expected to
break out in the next week. I doubt they'll just let us walk in
and take what we need, even if they don't use it."

Tau looked at the small groups of weren before them.
"Statement: then we shall have to procure/recover the mineral without their discovery/knowledge."

Cher'nath sighed. "All right, we'll wait for nightfall,
then move in, collect the stuff, and leave. If we're lucky,
we'll be in and out with no one knowing," Cher'nath said,
settling down to wait. Tau sat across from him, in a position where both of them could keep an eye on not only the
village but the surrounding jungle as well. Cher'nath
regarded the mechalus, who stared back at him, his metal-
veined face expressionless.

Tau spoke first. "Query: you feel manipulated/used?" he
asked quietly in formal weren. When he saw the surprise
on Cher'nath's face, he nodded. "Statement: the ship has
provided me with a complete glossary of your language
scanned from your companion/mate."

Cher'nath relaxed at the explanation. "Wouldn't you?"
he replied, his gaze flicking over to the village for a
moment.

"Reply: perhaps. Suggestion: if you evaluate our
actions, you know/understand we mean no harm. Statement: we needed/required your help, and this was
fastest/quickest way of obtaining assistance. Statement:
understand, if we knew of a better way to accomplish this
mission/task, we would have implemented it. Query: if you
were in this position, your ally/friend injured, lost on
unknown planet and hunted by hostile, superior enemy
force, what would you do?"

Cher'nath didn't reply for a few seconds, looking instead at the village again while he thought about the question. What if Ridyha was surrounded by enemies, hurt, unable to move? What if she were to die, not in battle, as was her right, but crippled and dishonored, and only he could prevent it? What would he do?

Cher'nath looked back at Tau. "Anything I had to," he replied.

Tau nodded slowly. "Statement: you understand lack of alternatives/options, then. Statement: your companion/ mate will return to you when this is over."

"I don't need to be assured of that," Cher'nath said. "I will make sure of it myself."

"Statement: regardless, it will be as I have said," Tau replied.

You've got that right, one way or another, Cher'nath thought.

The conversation died after that, weren and mechalus each choosing instead to concentrate on what they had to do. Night had fallen completely, and the village was dimly illuminated by reflected light from the larger of Spes's moons, Fides. One by one, the lights in the weren houses winked out.

Cher'nath waited for another hour, noting the time by the movement of the moon. He also noted the wandering pair of weren who walked a random perimeter around the village.

When he judged it was late enough, he rose, motioning for Tau to follow him. Pointing at the collector, he indicated that it should wait in the trees until summoned. The collector chirped softly and settled to the ground.

Cher'nath crept out of the copse of trees and paused, sniffing the air for nearby scent. He signaled Tau to follow him and started approaching the village, Tau following silently.

Moving a few steps at a time, the pair reached the out-skirts of the houses. Cher'nath and Tau quickly walked

down the main path to the village square and the pump in
the middle. Cher'nath checked to see that it was operational, then nodded to Tau, who signaled the collector to
join them.

After a few seconds, the round machine floated over
to the weren and mechalus. The collector extended a flexible metal hose from its side and inserted it into the
faucet. Tau turned the pump on, and the machine started
the extraction.

"How long will this take?" Cher'nath asked in a whisper.

Tau placed his hand on the collector. "Statement/esti-
mation: ten minutes to extract usable element amount.
Statement: suggest hide/wait in alley to reduce chance/
possibility of discovery."

"What about the collector?" Cher'nath asked.

"Speculation: if collector is discovered/noticed by the
guards, they will investigate it first, leaving them open to
neutralization," Tau said.

"Agreed," Cher'nath said, his fur already shifting color
to a mottled gray and black to blend in with the darkness.
The pair walked over to the nearest alley, a narrow gap
shrouded in darkness between two houses. Chuurkhna and
pistol ready, the weren and mechalus crouched down to
wait.

"Statement: I have sent collector a message/signal. Sent
message/signal follows: when extraction is finished, it will
depart/leave premises, as will we, and meet/rendezvous
back where reconnaissance began/initiated," Tau said.

Cher'nath nodded, scanning the square for any other
movement. Several minutes passed this way, the machine
noiselessly working while Cher'nath and Tau remained
alert. Just when Cher'nath thought they might pull this off
undetected, a snort next to their hiding place broke the
stillness. Light appeared in the open window above the
pair, and the front door of the house they were crouched

by creaked open. A shadow appeared on the ground near the door, then the huge form of a yawning weren stepped outside. Cher'nath and Tau exchanged glances, then watched the weren to see where he was going.

The weren stretched, his huge arms reaching for the stars, then slowly ambled towards the water pump. Looking over, Cher'nath saw that the collector was now hugging the ground, trying to be as inconspicuous as possible.

Cher'nath saw Tau move out of the corner of his eye, and he turned to see the mechalus raising his pistol. Quickly Cher'nath put his hand over the weapon and shook his head. Tau looked back at him, a quizzical look on his face, but Cher'nath only smiled.

By now the weren was almost to the pump. Cher'nath stepped out of the alley and waited, his chuurkhna ready. The weren, still apparently half-awake, bent over to turn the pump on when he noticed the metal tube that reached from the spigot to the strange metal machine on the ground next to it. Confused, he stared at it for a few seconds, which was more than enough time for Cher'nath to act.

The weren hurled his chuurkhna at his hunched-over target. The flat side of one of the end blades thudded into the weren's head, sending him sprawling. Dazed, the villager grunted and fell to his knees.

Cher'nath was already moving, sprinting toward the fallen weren. When he reached him he put all of the anger and frustration he had felt that day into a whistling uppercut that laid the other weren flat on his back. Cher'nath bent over the unconscious form, checking to make sure he was still alive.

The sound of footsteps behind him alerted Cher'nath to trouble. Looking back, he saw Tau a few meters away, running towards him at full speed. Before he could move, the mechalus jumped up on the weren's shoulders, launching himself past his surprised companion.

Cher'nath followed the mechalus's flight to see him
land, feet-first, on a smaller weren with a wickedly studded battle club in his hand. The mechalus and weren rolled
across the ground together in a cloud of dust. There was a
grunt, a snap, and then silence.

Cher'nath got up and looked around the square, searching for more attackers. Tau joined him a second later.
"Statement: collector is almost done/finished. One point
four processing minutes left." Cher'nath noticed that his
arm was hanging limply at his side.

"Are you all right?" he asked.

The mechalus nodded. "Statement: simple break/injury
acquired during combat/fight. Statement: internal repair
unit working." He motioned to the fallen weren Cher'nath
had knocked unconscious. "Query: why did you not permanently disable?"

"This mission is not undertaken specifically for my
clan," Cher'nath whispered, "therefore I cannot kill any of
the Rladh clan. *Ristath*, a state of open warfare, has not
been declared. However, since we are trespassing on their
territory, they may deal with us as they see fit. That's also
why the other weren didn't sound the alarm. There is more
prestige in capturing or killing an enemy single-handedly."

"Opinion: unfortunately for second enemy/opponent,"
Tau said, "he failed to count on second member of
infiltration party/team. Statement: opponent suffered
fatal/mortal injuries."

Cher'nath nodded. "You had no choice. Is the collector
finished?"

Tau bent down and contacted the collector again.
"Statement: almost. Twenty more seconds." He looked
past Cher'nath and his eyes widened. "Warning: take
cover!" he said, drawing his pistol and leaping past Cher'-
nath at something behind them.

The scream of a wounded weren and the crackle of a
charge pistol sounded like thunderclaps throughout the

village. Cher'nath spun around to see both Tau and another
Rladh weren crumpling to the ground in the doorway of
the first weren's home. Lights started appearing in nearby
houses.

Cher'nath turned Tau over. A stain was already spreading over his chest from the hole in his side. Tau shuddered
and tried to push Cher'nath away. "Command: go . . . get
collector back to ship . . . escape/leave while you can."

"No. We started this together; we finish it together."

Cher'nath hoisted the mechalus over his shoulder as if
he were a sack of soy germ just as he saw the roving patrol
appear at the other end of the village and start toward them.
Behind him the collector chirped once.

"Get back to the ship." Cher'nath ordered the collector.
"I'll try to delay them as long as possible. Tell the ship to
be ready when we get there."

The collector chirped several times, but Cher'nath had
no idea if it had understood him. Without pausing to see if
it was leaving, he took off for the forest, all too aware of
the angry howls and pounding footsteps behind him.

*   *   *   *   *

Ridyha paced back and forth in her room, pausing only
to stare at the darkness outside. It had been hours since
Cher'nath and the mechalus had left, and there was no sign
of them.

"Could you please try one more time to contact them?"

*Ridyha, I will try, although I am compelled to tell you
again that I was barely able to contact you. If they are even
a few hundred meters past that range, we will have no hope
of hearing from them.*

"Why is that so difficult?" she snapped. "Why can't you
locate them?"

*Because I'm a starship, designed for long-range scan-
ning in the relative emptiness of space. All of this ground*

*clutter obscures my tracking systems. We should continue
with your training.*

"No!" Ridyha took a deep breath, aware of the almost
overwhelming urge to break something. "Just try it once
more," she said, more calmly this time. "How are the external repairs coming?"

There was a barely perceptible pause as the ship multi-
tasked. *External repairs are ninety-eight percent complete.
A few more minutes and the hull will be at full strength.
Wait, I'm receiving a signal. Tracking.*

"Is it them?" Ridyha asked, peering out the view port.

*No. It is the collector. Cher'nath and Tau do not appear
to be with it.* The ship opened a portal for the collector to
enter and brought it into Ridyha's room. The collector
floated in front of Ridyha, chirping and beeping wildly.

"What's it saying?" Ridyha asked.

Just a moment. There was a pause as the ship spoke
with the computer. *Cher'nath and Tau were discovered as
they were collecting the element. Tau was wounded in the
village . . . wait at ship until they arrive . . .*

"What?" Ridyha said. "Absolutely not. I'm going after
him. Open a portal."

As she stalked towards the wall, the ship began, *I'm not
sure that's—*

The ship went suddenly silent, the walls of the room
turning a bright red, and the collector disappeared into a
hole that opened for it on the wall.

"What's happening?" Ridyha asked.

The ship's voice, which previously had been calm and
unaffected, spoke in a fear-tinged tone. *The Negationists
have found us.*

* * * * *

Cher'nath plunged through the forest with Tau slung
across his back. He heard the sounds of pursuit close

behind him and knew if he didn't cut back to the ship soon, he and the mechalus would both soon be dead. Cher'nath plowed through the chest-high bushes in his way, not caring about the trail he was leaving.

I hope they've had enough time to make those repairs, he thought as he cut over in the direction of the clearing. A war club slammed into the tree next to him, the near-miss inspiring Cher'nath to run faster, increasing the distance between him and his pursuers. He heard the whine of a laser pistol, and looked back to see Tau spraying the woods with blasts of light.

"Save . . . your strength. I'm not . . . carrying you . . . all this way . . . to have you die . . . on me now," Cher'nath panted.

"Statement: keep . . . running," Tau said weakly.

"One more hill . . . and we're there," Cher'nath replied. He could feel the fluids leaking from Tau dripping down his side as he ran, and he hoped they wouldn't be too late.

Cher'nath staggered up the last hill and stumbled to a halt when he saw what was on the other side.

The ship was still there, but now it was surrounded by more than a dozen large, four-legged robots bristling with what looked like sensor gear, robotic arms, and other scientific equipment. The ship was surrounded by a field of crackling energy that appeared to be keeping them at bay. Scanning the clearing, Cher'nath saw several other robots lying motionless on the ground.

"Tau, what in the name of *K'vast* are those?"

The mechalus wearily turned his head. "Reply: Negationist drones/workers. Addendum: robots carry out orders . . . for cyberminds. Speculation: should reach ship . . . if we're quick enough . . . and surprise them. Command: go now!"

Cher'nath looked behind him just in time to see the first Rladh weren burst from the trees. Without thinking, Cher'-nath leaped off the hill and bounded down the slope.

The drones reacted as one unit, several of them moving
to intercept the new target. With a grace that belied his
size, Cher'nath nimbly avoided the first two, but an arm
from the third clamped onto his leg and held fast, jerking
him to a stop. With a roar, Cher'nath slashed down with
his chuurkhna, severing the cerametal arm and shaking it
off.

The delay had been enough. Cher'nath saw his path
blocked by more of the robot drones. He knew both of
them would never make it to the ship.

"Tell Ridyha—" he began.

"Statement: I . . . know," Tau said.

Taking a few steps forward, Cher'nath dropped his chuurkhna as he lifted Tau above his head and threw the
mechalus toward the ship. Just before Tau would have hit
the energy barrier, it winked out and a hole appeared that
he sailed through. As soon as the mech disappeared, the
hole closed.

Cher'nath retrieved his weapon and looked around.
Spider-like mechanical bodies completely surrounded
him. Cher'nath straightened, gazed disdainfully at the
drones, and waited.

Before the drones could take a step toward either the
ship or Cher'nath, the clearing was alive with screaming
weren who swarmed out of the trees, descending on the
hapless robots and tearing them apart. Because the drones
had no defensive systems or armaments, the fight was
short and brutal.

Cher'nath met the first of the weren who had battled
through to him with chuurkhna raised and the battle songs
of his clan singing in his head. As he moved to engage the
first of several weren lunging toward him, he wore the
ferocious grin of one who would die in the most honorable
way a weren knew of, in battle.

Meanwhile, the ship, practically forgotten during the
one-sided battle, engaged its engines and rose into the air,

heading for the upper atmosphere and leaving the fighting weren and drones far behind.

Cher'nath swung his chuurkhna in a vicious sweep that cut the legs of his opponent out from under him. The enemy weren screamed in agony as his knees shattered from the blow. Cher'nath didn't stop to finish him off but whirled to face the next of several snarling warriors who surrounded him. He knew he was wounded, probably fatally, but he moved with incredible speed, mowing down anyone who got in his way. For a brief moment, he felt nothing but *chig'tanth*, pure battle rage. He was one with his ancestors, generations upon generations of warriors, dying in the only proper way they knew.

Out of the corner of his eye, he saw the flare of the ship's engines and knew that Ridyha, Tau, and the ship had escaped. Cher'nath held his chuurkhna above his head in the traditional symbol of weren victory. The Rladh paused for a moment upon seeing this, honoring his courage, then the entire group fell upon him.

Cher'nath's last thought as he disappeared beneath a screaming pile of weren claws and fangs was, *Farewell, my love.*

* * * * *

Later, Tau rested in a bed the ship had made for him. His wounds had been treated, and he was sitting comfortably. His attention, however, was not on his mending body, but on Ridyha.

She was in the room with him, staring at another bed similar to the one Tau was in. That bed's occupant, however, was no longer living.

Ridyha stared at Cher'nath's torn and bloody body. After the fight, she had made the ship go back and retrieve his body from the battleground. Tau, not able to help, had watched from the ship. He had counted seven dead weren around Cher'nath's body.

They had found Cher'nath draped in a rough pennant with a symbol on it that Tau recognized as a flag that had been flying at the Rladh settlement. Ridyha now held that same flag in her hands, turning it over and over. Ridyha had told him that weren clans often recognized uncommon valor in an enemy by covering him with their standard. Her eyes kept going from the flag to Cher'nath's body.

"He told me to stay here, even though I wanted to go and fight with him. His last thought was of me," Ridyha said.

Tau reached out to the weren beside him but stopped, letting his hand fall on the bed again. He had told her what had happened at the village and what Cher'nath had done.

"Statement: he did not want you to lose your life in a hopeless battle," Tau said. "Opinion: in that way, we both owe Cher'nath our lives. Opinion, confirmed: he was truly honorable."

"He was also my mate!' Ridyha growled. "It was my duty to fight beside him, but instead I was here and not at his side."

Ridyha, the ship said, *you and I both heard Cher'nath's final thoughts. We both know why he wanted you to stay here. He knew of your importance to your clan. There cannot possibly be dishonor in carrying out his final request.*

"What is important now that he is gone?" Ridyha said. "It was wrong of me to listen to him."

"Statement:" said Tau, "the past is done. Statement: Cher'nath is gone, and you and I will miss/remember him each in our own way, but we can cherish/honor his last days by remembering him as he would desire/want to be remembered: as a weren of honor who offered/sacrificed himself for his mate and companions/friends."

Ridyha looked at him strangely for a moment. "There's a lot more to you than just machine, isn't there?"

"Reply: I simply know/understand what you are feeling because, even though I only knew Cher'nath for brief/short time, I respected/trusted him, and I will also miss him."

The weren reached out, taking the mechalus's smooth hand in her own clawed one, and held it. The room was quiet for several minutes. Ridyha looked at Tau after a while. "Thank you," she said.

"Statement: no, thanks to both of you, without whom neither the ship nor myself would be alive/functional now," Tau replied.

Ridyha nodded. "Well, what now?" she asked.

The Negationists are still out there, said the ship. *We have lost them for now, but you can be assured that they'll still be looking for us.*

"I have the ideal place you can hide for now," Ridyha said. "I would like for you both to come to my village. I doubt the Negationists would try to move on a village full of upset weren. I must take Cher'nath's body back anyway, so he may receive the proper rites for the fallen."

Tau inclined his head in a small bow. "Statement: we will accept/take your offer of refuge/sanctuary. Intention: from there, we can analyze/extrapolate a plan."

"Who knows?" Ridyha said with a slight smile. "Maybe you will be leaving with an extra passenger. This ship could use a woman's touch."

"A woman's will—" he said.

—is stronger that the tightest fist, the ship replied. *Apparently, we are about to discover just how true that proverb is.*

Shaking his head, Tau had no choice but to agree.

About the Author

John Helfers is a writer and editor currently living in Green Bay, Wisconsin. His fiction has appeared in anthologies such as *Sword of Ice and Other Tales of Valdemar*, *The UFO Files*, and *Warrior Princesses*, among others. He is also the editor of the anthology *Black Cats and Broken Mirrors*. Other projects include co-authoring a fantasy trilogy and editing several other anthologies. In his spare time (what there is of it) he enjoys disc golf, inline skating, and role-playing games.

"The Life and Death of a Sleepwalker"

DEAN WESLEY SMITH

Renata Eamsden didn't know what she expected to greet her as the main entrance door to Compound 91-B slid silently open, but it certainly wasn't the smell. It choked her, as if someone had taken the air from her mouth, her lungs, and replaced it with something thick and rotten.

She pushed a step inside, then stopped, coughed, and stepped back, covering her nose as she stared down the long, dim hallway ahead of her. Doors lined both sides of the metal-walled corridor, open doors, black gaps like missing teeth. No one walked that hall, and it seemed so long as to vanish in the distance.

Beside her, Mi'chi Ipsilon, "Mickie" for short, the mechalus member of their group, touched her elbow gently. "Are you well?"

She shook her head, her stomach threatening to send her breakfast back up. Jonesy, the third member and the other human, looked like she felt. He was leaning one hand against the doorframe, clearly holding his breath. Only Mickie seemed unaffected by the intense smell.

She stepped back outside into the humid, almost searing heat of the morning and tried to catch her breath. Behind her, the others followed, and the door slid closed, holding the smell inside. She took two steps away from the building, her steps echoing off the hot concrete. She forced her mind to what she was seeing in front of her: city, paved streets, concrete, windowless buildings. She wanted to think about anything but that smell.

Around her, the city was seemingly deserted, but she knew the city's few residents very seldom went outside during the daylight hours. The three companions wore the planet's standard white, hooded UV blocking cloak that reached all the way to the ground, protecting even their feet as they walked. Under the robe, she wore only shorts and a thin blouse in a vain attempt to remain cool. Even her pistol felt hot against her side.

Her stomach was settling slightly. That smell had been a shock. Not in all her life had she smelled anything like it, so strong, so thick, so rotten.

Once, as a small girl, she'd come upon a dead animal while hiking. That smell had made her sick. This smell was worse. She could still feel it clogging her nose and filling her mouth.

Around them the air swirled, hot and humid. She had hoped, during the short walk from Arriver lodging, that the building would be cool. Now she preferred staying out here in the heat.

She moved back and leaned against the rough surface of the building, taking a few more long, slow breaths of the warm air, forcing her stomach to settle.

"I fail to understand what happened," Mickie said, staring first at her, then at Jonesy.

Mickie's black, wire-like hair normally shot straight back from his head, but under the hood, it just made his head look bigger. By human standards, Mickie was handsome as far as Renata was concerned, but the prominent veins on his face and neck made him clearly alien.

Jonesy, who was the scientist among them, shook his head. "Couldn't you smell that?"

Mickie shrugged, making his robe ride up and then back down with his powerful shoulders. "It was a human smell. I have smelled worse."

"Well, I haven't," Renata said.

She hadn't, at least not in her ninety-two years of memory. She hoped in the next ninety-two years to never smell it again, but she knew that wasn't possible. They were going to have to go in that building. It was the reason they had come so far.

This building and the others like it scattered around this area of the planet were the reason for all of the last year's travel, for leaving civilized space and coming to the Verge in the first place.

She pulled her hood solidly over her head, blocking out the intense glare. Why had the humans who settled this system even bothered with this hell of a planet? It made no sense to her. Most of the planet was blowing sand, with the only habitable band near one pole where temperatures remained moderate-to-hot by human standards. She had no doubt they would find the reason inside that building, if she could get herself to go back inside.

She smiled up at Jonesy, then turned to Mickie. "How about giving us another few minutes, then we'll try again."

Mickie nodded. "Reasonable."

Jonesy said nothing. Clearly, the thought of going back in there wasn't something that pleased him either.

Renata let her slight weight lean against the building a little more, making sure to keep her hood down so that it shaded her face, then she did her best to relax and focus. Going in that building might just be the most important thing she had ever done. She wouldn't turn back now, no matter what greeted her. She had come too far.

She let her mind focus around the coolness of the day she first heard about this Verge system. She and Tom, then her lover, were drinking coffee in a small, open-air cafe on the edge of a lake on Banisese II. They both had six days off from their jobs with the Concord and had picked that hotel, that cafe, to spend the time together.

She remembered Tom as a face, blue eyes, a warm smile and a nice laugh, but nothing more. Good company. Beyond that, her memory of him had passed into the years, except that he was with her that day.

She remembered that around the cafe the air had smelled of honey and was just warm enough to still be crisp but comfortable. The water of the lake was a bright, clear green, one of the most beautiful lakes she had ever had the pleasure to sit beside. It was one of those perfect afternoons, on a perfect vacation.

The man at a table beside them started telling his companion about a Verge world he'd heard about. "They've conquered death over the last few hundred years," he said. "Everyone on the planet is young. No one dies."

At first, both she and Tom had shrugged it off as too many starfalls for the guy, but he went on, until finally Renata could stand it no longer. She had turned and introduced herself.

"Renata Eamsden, coordinator for the Galactic Concord's study on life spans," she had said.

Her fulltime job was to study the other races who lived longer than humans, to find ways to extend human life spans beyond the standard two hundred years. She had taken the job ten years before after watching her grandfather wither from simple old age and die at one hundred and sixty-four—far, far too young. Those two years of sitting beside him, cleaning him up, watching him die, were the longest years of her life. The day she buried him, she swore to try to find a way to keep that from happening to her father and others. She had made it her life's work to turn back the aging process as much as she could.

Now this guy had said a human colony in the Verge had solved human death and dying over the last century, just since the Second Galactic War, so she had asked him to go on.

Luckily—or maybe unluckily—for her, the guy was nice and more than willing to tell her what he'd heard while on a mission back into the Verge. She'd gotten all the details, then cut her vacation short and gone back to work, forgetting about Tom.

The Concord records showed that the Hloewton system consisted of possibly six inhabited planets and was nothing more than a rumor from the *Monitor*'s visit to Zin Point in 2497. The inhabitants of that system had informed the captain of a world past the Armstrong system where rumor had it that people never died.

The *Monitor*'s records went on to detail how other neighboring Verge systems held only rumors of this Hloewton system, and with the destruction of the Silver Bell colony and the pressing business of re-establishing contact with the Verge, no further efforts had been made to contact this rumored system. No one seemed to even give it any more credit than any other spacer legend in that part of the Verge.

After finding that record, Renata dropped the entire matter, not believing the spacer. Clearly, he had sent her on a wild chase, telling her exactly what she had wanted to hear and ruining her vacation in the process.

Eighteen months later, a human woman named Iduna walked into her office and changed everything. Iduna stood well under two meters tall and had striking black hair and dark eyes. She had a smile that Renata loved immediately, and it felt to Renata that she had known Iduna before but just didn't know where.

It turned out she hadn't really known her. They had never even been on the same planet until now, but Iduna said she felt the same way, one of those bonds between two people that seemed to extend beyond the real world. Renata had never felt anything like it before, and it sort of stunned her.

After a short conversation, Iduna said she had heard that people were going to a Verge system called Hloewton,

where no one died. She then had told Renata that she had
a rare form of cancer, a form that didn't have a cure yet.
The disease would kill her within four years.

When Renata heard that, it felt as if someone had hit her
in the stomach, and the same feeling came back that she
had felt those years with her grandfather. Helplessness.

Renata could hardly listen as Iduna had gone on to say
that she figured that if she started soon, she'd safely make
it to the legendary Verge system of Hloewton before she
died. She had the money and no family, so there was no
point in her not going, to take the slim chance that someone there really could help her. She needed information
about the exact location of the system. Someone in the
Concord's bureaucratic system had sent her to Renata.

At first, Renata had tried to convince Iduna that the
Hloewton system was nothing more than a spacer legend,
but Iduna would have nothing to do with it. She was going,
and that was the end of it.

"Wouldn't you, if the situation was reversed?" Iduna
had asked.

Renata had to admit she would. Just before Iduna
walked away, Renata had said she'd help. Over the next
week, the two of them became fast friends. Eating every
meal together. After a few days Iduna left her hotel and
even moved in with Renata, sleeping in her spare bedroom.
Over the ensuing week, they worked through old records
to find out anything they could about the Hloewton system
and its people. The entire time Renata had the feeling in
her gut of someone hitting her over and over and over.

How was it possible that this bright, very much alive
woman could be dying? It didn't seem right and it certainly wasn't fair.

They discovered possibilities. The Hloewton system
might have been first settled by a large group of scientists
and their families, who had belonged to a strange religious
sect on Naigyun VII almost two centuries ago. The sect

believed that its members could live forever through their scientific advancements.

From what Renata and Iduna could discover, more and more people had gone in search of the Hloewton system during the expansion after the First Galactic War with the promise that they would never die. None seemed to have returned.

When they found those records, Iduna had wanted to leave at once. Renata had convinced her to remain one more night, and the two of them enjoyed one last dinner together. That night Renata had told Iduna that she would also go to try to find Hloewton a month or so behind her with a team. That way, if Iduna didn't find what she was looking for, at least there would be a friend there for her last days.

Iduna had cried at Renata's offer and given her a big hug, agreeing to leave messages behind, then with a quick good-bye, she had left the next morning. Again Renata's life had felt empty, the same way it had felt when her grandfather had died. Only this time, Renata didn't have someone to bury.

Renata put a request through to her boss, carefully documented with all the information she and Iduna had found, for a trip to the Verge to search for the Hloewton system. He passed it up the line without a word. The next thing Renata knew, she was assigned to find out about this Hloewton system and the claim of living forever. If her boss hadn't authorized it, she had been prepared to quit or take leave to fulfill her promise to Iduna.

One month and three days after Iduna left, Renata, along with Mickie and Jonesy, started out. Just under two years later, they left the Armstrong system, going into Verge territory beyond any area thought inhabited. One month later they arrived on Fearnleah, the main planet of the Hloewton system.

Fearnleah was a beautiful world with over a million inhabitants. It had scenic blue lakes and massive forests of high trees. The planet's main city was Gardenia, and she and her team went there first.

They discovered a number of things not really kept secret from anyone who wanted to ask. First, there were very few people over one hundred and fifty. There was no elderly population at all. All the elderly lived on another planet in the system.

There was no message on any record that they could find that Iduna had even made it there. It took them two weeks, but Renata finally discovered what happened to Iduna. She had made it there and had checked herself into a local hospital, which couldn't cure her, so they sent her to the other planet, where everyone supposedly lived forever. Her new address was Compound 91-B, the very building Renata now leaned against.

She shoved herself away from the wall and took a deep breath of the hot air. "Time to give this another try."

Jonesy nodded.

"Should I lead?" Mickie asked, moving toward the front entrance again.

"No, you follow us, just in case," Renata said.

"Just in case of what?"

"Just in case I pass out," Jonesy said, moving ahead of Mickie to stand beside Renata in front of the main door. "I wonder how long I can hold my breath?"

"I doubt it will do any good," Renata said. "Just get ready for the smell."

She was doing exactly what she told him to do: get ready for the smell. It wouldn't catch her by surprise this time, and she would handle it. She had to. Iduna was in there somewhere.

Renata stepped forward, and the sliding door of Compound 91-B whisked open, letting out a cooler draft of the thick, rotten air.

She forced herself to not think about it as she stepped inside, at first feeling like she was wading upstream through a wave of rot and death. Ten steps along the shiny, metal floor, she stopped, just short of the first open door.

Metal walls surrounded her. She was sure that, if there had been more light, the walls would have reflected their images. Indirect lighting above the ceiling made the entire hall seem more like dusk.

Two other halls went off at right angles, and she could see other halls branching off every thirty steps or so. This building was clearly designed with dozens, more likely hundreds, of long halls running parallel to each other. The only noise was her own breathing, shallow, not taking in much of the smell. The place was downright creepy and huge.

Jonesy smiled at her, but he looked pale. She imagined she did also. Only Mickie looked normal. How, she didn't know, but she envied him for his sense of smell.

"No one home," Jonesy said, staring ahead down the long hallway straight ahead of them, his voice echoing slightly

She knew Jonesy was just making conversation, since they all knew these compounds were automatic. They had discovered that earlier in the day. The buildings had no staff, just lots and lots of residents.

From her best guess, figuring one per room with as far as she could see down one hallway, there were at least a hundred doors. If there were a hundred hallways, that made it possible for at least ten thousand residents in this building alone. Somewhere in here was Iduna, living in this smell. How she stood it, Renata would never understand.

Renata nodded at the first open door and moved over to it. Inside were a bed and a nightstand, plus two empty chairs facing the bed. The rest of the room was just like the hallway: metal walls and indirect light above the ceiling, cold, sterile, and full of rotten, smelling air.

A man lay on a bed, seemingly resting. He was fully clothed, and his hands were beside him on the bed. Renata stepped inside and the light brightened slightly, just enough for her to see.

"Of all the gods," Jonesy gasped behind her.

Again, Renata's stomach fluttered, threatening to give breakfast back. The man's body had clearly been dead for years. His chest had caved in, his skin leathery on his hands, his fingernails long and curved. It was only his head and his face, with a little redness left in his cheeks, which showed any signs of life. Blood pumped through a vein in his forehead. Somehow, the man's body had died, but his head still lived from the neck up.

Renata had seen her share of cybernetics over the years, but never anything used like this. How could they keep only the head alive, and why?

Mickie moved up beside the bed and studied the man. "There are tubes and wires leading up through the bed to the back of his neck and head," Mickie said, "clearly what is sustaining this part of his body."

Mickie glanced around as Renata just stood, staring. She couldn't move. The thought of Iduna like this made her heart hurt.

Mickie picked up a helmet from a table next to the bed. "I suspect this is how you get in contact with the resident of this room."

He studied it for a moment, then replaced the helmet on the nightstand and opened up a medical scanner and held it over the man's body. "By my best estimate, he has been like this for approximately sixteen years," Mickie said. He held the scanner closer to the man's head. "He should last in this condition for approximately another thirty years."

Renata almost jerked. "You mean he won't live forever like this?"

"Not even close," Mickie said. "The brain is being kept alive while the body dies, but the deterioration is merely slowed, nothing more."

Jonesy backed out of the room, on the verge of breaking and running for the front door. She didn't blame him.

Renata looked at the two empty chairs, then at the helmet. "Let's move on," she said to Mickie.

The mechalus nodded and replaced the helmet on the nightstand.

For an instant, Renata thought the man's mouth turned down into a slight frown. More than likely, that was the way it had been when they came in. She didn't want to think of the other alternative.

"We've found hell," Jonesy said, as she moved back into the hallway and leaned against the wall outside the door.

"I'm beginning to believe you," Renata said.

"There are thirty-six buildings like this on the planet," Mickie said.

Renata looked down the seemingly infinitely long hallway, and shuddered. Thirty-six buildings, all holding upwards of one hundred thousand people, maybe more, impossible for her even to imagine.

"How is the energy maintained?" Mickie asked, staring into the room at the man. "Clearly blood pumps, and the electronics for the helmet seemed to be active. The energy at this scale would be enormous."

"One large mass reactor could cover it all," Jonesy said, "maybe two, but easily possible for such low energy devices."

Mickie nodded.

Renata reached in through a slit in her UV robe and retrieved her notepad. "Jonesy, start recording all this. I want a record of everything we find here. I have no idea what the Powers That Be back at Concord headquarters are going to think of this type of treatment for the dying."

"I know what I think of it," Jonesy said.

She flipped up a screen on her notepad. The words read, *Iduna Stickly. Compound 91-B. H-12, R-96.*

"Okay, Mickie," Renata said. "I need to find what this address would mean." She showed him Iduna's address on her notepad.

He nodded. "H-12, I would imagine, would mean hall number twelve."

"I thought it might," she said, "and R-96 means the ninety-sixth room on the right of that hall."

"More than likely," Mickie said.

Shoving her stomach down, she headed toward the main intersection of the hall they were in. "Watch for any markings to tell us what hall we're in."

"We're in number forty-two," Jonesy said, pointing at a faint number under the shiny metal beside the corner of the hallway.

Once he pointed it out, she saw it clearly. She moved down the cross-corridor until she saw that the next hall was marked *41* then kept going. It seemed to take them forever to get to hallway twelve. It was as if she were walking down a nightmare, everything the same, going on and on forever with no way to escape, covered in rot and dead, human flesh. Her desire to never let another person die as her grandfather had died had led her across light-years to this point. Now she was walking among thousands and thousands who were rotting just as her grandfather had rotted away, only they called this living. Humans hadn't been this barbaric to their elderly since the warehoused them in what they had blithely called "nursing homes" back in the late twentieth century.

At hall twelve, they started deeper into the building, the numbers beside the doors clicking off like a countdown to the end of her life. By the time they reached number ninety-six on the right, the hall still didn't seem to have an end in sight. They might have underestimated how many people were in each building.

She stopped outside of the address she had for Iduna.

"You sure you want to do this?" Jonesy asked.

She smiled at her friend. He knew how important Iduna had become to her in that short week. He wouldn't blame her for backing out now, but she hadn't come this far to turn around now.

"I'm sure," she said. "Just make sure you record everything."

"Understood," he said.

Renata glanced at Mickie, who only nodded. She forced her feet to move and went inside.

The room was the same as the first one, containing a bed, a nightstand, two chairs, and a helmet, except this room seemed to smell faintly of roses instead of decay. Iduna lay on the bed, a beautiful dress spread out over her legs and old-fashioned high heeled shoes on her feet. Her black hair had been combed and laid out over her pillow, and her face looked at peace with the world.

Renata stopped and stared at her friend while Mickie moved over beside the bed and scanned Iduna.

"She too has the wire and tube implants," he said. "A highly advanced cybernetic implant from what I can tell. From the level of decay in her limbs, I would say this happened recently, less than four months ago."

Renata nodded and moved over beside Iduna. Oh, how she wished she had had more time with her while she was alive, more time to learn why she picked such shoes, what her loves had been like, why she had no family. Now it was clearly too late.

Mickie picked up the helmet and handed it to her. The thing was smooth on the outside, with a single wire leading from the back of the helmet and into the nightstand. The wire was long enough to reach either chair.

To Renata, the helmet felt heavier than it really must have been. She knew she wanted to put it on, but was deathly afraid to do so, deathly afraid of what she would find when she did.

"Would you like me to test it?" Mickie said.

She shook her head no. "It might not work on a mechalus."

He nodded. "I agree."

She moved to a chair and sat down, holding the helmet in her lap and staring at Iduna. Why was she doing this? Why had this one woman forced Renata beyond the edge of human space to a building that smelled like the inside of a giant coffin?

Renata knew the answer to that question. It wasn't just Iduna, but also her grandfather's death that had brought her here, and the frailties she saw in her father's walk that brought her here. Iduna just represented all of them.

"Take this off of me if I don't do it myself in two minutes."

"Understood," Mickie said.

With a deep breath of the rose and rot smelling air, she put the helmet over her head. The room seemed to fade, as if the light was being turned down slowly.

"It's wonderful that you came to see me," Iduna said.

Renata turned her head to see Iduna sitting in a kitchen, an old-fashioned kitchen. The wonderful smell of a baking pie, apple pie she thought, filled the air, and Iduna was smiling the brightest smile Renata had ever seen from her.

Renata glanced around. She was sitting across the table from Iduna and on the table were two plates.

"Pie will be done shortly," Iduna said. "I hope you're hungry."

Renata knew that she was in some sort of virtual reality. She'd experienced them before, yet this one felt very, very real. Was that the real Iduna sitting across from her?

"I love pie," Renata said. She again looked around the kitchen, then turned back to face Iduna. "Tell me what happened?"

Iduna shrugged. "I got to Fearnleah just over five months ago. It took me another two weeks of searching for their secrets, without luck, before I finally wore myself out and checked myself into a hospital, ready to give up and die."

Iduna got up and opened what looked like an old oven door, then nodded and sat back down.

"A doctor there diagnosed my cancer," she said as she checked the pie and shut the oven door, "and gave me the same news I had already heard, then he offered me what he called 'eternal life.' "

"Eternal life?"

Iduna laughed. "You know. Live forever, just without my body. The doctor said he couldn't cure my body."

"But you don't live forever. This only slows the death of the brain, nothing more." To Renata, her words sounded harsh, almost too harsh.

"Oh, I know," Iduna said, her smile not breaking.

"You agreed to this?" Renata asked, the memory of the rotting human flesh smell blocking out the wonderful smell of pie. "What did they want from you in exchange?"

"Nothing," Iduna said. "They figured over a hundred years ago that putting their elderly, sick, and dying into this sort of life would be cheaper in the long run than caring for them until death, and nicer, don't you think?"

Renata didn't know what to think.

"Are you alone in here?"

Iduna laughed. "Oh, heavens, no," she said. She motioned for Renata to follow her.

Renata stood, wondering if she was also standing in the room with Iduna's body.

Iduna led her out through a beautiful living room to a front window. Yellow sunlight flooded in through the window, and outside a beautiful, tree-filled city spread out for as far as Renata could see.

"I can go out there anywhere," she said. "Meet anyone who has also chosen this path, make love to them, laugh with them, marry and divorce them. To me, it's as real as any reality I've ever been in, only better."

In the kitchen, a buzzer went off.

"Pies are done," she said.

She turned and headed back toward the wonderful
smell. Renata stood and stared out over the city, her mind
reeling with the shock of it all, then turned and followed.

"You're about to be interrupted," Iduna said. "Do come
back for pie. Bring your friend Jonesy with you, if you
want."

"How do you know that?" Renata asked.

"My body's still out there," she said. "I know what goes
on around it, somehow."

"So you knew I was coming?"

"Just a few minutes before, as long as you were in the
room."

At that point, the kitchen and Iduna started to fade,
again as if the lights were being turned out.

The smell of rot covered Renata again. She blinked and
looked up at Mickie.

"You all right?" Jonesy asked. "You didn't move a
muscle the entire time."

"I was fine," Renata said, staring at the body of Iduna,
then she glanced up at Mickie, who was holding the
helmet above her head. "I need another five minutes, then
we can go."

Mickie nodded and slowly replaced the helmet.

As Iduna's kitchen faded back into solidity in Renata's
mind, Iduna laughed and slid a steaming piece of apple pie
in front of her. "My grandmother's recipe."

"I can only stay for five minutes," Renata said.

"I know," Iduna said, "but you have time to eat a little
something."

Renata picked up the fork, not really believing she was
going to taste the pie, but she did, and it burnt her tongue
just slightly in the process.

After another wonderful bite of the delicious pie, she
looked at Iduna. "Can you tell me why you did this?"

Iduna finished a fork-full of pie, then nodded. "Because
of this," she pointed at the pie, "and all the other experiences

of life. I wanted to keep living, keep feeling and tasting pie, and loving, and meeting new friends like you."

"But your body wouldn't let you," Renata said.

"Exactly," Iduna said. "What is life, anyway? Is it tasting pie, or working, or loving?"

"All of those, and much more," Renata said.

"Exactly," Iduna said. "Over the years humans have spent entire lifetimes worrying about what happens when they die, and like you, years doing nothing but trying to add years. But if you don't live those years, what's the point?"

Renata sat for a moment, looking at her friend. "There's so much I don't know about you."

"Come back and we'll talk."

"But you're dead," Renata said, the words out of her mouth before she realized what she was even going to say.

"My body is dead," Iduna said. "My mind is still very much alive. I'm still here, enjoying the life I've been given for as long as it lasts. From what I understand, that time will be longer than my first life."

Renata stared at her pie for a moment, wanting to take another bite, yet afraid to, afraid to feel any more of this unreal world.

"Let me ask you this," Iduna said. "You told me about your grandfather. He's dead, but do you still remember him, the good things about him?"

"Of course," Renata said.

"Then he's not really dead, is he?"

Renata looked up into her friend's eyes. They were smiling eyes, yet sad eyes, but one thing they were for certain: they were living eyes.

"Do come back if you can," Iduna said. "My grandmother left me a hundred recipes."

"Can you get fat here?" Renata asked, smiling slightly.

"I don't honestly know," Iduna said, laughing. "Wouldn't it be fun to try?"

"It might be," Renata said.

At that moment, the room started to fade.

"Thanks, my friend," Iduna said, "for the help getting here and coming to check up on me."

With that, the metal room returned to full reality, pushing the wonderful smells and warmth of Iduna's kitchen away, and replacing it with the thick smell of rotting flesh and roses.

Renata stood and moved over beside the body of her friend. For the first time in her life, she finally understood that a human wasn't just a body to be preserved. There was much, much more than that.

"I'll visit again, soon," she said, knowing full well that she wouldn't be back for years, if ever, "and you're welcome."

She turned to her two friends and traveling companions. Both were looking worried, more worried than she had ever seen either of them look.

"I think we've seen enough," she said.

"Great," Jonesy said, clear relief in his voice. "Let's get out of here."

Renata looked around one more time. There was no eternal life here, just another form of death and dying. She headed for the door behind Jonesy as Mickie replaced the helmet beside Iduna's body. Outside, the hallway stretched in both directions, doors on both sides leading into rooms full of dead bodies kept alive for a little while longer by cybernetics and virtual reality.

The reality was the smell of rot and the lack of real people in this building. That was the reality of this place. Back in Old Space, she had a life, a job, people she cared about, people she hadn't yet met. For the time being, Renata was more than happy to live in that reality. Maybe now, thanks to Iduna, when Renata got home, she would learn how to really live in her world, the real world.

For the first time.

About the Author

Dean Wesley Smith has sold around one hundred short stories to various magazines and anthologies and is the author of over twenty novels. He's been a finalist for the Hugo and Nebula Awards and has won a World Fantasy Award and a Locus Award. He was the editor and publisher of Pulphouse Publishing and has just finished editing the Star Trek anthology *Strange New Worlds*.

"The Great Negotiator"

KRISTINE KATHRYN RUSCH

THE STARLINER was privately owned and privately operated. Fiona had
known that the moment she had seen it through the freighter's
portals. A fraal did not live four hundred years without learning
to recognize luxury, even if she rarely experienced it.

Her name was not Fiona, but that was what she called
herself—had called herself since she was twenty-three
years old, the year 2124, the year her life changed forever.
She did not tell her fellow fraal of her own name for herself; they would have laughed at her, using a human name
when her own had its base in tradition. A woman, be she
human or fraal or t'sa had a right to call herself anything
she wanted within the privacy of her own mind, and Fiona
was certainly better than the name the humans had saddled
her with in the last century: The Great Negotiator.

She hated that name, and it was the reason she was here.
The mid-space docking transfer from the freighter to the
starliner was as difficult as she remembered such things
being. Apparently, wealth did not ease that frightening
jostling or the feeling that with too much shaking, the ships
would simply come apart.

The handlers Shaunessy had sent, however, had been
extremely courteous, much better than the sesheyans who

had found her. They had been free sesheyans, originally
spies, who had been hired by Shaunessy to find her. They
had been cold and aloof and had said little. She had been
worried, at first, when they inquired as to whether or not
she had family. She no longer had any—her parents and
siblings had long since died, and she had never had any
children. In that answer, the sesheyans had known that they
had found the fraal they were looking for, and they had said
little more except that Liam Shaunessy wanted to see her.

Liam Shaunessy. She had heard of him, of course.
Everyone had. A former diplomat from a great family of
diplomats, he had been dismissed as one of the leaders in
the Concord after he had made a series of errors, each
more disastrous than the last, each leading to discord when
the Concord was attempting to form a lasting peace. He
had gone to Austrin-Ontis Unlimited and had made himself a large fortune, which his detractors said was what he
had been trying to do all along.

He had requested her presence, and to the surprise of
everyone who knew her, she had accepted. She had been
found before; once in the middle of the First Galactic War
and then later toward the beginning of the Second. Each
time she had refused to see the political leaders who
wanted her to negotiate a great peace. That she had
accepted Shaunessy's invitation frightened some of the
young fraal who believed it was a sign that a Third Galactic War was imminent. The middle-aged fraal thought her
acceptance a sign that she was beginning to lose what
holdings on reality she had. The older fraal simply nodded
and said among themselves that her decision made great
and tragic sense.

They all tried to talk her out of it, but she heeded none
of them. For 377 years, she had kept her own counsel. She
would do so now, as well.

The handlers had left her in a great suite, unlike any she
had ever seen in any sort of spaceship. Of course, it had

been nearly fifty years since she had been on a starliner, and that had not been a luxurious one, nor had it been human-owned. Strange to think she had forgotten how humans liked their comfort, but she had forgotten that. She had forgotten many things.

She walked through the suite's main room, saw that beneath the silk coverlets the furniture was bolted down. The shelves were built into the wall and also secured with sturdy bolts, only here the bolts were hidden by paint and decor. The air smelled faintly of incense and was warmer than the average spaceship. She wondered how Shaunessy had managed to get around clean air regulations for the incense, and then decided not to think about it. She was his guest, although she had not yet been given a room.

Fiona walked past the two couches and the long end tables, past the full-length mirror, which she did not look at, and stopped at the portals. Space looked different to the trained eye, or so she had been told, but her eye had never been trained. She had been raised to live on Earth among humans, to observe, to watch, and then—unexpectedly— to interact.

Her stomach fluttered at the memory, and she rubbed her hands together. Her hands were her reminders of all the years that had passed. She knew the others saw it in her face, the delicate web of wrinkles that made her pale skin look softer than it once had, the way her silver hair had thinned with time, the way her eyes seemed to have grown, to dominate all her other features. Once she had been a beautiful woman, pale and delicate—*as if you were made from moonlight instead of born on the moon*—but she was no longer.

A door opened behind her and her shoulders stiffened. No expectations, she reminded herself, and knew, with the increased beating of her heart, that the reminder would do no good.

"Hello." His voice was almost right. No Gaelic lilt, but the timbre was correct. She closed her eyes for a moment then turned.

He was taller than she thought he would be—all humans were—and she had to look up at him. She folded her long fingers in front of her long skirt.

His hair was black with a bluish tint—that at least was right, as was his skin, that creamy white particular to those with Gaelic blood. His eyes were the gray of an Irish winter sky, but their coldness was unfamiliar in a face that should have been as familiar as her own. Even her own looked strange to her these days.

He said her fraal name, massacring it as humans so often did. Then, in very bad Fraal, he apologized, saying he had been misinformed. He had thought that she spoke Standard.

"I do," she said in that tongue.

His relief was visible. He held out his hand, an old human custom that had, apparently, not died in the centuries. "I'm Liam Shaunessy."

Liam, she reminded herself. Liam.

She took his hand and before she could stop herself, she said, "Call me Fiona."

He tilted his head slightly, as if the name were strange to him, and so she laughed to cover her own embarrassment.

"It is so much easier to pronounce than my own," she said.

He did not let go of her hand. "You are the fraal they call the Great Negotiator?"

"Your people call me that," she said.

"Are they wrong?" he asked.

"History is always wrong, Mr. Shaunessy," she said, letting her thumb caress his forefinger. "It is always wrong."

* * * * *

Ryan Shaunessy laughed and settled into the great leather armchair in front of his desk. His office was large and filled with antique furniture. The only concessions to the modern age were in his reception area, behind a door now closed.

He was a single man, a young Prime Minister with, his people said, the career of a lifetime ahead of him.

"My da used to say that. 'History is wrong!' he'd shout, as if that would change things. Who'd be thinking one such as you'd agree with him?"

She did not smile, even though she loved his boisterous laugh. It invited more merriment. She was one of several fraal on delicate missions all over Earth, and she did not feel that laughter was appropriate, not at this time.

"So you believe me, Mr. Shaunessy?"

"Believe you? One of the fairy folk waltzes into my office, says that there have always been fairies, although in some places folk thought them gods, and in others, folk thought them extraterrestrials—and by God, those folk were right!—and now these leprechauns want to give us some sort of gravity induction engine and other newfangled technology so that we may go to the stars properly. Only you don't look so much like a leprechaun as you do Titania or Oberon's daughter, with perhaps a bit of Puck in your ancestry."

In spite of herself, she laughed. "There is some of Puck in my ancestry. He was my grandfather, and he visited your Shakespeare when he was just a boy."

"Well, the first thing you need to know, lass, is that he wasn't our Shakespeare. He was English, by God, and that's a vastly different thing from the Irish. I thought you'd said you'd been watching us for centuries."

"We have," she said.

"Then you should know," he said, suddenly serious, "that coming to the Prime Minister of Ireland with this offer is like asking for the world from the King of Nowhere."

"I understand your politics," she said, *"and others of my people have gone to see the heads of the European Common Union, and the President of the United States, and the Prime Minister of Japan. I don't think those visits will work."*

"Why is that?" he asked.

"Because to the humans," she said, *"the fraal have never been about politics; we have been about myth, and the only ones who have understood that have been the Irish."*

A slight frown touched his eyebrows. *"I still do not see how I might help you."*

She smiled. *"You will,"* she said. *"Believe me. You will."*

* * * * *

Liam Shaunessy took her hand and led her, as if she were a child, to a chair in the center of the room. This was a man who was not used to fraal, then, who saw someone of her slight stature as childlike or fragile, or worse, of lesser intelligence. The myths and misperceptions never really disappeared. They just acquired new names.

"Do you know why I asked you here?" he asked, easing her into the chair. Its silk cover was smooth, but the chair was hard, as most were in space. He did not sit—another difference then, from his ancestor. In no real way did Liam Shaunessy try to put her at ease.

"I have an idea," she said, "but I would prefer to hear what you want from you."

"You were the one who brought our peoples together." He ran a hand through his dark hair, leaving it to fall messily across his brow. "We are in a difficult time now. The Galactic Concord has brought a sense of hope to so many, a grand purpose, a vision, if you will, but many are resistant to it, and then there are those who destroyed the Silver Bell colony—"

"No one knows who they are."

His eyes brightened. "You know of that?"

She permitted herself a small, sad smile. Human life spans were only half that of the fraal. She didn't know how many generations of Shaunessys there had been between Liam and Ryan, enough to make Ryan one of Liam's distant relatives. She didn't know why she expected more similarities than there were. She had simply figured that, with the resemblance—

"Did I insult you, Fiona?"

She shook her head, even though he had. "You wish me to what? Preach to the unconverted?"

"In a way, yes."

"You'd better make certain that I'm converted."

"Aren't you?"

"The fraal are a diverse people," she said. "Not all humans support the Concord. Why would all fraal?"

"Do you?"

"What I believe and don't believe doesn't matter, Mr. Shaunessy," she said.

"Liam."

"Liam." She nodded, having been around humans so much that she understood their traditions, especially if those traditions had roots in British or American attitudes. "You should find out what I can do for you."

"What can you do?" he asked.

"I can't work miracles," she said.

"You did once."

"Says who?"

"My family."

She blinked once, closed her eyes for a second too long, and then opened them. "Your family is wrong."

* * * * *

"My people say that you should not eat fairy food,"
Ryan said as he cut her a piece of roast beef and placed it
on her plate, "but that you should always share your own
with them so as not to receive their wrath."

Fiona laughed. She sat at the linen-covered table in his
dining room and gazed through the windows at the rolling
green fields. Her people had always loved Ireland, for its
misty afternoons and its green hills, as well as for its
charming people. Her family, in particular, had tried to
make Ireland their home before the violent fear earlier
generations of humans had for the fraal forced the fraal to
move their installations to the moon and Mars.

"So," he said, placing a full plate before her. "I'm sharing with you."

She took the knife and fork as she had been taught, even
though such tools were not the ones she was used to. She
cut her food and took a bite. The beef was succulent, not
the tough chewy food her father had led her to expect.

Ryan sat down across from her. In the week that she had
been in his presence, he had been courteous and kind and
had given her more time than was, perhaps, her due.

Running Ireland, he had said to her on the second day,
is not like it once was. We're a unified country now and
small, insignificant by the world's standards. I'm more the
mayor of a small province than the head of a country.
Many of the decisions I make are simple rubber-stamping
of programs that have been in place since long before I
was born.

She had known that, of course, which was one of her
reasons for choosing him as her contact. She had begged
for this assignment, even though the older fraal had said
she was too young. Partly she had asked for the chance to
prove herself, and partly she had asked because she felt
that the elders were going about this in the wrong way.

The fraal had been in contact with the humans for centuries, but humans had a particular dislike to believing

that they were not the only intelligent species in the universe. Most humans had reacted with curiosity to the fraal, but some had reacted with violence, and the fraal had used their considerable psionic powers to make the humans' memories of those occasions fade, though not even the most powerful mindwalkers could completely erase memories. Now, it was felt among the fraal, that the humans could handle contact with another intelligent species— indeed, that the humans needed contact—and the fraal decided to provide it. After all, they had observed humanity for centuries. They believed they understood it.

They decided to talk to the human world leaders and to make their offer of technology and support known in that way.

Fiona, who had been fascinated with humans since childhood and who had, on more than one occasion, visited Ireland with her parents, believed that the humans would react as they always did to the fraal—with fear and suspicion—unless the fraal approached them correctly.

She knew that speaking to most world leaders was not correct.

"You seem quite at ease with me," she said to Ryan.

He smiled. She was beginning to like his smile. "A beautiful woman manages to get a meeting with me, and then, when the door is closed, claims to be a member of the Sidhe. Only the Sidhe are not, as we Irish always supposed, the Tuatha Dé Danaan, but instead an alien race that has been watching the wee and primitive humans since the dawn of time. Now what sane man wouldn't be kind to her?"

She laughed. "You could be wrong," she said. "Maybe we are the original Irish."

"You're saying that we're all Tuatha Dé Danaan, original Irish both of us? Or that we humans are the impostors?"

She shrugged. "Sometimes it just feels as if Ireland is as much our home as it is yours."

He reached across the table and took her hand. Her fingers were longer than his. "Tis said the Sidhe have no heart. Is that true?"

"If that were true," she said, "then I wouldn't be in Ireland."

He held her hand for a long time, running his thumb across her knuckles, his head bowed, his black hair so dark that the highlights looked a shade of blue under the lights in the ceiling.

"You seem so human," he said finally.

"Therefore I can't be alien?"

He did not reply. His thumb kept moving, though, back and forward, forward and back, its touch gentle on her skin.

"I was raised to be one of the ones who talk to you," she said. "I was raised with humans in mind, so that I would not be so threatening."

"Were the others raised so?"

She nodded.

"If they've been visiting world leaders, as you've said, why haven't we heard? This offer of technology, it is in our own best interest."

"You haven't announced anything."

He raised his head, a slight smile playing on his lips. "I'm the King of Nowhere."

"You've been waiting for the others to make an announcement?"

He nodded.

"Then you'll wait forever."

"You've heard from the others, then?"

She shook her head. "But I know."

"How do you know?"

"It's common sense," she said. "They've gone to unimaginative politicians. Let us take the Americans, for a simple example. They've seen us more often than you have in the past 175 years, and how have they responded?

With books and movies and television and netspec about alien invasions, mysterious abductions, and Unidentified Flying Objects. We're a threat, an anomalous threat. Now their president makes a national announcement saying we're real? Either he'll be laughed out of office, or the country will respond as its entertainment has claimed it will, with force. Most likely, though, it won't respond at all, because he won't have the political courage to make the announcement. Give us the technology anyway, he'll say, and we'll use it and give you credit. Well, we did that before in the twentieth century when we thought, perhaps, the human race needed some help to avoid a nuclear conflict. The Americans took the technology and never acknowledged us, only a few leaks into what passed then for their media: Area 51, Roswell, names that for them are as familiar as the Sidhe are to you."

"That's the Americans," he said.

"Do you think the Japanese will be any different? Or what of the European Union? Perhaps the African Union might help? They all have their stories of us, and in many of those stories, we're seen as threats. You started this dinner mentioning an Irish story that's much the same. Don't eat fairy food. Don't turn your back on fairies. Never leave your children alone lest fairies steal them. Never speak a man's name in a positive way without adding God Bless lest you open the door for a fairy to steal his soul."

His thumb had stopped moving. "You're very well informed."

"It's my people you're talking of," she said.

"Are the legends true?"

She slipped her hand from his. "That's for you to answer, isn't it? There are legends of elf maidens who steal a man's heart for sport. Perhaps I'm one of them."

"Perhaps you are," he said, his hand still clutching the air where her fingers had been. "Perhaps you are.'

* * * * *

"You were the one who united the fraal and the humans," Liam said, and there was a tone of begging in his voice, as if he didn't want her to contradict the things he had been taught.

"No," she said. "I am the one who opened the door so that they could talk."

"It is the same thing."

She shook her head. "It is a very different thing. Talking does not imply agreement. Others made agreement happen."

"Opening a door is a special talent."

"Yes," she said, "and I had help."

"Ryan Shaunessy."

She stood. It felt odd to have this man say his ancestor's name with such coldness, and his people had once believed that hers had no heart. Perhaps they should have looked to themselves.

She walked to the portal. She knew that the starliner had moved away from her freighter, had indeed traveled some distance, but she could not read the distance in the stars. Her inability frustrated her.

"I had heard that you were removed as one of the Concord's leaders," she said. She could see his reflection against the glass. His face, when he thought she couldn't see it, was as hard and distant as the points of light outside the portal.

He did not answer her, but he did not need to. She could hear the answer in his silence.

"So then, what am I?" she asked. "If I agree to help you, if I agree to help them, I become what? A bargaining chip for you? 'You will get the greatest negotiator history has ever known if you allow me back into the inner circle'?"

"You are very perceptive," he said after a moment.

"Why should I help you?" she asked. "Why shouldn't I

go to the Concord myself? Offer my services without going through you?"

"For the sake of Ryan Shaunessy?"

"You call on the name of a man you never knew to gain a favor from me?"

"You loved him, didn't you?"

She turned. He was staring at her with those dark gray eyes, those dead eyes. What had killed the spark in the Shaunessys? Or had Ryan truly been one of a kind?

"Didn't you learn the legends, man?" she said softly. "The Sidhe cannot love. We have no heart."

* * * * *

The dawn's light was pearly and diffuse as it came through the open floor-to-ceiling windows. The great house, Ryan's family house, had stood on this spot for centuries. She could feel the age in its stonework, in the arch of the ceiling and the waviness of the window glass.

The table behind her was covered with two dirty wineglasses, several empty wine bottles, two full coffee cups, and a half empty pot. Ryan still sat at the table, his shirt collar open, his hair tousled, his eyes at half-mast. Humans did not do well on no sleep, but she had forgotten that until this very moment, when she saw how vulnerable he looked.

They had talked through the night, nothing more, nothing less, but they had not spoken of the importance of gravity induction engines or the way fraal technology could give humans the stars. Instead, they had spoken of how they had grown up, and the differences between fraal and humans, the way the Earth looked from Mars, and how a man could love a country the way he loved a woman.

When the night sky was at its darkest, he asked her how to pronounce her name, and she told him. His lips stumbled over it again and again, until finally she smiled and told him that names were not necessary.

"Ah, but they are," he said and put a hand over hers.

"Then pick one for me," she said, "an Irish name, one you can pronounce."

He'd smiled and threatened to call her Medb, after the Queen of the Sidhe.

"One whose beauty is terrible to look at?" she had said. "I think not."

"The name of my grandmother, then," he'd said, "one of the finest women to come from these parts. Fiona."

Fiona it was, and Fiona it always would be. To him. To her.

She had taken the name, and they had christened it with wine, and they had laughed for what seemed like hours. An hour later, they switched to coffee, and the conversation had become slower.

And then, a moment ago, he had asked her: "What made you come to the King of Nowhere?"

The early morning sunlight brought with it a dew and a chill. She had gone to the open windows and stared out at fields she had always wished would be her own but knew that they never could. Her home was an isolated colony on Mars. Her world was a place she had never seen and her parents had never seen and her grandparents had never seen. It was almost mythical to them, the nomadic fraal, who had gone searching for something different among the stars.

"I do not think my peers have had such an easy time of it with their leaders," she said, without looking at him. "I doubt any of them have even had an audience yet."

"Why not demand one?"

"And risk the very thing they're trying to prevent, a negative human reaction?"

"Am I such a fool then to let a fraal through my door?"

She shook her head. "You're a man who expects to see selkies when you stare at the sea and who hears a banshee *in the wailing wind. You do not think it strange when a woman who looks like I do comes to your door and asks for your help. Instead, you talk with her, and when you believe it safe, you invite her into your office, and then your home. You're a man who still holds the myths in his heart, but who is rational enough to want to see their origins, to understand why they exist."*

"You knew all that about me before you came here?" he asked.

She turned. The morning breeze ran through her thin silver hair. "I hoped you'd be like that," she said.

He smiled then, his first real smile, just for her. "How then," he asked, in that serious tone he had used in their first meeting in his office, "may I help you?"

For the first time, she could see the temptation, the way her species had often gotten too close to his. The stories, the taboos, the ways that such intermingling could bring them all grief. For she wasn't used to such warmth in anyone's eyes, or conversations filled with such passion, nor services so freely given. She wasn't used to the way a simple look made her feel as if she really were made of moonbeams as he had said the night before, and she wasn't used to thinking of something other than the task before her.

She had to shake herself to concentrate on it.

"Keep me at your side," she said, "for two weeks, maybe three. All the while have your aides leak hints to the various media, have them run stories on legends from gods come to Earth to tales of the wee folk. Let the speculation about me rise, never answer questions about who I am. Then travel to the Americas and the European Union with me at your side and introduce me to the leaders there. Stage an event and allow the reporters to ask, one more time, who I am, and this time let me answer. I guarantee that all will be fine after that."

"You're asking a lot," he said. "If you are not what you say you are—"

"Then you are ruined," she said.

He nodded.

"And the legends of fairy come true."

"Not all of them," he said.

She waited.

He held his hands out in an apology. "I intend to keep a hold of my heart."

She felt a disappointment as keenly as she felt the dampness in the morning air.

He shook his head. "Intentions are nothing more than good will wasted."

"I thought you were afraid the fraal were heartless."

"If you were," he said, his eyes twinkling, *"you wouldn't be in Ireland then, now would you?"*

This time she smiled, just for him. "No," she said. *"I wouldn't."*

"It seems to me we're both taking risks, and if we succeed, we'll gain more than we ever had before." He got up and came to her side, then he put his arm around her, and she put hers around him.

In that moment, their alliance began.

*   *   *   *   *

Liam Shaunessy paid her passage on a different freighter and left her alone for the long journey home. Her cabin was a small one, a closet really, and when the human captain had realized how old she was, he had offered his own space, which she knew from experience would not be much larger.

She suffered the long journey in the cold, socializing when she could and eating as few rations as possible, since she felt the captain had been kind enough to do her a favor.

Most of the time she sat in the common area, staring out the only public portal, staring at the stars, and saying noth-

ing, thinking instead about becoming Fiona, about the
three weeks that had changed her life.

There was a legend among the fraal that a vibrant soul
traveled from one generation to the next, but she was now
convinced that in this, as in other things, fraal and humans
were different. She did not see any of Ryan in Liam
beyond simple genetics, and she had hoped to see Ryan
once again.

If she had, she would have accepted Liam's offer. She
would have tried to negotiate for his people as she had
once negotiated for her own, but she would have done so
because she understood the dynamics that made such
moments work.

History called her the Great Negotiator because she had
met leaders who had refused to see other fraal, because she
had made a speech at the end of those weeks that had
turned the tide of human opinion toward an acceptance of
visitors from the stars. Humans believed that without her
they would have turned down fraal help and never have
developed the stardrive, which led to all that followed,
good and bad.

But history, as she had told both Shaunessys, was
always wrong. It had been her ideas that had brought the
fraal and humans together, but ideas alone did not solve
problems. Ideas alone did not create great negotiators.

Great negotiators had a touch, a charm, a way of invit-
ing everyone to see the world their way. It had been Ryan
who let her walk beside him; Ryan who laughed at her
jokes and touched her lightly on the shoulder; Ryan who
risked the threats from legend and myth to lead his people
into this future, Ryan who had been the great negotiator,
not she.

Her own people did not have a name for her. She did not
have a place in fraal history. They forgot about her, as she
supposed was appropriate. She had not returned to them
for nearly forty years. By then, someone else had claimed

the credit, and the fraal had moved on to other things. At the time, she had not cared about credit. She cared about nothing at all.

No one had told her that human life spans were, at best, only half her own, and somehow that point had missed her in her early education. It was a point she would never again forget. Human life spans were short, and for her, love would only come once. It was silly of her to even hope that she would glimpse it once more before she died.

She leaned her head against the portal and looked into space. She was here, this freighter was here, because she and Ryan Shaunessy had convinced an entire world to look at legends in a new way. Their union had produced only one seed, and that seed had been a stardrive that had sent fraal and human beings into the universe. It was a great and terrible legacy, and one she had not acknowledged until now.

There were stirrings in the Verge and unseen enemies in the darkness. There was unrest and the talk of war, as there had been off and on through her very long life.

She had no family left, no real friends among the fraal, and her last dream had disappeared when she had seen the emptiness in Liam Shaunessy's eyes.

It was time to go to a place she had lived when she was young, to a place where dawn's pearly light would make her look like a creature of myth, to a place where she had buried her one true love.

She rose and left the portal. Finally, she had made a decision for herself. For the first time in three hundred years, she knew what she wanted.

She would pay the captain whatever he asked so that his stardrive—her stardrive—the stardrive that existed because she had met Ryan Shaunessy—could take her home. She would stand in the moonlight and hope that the ghosts that walked the Irish hills were no more myth than the fraal had been.

There was always truth in legends. The trick was in finding it.

About the Author

Kristine Kathryn Rusch is an award-winning writer whose novels have appeared on several best-seller lists. Her most recent novels are *The Fey: Victory* and *Hitler's Angel*. She has also co-authored *Star Wars: The New Rebellion* and several Star Trek novels with her husband, Dean Wesley Smith.

"Mind Over Matter"

Matthew J. Costello

Megan Rivers rubbed at the smeary porthole and looked out at the grimy little planetoid that was—unfortunately—her destination. The stupid chunk of rock didn't even have a name, just a string of letters and numbers. *Welcome to XJR3978.* It was like the code that they used to put on the back of old combustion vehicles back in pre-drivespace times. Now there were so many planets that they all had to get an officially registered number.

How romantic, Megan thought. *And be sure to visit our sister world, XJR3979. Make a vacation of it!*

It was like this throughout known space, and the Verge was only slightly better: worlds tumbling upon worlds, some with good atmosphere, some with bad atmosphere, some with no atmosphere. Some planets even supported native life forms, though with the stellar nations' expansion and use of "manageable resources," many of these new plants and animals were already on the fast track to extinction, but the only extinction that concerned Megan at the moment was her own.

She looked around at the other passengers in the ancient transport. The small ship, an old troop carrier from the look of it, was half-filled. The humans wore glum faces, probably miners and administrators back from a few

precious months of R&R, back to dear old XJR to work in
splendid isolation for another twenty-four months, which
was exactly what Megan wanted to do. A woman has to
make a living, and you used your natural talents—whatever they happened to be.

There was only one non-human, a mechalus, sitting
near the back. If Megan was likely to talk to anyone on this
little shuttle, it would probably be him. Talking, not to
mention working, with human miners was dull and boring,
but chatting with other species could be fascinating.

The shuttle bumped. Nice brakes, Megan thought as the
vehicle slowed down. Hope the landing is a bit more
gentle. She looked out the porthole again and examined the
planetoid, now much closer.

She was pleasantly surprised. The domed settlement
had an almost bucolic look. There was some genuine
water—an artificial lake she assumed—and big green
patches of grass that looked as though they had been transplanted from somewhere else, which they probably had. If
this was going to be home for the next two years, she could
do worse, *had* done worse as matter of fact.

A sleepy voice boomed over the intercom.

"Welcome to XJR"—a few seconds while the pilot tried
to remember or search for the catchy name—"3978. We'll
be landing in about three minutes, so please make sure that
your belts are tightly fastened.

No problem, Megan thought. As if I'd land in this thing
without being strapped in like a mummy.

The craft hit the atmosphere with a thud, burning
shielding that sent brilliant sparks screaming by the
porthole.

God, the captain's going to toast us.

The other passengers look totally nonplussed. Guess
this was a normal entry for this run.

A few minutes later, the ship straightened out, swooping into a smooth arc and curving around a large landing zone where Concord shuttles, massive mining transports, and private vehicles littered the giant landing zone.

Great, I'm here, Megan thought. Now all I have to do is find some work.

*   *   *   *   *

This turned out to be harder than she thought it would.

The massive entertainment center, a generic place of almost-pleasure, similar to hundreds of others that littered the known worlds, was nearly deserted. The bartender, a young woman, said that the big mines were "on hiatus," closed down with most of the workers put on furlough.

There had been a discovery in a nearby system that made this planetoid's treasure trove of rhodium not so rare anymore. The big corporations found the other system cheaper to mine, and since it was closer to the core of the Verge, transportation costs to XJR3978 were deemed no longer expedient. The big businesses were moving on. If anything remained of XJR3978's mining facilities in a year, it would be left to the independents, which could be good or bad, depending on your point of view.

Six months ago, the Living Resources Administrator of *Callocorp,* one of the big mining companies, had told Megan that her skill was needed by his firm on XJR3978, but now things had changed. According to the bartender, *Callocorp* had moved out five weeks ago and wouldn't be back.

"What *is* your skill?" the bartender asked.

Ah, here was the hard part. Always hard telling people . . . *here's what I do.*

"I'm a Finder," Megan said. She waited to see if the woman knew what that was. When no flash of recognition bloomed on the woman's face, Megan said. "You know, I have a bit of psi. They use me to find which piece of rock might hide all the nice sparklies." She took another sip of the purplish drink, feeling a bit of a buzz. "It's a living, sometimes anyway."

"A mindwalker?"

"Oh, you thought only the fraal had that? No way. There always have been a few humans who had some too."

"That always spooked me. About the fraal, I mean."

"The fraal? They don't bother me. Hey, they watched us for centuries, nice and peaceful. No, I don't worry about them."

God, Megan thought, I'm talking so much. I must be desperate for some human contact. After that last stint, I should just shut up. Live and let—

"So, who *do* you worry about?" the bartender asked.

Megan scanned the nearly empty bar area. It seemed more like a giant meeting room, but its emptiness gave it all the coziness of a docking port. There were a few t'sa squabbling excitedly at a table in the back. A few humans, probably bosses and drill operators, sat here and there over a couple of tables, staring glumly into their drinks. Okay, she wasn't going to offend the species she was about to name.

"The weren," Megan whispered.

"Oh, yeah." The bartender nodded, smiling. "Don't get too many of them passing through here, though. Every now and then a band of contract workers will pass through, but they never stay long"

"Good for you, I guess," Megan said as she stared into her drink. "The way they're always fighting each other, and well"—for some reason, her thoughts were unusually cloudy; how many drinks had she had?—"uh-huh, I know what you're thinking: the way they look, right? Pretty damned scary."

"You bet." The bartender nodded amiably and refilled Megan's glass. "You ever work with them?"

"Sure. I go where the work is."

"But they're not dangerous, right? I mean nothing that's going to affect us here?"

Another sip. What the hell, Megan thought. It's only a bartender.

So she told the nameless bartender what she had seen and heard on Spes. It was good to tell someone at last, someone who couldn't do anything to make Megan's life difficult, because that's the last thing she wanted. The bartender gave her another drink on the house.

* * * * *

Megan thought she was dreaming, but as the haze behind her eyelids faded, the man still stood over her, his face tight, serious—this was definitely not one of those nice cozy dreams. She was lying on her rumpled bunk in the back-alley room she had rented after hitting town. Weak daylight came in through the open door.

The man shook her, making sure she was awake, then he spoke. "Megan Rivers?"

Megan nodded as best she could from her prone position.

The man took out an ID card, silvery and official looking. Megan sat up, oblivious to the fact that her T-shirt clung to her thin frame a little too tightly. The card looked dammed official.

"Concord Intelligence," she read aloud. Underneath she saw the not very flattering picture and a name, Lieutenant Gregory C. McShane. "Is this about my credit problems? 'Cause if it is, I just want to say—"

"I'll step outside." Lieutenant McShane didn't smile. "Please get dressed. We have something to discuss."

There was a long pause while Megan tried to think what stupid thing she might have done to inspire this visit, then she remembered. The *bartender*. Talking about the weren. God, the blue meanies—those potent drinks strike again.

Megan nodded. At least she knew what the Investigator was going to talk about.

* * * * *

They walked around what passed for a promenade that girded the residential section of the settlement.

"You're not a marine?"

Greg laughed—finally. "I was. This is a promotion. I thought it would be safer."

Megan nodded.

"So," Greg said as though he judged them far away enough from any listening ears, "tell me what you told the bartender. Leave nothing out."

"Now that's annoying." Megan said. "Why did she—"

"She works for the Concord, on the payroll. It's one of the ways we watch what's happening in the Verge."

Something to remember, she thought. "Okay, but I really don't want to get involved."

"Of course." He smiled, but it held little warmth. "Just tell me what you know, Miss Rivers."

"Okay." Megan took a deep breath. "I was on Spes. The Borealin terraformers there thought my talents might be useful for some of the research they've been doing. I told you I'm a mindwalker, right? A Finder, nothing major, just now and then, I get a pretty clear picture of things—"

"And on Spes?"

"Right. I met a worker, a weren who had been sent with a survey crew to a distant weren outpost, and was he scared. He emanated fear. What I picked up scared me. Something's going on at this outpost. I figured it's not my business. I'd just do my readings on the interior of the rock, then claim my pay and get the hell out of there."

Greg looked at Megan. Not a bad looking guy, she thought. Not exactly her type, she didn't usually care for "the authorities," but he did have interesting eyes.

"What happened?" Greg asked, breaking her reverie.

"The weren was operating a mining suit, trying to take some core samples from the secondary rock strata. I was there, telling him which tunnel to search when he tapped into some kind of gas pocket. Shot him back against the wall. Everyone ran to get him out, and when he regained consiousness and saw me, he went crazy. Ever see a weren go into hyperdrive? Yikes."

"What triggered that?"

Megan looked away. Time to throw down all her cards. If she held out on him, he would probably know. She couldn't remember what she had and hadn't told that backstabbing bartender.

"Well, I picked up the guy's *whole* story. He knew I was a mindwalker and he knew I got his whole tale. He grabbed me with one of those clawed hands and said to not tell anyone, which I didn't . . . until last night. I'm such an idiot."

Again Greg laughed. "Hey, you might get a medal out of this."

"Medals? I don't need medals. I need money."

"That can be arranged too. His story?"

Megan took a breath. "In this outpost, a weren chief named Hatala is doing this, well . . . experiment."

"Go on."

"He's captured some fraal, and he has people examining them, trying to see where they get their psionic powers."

"Let me guess the rest. He wants to create weren with mindwalker abilities?"

Megan nodded.

Greg smiled and said, "Listen, Megan, that's nothing new. Researchers have been trying to replicate psionic abilities for years with limited success. What had your friend so spooked?"

His smile and increasing good humor helped to put her somewhat at ease, but the guy was Intel; there was no way she would trust him too far. She swallowed and said, "I wouldn't call him a friend exactly. In the medevac on the way back to the station, he told me that if I told one person what I knew that I wouldn't live to tell another. That was bad enough, but he was dead less than twenty-four hours later. Due to his 'injuries' they said, but he wasn't hurt that bad. Still, I don't like taking chances, so I got the hell out of there."

"You're stalling, Megan," Greg said. He still wore the smile, but his gaze held a hint of frustration as well. "You still haven't told me what you read from the weren."

"Listen, I'm not stalling. You said you wanted to hear everything, so this is it."

"You're right," he agreed, though he didn't hide his insincerity too well. "Please continue."

"This guy, the weren, I got something from him that had him really scared. Hatala's researchers had some success—a lot, actually, led by some disaffected Orlamu geneticist who's joined him. Hatala is planning on subjugating nearby weren settlements, unifying them . . . and eventually taking all of Spes."

"You didn't think that this was important for the Concord to know?"

Now Megan looked away. "Of course I did, but I've got enough troubles of my own. I don't need to get mixed up in this."

Greg took a step closer. "You've seen the weren up close. Tell me, do you want an army of psionic weren mindwalkers running around?"

"Of course not, but I don't want them after me either. Better for me to just shut up and disappear, no harm done."

"We can protect you, Megan. Hatala is certainly ambitious and ruthless, and he may even be cunning, but he's not the Concord. He stands little chance of conquering Spes with a major Concord outpost in the system, but he could pose a serious threat to local settlements. The Concord cannot allow that. Still, we can only act if we have proof."

Megan's eyes flashed. She was picking up something

now . . . something that made her feel cold.

"Proof? Like what kind of proof?"

"Evidence of the kidnapping of a fraal and the experiment, then we can call in the marines and shut down Hatala before it's too late."

Megan nodded, then added, "Good luck."

Greg smiled. "Right. I'm sure we'll need it."

Megan's mouth fell open.

" 'We'? Listen. I told you I can't get mixed up in this right now. I've got problems of my own. And I'm no Intel agent! What the hell do you—"

"Hey, at least it's a way to solve your money problems," Greg said with a grin, but the smile suddenly faded as he continued, "Besides, I'm not giving you a choice in this matter. I checked you out, Ms. *Rivers,* also known as Mary Kasselman, Madeline Rivers, Madeline Benoit . . . I could go on. You're wanted in Tendril and Aegis—petty stuff mostly, but they'd still like to have you back. Help me out, and I'll see what we can work out. Refuse, and I'll take you into custody right now. You'll be safe from Hatala's men all right, but somehow I don't think you'd care for the safety of a prison cell."

Megan stared at him dumbfounded. Damn, she thought. Damn, damn, damn, damn.

"When do we leave?"

* * * * *

Megan and Greg spent the first part of their journey onboard a Star Force cruiser that took them all the way to Arist in Hammer's Star. She was confined to her quarters, but Greg tried to keep her company, though most of his visits consisted of going over aspects of their upcoming mission. From Arist, the two of them proceeded in a small ship with barely enough room for the two of them.

As they entered Spes's atmosphere and began to home

in on the outpost, Greg started drilling her on their cover
and what they were going to do once they landed. They'd
only been over it a dozen times already, but her stomach
was beginning to jitter with nervousness. This was it, the
real thing, no turning back at this point.

"You're a mindwalker who specializes in mineral
deposits, right?" Greg said as he transmitted their beacon
to the outpost. "There's no reason you wouldn't drift back
here for work, right? I'm your . . . friend. I brought you
here."

"Yes, my chauffeur, so when we get to the weren outpost . . . then what?"

"I haven't figured out that part," Greg said as the outpost's reply beacon came through. "Okay. Looks like they
picked us up."

Greg steered the ship over the outpost. To go along with
his warlike nature, Hatala's outpost consisted of several
fortified structures linked to another, sprawling a kilometer in all directions. Interspersed throughout were houses,
storage buildings, market stalls, and open lots, with the
settlement's crops in the fields outside of town. Megan was
in no rush to see the fortress any closer. The area had a
dismal reputation among the other settlers in the vicinity.
The ship dipped down suddenly.

"Sorry," Greg said. "I'm used to bigger ships. This is
like a toy."

"Nice. I just I love traveling through space in toy."

The ship soared above the outpost. A gruff scratchy
voice speaking Standard suddenly broke the comm silence.
"Approaching vessel, identify your ship registry and purpose of visit."

Greg pointed to Megan.

"Megan Rivers. I'm a mindwalker specializing in mineral location. I'm looking for work, and I thought I might
be of service to your mining operation out here. I request
landing clearance at the spaceport. Ship registry coming

through now."

Greg transmitted their craft's registration. The speaker went quiet. Several seconds went by and still nothing. Megan looked at Greg. Was the request being considered; were they checking on the ship?

"Don't worry," Greg said reassuringly, "they'll buy it. The Concord paid a lot of money for our false registry. Relax and enjoy the view."

The comm crackled to life again. "Permission to land, but don't count on finding much work here. You are authorized for twenty-four hours. If you want to stay longer, request again."

Megan whispered. "Can't wait."

Greg flew a few thousand meters over the fortified settlement. Below in the streets and alleys, the weren took no notice. Megan looked over the creatures. It was hard not to physically react to their hulking, brutal appearance.

"Ah, there's the spaceport."

Megan turned to Greg. He handed a small weapon to her. She laughed. "Sorry. I don't *do* weapons. 'Peace and love' have been the motto in my family for generations."

"Take it. It's a small charge pistol with a seven round clip. The safety's that button just above the trigger. Hide it in your pants leg. You may be happy you did."

Megan took the small gun; it was heavy.

I hate this, she thought. The only plus was that the Concord would clean her record, wipe out her debts, and give her twenty thousand Concord dollars, a year's worth of financial go-juice, if she was careful. It was a definite plus, but the pistol seemed to indicate that there was a chance she might have to shoot something. If that was true, someone might shoot at her.

That's a definite minus. A big one.

* * * * *

The ship landed at the small spaceport near a cluster of weren homes. After Megan and Greg exited the ship and locked it behind them, a few curious weren ambled over to gawk, probaby to see if they were traders bringing in new wares. Megan smiled and explained that she was just searching for work. Greg stood to the side, acting as though he was merely her escort.

The heat was oppressive. Megan had grown too used to the environment controls of space stations and domed settlements. She suddenly realized how long it had been since she stood on a planet beneath open sky.

"Okay, " she whispered, "now what?"

"How good are you?"

"At what?"

"How good are you at your mindwalking?"

Megan sighed. If Greg was depending on that, they were in big trouble. "I'm . . . okay. I get flashes, not a lot of control though. The usual. Why are you asking me that *now?*"

Greg ignored her question and said, "What about pushes?"

"God."

"Can you push?"

"Once in a really big while I can give someone a nudge. Never tried it on any non-humans though."

"But you've done it?"

"Yes."

"Good. I'll tell you the plan while we walk."

Megan and Greg started toward the center of the settlement. They passed a few open markets and training areas where weren practiced their fun and games. Nearly all of the games seemed to center around fighting or shooting. Though the tusked creatures looked at the humans with suspicion, none said anything to them as they wandered through the streets. They saw only two other humans in the entire place—two grubby traders haggling with a merchant over a bundle of textiles.

By the time they reached the center of the outpost where Chief Hatala's Council Chamber lay, the hot afternoon was turning to warm evening. It would be full dark in a couple of hours.

The Chamber itself was in the midst of several outlying buildings, and a pitted and cracked wall enclosed the entire area. Fierce, suspicious-looking guards patrolled the area. Every one of them carried at least one gun, and several had wicked-looking chuurkhnas as well.

As they walked across the open ground to the main gate, Greg told Megan what he had in mind for getting inside.

"I see why you gave me the gun," she said in response, her mouth suddenly dry.

"We won't use the weapons, not unless we have to, and I hope we won't have to."

They approached the gate where they were stopped by a huge weren. Megan explained that she was searching for work and wished to petition the council to utilize her skills. The guard waved them through lazily, not even bothering to search them.

They entered the outlying buildings. The narrow pathways were filled with weren in an assortment of uniforms, outfits that did little to hide their ferocious, animal-like nature. Gone were the market stalls, the idle passersby, and children. Every weren they now passed was a soldier. Most eyed the two humans suspiciously, but none stopped them or said anything.

"You know where to go?" Megan asked.

Greg nodded. "Yes. We have maps—they're probably a bit outdated though. It's been a while since we sent a survey drone over this area, but at least it's something."

A weren suddenly stepped into the path, cutting them off. Megan feared he might have heard them talking. The creature's uniform was filled with badges and medals and looked more official than anything they had seen so far, and a gigantic charge rifle was slung across his back.

The weren barked, "This area is restricted for those on official business with the Court of Chief Hatala. You have no business here and must go back."

Megan spoke. "I worked the Revik asteroid belt further out in the system—"

"I *know* where the Revik belt is, girl. State your business and be done, or I will have the guards throw you out."

"Yes, yes of course. I'm a Finder. I can sense mineral deposits—"

The guard crossed his arms over his massive chest, pulled himself to his full height, and growled warningly.

"I, uh, I learned s-something of importance th-that Chief Hatala will want to know."

She had to do it now . . . to deliver a slight mental push to make this lumbering creature agree to allow them to continue.

"It's important that I continue"—and she pushed with her will, terrified that this huge beast might somehow know what she was doing—"to your chief's audience chamber. He must see me."

Megan thought her own voice must have sounded decidedly unconvincing, but the lumbering weren nodded and moved aside.

They passed more guards on the way, taking wrong turns and hitting dead ends, but Megan grew so confident wandering through the rambling city that she asked directions from a weren whose tusks glinted as he nodded and pointed out the way to go.

"Hey, at least they're buying our story," Greg said.

"Or they're incredibly dense."

"I wouldn't count on that."

The easy part ended as soon as they came to a large building with a huge metal door. A half-dozen heavily armed weren guarded the entrance. Their weapons were outdated, GW2 charge rifles mostly, but lethal nonetheless.

Megan turned to Greg.

"Game over, hmm? No way I can give those guys a push."

"Try it," Greg said.

"Are you insane?" she whispered. "There are *six* of them there!"

"Listen," Greg replied quietly. "It's too late to turn back now. If we tuck tail and run, they'll know something's up. Just try it, Megan. Trust me."

They stopped at the gate while three of the guards walked over. The guards shook their heads in a typical way of the weren, a warning head bob. All but one of them readied their weapons.

The largest of them, an old grizzled creature with a chipped tusk, stepped forward and said, "What do you seek at the Chamber of Hatala, Chief of the weren of Spes?"

Megan started speaking, adding all the mental force she could, while Greg looked on. "I have some information for Lord Hat—"

"*Chief* Hatala!" one of the other guards shouted. "We have no *lords* here."

"Y-yes, yes, of course," Megan went on. "My apologies if I have offended. I recently stumbled upon some information that Chief Hatala must know, but the information is dangerous and fit for the ears of Hatala alone."

Megan felt something. It was similar to the feeling she had when picking up mental images from others, but no images came, just a slight nudge, a tickling at the base of her conscious mind. She glanced over to Greg, trying to tell him with her eyes that this wasn't working. Maybe these guards were smarter or maybe it was simply the fact that there were more of them.

"You may give your news to me, little girl," said the weren with the chipped tusk. "If I deem it worthy of the chief's attention, you may see him, but I will not trouble him unnecessarily."

The other guards added some growling noises to their refusals. Things were getting tense.

"It's no good." Megan whispered to Greg. "They don't care. They won't—"

In one fluid motion, Greg pulled a slender pistol from inside his jacket and pointed it . . . right at Megan. Every guard raised his weapon as well, three aimed at Megan and three at Greg.

Her jaw fell open "What? What is this?"

Greg spoke quickly but calmly. "This woman is a spy posing as a free agent. She's hear to learn Chief Hatala's plans for Spes and deliver the news to the Concord."

Megan shook her head. "What are you doing? Is this a set-up?"

Dumbfounded and terrified, she turned to leave, but four bulky weren blocked her exit. They grabbed her arms and quickly led her deeper into the structure, through more halls and corridors. Every few minutes Megan said, "I don't believe this."

Greg, accompanied but unrestrained by two weren, said nothing. They reached a massive hall, lit by torches and adorned with giant tapestries showing weren battle scenes. The air in the hall was cool, a pleasant change from the outside heat; the weren obviously had environmental controls. But the air was thick, smoky, and unpleasant. On the far end of the room, standing beside a large steel table was a weren who was obviously the leader. . . Chief Hatala.

He was the most massive being Megan had ever seen, easily two-and-a-half meters of solid muscle covered in thick black and gray fur. His tusks gleamed a dull red in the light of a few lamps. His braided beard hung well below his chest, and golden earrings dangled to his shoulders.

"What have we here?" Chief Hatala wasted no time. "New pets perhaps? Tell me what this is about. Now!"

Megan spoke up quickly. "Here's the deal"—she looked around at the weren—"this jerk here is with the Concord—"

Greg tossed a silvery plastic card across the table to Hatala.

"Take a look, Chief Hatala. It's a phony. I had it made in Lucullus. Makes life simpler. She didn't even look at it closely."

"What?" Megan said. "That ID's not—"

Megan looked over at Hatala and watched him turn the card over in his hands. Then the chief laughed, a great roar that hurt Megan's ears.

"This stupid fake works for you?"

Greg nodded. "In most places, yes. Everyone's so scared of the Concord . . . you'd be surprised."

Hatala threw down the card into the fire, then barked. "Not here, human. On my world, I fear *nothing*, not any other weren clans, not humans, not any other species." Hatala stood up and raised his arms over his head. "We will rule over all the weren someday, and it begins here."

The chief walked over to a massive cushioned seat positioned in front of the hearth. He sat and continued, "Well, little human, that explains who you are *not,* but I still wait to hear who you are."

"Listen, please—!" Megan shouted.

One of the guards cuffed her lightly on the back of the head, cutting her off. Hatala smiled and said, "You will have your turn in a minute, little one. Now, you"—he gestured at Greg—"who are you, and why are you here? Impress me, or I'll let Dreneg here use you for target practice."

"It's quite simple, Chief Hatala," Greg said. He smiled, but Megan could see the nervousness in his eyes. "I'm a bounty hunter, plain and simple. I'd been tracking this little minx for a, uh . . . a *businessman* . . . on Penates. I caught up to her on a run-down little mining operation, and—much to my surprise—found out that she had some information concerning you, valuable information, dangerous information."

Megan looked at Greg in shock. Had she truly been that stupid? Greg's eyes darted from watching Hatala to Megan. Megan tried to think of her options, if she had any left. If she tried to run, she might make it all of three meters before one of the weren guards slashed at her feet and brought her down . . . if they didn't simply shoot her outright.

Could she try to convince Chief Hatala that Greg was lying? Was he lying? Was he really with the Concord, or was this whole thing designed to get something from the weren warlord?

"Let me tell you what I want, Chief Hatala." Greg said.

"You want?" Hatala laughed. "You haven't brought me anything but a stupid human female. No one will miss her if I throw her into a Mong Pit and watch the show!" More laughter, while Megan wondered what the hell a Mong could be. It didn't sound good, whatever it was.

It was true enough—no one would miss her. She prided herself on being a loner, a pioneer. Now, standing here, she knew there was a downside to being so alone, so free.

Maybe, she wondered, I should just tell what I knew, come clean and hope for mercy. Tell Hatala everything and promise to keep my mouth shut.

Greg interrupted her desperate thoughts.

"Chief Hatala, I brought you someone who knows your very important, very secret plans for war, your dream of uniting the weren clans of the Verge into one powerful nation under your rule."

The guards made growling noises while Hatala bobbed his head, none too happy about this.

"Secret plans? Secret plans!" Hatala bellowed. "What secret plans are you talking about?"

Greg smiled. "Your plans to use the fraal to transform your weren warriors into battle-ready mindwalkers."

With more head bobbing, Hatala took a step closer to Megan. She backed up into the barrel-chest of one of the guards.

The weren leader lowered his head so he was eyeball-to-eyeball with Megan. He opened his mouth as though he wanted to bite her head off. Instead, he simply barked once, a terse humorless laugh.

"Kill her."

Megan turned, but the guards were right there. She thought of her pistol. No one had removed it; they hadn't even searched her, but there was no way she could reach it in time, not with the guard holding her.

"Wait," Greg said. "I discovered only very little of what she knows. You don't know who told her or what they told her—and more importantly, how many people she told. You should find out who else knows, and I'll be more than happy to track them down and kill them for you—for a modest fee, of course. You certainly don't want the Concord getting wind of your plans."

The weren leader tilted his head left and right. Megan could barely breathe. The thick air in the room, the heavy breath of her guards, and the fear all combined to paralyze her thoughts. Then she *felt* something else, as if something or someone was giving the weren warlord a psionic push. Hatala seemed to hesitate, confused. Something wasn't right.

Greg stole a sidelong glance at her and winked. What's going on here? Her mind screamed. Think, think, think. Greg, a bounty hunter? How?

Then it all came together in her mind. How could she not have seen it before? Greg couldn't be a bounty hunter. They'd spent two starfalls getting here in a Concord Star Force cruiser. She held no admiration for Star Force, or the Concord for that matter, but she knew that they didn't let bounty hunters hitch rides through the Verge.

The gun, Megan thought. Greg had voluntarily given her a charge pistol. He would never have done that if he was merely delivering her as goods to Hatala.

"So," Hatala announced, breaking her train of thought,

"we torture her, make her speak. Even better."

Right, sure—sounds good to me, Megan thought. She had nothing to lose now. She jabbed an elbow into the nearest guard's gut. The blow was strong enough to send the unprepared weren reeling backward despite his superior size, then Megan looked for an opening between the guards. She dodged to the left of one, then dipped under another guard's weapon.

The third guard reached out and snared her around the neck with his great, clawed hand. He grabbed both her wrists and yanked her around to stand in front of Hatala.

So much for my escape, Megan thought. The guard's grip was strong as steel; her struggles were futile.

"You don't have time for torture," Greg said, "enjoyable as it might be. There were Concord agents at the mining settlement. I saw her speaking to at least one of them, and there could have been more. Every minute you wait, your plans could be getting exposed."

Hatala turned away from her to Greg and asked, "What do I do?"

What's going on with him? Megan wondered. What's with this great leader taking marching orders from a human?

Megan looked at Greg. Was that a hint of a smile at the corner of his mouth, almost imperceptible? There's something else going on here, she thought. Greg is doing something.

"Oh, it's easy, Chief Hatala. You can get everything she heard, who she told it to and, more importantly, the traitor who told her."

The weren leader faced them, alternately eyeing Megan and Greg.

"How?"

Greg waited. Everyone waited. Even Megan didn't have a clue what he was about to suggest, just as long as it didn't involve the Mong Pit.

"Easy. If I may be so bold, Honored Chief, I'm aware that you have fraal here . . . as your guests, of course. Bring them up and let them probe her mind. She's psionic, too, though of a very low level. The fraal should have no problem finding out everything you need to know, then you can kill or torture her at your leisure and pay me a reward or send me out on contract to do clean-up."

Hatala walked slowly to the far end of the great hall. When the weren chief reached the end, he turned around and raised one massive hand. "Yes. We will do that, but if she is only a low level mindwalker as you say, one fraal will be sufficient.." He gestured to two of the guards. "Bring one of our guests here, the one called Tm'laa, and hurry. My head aches and I tire of this nonsense."

The guard left, Hatala sat down, and for a few minutes nobody said anything.

* * * * *

As soon as the fraal shuffled in, Megan's heart sank. The creature, forlorn and dressed in ragged clothing, moved slowly as though his legs had been hurt. Purple blotches dotted his smooth skin, and the dark, almond-shaped eyes looked around with none of the glitter that fraal eyes normally produced.

"Welcome, Tm'laa," Hatala shouted mirthfully. Megan saw Tm'laa nod. If there was any rebellion in the creature, it had been snuffed out. Still, the guards all eyed Tm'laa nervously, even though he was less than half the size of the smallest of them, and two rifles were aimed at the fraal at all times. He would do exactly what the weren leader asked.

"Tm'laa," Hatala said, "you see this human here, this woman. She supposedly knows things about the project you have been helping us with. Find out everything she knows, find out who told her, and find out who she has told."

The weren leader looked to Greg for approval. The guards looked none too happy about this. Megan caught them exchanging nervous glances.

Yes, Megan thought—Greg is doing something to Hatala. She looked at Greg, knowing for certain now that the man might have more than a little psionic ability himself. She remembered the ease with which the guards had allowed them into the compound. It all made so much sense now. She had been a fool not to see it before.

"Tm'laa," Hatala asked, "do you understand?"

Another nod. "I do, Chief Hatala."

"Tm'laa," Hatala said gravely, "no tricks. You remember what happened the last time? My mercy is at an end. Do as you are told."

The fraal nodded sadly and closed his eyes.

Megan thought she might be able to block the probe, but—in the long run—it would be of no use. The fraal were famous for their mindwalking abilities. This creature would dig his way into her mind all too easily, peeling away barriers, getting down to her secret, guarded thoughts.

Given enough time, this Tm'laa would have everything she knew.

Then Megan saw something. Greg moved a halfstep toward his nearest guard and dropped his hand to his side. The hand was open, relaxed, and completely nonthreatening, but Megan knew that Greg was about to make his move.

She braced herself for the probe. Instead, she felt something else. It came in bits and fragments at first, but then, she could sense the entire message, and it wasn't from Tm'laa. Somehow Greg sent her a message: *Get ready to go for your gun.*

Megan tried to imagine a response. *What is this? What are you doing?*

What came back, in bits and chunks, was only the command, *Get ready,* and, *When . . . say "now."*

"Tm'laa," Hatala said, "what do you see? Tm'laa?"

Megan knew that Tm'laa wasn't probing her at all. Greg must have gotten a message to the fraal as well.

"Yes," Greg said in Standard, "tell us what you see . . . *now.*"

For a second Megan almost didn't move. Greg said the word "now," and it seemed to float into the room and then vanish, a green light ignored. Not daring to breathe, she felt her heart beat once, then she moved. Trembling, she reached down to her pants leg and pulled out the tiny charge pistol.

In the same instant, the guard next to Greg began to fall, clutching at his temple and crying out in pain. The heavy rifle forgotten, Greg grabbed it, aimed, and fired. Megan heard the deafening *crack* of the rifle, felt the intense heat of the plasma trail as it sliced past her, and the guard behind her collapsed with a shattered, bleeding chest.

The other weren were taken completely by surprise. Greg shifted his aim and squeezed off another round. Another guard fell dead just as two others fell to the floor, clutching their heads and wailing in agony.

Chaos erupted.

One of the guards raised his rifle and was about to cut Greg down when Megan fired her own weapon. She meant to catch the creature in its shoulder, but she shot a little to the left and too high. The weren's head vaporized in a cloud of red mist and shattered bone.

The rest of the guards had shuffled back and were about to open fire when Greg yelled, "Stop!" Everyone froze. Greg had his charge rifle aimed directly at Hatala, only centimeters from the chief's throat. "Anyone moves and your chief loses his pretty head."

For a heartbeat, no one moved. Three weren were obviously very dead, and two more still writhed moaning on the floor with blood trickling from their nose and ears. The remaining guards, wide-eyed and afraid to twitch, looked first at one another, then at their chief for guidance.

Hatala spoke. "More guards will come, little human . . . in tens, in hundreds. You will be surrounded by weren, *my* weren. There's no way to go."

Greg nodded. "Yup—it would appear that way, but I think we'll have a bit of help on our escape." Megan saw Greg look at the fraal. "Ready, Tm'laa?" The fraal nodded. "Okay, everyone put down your weapons nice and easy, then lie down on the floor, belly down and face to the floor."

After a nod from their chief, the three remaining guards set their rifles ever-so-gently upon the floor and lay down next to them.

"Now you, Hatala." Greg pulled his weapon away from the creature's neck. Hatala lay down. "This is a big hall. I'm not too sure which door we'll leave by, you know, but whatever door it is, if I see one of you even try to take a peek at us, your head will become part of the wall in this charming room. Understand?"

The weren nodded.

Tm'laa spoke in Standard, in calm, almost soothing tones. "Others are coming from there"—he pointed to one door, then another—"and there. Soon. Our time is gone."

"Right." Greg came over to Megan. "You okay?"

"Just great. Can you tell me what this has been about?"

Greg laughed. "Sure, but can it wait until we're off this rock?"

"*If* we get off this rock."

"I suggest," Tm'laa said, "that we get moving now, that way." Tm'laa pointed at a door, and Megan started running, followed by a limping Tm'laa. Greg ran backwards making sure none of the weren looked.

One guard did, raising his head just a bit. Greg didn't hesitate. He shot and in an instant the weren was minus that head.

"Getting messy in here," Megan said.

They ran through the door and into a labyrinth of hallways. After several twists and turns, they stopped to allow Tm'laa a rest, his breath wheezing in broken gasps. Greg looked down each hall and when he saw no one approaching, he touched the back of his right wrist. The back of his hand popped open, revealing a small transmitter.

"You're cybered," Megan whispered, "and a mindwalker unless I miss my guess. I'm convinced that you're no common bounty hunter, but are there any other secrets you're not telling me?"

"Lots," Greg said with a smile as he keyed a commcode into the transmitter, "but there'll be time for that later." A small light on the comm flashed green and Greg said, *"Hadrian* this is GM-In one. Execute. Repeat: execute."

Angry shouts and cursing began to drift from the hall behind them.

"Time to get outside," Greg said. "Tm'laa, can you make it? We're almost there."

The fraal nodded, still too out of breath to speak. He pointed to the left hall, and they kept running. At times Tm'laa would stop them, sensing that someone was coming. Other times he urged them to move quickly to avoid a party of guards racing toward them.

Gradually they made their way to a back door. Two alert guards there yielded to the logic of Greg and Megan's charge weapons, and then they were out.

Only the barest hint of daylight remained in the sky, though the air was still uncomfortably warm. Megan thought they were actually going to make it.

"Which way is the ship?" she rasped as they bounded down a darkened, narrow street.

"No time!" Greg said as a small party of weren rounded the corner in front of them "Everybody down!"

The three of them dove into a small alley just as a round of bullets slammed into the wall. The alley was dark, but Megan could see that it ended in a high wall only a few meters away. They were cut off.

"I'm sorry," Tm'laa told them. "There were just too many, and I'm tired, so tired. It was hard to tell which way was dangerous."

"It's okay," Greg said. He popped a few shots down the street, not aiming, merely to discourage their pursuers from coming any closer. "You did a good job."

Another round of charge fire slammed into the building covering them, sending splinters of stone and plastic flying into the street

"What do we do?" Megan asked, wide-eyed with fear.

"We wait," replied Greg. "Sit tight."

Megan studied Greg in the dim shadows of the alley. He seemed completely relaxed. Is this how you face death, she wondered.

"Wait? Wait for what?"

The weren warriors couldn't be more than meters away, and they continued to litter the street with bullets.

"Shouldn't we run?" Megan asked.

"And miss the fun?"

"Fun? What—"

Just then, a sonic boom shattered the darkening sky. Everyone looked up. A fast-moving cloud, sparkling with many lights, descended upon the settlement. Except, Megan saw, it wasn't a cloud after all, more like a Concord cutter.

In seconds it went from a distant object high in the sky to a massive metallic warbird floating a dozen meters above the town. The ship hovered for a heartbeat, then opened up, disgorging dozens of small metal-clad shapes with dizzying speed. In seconds, heavily armored and armed marines descended into the streets, floating down in their induction-powered armor.

Greg came close to Megan and Tm'laa.

"In the old days, they called it 'the cavalry to the rescue'."

"Does this mean the mission is over?" Megan asked.
Greg nodded.

"Thank God," Megan gasped. "Now can I get paid?"

*   *   *   *   *

Megan sat in her small quarters in the Star Force cruiser
Hadrian bound for Bluefall. She had been aboard for two
days and had slept most of that. As promised, Megan's
account now had twenty thousand Concord dollars, a
"reward for service to the Concord and the inhabitants of
Spes," et cetera, et cetera, and her record was in the
process of being expunged by some Concord Administrator in Tendril. All that now remained was the decision of
what to do next.

Putting the matter aside for the moment, she picked up
a small envelope that had been waiting in her message box
when she awoke. In a small, very precise hand, it read
simply, "Ms. Rivers."

She opened it. It was from Tm'laa, and the fraal had
actually taken the time to write it all out by hand.

Ms. Rivers:

*By the time you read this, I will most likely be on my
way elsewhere for a long period of rest and recuperation,
but I did not want to leave without taking the opportunity
to thank you. You were instrumental in saving my life, and
that is a debt I shall not forget.*

*Please allow me to begin to repay that debt now with a
bit of advice. Take it from a fellow mindwalker that you
vastly underestimate your own potential. The mind is like
any part of the body: it will grow stronger with exercise
and more skilled with practice. I will not tell you not to
fear. There is reason to be afraid; the mind is not a child's
plaything, especially for a mindwalker. Remember that an
untrained mind is even more dangerous for you than for*

*most. Take care with your future endeavors, and until we
meet again, may the Divine Unconscious guide you on
your way.*
    Sincerely,
    Tm'laa

Megan smiled fondly and put the letter away. She was
about to leave for the galley when there was a knock at the
door.

"Come in," she said.

Lieutenant Gregory McShane entered the room. "Good
morning," he said.

"Good morning to you," she replied. "How is our friend
Hatala?"

Greg smiled. "Grumbling, fuming, and generally heap-
ing curses upon anyone who comes near him, but he won't
harm anyone in his cell. He'd better get used to close quarters where he's going, though."

"Well, I can't say that I care much whether he likes it
or not. As long as he's well away from me, I'll be happy."

Greg cleared his throat, looked at her rather sheepishly,
and said, "Well, you'll be in no danger from Hatala, that's
certain. However, I do have something of a proposition for
you."

"I'm not sure I like the sound of that," she said, looking at him through narrowed eyes. "Your last 'proposition' nearly got us both killed. Do I have a choice in this
one?"

"Of course." He looked rather abashed. "Listen, Megan,
I truly had little choice in lying to you. I needed you to get
to Tm'laa."

"Why? Why me, and why Tm'laa?"

Greg sat down in a nearby chair without invitation and
said, "Tm'laa is a Concord Intel agent whom we planted
in Hatala's little 'organization' in hopes of finding out
what was going on. When he disappeared and I heard your

tale, especially the part about an Orlamu geneticist experimenting with psionic abilities, it wasn't hard to figure out. Tm'laa is a devout Orlamu, and his cover on Spes was as a geneticist working for the Borealin terraformers."

"But why drag me into all of it?" Megan said with some heat. "What the hell did I do to deserve that? You seemed to do just fine on your own."

"Time was short." He shrugged his shoulders. "I had to get Tm'laa out before they killed him, or before he actually had to begin helping Hatala in order to stay alive. You may not have noticed, but this part of the Verge is nigh on the back ass of nowhere. If I'd taken time to call in an experienced undercover agent, Tm'laa might be dead now."

"You still didn't have to lie to me."

He sighed in resignation, then said, "Would you have come with me if I'd told you the truth?"

She blushed and shuffled her feet but refused to drop her gaze from his.

"Yeah, that's what I thought," he said smugly.

Dropping that line of questioning, she hit him with another. "Why did you lead me along, convincing me to try my psionics on those guards when you were the one doing the pushing all along?"

"I had little choice, Megan. I had to distract them. If Tm'laa had actually been able to teach some of Hatala's people psionic defenses—unlikely I'll grant you, but I wasn't going to take any chances—then I had to point the suspicion elsewhere so I could hit them myself."

Megan gasped at that, her jaw dropping. Greg's smug smile only infuriated her more.

"You mean you painted a target on my forehead, you bastard!"

"Bluntly put, but yes. Listen, Megan, I really didn't think Hatala's people had had enough time to prepare any sort of defenses against your psionics, and I didn't think that the other fraal captives were likely to help him willingly. It was a precaution only."

That didn't help much in Megan's mind. Greg had still lied to her, used her, and gambled with her life.

Greg cleared his throat. "Listen, Megan, you've turned me off the reason I came here in the first place. I have a proposition for you."

"Not damned likely," Megan said as she sat in the small chair across from him, "but go ahead."

"Remember on XJR-whatever-it-was how I told you that the Concord employs free agents throughout the Verge to help keep an eye on things?"

"Yes."

"Well," Greg said, "based upon my report of our mission, the Concord would like you to work for them. You'll be given a small driveship and a modest expense account. You can set yourself up as a licensed Concord mining agent, or do whatever you want."

"What's the catch?" she asked. This all sounded too good to be true.

"Don't look so suspicious!" Greg laughed. "Given your past record, you aren't going to get much of a security clearance. You may occasionally be asked to relay info or supplies to other agents. The catch is that you have to report your current location to your contact and relay any pertinent information to him on a timely basis."

"Just who is my contact?" She was afraid that she already knew the anwer to that.

"Me," Greg said with a smile.

"Oh, hell, that's just great."

"Take it easy, Meg." There was more than a hint of condescension in Greg's tone, but he was still smiling. "I thought we worked pretty good together."

Megan looked away for a second.

"Just how 'modest' is this expense account?"

"You won't be rich," Greg answered, "but your days of

hopping back and forth between grimy mining colonies would be over. You don't even have to continue your work as a Finder. Hell, I don't care if you want to become a lounge singer on Bluefall. You might look good in a skin-film dress."

"Up yours, McShane."

Greg laughed. "Sorry. But seriously, Megan, you can do as you like. Tm'laa was rather impressed with your performance. He even expressed some interest in working with you after he's recovered. You've got potential, kiddo. Keep clean and you could go places."

"Greg," she sighed.

"Yes?"

"Let's start over. My real name is Mary Agnes Rivers, but don't you ever call me that. When we work together, it's Megan or Meg."

Greg laughed, and then Megan laughed too.

About the Author

Matthew J. Costello is the author of more than sixteen novels, several film novelizations, and numerous non-fiction works, including collaborations with F. Paul Wilson and Craig Shaw Gardner. His articles have appeared in publications ranging from *The Lost Angeles Times* to *Sports Illustrated*. He scripted *The 7th Guest*, the best-selling CD-ROM interactive drama and its sequel, *The 11th Hour*.

"He's a Good Little Boy"

Michael A. Stackpole

THIS WAS NOT the day I needed this happening. Actually, I didn't need it at all, but since I made my living handling things most folks don't want to handle, this problem fell to me anyway. I had just come off a full day of shifting rubble and pulling miners out of a hole in the ground owned by the Pyritix Corporation. Added to that was that fact that my new Concord Field Administrator was making a surprise visit to my sector, so being called out to the mechalus enclave to deal with a problem really wasn't what I'd been looking forward to.

The report I'd received—which came in just as I was forcing the top button on my best uniform jacket closed—didn't make much sense to me. Ronald Aspan, the local district director for Pyritix Corporation, was accusing his son's spark nanny of kidnapping the boy. I knew Aspan had a spark watching over little Kenny—his father called him "Punt" for some reason, which always struck me as a weird nickname—but that wasn't unusual. A lot of mechalus from the enclave worked in Pyrton as menials, and many folks favored them for childcare.

A spark kidnapping the kid didn't ring true to me, mainly because that's a pretty aggressive act, and most of the local mechalus tended toward pacifism. This was especially true of the sparks at the enclave. Their leader, Avi Hausoc, had a bunch of them involved in some project she referred to as "the work." Her people all lived at the enclave but came down to Pyrton to scavenge around for old, busted tech, which they repaired and sold or somehow incorporated into "the work." Kidnapping a child just didn't fit into the pattern I'd gotten used to over the last year.

I'd been out to the enclave before, at least once a month. The sparks were pretty good at finding and fixing all sorts of things, including quantum rifles and other weapons that will ruin a guy's day if he finds himself in front of the trigger.

Cruising on up over a hillcrest, I could see the enclave nestled there between two ridges. At this distance, it looked very much like the stump of a tree that had been blackened by fire. The thick central tower grew upward, the farther edge of it stabbing higher into the sky. At its base the tower broadened into the compound's main building. Tunnels that bumped up through the greensward like humps of a sea serpent connected it with smaller outbuildings. In broad daylight the compound sparkled a little bit and maintained a sharp contrast with the red-rock formations on either side of it. At night a legion of little lights winked on and off as if the building itself was reflecting the starry sky.

A series of several ground-huggers bearing some of Pyritix Corps' own house militia came racing along down the unpaved road. I saw mostly men jammed into the last two vehicles, but the shaggy, hulking forms of two weren stood out in the back of the first flatbed worming its way along the dirt track.

I shook my head as I throttled the skybike up and raced across country toward the enclave. It made sense that Ronald Aspan would call out his company troops to try to get his son back, but either of the weren he kept as part of his personal security detail would have been enough to do the job. The raw display of power didn't really surprise me—I'd gotten used to Aspan flaunting his power over the last six months. I didn't like it, but I'd gotten used to it. I just hoped I could prevent things from getting decidedly messy.

My skybike got me to the enclave about a minute and a half before the Pyritix vehicles arrived. I slew the skybike around so it blocked the path to the compound's doorway, but rolling over it would have been simple. I decided to trust in the fact that Aspan really didn't like Concord authority meddling in his affairs, and that killing me would bring a lot more of that down on him than I could ever do by myself.

I got off the bike, left it in hover mode, then straightened my uniform. Watching the trio of troopcarriers roll up the hill toward the compound, I felt decidedly naked. While the Concord uniform did fit me—albeit tight at the shoulders and loose at the waist—I would have preferred some heavy assault gear. The uniform might command some respect, but it wouldn't stop beams or bullets.

I did shuck my stutter SMG out of the skybike's scabbard, extended the stock and let the whole thing dangle rather casually from my shoulder by the strap. I'm big enough that the gun almost looks pistol-sized in my hand. I picked it up to emphasize that fact as the first vehicle slowed. I checked the weapon's battery, smiled, then leisurely lowered the weapon.

Ronald Aspan got out of the lead carrier's cab as the other two vehicles fanned out and moved forward a bit before stopping. He shot the cuffs on his gray jacket, then picked a piece of lint from his right shoulder. Slender and slightly taller than average, Aspan had a face that had been assembled out of an under-abundance of jaw, an over-abundance of forehead, and a nose that had never been broken. Somehow, all of his features seemed to have been sharpened until they looked as if his face could split rock.

It was a theory I'd wanted to test on a number of occasions.

Korphyr and Lenguila, the two weren, came over the cab of the vehicle and dropped into position two steps back and one on either side of Aspan. Weren, as a rule, are huge creatures with massive arms and shoulders. Their forward-thrusting heads rest on bull necks that are covered in a thick mane that runs from forehead to mid-spine, and the males' underslung jaws sport two mighty tusks. While they're capable of civilized and even philosophical discourse, their real talent comes in the area of combat, and the two Aspan retained were no strangers to fighting.

They followed him at a respectful distance as he approached me, their tusked heads swinging side to side as if they thought I'd brought an army with me. Korphyr clearly decided I was alone, which brought a grim smile to his jet-black face. Lenguila, on the other hand, tightened his eyes warily and continued to look for trouble.

"Constable Walgrove, how good to see you here." Aspan's tone of voice made it clear he was not pleased to see me at all. "I trust you have come to help me recover Punt."

I stroked a hand across my jaw, emphasizing the fact that I had enough of one for the both of us, with a bit left over. "I understand there is some trouble. I'm here to see we get it settled. Wouldn't like to see blood spilled here."

"Not blood," Korphyr growled. "Sparkweep."

I eyed Korphyr coldly as his clawed hands twitched open and closed.

"You're not much of a calming influence here."

Aspan lifted his chin and sniffed. "Being calm in the face of having my son stolen from me is not something I desire in my employees. They'll do what I tell them to do. Now are you going to get my son back from these sparks, or will my people have to do it?"

Before I could address his threat properly, the compound door behind me creaked open. Aspan flinched and

Lenguila interposed his body between the door and his master. Korphyr lunged forward but stopped beside my bike. I think it was less the SMG I had jammed into his armpit that stopped him than the sight of Avi Hausoc coming into the daylight.

The mechalus, as a species, are strikingly similar to humans in form, but as the enclave's leader stepped into the sunlight, there would be no mistaking her for the same species as Aspan. Her flesh had the hue of blue steel, but silvery ribbons of circuits ran through it, flashing and glinting in the light. Her hair, which she wore very long, had curled itself into long, thick locks that seemed more carbon filament than protein. Her features had a delicate simplicity to them, and her slender form moved with a sensual grace that made her beauty undeniable. Even so, the mechanical parts of her made her inaccessible and a bit forbidding, as if even thinking of her as sensual were somehow improper.

She raised a slender-fingered hand and opened it in greeting. "Introduction: welcome to our compound, the Aleerindos. I am Avi Hausoc. Welcome, Walgrove, Carey, informally, Catch."

I turned toward her and nodded. "Thank you. I wish I was here under other circumstances."

Avi looked past me toward Aspan. "Greetings to you, Ronald, sire and creator of Kenneth."

Aspan stepped out from behind Lenguila. "I want my son, now. Don't deny you have him."

"Query: why would I deny the obvious?" Avi waved her left hand toward the doorway. "Statement: Kenneth awaits twenty meters within. Come."

Aspan flicked a hand against Lenguila's gray-furred shoulder. "Fetch Punt, and be quick about it."

I held up my left hand while keeping the stutter gun pressed against Korphyr's chest. "Don't be thinking I'm letting either of you in there."

Lenguila dropped into a crouch. "Hurt Korphyr maybe, but I will reach you."

I ground the gun's muzzle a bit deeper into the black weren's rib cage. "I've fought weren before. I know you have *nervi plexi* like other living creatures, and one of them is right where I have my gun pointed. One whisper and Korphyr will be curled up and mewing, leaving me plenty of time for you."

The gray weren dropped his jaw open in a grin. "Plexus is easy shot at close range. Not me. Not when I'm moving."

Avi Hausoc opened both her hands. "Statement: Constable Walgrove, we will allow the entry of all parties into the Aleerindos, but they must come unarmed."

"An unweaponed weren is hardly less dangerous." I let the stutter SMG slip away from Korphyr's torso. "Am I to be stripped of my weapons as well?"

She looked away distantly for a moment, then nodded. "Reply: you may come, unarmed. The weren and Ronald, sire and creator of Kenneth, may come too. The others shall wait."

Aspan smiled briefly in my direction. "Avi Hausoc's wisdom is quite evident."

I holstered the SMG on my skybike and said nothing. I did pop open the storage compartment and slipped onto my left wrist a compact weapons-scanner. I played it over Aspan and the weren but got nothing in the way of handhelds or implants. The lack of implants didn't surprise me—Pyritix Corp had a company policy against such things in employees that supposedly was based in some incidents during the Cyko Riots. Rumors suggested that the bias was actually an Aspan family quirk. If so, more power to them—I never liked the idea of having machinery grafted into a person. The sparks are born that way, which is different in my mind.

I let Aspan and the weren go into the building first,

figuring I could block the way out if they tried anything stupid. The entryway proved narrow enough that the two weren needed to twist one shoulder forward so they could pass through it, and even at that, little wisps of fur clung to mismatched joints of the polymer paneling that lined the corridor.

Me, I just felt the occasional tug at the shoulders of my uniform.

The entryway opened into a tall, airy rotunda at the tower's base. The floor had been finished in black marble, with a tracery of white worked through it. The black polymer paneling extended from the entryway and up and around to cover every surface in the cavernous room. The joints here matched seamlessly, making it appear as if the whole room had been glazed.

Though the lighting had been kept deliberately dim, lights flashing from behind the panels gave the room enough life to dispel any cold, funereal airs. Little lights, all gold and red and green, flicked on and off in wonderfully flowing patterns. Waves of illumination broke and swirled into little eddies that died in the dark, then another spark somewhere would explode outward and become a new cyclone of light that would wash over the room.

This was "the work," a living, ever-expanding sculpture that was equal parts memorial and monument, celebration and exploration. I felt a little chill run down my spine, knowing every bit of this creation had been taken from items discarded as useless. Things ugly, broken, and abandoned had been melded together into something breathtakingly magnificent.

In the center of this lightstorm stood Kenny Aspan. Two sparks stood with him, one with her hands on his shoulders, the other, a male, crouched beside him. Both of them looked young—with mechalus it's often tough to tell, but they didn't project as much strength as Avi Hausoc did. Kenny appeared quite small in comparison to them. I think

he was all of four years old, but he seemed a bit stunted
growthwise to me. His head, which was covered with a
close cropped shock of blond hair, seemed a bit oversize
for his body. Genetics had softened his father's sharp features but hadn't given the kid much more than his dad had
in the way of a chin. The big blue eyes, though, had occasional flashes of curiosity that helped dispel a generally
sad expression.

Kenny's sad expression seemed to deepen when he saw
his father.

Ronald Aspan crossed his arms over his chest. "Punt,
come here."

The little boy looked at his father, then once, quickly,
shook his head.

Aspan snapped his fingers and pointed at his son with
his right hand. "Punt, come here, now!"

The snarled command started one of the boy's feet forward, but it returned to its mate quickly enough.

Aspan then turned on me. "Constable, do your duty. Get
my son."

The imperious tone of his voice made me sorely
tempted to slug him one, but I kept my urge in check. I
knew it would upset Avi Hausoc, and with his chin being
so small a target, I knew I could have missed, which would
have upset me. Instead I ignored him and positioned
myself in the middle of the four meters separating father
from son. In doing so I glanced at my weapons-scanner
and got nothing beyond what I'd expect from the two
sparks, and the boy proved to be as blank as his father.

I looked up from the scanner to the mechalus leader.
"The boy is here. His father is not happy. What's going
on?"

Avi Hausoc's hands fell to her sides, and her body
locked up almost as if she had become inanimate from the
neck down. "Kenneth has just passed the fourth anniver-
sary of his nativity. He is special to us. We wished to

engage him in a *fliidrun*. Ronald, sire and creator of Kenneth, agreed to this."

I glanced at the boy's father. "Did you?"

"Yes, but I changed my mind." He folded his arms across his chest again. "I have that right as a parent."

"You informed them of your change of heart?"

"After I learned the details of what a fliidrun was, yes." Aspan's eyes narrowed. "I did not think it appropriate for someone his age."

I frowned. The sparks working on Hausoc's work had developed some interesting rituals and the fliidrun was one of them. At ages corresponding to powers of two, they spend four days in what amounts to a Faraday cage. It isolates them from all electromagnetic radiation, producing the rough equivalent of total silence for them. It is supposed to help them center themselves and build up a sense of self. Back when I turned forty, Avi Hausoc insisted I go through a fliidrun, even though my age wasn't right. It was about as peaceful a time as I'd ever had on this rock.

I really couldn't see what harm it could do to a boy Kenny's age, but I also couldn't see any reason why Aspan's son shouldn't be returned to him.

I pressed my hands together. "Look, I got this job as a Concord Constable in this district because I have the tools to keep the peace, not because I understand all that much of the law. What I do understand of it tells me that keeping the boy here is, at its very least, custodial interference. You really need to give the kid back."

Avi Hausoc's eyes flashed silver for a moment. "Statement: consultation of expert systems indicates your reading of the statutes are correct. Conflict: reading of other statutes indicates an overriding interest that negates the statutes you cite, specifically GC14872.23.153."

I blinked. "I'd have to go to my bike to find that statute."

"This is ridiculous, Walgrove. Get my son and give him to me now!"

My head came around and I poked a finger against Aspan's breastbone. "Take it easy. The boy's safe."

Korphyr slapped my hand away from his master's chest. We glared at each other. I'd have held that stare until the local sun went nova, but I noticed another person coming into the rotunda behind them. My eyes flicked that way, and both weren't spun, arms wide, claws extended, which made them look rather ridiculous.

The woman they faced could easily have been described as petite, but the word would have been oversized on her. Her black hair had been drawn back into a tight knot at the nape of her neck. Her large, dark eyes had a slight slant to them, but were quick and inquisitive. Her high cheekbones and strong jawline sharpened her features a bit, but that just gave her face a hint of a predatory cast. Her mouth had full lips and her slender nose supplied her an aristocratic bearing.

She wore a Concord Field Administrator's uniform—the kind an official tends to wear when she wants to impress the locals with her office. As she walked forward in the skirt and jacket, I caught just a hint of uneasiness, which suggested she liked her uniform little more than I did mine. Still, her fluid gate and the lack of hesitation in it impressed me.

She moved toward the center of the room, slipping between Lenguila and Aspan, then bowed her head toward Avi Hausoc. "Statement: my apology for intruding here. Introduction: I am Victoria Moorcroft, Concord Field Administrator. I was informed of this situation as I was coming to Pyrton, and I diverted here. Request: I would be of any and all assistance in this matter."

Aspan stroked his chin for a second—taking it real slow to make it last that long—then graced Moorcroft with an unctuous smile. "At last, someone who will do what is required. That is my son, Kenneth, over there. I demand his return."

Avi Hausoc shook her head. "Statement: we cannot permit the boy's return to Ronald, sire and creator."

I sighed. "This is the impasse we were at when you came in. The sparks . . . uh, mechalus . . . cite some law that prevents them from turning the boy over to his father."

Avi Hausoc nodded. "GC14872.23.153."

Moorcroft's chin came up. "Interesting. Query: details."

Hausoc stiffened. "Statement: To provide those details would violate article seven of the Bill of Sapient Rights that was part of the Galactic Concord."

Moorcroft's eyes became slits, then she grabbed my right sleeve. "Your indulgence, please, while I confer with Constable Walgrove here."

She tugged me back away to the far side of the rotunda, then stood at my left, positioning herself so she could watch everyone back in the middle of the room. She studied them in silence for a moment, then drew an overthick stylus from inside her uniform jacket and tapped it absently against her lips.

Without looking at me, she began to speak in a low whisper. "This is not how I intended to first meet with you, Constable Walgrove. You have my apologies. The last thing I would want to do is to undercut your authority in this region."

I detected a lot of sincerity in her voice. She hadn't needed to pull me aside or tell me what she had. Her predecessor never had exercised such discretion, but then he had always seen me as little more than a mercenary who wanted a position where he could give orders rather than take them. He decided I was ambitious and therefore dangerous, whereas I really was just tired of being shot at on worlds floating around stars I'd never heard of before.

"No problem. Call me 'Catch.' Most folks do."

Moorcroft gave me another quick glance, sizing me up again. "Your file doesn't explain the nickname."

"No, ma'am, it doesn't."

A grin tugged at one corner of her mouth. "Okay, Catch, what's your read?"

"Daddy's being a bit overprotective, and I can't factor the article seven comment by Hausoc. That just popped out of nowhere at me. What kind of privacy issue can there be here with the kid?"

She nodded. "You know what GC14872.23.153 is?"

I shrugged. "Criminal complaint, but that's all I can figure out. I tend heavily toward the peacekeeper part of the job, cruising past the lawman thing, I'm afraid."

"Criminal neglect and mistreatment of a minor."

"Criminal neglect?" I scratched at the back of my neck. "Aspan has 'round the clock help for the boy. There's someone always there."

"You know this because . . .?"

"Daddy likes to spend a fair amount of his time in the dimmer regions of Pyrton, in some of the clubs where moral entropy is viewed as a sport, not a character flaw. Some of them don't allow his weren in, so when he gets into trouble, I get a call."

"I saw no mention of such things in the file on him that I reviewed while incoming."

"I file the reports, but a lot of my help is local and has kin employed by Pyritix." I smiled. "Besides, he foots the bills for the destruction he causes. I know of a laundry-man who sent a child to an offworld academy based on cleaning up Aspan's wardrobe."

"Aspan's conduct doesn't keep with the Pyritix Corp image: 'Family products by families for families.' "

"Families need paychecks to buy family products by families for families." I shrugged. "Pyritix pays well and most folks prefer that to unemployment. This is still pretty much of a frontier world. The image thing is more impor-tant on core Concord worlds."

"Indeed, it is. Very important."

I winced at the edge in her voice. One of the big problems with the Galactic Concord is that a lot of their officials don't get that while the leadership of many worlds signed on to the treaty ending the war, the majority of folks on those worlds really didn't care. Their daily struggles to stay alive and claw a living out of some dusty world orbiting a dim star meant that the Concord would be important to them only if it helped them. As I often hear in these parts, the biggest lie going around today is, "Hi, I'm from the Concord, I'm here to help you."

Folks tolerate me butting my nose into their business because I have a direct impact on their lives: I get them out of trouble, put them away for trouble, or get rid of folks causing them trouble. Ronald Aspan and his weren didn't like me because I wasn't afraid of them and wasn't dependent upon them, so they couldn't control me. While I was part of the Concord apparatus, I was really just a very small local cog who would be more trouble if killed than if left alive and tolerated.

Administrator Moorcroft was beginning to sound as if she thought the Galactic Concord's image needed some burnishing in this region. She was right, but getting Ronald Aspan in trouble for carousing was pretty much a minor thing when compared to a mine collapse that killed a half-dozen folks not a day earlier. I started to open my mouth to point this out to her, but she waved off my comment.

"The mechalus here salvage discarded things to include in the Aleerindos?"

My jaw dropped open with surprise and I snapped it shut again. "You know about 'the work'?"

She gave me an irritated frown. "It is one of the more unique aspects of my sector, why wouldn't I know about it?"

"No reason at all. The answer is yes."

Moorcroft nodded for a second as reflections of the work's light flashed across her hair. "I have a play to make

here. Back me. Watch Aspan." Before I could reply, the
tiny woman marched back to the center of the floor.

I trailed after her, raising my chin and giving Aspan my
best you-are-pathetic stare.

He looked at me, sniffed, then arched an eyebrow at
Moorcroft. "Well? I'm waiting."

"I need a piece of information from you." She pointed
at him with the stylus in her right hand. "You are Kenneth's custodial parent. What about his mother?"

"We're separated. Punt's mother is on Alaundril, last I
heard. At least, that is where she was two years ago when
we parted ways."

Moorcroft turned from Aspan and dropped to one knee
in front of Kenny. She reached out to stroke his face with
a hand. The boy smiled slightly, turning his face toward the
hand stroking it, then he stepped back against the thighs of
the spark female behind him. The mechalus' hands glided
over the boy's shoulders protectively.

Moorcroft straightened up again. "I have a problem, Mr.
Aspan, and it comes down to this: you say the mechalus
here have kidnapped your son, but they maintain you are
neglecting and abusing him."

"That's nonsense." Aspan snorted angrily and flicked a
hand toward the sparks. "What would they know about
human relations?"

"A question I would have asked before I hired them to
watch my child, I think." Moorcroft's riposte surprised
Aspan, and she burrowed in while she had the chance. "I
noted in your datafile, Mr. Aspan, that you have made
something of a change in your life recently. Up to five
years ago, before you met and wedded your wife after a
whirlwind courtship, you were quite the playboy."

"I enjoyed life, yes. That has nothing to do with this."

"No? Then it was true love that ended your wastrel
ways?"

Aspan's blue eyes narrowed to slits. "I had grown up a

child of privilege and did not realize what was truly important in life. My wife helped settle me down and provided me with my son. After she left me, Punt and I came here to reconstruct our lives. We'd been doing quite well until this incident. As your constable knows, there are no charges against me. I care for my son, I provide for him."

"Rumors of your grandfather assigning you to this facility to see if you could apply yourself to making it succeed are untrue?"

Aspan's expression soured. "He offered me a choice of positions. I chose this place since it was the most difficult to manage. I chose it to prove myself."

"Your grandfather would not be worried about how you would throw away any of the family trusts bestowed upon you?"

Aspan's nose wrinkled with disgust. "You have a small mind, Moorcroft."

"One I use to its fullest, Mr. Aspan." Moorcroft regarded him coldly for a moment, then looked over at Avi Hausoc. "I am now placed in an interesting situation. You allege abuse, but will not speak of it because of privacy issues. I have to assume your allegations are baseless unless you allow me a test."

The mechalus leader nodded.

"I've read of your life here and of your fliidrun rituals. I would have you put the boy through one, commencing now." She glanced at Aspan. "You have no objection to this?"

He shrugged. "Would it matter if I did?"

"I'd certainly ask the constable to log your protest."

Aspan opened his hands. "Then there really is no purpose in protesting, is there? Bear in mind, you will be responsible for any adverse effects of this spark thing you put him through."

"I'll accept that responsibility." She looked at the mechalus. "You agree?"

Avi Hausoc nodded, but the female behind Kenny dropped into a crouch and hugged the boy to her chest. "No! Objection: no fliidrun for the boy."

"Ha!" Aspan thrust a fist into the air triumphantly. "There, she defies you, Administrator."

"As well she did, Mr. Aspan." Moorcroft's voice dropped into an icy whisper. "She saved your son from death."

Something nasty flashed through Aspan's eyes, then he snapped his fingers and pointed at the boy. "Get him. He's mine."

Korphyr rushed forward, and I leaped at him. He had his head low as he drove at the sparks, so I grabbed his tusks to avoid being disemboweled, then started to twist his head to the side. He snarled and brought his head up, lifting me from the ground. His arms closed around the small of my back and his hug tightened in an instant. He jammed his jaw against my ribs and slowly started squeezing so hard I figured my guts would plop out of my mouth.

Pain shot through my body like lights storming through the Aleerindos. I knew I was seconds away from hearing bones popping. Bits and pieces of my life began to flash before my eyes, and I clung to those snippets that dealt with fighting weren close-up. The standard advice was "don't," which, while ironic, wasn't very useful at the moment. One tiny piece was, though, and I put it to use.

I reared back, then curled forward, driving my right elbow into the thick muscles between Korphyr's neck and left shoulder. He grunted and his grip slackened, so I did it again. His grunt rose into a bit of a squeal, and we started to fall toward the ground. I slammed my right fist into the point of his chin. That punch slackened his jaw and broke his embrace.

He landed hard on the ground, bounced once and rolled onto his back. His arms lay limply on the ground and his eyelids fluttered as I landed beside him. Despite the pain in my back and the numbness in my legs, I tried to heave myself to my feet. While I might have put Korphyr down, Lenguila could still tear me apart, and given that I couldn't see him, I had that sick feeling that he was coming at my back. I spun and stumbled onto my knees.

I saw Lenguila's clawed right hand reaching for me. Fortunately, he reached for me from the floor. He lay on his left side with his legs drawn up against his belly. He pressed his left hand to his ribs and wore a grimace on his face that would have made him truly frightening, save for the mewing sound he was making.

Moorcroft twirled the stylus through the fingers of her right hand, the narrower end trailing a wisp of smoke matching that curling up from between Lenguila's fingers. She nodded toward Korphyr and me.

"Good, you know about weren plexuses. Useful knowledge to have out here."

"As useful as having a pulse baton's guts built into something that looks like a stylus." I rubbed a hand over my back. "Fancy toy."

"The Concord loves giving its officials new toys." Moorcroft slipped the thing back into her pocket. "One charge, maybe two. Useful when enemies aren't expecting you to be armed."

I glanced from her to Lenguila. The downed weren frowned, then closed his eyes and let his head loll to the floor. For her to have dropped him, she'd have to be very quick, very skilled, very lucky, or some combination thereof, even with the pulse baton there. I shuddered and struggled to my feet.

Moorcroft moved past me and walked up to Aspan, invading his personal space as if she were a weren herself. "We have an interesting situation here, Mr. Aspan. Agents in your employ have attacked Concord officials. I don't think that would play well at Pyritix Corp's headquarters, and I *do* know *that* report will go through." She glanced at her chronometer. "You'll be recalled in what, less than a month? Your work here will be a failure, both as a corporate executive and as a parent, since you're hardly the sort of moral example the Aspan family wishes to project."

Aspan's beady eyes narrowed. "I sense a compromise in the offing."

"Indeed, you sense correctly." She pointed to his son. "You could, of course, entrust your son to the mechalus here so he can experience the life of a different species. You would be exposing him to the family values of the mechalus, which would be a great cultural benefit to him and to the next generation of Pyritix's leadership. This would allow you to concentrate on your work, which will keep you very busy and allow him to learn from the mechalus enclave here. After all, he has so much in common with them that this stay would be of great benefit to him."

"If I don't agree?"

"As district coordinator, I will immediately have the boy placed in protective custody since you will be arrested for assault. I will ask Avi Hausoc if she and her people would keep him until the situation is resolved. You would be removed as custodian of record until such time as you are cleared of charges. It could take a couple of years, during which time you would have to remain here in Pyrton."

"You overestimate the prowess of Concord legal officials here." Aspan yawned. "I'll have the boy back before your posting to some even more distant world comes through."

Moorcroft's eyes became dark slits. "Ah, but then the whole seedy story of what you've done to your son will come out."

I gave Aspan a cruel smile. "What would that story be?"

Moorcroft accepted my leading question with a gracious nod, then folded her arms across her chest as lights whirled and cavorted around her. "Pyritix Corp and the

Aspan family have an almost pathological hatred of cybernetics, to the point where they have actually discharged employees who have resorted to using cybernetic replacements for severed limbs."

I let mock shock contort my face. "Not Pyritix Corp? 'By families for families'? That Pyritix Corp?"

"The very same." She began to pace her way around Aspan, who remained motionless. "I know this because an employee was a friend of my father's who lost his leg as the result of a jet-ski accident. He lost his job before he left the hospital. Needless to say, they don't buy Pyritix Corp products any more."

Moorcroft tightened her circle and tapped Aspan's shoulder with a finger. "Avi Hausoc's referring to you as Kenny's 'sire and creator' surprised me. Among the mechalus, the word 'creator' has a host of meanings, many of which refer to the individual who has made something or someone better. When she refused to specify how you were endangering your son because of privacy, I had to wonder what she knew of the boy that was so secret she could not mention it in front of his father or two Concord officials. There seemed to be only one logical answer: the improvements you added to your son."

I blinked and glanced at Kenny. "The boy is cybered? Can't be."

"It's the truth, isn't it, Aspan?"

The boy's father said nothing.

I shook my head. "I don't believe it. I scanned Kenny and his keepers when I came in here. They were normal for sparks . . . uh, mechalus . . . and he was negative for any chips. I got no RF signature traces from him."

"Right, because his replacements are very special, very expensive, and unlike most cybernetic replacements, small enough to be heavily shielded." She smiled at the boy. "He's not carrying enough parts to be fully functional on his own. His father has all the programming running on computers elsewhere and being radioed to Kenny, isn't that right?"

Aspan shrugged. "I don't know what you're talking about."

A cold chill ran up my spine. "Putting the kid in a Faraday cage for the fliidrun would cut him off from all outside radio contact. It would isolate him from the programs that make him work. What's wrong with him?"

She shook her head, then looked back at his father. "An accident probably—you would have had serious trouble trying to hide some sort of congenital defect from the rest of the Aspan clan. I suspect, if we check, we'll discover that your grandfather laid down the law to you. He told you to settle down, raise a family, or be cut off from the family's wealth. Money has probably been set aside in a trust that has a time-limit—five or ten years, which is probably why you and your wife are just 'separated' instead of divorced."

"And why you keep the boy alive with chips." I glared at Aspan. "You were willing to go along with Administrator Moorcroft's suggestion about putting Kenny through fliidrun because his death would be on our hands and would free you of all responsibility for the situation."

"Fascinating conjecture, Constable, but even more ephemeral than the Aleerindos." Scorn echoed frostily from the black walls. "That fanciful tale will merely titillate some and anger others, but it won't hurt me."

Aspan was right, and I knew it. It was the sort of scandal tale that brightened the lives of folk by making them seem better than whoever had the misfortune of being the gossip-victim that week. Properly spun the tale could become one of a father's devotion to his son—devotion that led him to risk his family's anger and being cut off from their wealth, just to keep his son alive.

"It's not you I'll hurt with the story, Aspan, at least, not directly." Moorcroft dropped to one knee in front of the boy and looked back over her shoulder at his father. "This story, when leaked to major financial analysts, will suggest a future power struggle within the Aspan family, which should rock confidence in the Pyritix Corp's future. Investors get scared, stock prices drop, worlds back out of trade agreements because they think the company is in trouble. Employees discharged because of cybernetic-enhancements sue the corporation because of the Aspan family double standard. It will cause a lot of trouble, and the easiest solution is removing you from having anything to do with the company. Forced to choose between you or future prosperity, what do you think the family will do?"

Aspan winced as she outlined her scenario. His hands curled into fists, and he trembled for a second as if he was going to lunge at her, but then his shoulders slumped. He lowered his head so his chin almost touched his chest, then his voice went lower. "If Punt lives here, I am still parent of record?"

Moorcroft nodded. "You are."

"And the story . . .?"

She straightened up. "I won't be calling a broker to tell him to sell Pyritix stock short."

"Well, then, I see myself as having little other choice than to go along with your coercion. So be it." Aspan waggled his fingers at his son. "Be good, Punt. Daddy will come for you in due time."

The smug smile he wore was just too much for me. I reached out and grabbed a handful of his tunic, yanking him over so we stood nose to nose. "Two things, 'Daddy.' 'Due time' means you visit every week for at least four hours. I'll bring you out here myself."

"I might not be avail—"

I snarled and smacked his chin. "I said I'd bring you out here myself. That wasn't an offer, just a statement of fact. You'll be here. It's up to you just how much it will hurt."

"And the second thing, Constable?"

I did my best to ignore the contempt in his words, largely because of the fear I saw in his eyes. "Second, if I'm called in to help you home because you can't help yourself, you'll wake up in the morning in a lot of pain. I'm betting you'll stumble over every step between where you are and where you're going, understand? You don't want to be in a position where I'm your guardian angel."

I gave him a shove backward. He caught his heels on Korphyr's body and crashed down to the ground. A bunch of mechalus males descended on him and the weren, hauling them out. Opposite them, the two mechalus who had been with Kenny led him off deeper into the enclave. Avi Hausoc nodded to us, then trailed after the boy.

I waited until Moorcroft and I were alone before I dropped to my knees and pressed hands to my back. I looked up at her and winced as I kneaded bruised muscles. "I don't get why Aspan would consent to the fliidrun this time, when he balked the first time. His son would have ended up dead if the mechalus had put the boy through the ritual the first time and he would been shed that responsibility."

"His later consent does seem a contradiction." Moorcroft scratched at her chin with a finger. "I think he gave consent before he knew what the ritual was, then panicked and withdrew it when he figured his son would die. After that he regretted the snap decision that saved his son's life, and given a chance to be rid of the boy again, he jumped at it."

"Makes sense in a twisted little Aspan way. What's to stop Aspan from killing the computer that's keeping his son alive? The boy dies now and his death is on your hands. He could be out there now putting in a call that terminates Kenny."

She shook her head. "When I watched Kenny's eyes, I saw he wasn't following the lights as they flowed through the Aleerindos but was watching where they would flow.

The mechalus work was already in tune with him, telling him what was coming next so his eyes would be ready for it. They already are able to control his processes and keep him alive."

I nodded slowly. "Avi Hausoc wouldn't have allowed the boy to be taken from his father if a shut-down would have killed him."

"No, she wouldn't." Moorcroft opened her hands. "I think the mechalus see Kenny as part of 'the work.' I believe they intend to salvage him, just as they salvaged most of the stuff here. The mechalus working on the Aleerindos are more than just artists creating the work; they are part of it, too. It lives, a combination of biology and technology, just like Kenny. As they work with him, he will come to understand this is the most perfect place for him."

I slowly stood again. "Now the boy will be cared for, which is good, but Dad will get his money for doing nothing. I don't like it."

"Neither do I, which is why we'll make sure it doesn't happen." Moorcroft gave me a smile that was pure ice. "Aspan's a snake and for him, an agreement today is just something to break tomorrow."

"That's my read. So, how do we cut dad off from his money?"

"Easy. Once the mechalus programs going into Kenny are refined and running perfectly, we'll have Kenny file a petition to become an emancipated minor. Because of the work Ronald did on him, the boy can function at a much higher level than someone his age, so passing any test for emancipation will be easy for him." She laughed lightly. "Since you and I will administer the test . . . "

"We know the results will be right." My smile broadened a great deal as I imagined the look on Aspan's face when his plots collapsed in on themselves. "Doing that might not make you very popular with some folks. Pyritix

Corp does have influence in the Concord, you know."

She nodded and started walking out of the Enclave. "Oh, I do realize that, but if I was trying to be popular, do you think I'd ever have gotten this assignment?"

"Good point." I started shambling after her. "So, you know a lot about mechalus culture, the Concord legal system, and you can drop a weren with a toy. Pretty formidable."

"Thanks."

We emerged into the sunlight and saw only the faintest hint of dust from Aspan's retreat. "If you're that tough, how did you get stuck with this assignment?"

Moorcroft shrugged easily. "A long story, of which you'll probably hear more than you ever wanted to. Still, that's not important."

"Oh, and what is?"

"Should be obvious, Catch." The grin she gave me was all predator. "What's important is figuring how to get off this rock, and I'll do it. That's what being formidable is all about."

About the Author

Michael A. Stackpole, an award-winning game designer, was born in 1957 and grew up in Burlington, Vermont. In 1979, he graduated from the University of Vermont with a BA in history. In his career as a game designer he has done work for Flying Buffalo, Inc., Interplay Productions, TSR, Inc., West End Games, Hero Games, Wizards of the Coast, FASA Corp., Game Designers Workshop, and Steve Jackson Games. In recognition of his work in and for the game industry, he was inducted into the Academy of Gaming Arts and Design Hall of Fame in 1994. He's the author of the *New York Times* best-selling series of Star Wars X-Wing novels, and the fantasy novels *Once a Hero* and *Talion: Revenant*.

"The Ninth Cylinder"

PHILIP ATHANS

ACTUALLY FINDING the right asteroid in the crowded Galsworthy Belt was only the first hard part in a day that Jessica Belwe knew would be full of hard parts. Though she knew her way around a sensor station—she'd actually scratch-built *Esilio*'s sensor package herself—it had still taken her longer to pinpoint this particular rock than she'd hoped. She had been the only one on the ship, including her pilot Durante, who'd noticed the delay though, and *Esilio* was decelerating fast now in the right direction.

"All I'm saying," her brother Jonathan, the third of the three people aboard the Trader-Class starship continued, "is that Alitar could use someone with your contacts, your ability to—"

"Make money?" Jessica interrupted, knowing she was being hurtful without having to notice the look on her brother's face. She'd always found Jonathan cute, silly, and rambunctious. No matter how grown up either of them had become, it just wasn't easy for a big sister to take her little brother seriously. Jonathan's boyish looks and skinny, short body didn't help. He looked much the same as he did when he was twelve, which was the last time they'd actually spent much time together. He'd contacted her after

eleven years of not seeing one another to ask for help getting off Alitar. He was in trouble there now but wouldn't
tell her why. She wanted to press but figured she'd leave
him his secrets, if he'd leave her hers. There didn't seem
to be much between them anymore but secrets.

"Not much call for that in the occupied territories,"
Durante chimed in, seeming strangely cheered by his few
weeks with Jessica and Jonathan's sibling give-and-take,
"making money."

"That's not what I meant," Jonathan sighed, "and you
know it. Alitar is in trouble, Jessica, and you have the contacts, the hardware, and the money to help. We were born
there, we grew up there . . . we owe those people—"

"Spins at one for two three point four," Jessica said to
Durante, dismissing Jonathan with this interruption. "Solid
nickel-iron . . . eight klicks rough."

Durante looked back at her from his couch a good three
meters ahead of Jessica's station with narrowed, accusing
eyes. "I know, Captain," he said. "That's one spin every
twenty-three point four minutes. Now let your brother
finish. I'm always curious to hear about other people you
owe."

"Secure it, Durante," she said, ignoring the snide laugh
he offered in return.

Jonathan stopped talking, as Jessica noticed he'd learned
to over the weeks spent caught between his sister and her
bantering pilot. He had that look on his face again, that look
that told her Jonathan could tell how Durante felt about her.
The gruff pilot kept his heart on his sleeve, and like everyone else who met them, Jonathan guessed that the only one
in the Verge who hadn't seen it there was Jessica. He
guessed wrong. Granted, they were an unlikely couple and
had never been together in any but a very professional,
mutually-profitable way, but Durante's attraction to her fed
her attraction to herself, and Jessica figured they could stay
in that comfort zone for at least a few more years.

Physically, they had nothing in common. Durante was
all head with scars tracing patterns in his makeshift crew-
cut. He had a hard, tight, scrappy body that barroom
brawlers and women alike avoided. Age and too much time
aboard a ship had started to turn his skin as gray as the
stubble on his head. His left arm was an obvious piece of
strong and functional cyberware. When Jonathan asked
what happened to his real arm, the only answer he got was
a grimly amused smile shared between Durante and
Jessica.

Jessica, on the other hand, was a classic beauty. She
was taller than Jonathan, with an athletic build and subtly
Asian features. Jessica knew her looks were an advantage
in her business, and she cultivated her beauty. Impractical
as it was, she kept her shiny black hair long and straight
and took time to wash and brush it every morning before
coming out of her stateroom.

"Density zero point eight," she reported, again unnecessarily as *Esilio* continued to fall under Durante's skillful
control toward the rolling asteroid.

The pilot didn't look up or even move. Contrary to popular opinion, he did know when to shut up. Unfortunately,
Jonathan didn't.

"What are we buying here, Jessica?" he asked.

She took a couple deep breaths and flexed her fingers,
calming herself for the transaction they'd come all this
way to complete. It unnerved her a little having Jonathan
along. She knew he'd been working back home on Alitar
for some kind of resistance cell or terrorist group, trying
to kick Galvin off the planet. It was a losing battle, which
is why Jessica hadn't bothered to stay around to fight it
herself. Growing up in the city of Teminin on the south
coast of the Yellow Pan so close to the occupied zone, Jessica and Jonathan had been exposed to the war early and
daily for most of their lives. He'd only been a kid when she
left, but little Jonathan was already starting to repeat the

sort of anti-Galvin propaganda the company chaplain had mouthed over their father's grave.

Jonathan had been up to something on Alitar, but that was war, with propaganda and brainwashing and hope and nationalism and pride and all those other things that made you think you weren't just killing someone over a scrap of stuff. In her line of work, Jessica always put the scraps of stuff first and chose who she shot at very, very carefully, at least, most of the time.

She didn't feel good about having to use Jonathan the way she was planning to use him, but she still couldn't see any rational alternative and was just too afraid to openly ask him. He wanted to be a soldier or a revolutionary or a martyr or something, but maybe when all this was over he'd start to realize how things really worked.

The trade she'd come here to do was with a group of mechalus she'd never met or done business with before. She had a plan, a way to work the deal and maybe keep both what she expected to trade for and what she expected to trade with. It wasn't going to be easy, and it required three. Everyone else had run out on her the second the money started drying up. When Jonathan and the opportunity came along at the same time, she just couldn't *not* do it. She told herself again that her brother would never be in any real danger, that she and Durante had done it before, maybe half a dozen times, and no one had been hurt.

"Mass zero point zero zero zero three three—"

"Jessica," Jonathan said, standing over her now where she sat at the sensor station. Durante was the wings and she was the eyes. Jonathan was useless on her bridge, so she continued trying to ignore him.

"—seven four," she continued without pause. "Surface gravity zero point zero five nine—"

"Our people are dying, Jessica."

"—nine eight two two," she finished.

"Let's call it point oh six," Durante said, "just between friends."

Jessica looked up at the pilot and had a hard time not meeting Jonathan's stern gaze. She had a hard time, but she succeeded.

"If you're about to tell me that it displaces seven point three four eight billion tons," Durante added, "don't bother."

"E.T.A.?" she asked him quickly, sharply.

"We could have used you," Jonathan interrupted Durante's answer, "on Big Slate."

Jessica had to look at her brother now. "You were at Big Slate?" she asked, her voice low.

Jonathan nodded and Durante said, "Six minutes."

A cold electronic chirp drew Jessica's attention back to her console. She said, "I've got something," at the same time Durante said, "You got something."

She took a silent minute to study her console carefully.

"Talk to me, Skipper," Durante said. His voice was different now, not nervous, but clear.

"Drive cutter," she said, too loudly for even the comfortably big compartment. She cleared her throat and continued, "Irregular profile. It's not in the grid . . . it's them. It must be them."

"Nobody else'd be creeping over the lip of this particular pebble," Durante offered, looking back.

"Go to three three three mark one nine," Jessica told him.

"Roger," Durante returned, "matching 'em."

Jessica stood and brushed past her brother, leaving him to look at her receding back as she crossed the length of the bridge in only a few long, fast strides.

"We should have the weapons powered up," Jonathan offered feebly, "don't you think?"

Jonathan didn't hear Durante laugh. Jessica's fingers flew across her console and brought sensor functions up on

the panel in front of her. There was another electronic chirp
from the station next to Jonathan and it went mostly dark.

"They won't shoot at us right away, brother," Durante
told him, his tone only a little condescending. "Almost
nobody shoots at us . . . right away."

It was Jessica's turn to laugh. "Never did get that severed induction governance coil locked down," she said.

"You mean, we have no weapons?" Jonathan asked.
"The mass cannon doesn't work?"

"Easy, brother," Durante said. "Why'd you think
there're so many empty seats up here?"

Jonathan looked around and counted six empty
couches, six unmanned stations. He'd wondered about it
once, weeks ago, but hadn't thought to bring it up.

"Are all these—" Jonathan said, stopping abruptly at
the sudden feeling of rapid deceleration.

"Burn's good," Durante reported flatly. Jessica looked
up, trying to make out the still distant ship against the star
field. "There it is."

It was obvious that, at some time in the distant past, the
other ship had been a sleek, fast drive cutter molded with
smooth edges and a gentle, stout lifting-body shape meant
for atmospheric entry. Now it was a rounded triangle bristling on all sides with lumps and boxes and antennae and
dishes. Jessica had her doubts that the thing could ever fly
in atmosphere, but then it didn't have to out here. She studied the outline carefully, unconsciously nodding to herself
as she took note of the more obvious retrofits.

"Multiband radar," Durante said, only half a step behind
her. He pointed out at it, but the characteristic antenna was
still only visible on a screen in front of him. Jessica didn't
bother to follow his finger. The cutter tilted into the dim
sunlight and there was no flash against its too-dull upper
wing surface.

"They coated the planes with solar cells," Jessica said,
as if explaining it to herself.

"Yeah," Durante concurred, "yeah, they been busy with that boat. See the tile intersects?"

Jessica nodded and said, "They armored her."

Jessica sighed and Durante swore at the same time.

"What?" Jonathan asked. "What is it?"

"You see it too," Jessica said to Durante.

"Freakin' deflection inducer," he said. "Damn."

"It's okay," Jessica told him, almost believing it herself.

"Oh yeah," Durante replied, "yeah, that's great. That's just great."

"It's okay," Jessica told both of them, "we can't shoot at them anyway."

"What?" Jonathan asked, his voice coming to a thin edge. "Is that supposed to make us feel better?"

"There's more," Durante said, "much more."

Jessica knew why Durante was nervous. If the other ship was equipped with that level of hardware, the obvious stuff was certainly only part of what this little cutter had in store for them. She sighed and traced a pattern across the lights of her console. The little screen directly in front of her went blue. The single bright white word *OPEN* faded onto the blue field.

"We're here," Jessica said, making her voice a little louder, a little clearer. "Let's do it."

The blue screen was replaced by a face mostly obscured by shadow and interference. Only Jessica could hear the voice reply, "Emmennex. You have the currency."

"Belwe," she replied quickly. "I will accept delivery of the package on the rock."

There was a pause, quickly filled with Jonathan saying, "What'd he say?"

Durante had been at this point with Jessica more than enough times to know it was time to shut up and let her do what she did so well. "Secure it, brother," he told Jonathan. "Let her buzz."

"Make your landing," Emmennex, the voice on the

other end of the laser transceiver, said. "We will follow."

Only Durante could see Jessica smile. The fake anger in her voice fooled Jonathan, who grimaced when she said, "As if. You set, and I'll be right with you."

There was only a brief pause before the answer, "I don't know you."

"You know who I am, and you know people who know me," she said. "I'm in the biz, you're just a newbie. Land."

"Jess—" Jonathan began to say, then thought better of it.

"I do not know 'biz' or 'newbie,' " the voice said into Jessica's ear, "but I will not be landing first."

"Okay," Jessica said with a sigh, "tell you what. Say a number between one and ten and so will I, then have your computer randomly generate a number between one and ten."

She had to look at Durante and his smile almost made her laugh. Seeing that made Durante laugh.

"Whoever comes closer," Jessica continued, "without going over, wins."

There was a long silence on the transceiver that Durante laughed all the way through, then the voice said, "Four."

"Six," Jessica answered, making Durante laugh even harder.

The voice came back almost immediately with, "My computer says five. I will stand by while you make your landing."

Jessica managed not to laugh long enough only to acknowledge the message and sign off.

"You are going to get me killed," Durante said. "You are definitely going to be the cause of my death."

"What is this?" Jonathan said. Jessica had almost forgotten he was there. "Is this what you do for a living, Jessica?"

Durante was busy matching the asteroid's spin in preparation for landing, so Jessica answered him, "I knew they were going to lie and make me land first. I want them to think they have some kind of advantage."

"Why is landing first an advantage?"

"It isn't, necessarily," she said, "but they seem to think it is."

"If the deal is square," Jonathan said, amazing Jessica with his lack of experience, "why does it matter? What's the problem?"

Durante paused long enough to look up and back in the direction of Jonathan's station and said, "There's always a problem, brother."

Durante piloted *Esilio* in a slow, dangerous dance with the spinning asteroid. There was no sensation of stopping or landing save for the tiniest vibration in their seats. The hardest thing, the thing that made even Jessica dizzy, was the odd, ill-defined point when the tumbling rock became a flat surface, when a grain of sand became the world, and the stars started spinning over a solid, sharp-horizoned wasteland.

"Damn," Durante breathed. "Hot shots."

The drive cutter was landing. They could see it drifting toward them. Viewscreens all around the bridge compartment showed dizzying images from different angles of the cutter sliding sideways over *Esilio*, spinning to face the opposite direction from the trader. A small cargo door opened in a smooth spot under the cutter's port side wing and Jessica could just make out a figure—no, two— silhouetted against the bright yellow interior light. The cutter skimmed to a light landing no more than twenty meters off *Esilio*'s port side.

"A little close," Durante remarked.

Jessica shrugged and stood. "Secure the bridge," she said, "we're on."

Durante sighed at having been ignored, or so Jessica figured, and followed her through the open airlock into the weapons pod. Jessica stopped at a console there, reached under it, and produced a rather impressive render rifle.

Jonathan followed Jessica and Durante through the next set of open airlock doors into a brightly-lit corridor running the length of the ship. The doors closed behind them.

"You're going out there?" Jonathan said as they passed a four-way intersection that led to the crew quarters. "*Both* of you are going out there?"

"Worry not, brother," Durante said as they passed through another open airlock that once again cycled closed behind them, "you get the safe duty."

Something made Jessica suddenly want to stop Durante from continuing to tease her brother. She shuffled a couple of steps, deciding back and forth several times whether or not to stop. She could tell Durante sensed her hesitation, but they continued on through the crane control compartment and into the port side cargo bay while Jonathan asked, "Safe duty?"

"Yeah," Durante said as the three of them stopped in front of a line of soft e-suits hanging from a rack that had been crudely bolted to the forward wall of the cavernous cargo bay, "you don't have to follow your sister on one of her—"

"Damn it, Durante," Jessica broke in, setting her rifle to lean against the wall and reaching for one of the e-suits.

"Oh," Durante breathed, "damn."

"What's wrong?" Jonathan asked.

"Self-seal's expired again," Durante explained, his voice sounding like an apology.

"Yeah," Jessica said, angry, "since Lison." She stuck her finger through what could only have been a bullet hole in the left arm of the e-suit.

"Damn," Durante said, "that was cold, I'll tell you what."

"He can wear one of the other ones," Jonathan offered, then stopped when he saw the looks on both their faces and continued more quietly, "can't he?"

"Can't you?" Jessica asked Durante quickly, sharply.

She could feel gooseflesh slide across her arms in waves and almost stopped it right there, but there was desperation at work here. She only had this one chance, this one deal to save her skin, so she let it go on.

"No," Durante answered, "I can't, and you bloody well know that, Captain."

She threw him the suit and started to say, "There's nobody—"

"I know there's nobody left," Durante interrupted. "I can't wear any e-suit but my lucky e-suit . . . not on a rock like this, not with mechs on the line . . . not with one of these deals of yours going down, okay?"

"Mechs?" Jonathan asked.

Jessica looked at her brother, reached a hand out to her left, grabbed another e-suit off the rack, and handed it to him. She turned to Durante for a second but was looking at Jonathan when she said, "Sailors," in a voice full of both irritation and affection.

"What are mechs?" Jonathan asked, breaking the mood. "Who are we dealing with here?"

Durante snorted, but Jessica couldn't tell if the pilot was amused or frustrated, relieved or disappointed. He stepped back into the airlock leading into the crane control compartment, taking his lucky e-suit with him.

She stopped him by calling his name. He turned around to face her, his right hand obviously reaching for something behind the doorframe, in a compartment in the little airlock.

"Listen," Jessica told him, "you remember what happened at Lucullus's Arch, okay?"

"I remember," he said.

"You sure?"

Durante found what he was looking for, a hand-held magnetic clamp, and tossed it to Jessica. It was heavy and she had a hard time catching it.

"I'm sure," Durante said, eyes locked on Jessica's. "It'll be lighter outside," he added, nodding at the clamp. The door cycled closed and he was gone.

Jessica didn't watch Jonathan struggle into his e-suit. Instead she crossed to the otherwise empty cargo bay to a blue plastic tarp covering the bay's lone cargo and started to unhook the straps holding the tarp to the floor. She paused before pulling the tarp off, Jonathan watching her silently, and stopped to put on her own e-suit. Her hands and body flew through the process with practiced ease, and she was ready for vacuum well before her brother was. Jonathan was pretty sure he had his helmet on right when Jessica finally unveiled her cargo.

"The currency?" Jonathan asked, suspiciously eyeing the nine slim silver-metal cylinders. Each had only two markings: a simple numeral one through nine and the universal symbol for radiation.

Jessica turned around and looked at him. "Thi—s biz—ess, Jo—tha—" she said, her voice breaking up in his helmet.

She crossed to him quickly and he flinched when her arms came up to help him with his suit. Their eyes met for the first time in too long and she finally offered him a reassuring smile. His response was to sigh, close his eyes, and let her fix his suit.

"There," she said, her voice loud and clear now in his helmet, "now your eyes won't pop out when I open the door."

He forced a laugh, then said, "What's radioactive?"

She turned away from him abruptly and went to retrieve her rifle.

"Jessica?"

"We'll make the deal halfway between our ship and the mechs'," she said, waving him toward the cylinders. "I'll push the cart, you cover me—and Jonathan," she turned to face him and tossed him the rifle, "look mean."

He caught the rifle and was surprised by its weight.

"It'll be lighter," she said, "outside."

Jonathan stood there for a few minutes, looking at the rifle, then up at his sister as she worked the cargo door, draining the bay of air before opening it. He couldn't hear the door roll up to reveal the blasted, dead landscape outside, couldn't hear anything but the roar of his own breathing and the thin hiss of the open channel to Jessica.

She walked to the stack of metal cylinders tied onto the platform. She lifted the platform easily and began to slide it across the floor on an invisible gravitic cushion.

He looked up and shivered when he realized exactly how close the other ship was. It was ugly, all studded and bristled with line-interrupting additions. It was a mean, diseased-looking ship.

"Stay close to me, now," Jessica told him, startling him into following her. "Mind the change in gravity."

"I've never killed anybody," he said sharply, embarrassed but not sure why.

"I thought you were a terrorist," she answered without turning around.

She spun the grav cart around, facing him, but looking down and behind her as much as her helmet allowed. She hopped off the lip of the cargo bay door and took a long time to disappear as she and the cart dropped to the surface as slowly as a feather fell on Alitar.

"Actually," he said, moving to stand on the edge of the door, "I just write computer viruses."

She waited for him to settle onto the surface of the asteroid but didn't see his face blanch from the sudden drop into a near weightless environment.

Computer viruses? she thought, Big Slate?

She'd taught him everything he knew about computers when they were both kids, at least she thought she had, until now. Knowing she could never write a virus like the one that cracked Galvin's net on Alitar and paved the way for the successful Big Slate offensive impressed her, but it

also scared her a little somehow. She looked up at him and
met his confused, anxious gaze.

"Multiplex Cow?" she asked him. Everybody who
knew anything about dataware had heard of it.

He nodded.

"Listen," she told him, "we're going to be just fine. I
don't know these guys . . . they're a bunch of mechalus
mercenaries or something . . . but they have something I
want, and I have something they want." Her eyes followed
his to the containers. "We have some mutual friends, these
mechs and me, and I have some insurance of my own,
okay? I don't want you to worry."

His eyes brightened and he smiled a little, but his grip
on the rifle was still stiff and unfamiliar. The mechalus
would recognize that, but Jessica honestly didn't think it
would matter. "Thanks," her brother said.

"Good, now keep quiet."

She turned and pushed the cart in the direction of the
mechalus' cutter. Jonathan had trouble following her, even
keeping his footing at first. He was concentrating on his
feet so much that he didn't see the mechalus party emerge
from their ship, sliding a big, sealed cargo container in
front of them. Jonathan had trouble stopping when he saw
his sister bounce to a halt in front of him. He managed not
to gasp when he saw the mechalus party only a few steps
in front of him.

They seemed huge next to Jessica and Jonathan, though
they weren't quite as big as the weren he'd seen on their
last refueling stop at Hanover Station. They were wearing
e-suits, of course, but they were hard suits, at least in
places, and studded with a similar array of add-ons and
subsystems as their ship was. Behind their faceplates were
bizarre faces trimmed in circuit points and plates of what
might have been some kind of skin-grafted armor. One of
them looked like a woman, though Jessica couldn't be
completely certain. "She" was holding a render rifle that

looked exactly like Jonathan's, and she smiled at him when she noticed him noticing the gun. The expression made Jessica feel cold.

"Jessica Belwe," she said simply.

"Emmennex," the bigger of the two, the one standing closest to the unmarked cargo container answered. "I will inspect the currency."

"I want to see the missiles first," Jessica said flatly. Jonathan looked up at her. She was surprised and disappointed by his reaction. What did he think she did for a living?

A sound came over the radio that must have been a laugh. It sounded like a klaxon buried in metal shavings. Both Jonathan and Jessica shivered.

Emmennex casually released two clasps on the side of the cargo container and it tumbled open in the low gravity with a flick of his gloved finger. Inside were the unmistakable, sleek shapes of ship-to-ship missiles, ten of them, their nose cones tapering to a point that seemed sharp enough to puncture an e-suit. Jonathan couldn't take his eyes off them; they were beautiful and horrifying, each one capable of killing dozens, hundreds, in a ball of super-heated plasma.

"Query: you like, bodyguard?" the other mechalus asked him. Her voice was thinner than Emmennex's, obviously a female. "Speculation: pretty are they?"

Jonathan nodded and looked to his sister, who had approached the missiles. Emmennex stepped aside—actually slid in the microgravity—to let her get closer. Jonathan could see that she was reading a small string of numbers off the side of each missile.

"Query: you have a name, bodyguard?" the mechalus woman asked him, her voice unsettling even without the teasing, flirting edge.

"Do you?" he asked, with a sharp edge in his voice, "bodyguard?"

"Reply: Veertsen."

"Jonathan."

"Great," Jessica broke in, "now that we all know each other, let's get it done."

She bounced aside and Emmennex came forward, his eyes locked on the cylinders. "Bomb grade?" he asked. "All of it?"

"As promised," was Jessica's response. She noted the meaning-heavy glance the two mechalus exchanged, and she saw Veertsen's hand tighten slightly on the grip of her render rifle. "But with one thing more," Jessica added.

"There was an agreement reached," Emmennex said too quickly, too suspiciously.

"Yeah, there sure was," Jessica replied, "but I don't know you well enough to expect you'd keep it, so I have some insurance."

"Emm—" Veertsen started to say before he silenced her with a wave of his hand. The movement made the soles of his boots drift a few centimeters across the hard, pitted rock.

"Tell me," the mechalus said.

Veertsen moved suddenly to one side and Jonathan gasped, though her rifle never came up. He fumbled with the grip of his own weapon and nearly lost his precariously light footing. The mechalus woman was looking at *Esilio* with narrowed eyes, ignoring Jonathan completely even though he'd actually come close to killing her accidentally. Jessica, alerted by the sudden movement, saw Jonathan accidentally disengage the render rifle's safety.

Emmennex didn't look away from Jessica, and she knew he either trusted Veertsen completely or not at all. "You were saying?" the mechalus asked.

"The cylinders contain exactly what you came here to trade for," she told him, "nine loads of refined plutonium-239—bomb grade 'P'—enough for . . . well, enough. But the cylinders are my little creation. They each contain, along with the plutonium pellets, a self-contained ARIES system that'll clean the pellets if it has the chance. In less than a minute you'll have nine cylinders full of nothing: plutonium-239 converted to a mixed-oxide fuel state, and there's no going back from there."

"And?" Emmennex prompted, his voice still patient, almost detached.

He glanced at Veertsen, who finally turned her attention away from *Esilio* and nodded. Jonathan brought his rifle up to his chest, and Jessica drew in a sharp breath.

"Jonathan," she said. "Easy. We still have a deal here."

"Query: do we?" Veertsen asked.

Jessica didn't acknowledge her. "The ARIES won't activate unless a signal is sent from my ship. If we don't get back there safely with the cargo we came here for, you get nothing. The cylinders and my ship are already linked by a tight-beam carrier wave. If that beam is broken, the process starts, and you get nothing. When we're safely away I'll transmit a signal that will permanently disable the ARIES processors, and we're all happy. Is there anything about that you don't understand?"

There was a long silence then, a silence you can only find on an eight kilometer long chunk of rock drifting through the middle of the ass-end of space. Jonathan locked his gaze on Veertsen, who simply closed her eyes.

Jessica locked eyes with Emmennex, who offered her an artificial, practiced smile in return.

"Boss," Durante's voice sounded in Jessica's helmet. The signal had that too clear, tinny sound of a tight-beam laser link. She felt reasonably sure she was the only one who could hear him. "It's Far Sky all over again."

Jessica forced her face to remain impassive as her heart started thumping wildly in her chest. She didn't answer her pilot. If Emmennex saw her mouth moving behind her faceplate but heard nothing, he'd know something was going on. Instead, she reached up slowly and touched a small recessed button on the side of the first cylinder. Identical panels, no more than a few centimeters square, silently slid open on the side of all nine of the silver metal cylinders. There were three small indicator lights behind each panel, one green, one amber, and one red. The amber lights were flashing on eight of the nine cylinders. The ninth was burning steadily green.

"Wait—" Jessica started, but Veertsen's sudden movement interrupted her. There was a burst of noise in her helmet. She spun in time to see the mechalus woman slip gracefully around Jonathan and strip the render rifle from his hands in a single fluid motion. The sound she had heard was Jonathan's breath being driven from his lungs by Veertsen's knee in his back.

"Jessica!" Jonathan said hoarsely.

The mechalus woman had his left arm behind his back. His feet had come off the ground, and she was holding him helplessly in front of her with one hand, the other still tight on the grip of her render rifle. Jonathan's weapon was spinning slowly away, arching incrementally toward the surface of the rock.

"It's okay, Jonathan," Jessica said, holding her hands up as if trying to ward the whole situation away from her.

Emmennex still stood unarmed in front of Jessica. When she looked at him, she couldn't read his face at all. "Query: why is this?" he said slowly.

She didn't know for sure why the cylinders had begun to reprocess the plutonium, but she had one good guess. The mechalus must have tried to jam the signal and succeeded. When the carrier wave was broken, that was it. Jessica eyed the ninth cylinder and kept her gaze locked there until Emmennex reluctantly followed it. Veertsen was getting restless and Jessica could hear Jonathan's breath over the comm link, loud but steady. He was afraid, but he was still trusting her. She silently cursed herself, knowing she might not be able to save him. This

Emmennex, whoever he was, had made one mistake. She couldn't count on him making another.

"There's still one cylinder's worth," Jessica said finally.

"Not enough!" Veertsen answered, her voice rough, angry.

"Veertsen," Emmennex said, "command: maintain."

Jessica thought she could hear the mechalus woman sigh, but it might have been Jonathan she heard.

"She is right, of course," Emmennex said. "One cylinder is not enough for these missiles. You have made our deal into nothing."

"I have done nothing but protect myself, Emmennex," Jessica said, "and you know it. I told you what would happen if you blocked that signal."

Emmennex turned his head slowly to look at Veertsen, but spoke to Jessica. "So here we are," he said, "both of us with—"

They couldn't hear *Esilio*'s cargo door begin to close, but Emmennex detected the faint change in lighting as the interior illumination from Jessica's ship began to fade. He stopped talking and grabbed for the cylinder. Jessica let him have it, though she hoped her hand coming up with a heavy metal object would make him think she was grabbing either for him or the cylinder. She couldn't tell if he did or not, but he took the cylinder in one big hand and launched himself off the rock in a single long, controlled stride.

The object in Jessica's hand wasn't a weapon. It was the magnetic clamp. She set it to the side of the missile container and felt it grip on. She was looking at her brother, still in the grip of the mechalus woman. Veertsen had turned to watch Emmennex's escape. A series of electronic tones sounded in Jessica's helmet. The mechalus captain was communicating with his bodyguard and Jessica hoped he was telling her to leave Jonathan and protect the missiles, but the mechalus woman's grip remained firm.

"He's got the cylinder," Jessica said to Veertsen, "Leave my brother and you can have your missiles back."

Veertsen looked at her and smiled. Jessica could see the shadowy figure of Durante slide through *Esilio*'s slowly closing cargo doors. She pointed in the direction of the mechalus's cutter and Veertsen followed her finger. They both watched Emmennex suddenly fall more quickly as the artificial gravity in his ship's cargo bay dragged him down.

Jessica didn't say anything when she felt the gentle nudge at her side. She reached around slowly and took the hooked end of the cable Durante had shot at her from *Esilio* in one hand. She tried to get it up and click it closed onto the clamp stuck onto the missile container before Veertsen turned around, but she didn't. The mechalus woman saw her hook the cable onto the container and knew she'd have to fight to get her boss's missiles back.

Jessica's heart stopped. What she saw next, she saw in the slow motion of a glass falling off a counter, a set of keys falling into a sewer grate, or a brother being shot in the back with a render rifle. Jonathan's body seemed to collapse in on itself, and there was a sudden loud burst of static, then his signal went dead. Jessica opened her mouth to scream or cry or shout or something, but no sound came out. She knew he was dead and knew she'd be next if she couldn't get her body to move. She almost couldn't, and when she did finally move forward, she wasn't sure if it was out of pure self-preservation or the beginning of a desire to try to set things right.

Jessica crossed the empty distance between them quickly and had the mechalus's render rifle in her hand half a second before Veertsen fired again. There was no noise and little light, but even through the thick glove of her e-suit Jessica could feel the weapon vibrate as it rattled through its random sequence of gravity induction cycles. Jonathan floated free and there seemed to be movement there. It looked like parts of his e-suit, the legs especially, were flapping in a breeze as he fell, though there was no air around them. It was muscle spasms, death tremors, but some people might have thought the motion reason enough to hope. Jessica didn't have time to think he was alive, though. Veertsen was fighting.

The mechalus was too strong for her, and the only reason Jessica lived long enough to realize that was that she'd managed to get in close fast enough so that the mechalus couldn't get her rifle into play.

"Your fault," Veertsen sneered through the comm link, "it's your fault this ended so."

Jessica didn't need to hear that. She knew it all too well.

Veertsen twisted and sent them both tumbling off the surface of the asteroid. Jessica had that turning, falling feeling that she always hated about E.V.A.'s. It almost seemed like they'd launched off the rock for good. It didn't take much to escape this little rock's gravity well—more than that, but not much more. Stars spun across her vision and she realized all she was doing was holding onto the mechalus who killed her brother; not fighting, not wrestling, just holding her. The stars turned into liquid blotches like tiny blue-white nebulae and she knew she was crying. She held on tighter. No matter how hard she tried, Veertsen couldn't pry Jessica off her back.

"No one has won here, bitch," Veertsen said. "Let me go."

Then Jessica got mad. Of course no one here won, but some lost more than others. She'd lost more than the mechalus. Her brother, the last family she had in the whole, cold universe was dead, and the missiles probably wouldn't make it into her hold, which meant they wouldn't make it to Hurricane and she wouldn't get paid. If she didn't deliver the missiles that would be it for her. Even Durante wouldn't stay with her. She'd be broke, no ship, nothing. Done.

She'd made her own way, of course, and she knew that too. By the time the two women, Veertsen still struggling, Jessica still just holding on, came to rest on the hard surface again, Jessica knew there was only one thing left to live for, one last victory, hollow as it may be, one last chance to walk away a winner, in more ways than one.

The hollow click of her helmet against something snapped her out of it. It was the render rifle that Jonathan had dropped; it was right under her. She let go of the mechalus and scooped up the rifle in one motion. She'd never have thought she'd be able to move that quickly, that gracefully, but she did. She brought the rifle up and saw Veertsen doing the same thing with hers. She didn't wait to aim, just squeezed the trigger and there was a flash, and the mechalus woman came apart in front of her. Jessica didn't look at the mess and ignored the pieces of hardware and wetware that sprinkled across her faceplate and e-suit.

She launched herself into the black sky and overshot the missile container, coming to rest only barely close enough to grab hold of the slack cable.

"Durante!" she screamed. Her voice sounded shrill and panicked, old and tired all at the same time as it echoed in the confines of her helmet.

Durante didn't answer. He didn't have to; he knew what to do. Jessica pulled lightly on the cable and that was enough to swing herself onto the top of the missile container. She scrambled to close it as she saw *Esilio* pop off the surface of the asteroid in a shower of sparks and super-heated metal flakes. She couldn't get any leverage, weighing nothing, pushing against something that weighed nothing, and the container wouldn't close.

The cable went taut and in less than a second the container was off the surface too. Jessica tightened her grip and shifted to one of the container's strong handles. She expected some kind of wind or something to make it harder to hold onto the container, but of course there was no wind. The acceleration as *Esilio* left the rock behind was enough.

The container was spinning madly, connected to *Esilio* only by the slim, strong cable. Jessica couldn't do anything for the first few seconds but hold on and scream. The missiles, locked into a tight, cushioned rack in side the container, stayed put.

The stars stopped spinning, the asteroid started spinning, and she looked back. They were accelerating rapidly away, but she thought she could still see Jonathan lying there, stuck to that rock.

The mechalus ship was powering up.

"Eyes!" Durante shrieked in her comm link, and she immediately closed her eyes tight and pressed her faceplate against the hard side of the missile container. Everything went white and she screamed again. She felt heat her e-suit could never possibly fight off, and then she just lay there waiting to either live or die.

"We're clear," Durante said, and she stopped screaming.

She turned around, still holding tight to the madly-spinning container. When it rolled around to face the asteroid, she saw that all that was left of the rock and the mechalus drive cutter was a seething yellow ball of superheated plasma. The ninth cylinder Emmennex had brought aboard his ship wasn't filled with bomb-grade plutonium and an ARIES system like the other eight cylinders. It was full of bomb-grade plutonium and a trigger.

Had she won?

She had the missiles, but her brother was dead. No matter what she did now, sink or swim, she knew that was her fault.

"Pull me in, Durante," she said, her voice hoarse and weak from the screaming and the crying and the dry, recycled air of her e-suit. "Then set a course for Algemron."

There was a silence as Durante weighed the next few

years of his relationship with Jessica against his own need
to make a living.

"So," he said, "we're not going to deliver this cargo to
Hurricane?"

"No," Jessica answered, "there are some people I know
who could use them more."

Durante didn't say anything, he just set a course for
Algemron.

The container's spin began to slow as the cable pulled
in toward *Esilio* and Jessica got only one last look at the
cooling ball of sun-hot gasses that was her brother's grave.

"Jonathan," she said, "wait'll they see my Multiplex
Cow."

About the Author

Philip Athans. What can I say about Philip Athans? Women want
to be with him. Men want to be him. He currently lives in the
Seattle area with a couple of really lucky gals. And yes, he is one
damn fine lookin' man.

"A Killing Light"

ROBERT SILVERBERG & KAREN HABER

*N*IGHTBIRD DROPPED out of drivespace with a silken purr and a flash of rainbow colors.

Lila Artemis, captain of the merchant ship, smiled as the physical universe winked back into place around her vessel. She gave her helmsman, Savaan, an appreciative glance. "Nice going."

Artemis always felt better after starfall when she could see the stars in her viewscreen again. She found the impenetrable blackness of drivespace unsettling.

Savaan, a fraal who was considerably taller than most of his kind, nodded with his usual self-satisfaction but kept his concentration on the navigation boards, scanning relentlessly.

"Well, Savaan," she asked, "where exactly are we?"

The fraal took a moment to scan a final readout before replying. His large, pupiless eyes reflected his station's small vidscreen with an eerie bluish light. "We're on the extreme outer edge of the system, Captain, not one of *Nightbird*'s better starrises."

"How long to Grith?"

"At our normal cruising speed, we'll reach port in a little over fourteen hours. I can get us there sooner if you wish."

Artemis considered his suggestion. They were at the very edge of the Corrivale system and anyone could be out there, waiting for a chance to prey upon unsuspecting vessels. Still, this wasn't Lucullus, so they should be all right as long as they kept their eyes open.

"No, Savaan," she told her helmsman. "Let's not look like we're in any hurry. Normal cruising speed will be fine. Just keep your eyes open."

Behind Savaan, T'Suimera, the t'sa who was head of security, was scanning the ship's aft screens, keeping watch for stray asteroids, pirates, and anything else he deemed out of the ordinary. Like most of his lizard-like people, T'Suimera set to his task with eager determination. If so much as a stray chunk of interstellar ice came near *Nightbird*, the t'sa would know about it.

Captain Artemis was concerned about threats outside the ship, but she was even more worried about internal matters, specifically her cargo.

"T'Suimera, how did our passengers fare?"

The t'sa entered a series of commands on his console, his clawed fingers clicking across the keypad. "Heat signatures normal. Atmosphere and gravity are at optimum levels. All life support systems are functioning normally. All seems secure."

The knot at the core of her stomach eased. Although *Nightbird* ostensibly carried plumbing supplies for a research facility on Grith, she had a clandestine purpose as well: to ferry sesheyan refugees out from under the clutches of VoidCorp. There were eight such refugees now hidden deep within the ship's cargo bay. Lila reminded herself that they were undetectable and secure. Nevertheless, she wouldn't rest easy until they had been safely delivered to Grith.

"Should we let our passengers out?" asked Savaan.

"Not just yet," Artemis replied. "Grith is still several hours away. A lot can happen in those hours. As far as I'm concerned, we're not safe until we're actually on the ground, and even then we'll need to keep our eyes open."

The t'sa continued scanning, his legs dangling from the edge of his seat. He was perched on what Lila had come to think of as his high chair: a padded seat raised a good half-meter above her own. What else could you do if you had a t'sa working security? The jittery little lizard folk hadn't the reach of larger humanoids.

"Captain, there's a yellow light on Bay Door Eight."

She didn't like that. She left her chair and peered over her security chief's shoulder. "Check it."

Captain Artemis towered over both her navigator and her security chief. A strapping redhead, Lila had reached full adult height by the age of eleven. After twenty years of knocking around the Verge, first with her parents and later as the captain and owner of her own commercial rig, she had learned to take her ship seriously when it said that it needed attention.

The more Lila Artemis thought about it, the less she liked that yellow light. "I'm going down to Deck Three," she said. "I want to double-check the cargo bay personally. Savaan, you have the bridge."

The fraal nodded.

Lila moved through *Nightbird* like a proud trader surveying her shop. The ship was built for efficiency, not beauty. It had the rough-and-tumble look of the merchant freighter that it was, patched and repatched, dented here and there by meteors that had slipped through the ship's deflection inducer. Nevertheless, Lila loved her vessel and wouldn't have traded it for a fleet of new cruisers.

Deck Three held the shuttle and cargo bays, vast echoing spaces now remarkably empty. Their "cover cargo" of plumbing supplies took up less than half the space in one bay. Lila peered inside the cargo bay and stared at the far wall. She knew that beneath the padded bulkhead was an escape pod set into the wall of the ship. Carefully adapted to special use, the pod had been armored and stealth-shielded. It was a world unto itself, a safe room with its own food supply and life support system. Once inside, the occupants would be cut off from all activity in the main section of the ship, and thanks to a scan-reflective hull, undetectable. This was especially useful in the Verge where ships could be caught and boarded with little or no warning. Right now, the pod held eight sesheyans on their way to a new life.

Lila patted the bulkhead beneath where her passengers were hidden. If she did nothing else, she thought, she had at least been of use to these poor folk.

The sesheyans were by human standards nightmarish in appearance, with bulbous eight-eyed heads, clawed limbs, and powerful leathery wings. All in all, they looked like large bipedal salamander-bats. Creatures of the night, they preferred to live and work in twilight environments similar to that of their homeworld. They were a peaceful folk who, left on their own, would have pursued their aboriginal traditions, roaming their dim jungle world in great tribes. However, many sesheyans were skilled hunters and trackers, and those who took to their new life offworld often became quite skilled as bounty hunters or assassins.

Unfortunately, Sheya, the sesheyans' homeworld, had the bad luck of orbiting a star whose system had been seized by VoidCorp.

VoidCorp. The very name left a bad taste in Lila's mouth. All citizens of VoidCorp were considered Employees—indentured servants if the truth were told—by the megacorporate stellar nation.

She had watched from afar as VoidCorp swaggered through the Verge, absorbing planets and lives. Better, she thought, to collide headfirst with an asteroid than become an Employee-for-life of VoidCorp.

Only on Grith, a moon of Hydrocus in the Corrivale system, were sesheyans free to live as they wished. To this world with its orange skies and seemingly endless jungles, a group of sesheyan settlers had been ferried long ago by mysterious aliens, now vanished. Some of the settlers' descendants survived in shantytowns and shacks in Diamond Point, Grith's major city, where they maintained a tense alliance with the city's ostensible administrators, the Hatire colonists of the Colonial Diocese. Many other sesheyans of Grith had "gone native" and returned to their aboriginal lifestyle in the jungle. Exactly how many sesheyans roamed the jungles of Grith, no one knew for certain, which made it a perfect haven for sesheyans fleeing the servitude of VoidCorp.

It was to Grith Starport at Diamond Point that *Nightbird* was ferrying her passengers. The eight sesheyans in the pod had signed on with Captain Artemis for a trip to a new life of freedom, far from the tentacles of VoidCorp. The chief of the Diamond Point Port authority, a sesheyan named Se'Tali, would receive her cargo and help to ferry them to their new life of freedom.

She pursed her lips over the thought and, deciding that all was well in the bay, strode back to the lift. Moments later she was on the bridge.

"Savaan," she said. "How soon do we make planetfall?"

"ETA at Diamond Point Spaceport in approximately thirteen point seven-five hours."

"How long to unload?"

Savaan paused to glance at her. His huge dark eyes were unreadable. "Assuming that there are no problems with the Aanghel syndicate and its operatives, no more than forty minutes. Of course, that does not include clearing our plumbing supplies through customs."

"Please, gods," T'Suimera said, "no problems with the Aanghels. I thought the Hatire ran the spaceport."

"Only nominally," Lila replied. "The sesheyans are contract workers, which means that the Aanghel family controls them—and through them, the spaceport."

The t'sa forced a grin. "The Aanghel family makes me nervous."

"Everything makes you nervous," Lila said, "which is why you're such a good and useful security chief."

T'Suimera gave an exaggerated bow from his perch.

"How's the stardrive?" Artemis asked. "How long until we can starfall again?"

Savaan brought a new display up on his vidscreen. He scrolled through several pages and said, "It seems that *Nightbird* has done rather well in that area at least. We should be able to starfall in just over sixty-one hours."

T'Suimera snapped to sudden attention, the crested scales along his spine standing out at right angles from the rest of his armored hide. "Heads up, everybody. Vessel approaching at 2.0 AU on direct interception course."

"Warn him off," Lila said.

"I've tried. He's ignoring our signal."

"Change our heading," she said. "Evasive action."

Savaan did so, and Artemis watched their course layout on her vidscreen. The green light that was *Nightbird* veered off her arrow-straight course. A few heartbeats later, the red light that was the other ship turned to pursue them.

"They're matching us," Savaan said, "move for move."

"We're being signaled, Captain." T'Suimera glanced at her over his shoulder. "It's a VoidCorp cruiser, bearing markings CL 351." He ran the numbers through the system registry. "It is a verified patrol craft out of Iphus."

VoidCorp! Lila kept her voice level although her heart was pounding. "Give them standard ID and ask them what they want. And T'Suimera, get those deflection inducers ready."

"Aye, Captain." T'Suimera processed the communiqué. The reply came back almost immediately. "They request course heading and cargo list."

"Tell them it's none of their business. Politely."

"They insist," the t'sa said after a moment of relaying messages. "They are, of course, better armed, but we could take the chance that they won't fire upon a private merchant vessel. It's in direct contravention of the Treaty of Concord."

Savaan obviously couldn't resist twitting his shipmate. "With all due respect, T'Suimera, VoidCorp will do whatever is in their best interests, which includes firing upon a merchant ship."

"Knock it off, you two," Lila said. "T'Suimera, tell them where we're going."

The t'sa transmitted the information and listened intently to the reply over his earpiece. "They claim to have search rights for all incoming vessels bound for Grith. They're stopping and boarding all ships coming into this system."

"On whose authority?"

"Their own. They claim Corrivale, you know."

"That's disputed," Lila said. "Their claim's based on holdings that were destroyed in the Second Galactic War. As far as the Concord—and we—are concerned, this is an independent system."

Maddeningly calm, Savaan said, "Of course, I agree with you, Captain. However, it is dangerous to disagree with someone who is holding you at gunpoint."

T'Suimera's eyes glittered. The effect reminded Lila of the ship's running lights. "For once I agree with that uppity fraal, Captain. We're outgunned five to one, we can't outrun them, and they're requesting permission to board . . . again."

Savaan sniffed. "As I see it, we have no choice."

"More risk if we don't allow them aboard, Captain," said T'Suimera. "If they disable us, we'll never get home. And the cargo is well stowed and secure. You checked it yourself."

Lila raised her voice. "I don't remember asking your

opinions, boys. I don't like letting VoidCorp thugs aboard
the ship, but I don't like the idea of the *Nightbird* floating
around in pieces, either. All right. Permission to board is
granted . . . reluctantly. Slow *Nightbird* to nominal boarding speed and transmit the code for our airlocks to those
bastards."

*   *   *   *   *

The VoidCorp security detail was big, mean, and ugly.
They looked more like mercenaries than corporate patrol.
Lila had seen weren that were more attractive.

The team leader, a no-neck thug with only a thin stubble
of black hair, took one look at T'Suimera and his face
creased into a nasty smile, as if to say, "That's your security chief?"

T'Suimera, in turn, was polite in the sarcastic extreme.
The only sign of tension was his reversion to his T'sa
dialect speech patterns as he examined the patrol's ID
"Your credentials? Fine/good/yes. Everything here seems/
looks/is in order. How long will this take? We're already
overdue/tardy/late for our designated landfall."

"Your schedule is of no interest to VoidCorp," said the
no-neck. "I suggest that you anticipate delays."

T'Suimera grinned his most feral grin, the kind he saved
for special enemies. "I assure you that nothing/zilch/nil
whatsoever is out of order on this ship, absolutely nothing."

"Then you have nothing to worry about," the leader said
with a condescending smile. "We'll make our own determination. Your course heading is for Grith. What business
do you have there?"

"May I ask what concern/business/interest that is of
yours?"

"Grith is in the Corrivale system. VoidCorp owns the
Corrivale system." The thug's recitation had the singsong
lilt of rote memorization.

T'Suimera shook his head. "Not yet they don't. The Concord deems this an independent system."

"Negative. This system has been reclaimed. This"—the thug gestured with his sabot pistol—"provides any additional authority I require. What are you planning to trade on Grith?"

T'Suimera eyed the pistol but never stopped grinning. "Plumbing supplies. You may check/see/study our cargo manifest. Perhaps you'd like to take/carry/have a Bertek quick-flush as a souvenir?"

The VoidCorp brute ignored the suggestion and made as if to walk right over T'Suimera, but the t'sa held his ground, his tail whipping from side to side with an audible crack. His black *det'sya* tattoos showed in high relief against his pallid hide.

At the last moment the VoidCorp squad leader yielded ever so slightly and sidled past the *Nightbird*'s security chief. T'Suimera's smile widened to show even more teeth than before as he clicked them open and shut once.

Lila Artemis watched the proceedings from her throne-like captain's chair. Outwardly, she was calm, even impassive. Arms folded across her chest, she sat calm and composed above the fray, but inside she seethed. Here they sat dead in space while these bastards snooped all over her ship. What if they actually managed to find her precious passengers? This far out in the system with no witnesses about, who would care to investigate if one lone merchant vessel met with an "accident"?

No, they wouldn't find them. They couldn't. She told herself that the refugees were well hidden. The VoidCorp scanners would pass right over and never see them.

She hated the men who swarmed through her ship, hated the risk they posed to the poor desperate sesheyans she was transporting, hated the company that employed them, and hated the galactic order in which an abomination like VoidCorp had been able to flourish and subjugate so many citizens.

Someday, she thought, someday, VoidCorp, your hold
will slip. Your corporate state will come apart and scatter
to the four quadrants. Your very name will be outlawed,
anathema, and oh, that I be allowed to see that day. Please,
gods, soon.

VoidCorp's team prowled the ship, stem to stern, shining lights into dark corners, rapping at walls, prying at
insulation, scanning and re-scanning every passageway
and cargo bay, and generally annoying the hell out of
everybody. At 1400 hours, they gathered on the bridge.
Some looked no more than bored, but their leader was positively furious.

Lila stared straight ahead, rigid with tension, refusing
to meet the gaze of either Savaan or T'Suimera. She was
considering what she would do if the VoidCorp squad
attempted to take control of *Nightbird*. At the thought, her
hand moved slightly closer to her sidearm.

"We've found nothing," said the neckless squad leader,
"nothing at all." He glared at Lila and her crew with obvious chagrin, as though it were somehow their fault.

"Just as you were informed/told/briefed," said
T'Suimera, "six hours ago."

The VoidCorp thug grunted and gave the order for his
team to disembark.

Lila made a great show of ignoring their departure,
turning her back and addressing her fraal helmsman.
"Savaan, as soon as we're squared away and secure,
resume our heading, and let's try to make up for lost—and
wasted—time."

The airlocks slammed. As the VoidCorp ship broke contact and veered away soundlessly, the three crewmembers
exchanged smiles of relief.

"Well," Artemis said, "it looks like that high dollar
stealth equipment we installed was worth it. Remind me to
take Kelso out for a drink when we get back to Tendril."

Soon the VoidCorp ship had dwindled to a speck in the *Nightbird*'s aft screen. Savaan added power to their own engines and they shot away toward the distant star that was Corrivale. With each light-hour they put between *Nightbird* and the VoidCorp ship, Lila's mood lightened. Space had a cleansing quality that she savored, especially at times like these.

"On course for Grith," said Savaan. "At present speed we'll arrive in just under ten hours."

T'Suimera cut in, suddenly. "Captain, I'm getting peculiar energy readings on Deck Three."

"Source?"

"Difficult to pinpoint, but I think it's near the cargo bay."

"The cargo bay? Can't you be more specific?"

"No. It's fading." T'Suimera blinked at her. "Now it's gone. I'm not sure what it was."

"Any damage?"

"None that I can detect."

"Make a note of it." Lila spun on the helmsman. "Let's have a look at our passengers. Yellow lights in the cargo bay not ten minutes after those thugs left seems damned coincidental to me. Savaan, you have the bridge. T'Suimera, you're with me."

The t'sa suspended his boards and was behind her in an eyeblink.

As soon as they entered the cargo bay, T'Suimera began tearing away the bulkhead camouflage. Great chunks of insulated framework came loose in his sharp claws. Beneath, gradually coming into the harsh yellow light of the cargo hold, was the black and rounded hull of the escape pod.

Lila pulled the loose chunks of insulation free. In a moment she would see the faces of those she had freed.

T'Suimera neutralized the pod's security field and lowered the illumination levels in the main bay to twilight.

"We might as well make them comfortable," he said.

Lila nodded her approval.

In the gloom, the t'sa triggered the pod hatch, and the door slid back with a soft hiss.

There was no movement from within.

"Hello?" Lila said. "We've arrived in the system."

There was only darkness and silence.

T'Suimera pulled out a small flashlight and aimed it at the pod interior. Lila was standing behind the t'sa and couldn't see past him into the pod.

"By K'san Ch'Nak!" T'Suimera exclaimed. "They're dead!"

"No!" Lila shouldered past him and entered the pod. At first, in the minimal light, she could barely make out the shapes of her "cargo," then she saw them.

Sprawled in a motionless heap were seven sesheyans. An eighth lay against the far wall. Most of the dead still wore their protective goggles, although at least two of them had apparently torn them off in their death throes.

Lila Artemis stared at the limp figures, and her emotions roiled. She had promised these desperate people safe berth and passage. That had been her duty and her vow. Somehow, she had failed, and they had died.

Her voice was rough around the edges as she said, "All dead, T'Suimera? You're certain?"

"This one's still breathing." He gestured toward the sesheyan collapsed against the wall and activated a medical scanner he had brought along.

The sesheyan was obviously dying. His wings shivered with minor convulsions and his jaws worked, although no sound came forth save a terrible groan. In a wavering voice, he said, "The light. Ka'itei's terrible liiiiight." Still groaning, he toppled sideways and half-slid, half-fell off the bench.

Lila reached for the dying being, but T'Suimera stopped her. "Captain, it may not be safe. I'm getting

strange residual energy readings . . . all over the board.
There's a fair amount of low-level radiation in here."

"Anything like the readings you noticed before?"

"Yes. Captain, you're not shielded."

"Neither are you." She ignored T'Suimera's warning
and cradled the dying sesheyan in her arms. "Can you hear
me?"

There was no response other than a muted groan. As
Lila watched helplessly, the sesheyan stopped moving. She
didn't require T'Suimera's scanner to tell her that the last
of her passengers was dead. Gently, she lowered him to the
ground.

"Put them all in stasis," she said, "and get the medtech
'bot in here. I want a full analysis. What killed them, some
fast-moving virus, mass seizures? We've got to be able to
explain their deaths to the Diamond Point Port Authority.
To do that I need some answers." She took a deep breath.
"Full decontam for you and me, and seal off this deck. We
don't know if what killed them is a threat to us."

She stormed out of the pod and sought out the nearest
intercom. "Savaan, this is the captain. Our passengers are
all dead, and T'Suimera says there's low level radiation
throughout the bay. Seal off the bridge. The chief and I are
going to decontam. Reduce our speed to one half normal
cruising speed. We need to buy ourselves some time."

"Captain, I—"

"Just do it, Savaan. Artemis out."

* * * * *

Stoically, Captain Artemis and T'Suimera endured the
exam. Probed and pricked, they shared sour looks while
awaiting the medical robot's results.

The report was, in part, reassuring. There was no trace
of microbe or contaminant that could endanger *Nightbird*'s
crew, but that left the mystery of the sesheyans' deaths

unanswered. The Diamond Point Port Authority was
getting impatient for information. Following procedure,
Savaan had contacted Diamond Point not long after
Artemis and T'Suimera had left the bridge. *Nightbird* had
been expected several hours ago.

"How long can we stall them?" T'Suimera said. "They
have a right to know what's going on."

"Yes," replied Lila, "but not before we do. I don't want
any police, no matter how friendly, snooping around my
ship before I have some notion of what's happened."

The medtech robot's analyses were unsettling. Some
sort of energy pulse had apparently killed the refugees as
they huddled in their hiding place. Source: unknown.
Energy composition: unknown.

"Too many unknowns," Lila said.

"Regardless of the cause, we must allow the Port
Authority access to the victims," said Savaan, who had
rejoined them when it became evident whatever had killed
their passengers was no longer dangerous. The fraal was
as tight as a strung wire. "They will want to conduct their
own investigation. To delay is highly improper."

"Whose side are you on?" Lila bristled at the thought
of more strangers on her ship snooping around.

"We can't risk losing docking privileges," T'Suimera
said.

"Don't tell me things I already know." She hated to con-
cede that Savaan was right.

"Port Director Se'tali is demanding an answer for our
delay," said Savaan. "To say that he is becoming suspicious would be stating the obvious."

"Tell him about our little visit from the Corpses.
Explain to him that we've experienced engine difficulties
since their visit. As a sesheyan, he won't have trouble
believing that VoidCorp might sabotage our ship."

"You don't really think he'll believe that?" T'Suimera
asked.

"I don't care if he believes it or not," the captain said tersely, "as long as we can buy ourselves some time. We can't land until we know what killed those sesheyans."

"Captain, if I may"—Savaan obviously knew he was testing Lila's patience—"we have nothing to fear from landing. We have done *nothing* wrong. If anyone is suspect here, I believe it is those VoidCorp thugs. The authorities on Grith might even be able to help us determine the cause of death."

Artemis sat silent for several moments. The fraal made sense, but landing on a world full of sesheyans in a ship with eight dead sesheyans made her uneasy. Out here in the Verge, people could disappear without too much effort. Still, Savaan was right. *Nightbird*'s crew was innocent. If the VoidCorp thugs had indeed killed the sesheyans, then the Port Authority of Grith might be their only ally short of running to the nearest Concord outpost.

"How long until the stardrive has recharged?" she asked Savaan.

"It would be just under fifty-one hours now."

"Very well." Artemis sighed. "I'll contact Se'tali and explain to him what has happened. T'Suimera, get down to engineering and see if you can get the drive recharged any quicker. Savaan, proceed to Grith on a vector that will put us there in twenty-four hours. That should give us time to try to find some answers of our own."

* * * * *

Se'tali did not take the news well. He was enraged, and though he assured Artemis that he did not suspect her or her crew, he insisted that *Nightbird* proceed to Grith at top speed. Lila declined, saying that they were experiencing problems with their induction engine and were now at the safest speed their computers would allow. The sesheyan obviously didn't believe her, but Lila knew he could do nothing about it.

Savaan took her orders to heart, and they arrived at
Grith precisely twenty-four hours later, requesting a berth
assignment at Diamond Point Spaceport.

"Welcome, *Nightbird*," came the reply from Port Central.
"Take berth 9-A. You are now under the authority of the
Colonial Diocese. All local laws apply to you and your crew."

"Acknowledged," Savaan replied noncommittally.

The fraal nimbly steered them to rest between two large,
timeworn cruisers and shut down *Nightbird*'s main drive
engine. He seemed extremely pleased with himself.

The visit from the head of port authority was prolonged
and uncomfortable. He was not amused by the deaths of
his fellows. Se'tali, the port chief, greeted them with what
he diplomatically called "an escort," but the bulky scanning equipment they carried gave them away for what they
truly were: investigators.

"Captain," he said as his crew dispersed through the
ship. "This is a very grave matter." He had obviously been
offworld: his grasp of Galactic Standard was excellent, and
he spoke with none of the usual sesheyan accent. "I regret
to inform you that your ship is restricted to dock until further notification."

Lila felt her hackles rise. "On what grounds?"

"Pending a full resolution of this matter. Our people
have died, and we want an explanation. Your craft was the
site of the crime, though as yet we have no reason to suspect you or your crew. We don't want you to leave while
we're still pursuing our own investigation. The scene of the
deaths must remain undisturbed."

"We're already cooperating fully."

"Indeed, and I urge you to continue to do so."

Lila gave him the equivalent of T'Suimera's killing
grin.

"My team is putting them in stasis now. We'll—"

"We've already taken care of that," Lila interrupted.

"You've disturbed the bodies?" Se'tali said with a hiss.

"We had to. We had no idea what had killed them, and the rest of us might have been in danger. Due to our unexpected engine troubles, we had no idea we might be out there."

"How fortunate that you were so suddenly able to correct the problem," Se'tali said.

"Indeed," Lila replied with a perfectly straight face.

"I would be happy to have my own technicians examine your engines to try to find any problems," Se'tali offered with a deprecating bow.

"Thank you," Lila replied, "but my chief already found and corrected the problem."

Se'tali watched her for a moment more, obviously suspicious, but unwilling to press the matter.

"Well, Captain," he announced after a moment, "we will try to be as little of a nuisance as possible. We will conduct a preliminary examination and inform you of our findings. We prefer to do this in situ. The less that is disturbed, the easier we will be able to gather accurate evidence."

Lila ground her teeth in frustration while Se'tali looked on.

"Fine," she said, "but your teams are to be escorted by my crew and myself at all times. I won't have *any* unauthorized persons roaming about my ship with impunity. They are not to touch *anything* without permission. If they need information, they will request it from one of us, and we will cooperate fully. Is that understood?"

"Including yourself, your crew is only three, Captain. Restricting our investigation to three parties will only cause delay."

"I'm in no hurry, Mr. Se'tali."

*   *   *   *   *

Eight hours later, after an exhausting search of every square centimeter of the cargo bay and a good part of the rest of *Nightbird*, Captain Artemis confronted Se'tali as the sesheyan and his team of investigators prepared to leave.

"Does your 'escort' have any findings so far?" she asked him pointedly.

"Yes." His eight-fold gaze bored into her. "At least two of the victim's brains bore a residual psi-resonance signature similar to that associated with the fraal."

She glared at Se'tali. "What exactly are you suggesting?"

"You have a fraal navigator, do you not?"

"I do. Savaan, my first mate."

"We will want to question him."

"Now wait just a minute." She couldn't believe what she was hearing. "You can't seriously consider Savaan to be a suspect. He was on the bridge the entire time."

"Under our laws, everyone is suspect until proven innocent."

"Your jails must be full."

"Actually, we have very little crime."

Lila Artemis knew that most sesheyans on Grith were up to their third set of eyes in crime. She gave Se'tali a sardonic half-smile. "I'm afraid I can't permit my first mate to be removed from his post . . . for any reason."

"Captain, I remind you that you are in our territory and under our jurisdiction. Our laws take precedence, especially when sesheyans have died as a result of your negligence."

"Our *negligence?* On what evidence are you basing that accusation?"

Before Se'tali could reply, Lila heard two swift drumbeats, or rather, she felt them.

Snap. Ka-bam.

Magnetic dock grapplers had attached to *Nightbird*, tethering her in place.

She kept her tone civil only with great difficulty.

"Inspector, I strongly protest. This is an act of extreme aggression."

"Under our laws it is seen as merely taking a precaution." His expression was insufferably smug.

Lila felt her self-control eroding. "I demand that we be permitted to consult a legal representative immediately. The Concord Directives are clear on this matter. All discussion on this matter must cease until we have appropriate legal representation."

The sesheyan stared at Lila Artemis; his eight eyes open wide beneath his protective goggles. "Our laws are not subject to Concord auth—"

Lila rode right over him. "My ship's log will show that you initiated a conflict with us, grappled the ship without warning, and made no effort to respect the Treaty of Concord regarding legal representation. Now get the hell off my bridge before I toss you through the nearest airlock."

"This won't save your helmsman," Se'tali said. "The psi-resonance signature is quite distinct. A fraal was involved in this crime against our people, and your helmsman is the only fraal on your crew."

Lila gestured, not gently. "We have nothing further to say until our lawyer gets here."

The sesheyan and his team hurried away with bad grace. Lila bit her lip, knowing that she had done nothing to resolve their problems, and time was on the side of the sesheyans.

Time. On whose side? The sesheyans? Maybe not. Time, she reasoned, could be many things to many people: an obstacle, a long journey, or a refuge.

*   *   *   *   *

The next morning on the bridge, T'Suimera gave her the bad news. "The sesheyans say that although they've located a Hatire lawyer to serve on our behalf, he's been delayed. They order us to yield Savaan to their custody immediately or bear the consequences."

"Those bastards," Lila said. "I suppose that means guns."

"At the very least."

"Our deflection inducers are the best."

"But not strong enough for a prolonged onslaught," said the t'sa, "and it's not safe to do much shooting at dock—ricochets could take out other ships. Of course, that's a factor in our favor, but then there's the grapplers to consider."

"Captain," Savaan said, "I shall surrender to the authorities. I don't want to put the ship in jeopardy."

Lila glared at him. "Honorable sir, if you take one step off this ship, I'll have T'Suimera lock you in your room and put you on kp duty for the next two years. Nobody is surrendering to anybody. Understand?"

The fraal nodded. "Yes, Captain."

"You're not going any place," she said, "especially into that jungle out there. You know how you dislike humidity." The decision, as it hit her, brought a smile to her lips. "Besides, our destination isn't a place, exactly."

Both Savaan and T'Suimera were watching her with obvious confusion. A sensor on the security board beeped and the t'sa turned toward it. "Captain, the sesheyans are readying a boarding party. They mean to take us by force."

"Power up the deflection inducers and lock us in," Artemis ordered.

"It appears that we're out of time," Savaan said.

Lila Artemis wanted to laugh aloud. "You're wrong, Savaan. In fact, you couldn't be more wrong." She stood up. "And by the way, you're relieved of duty."

The fraal faced her, astonishment evident on his long face. "Captain—"

"That's an order, mister."

She saw the dawning of a question in his deep eyes, and perhaps the genesis of fear as well. Savaan knew her, knew her well, and therefore he knew that she was not in the habit of betraying or selling her crewmembers, even if it cost her the ship. But the shadow of doubt was there, and that hurt her.

"Report to your quarters, Savaan."

He left without another word, and she watched him go. He would understand soon enough.

"Shall I shut down his station?" asked T'Suimera.

"No." Without another word she settled into Savaan's chair, noting in passing that the long-limbed fraal's seat fit her comfortably.

There was the sound of far-off thunder and the ship vibrated slightly.

"Captain," T'Suimera said. "We've been fired upon."

"Status?"

"The inducer deflected it. No damage." The t'sa paused, then smiled. "Correction. Damage to the dock, from a icochet."

"That'll teach them to fire on a protected ship."

"They're slow learners," T'Suimera said an instant before several rumbles jolted the ship. "Firing again, and deflected again."

"Good. Use this confusion to repolarize the grapplers so that our hull will repel them. Small pulses, T'Suimera. Don't arouse suspicion. Just get those damned things off of us."

The t'sa grinned broadly. "Aye, Captain."

"Meanwhile, I want to take a look around." She activated the main scanner. "The sesheyan forces are massing on the dock. Don't those fools know they could get hurt by deflected gunfire? Well, that's their problem." She keyed up a 360 degree scan and froze it at the halfway point. "I see that we've still got access to the launch points. T'Suimera, what's happening with those grapplers?"

"Working on the last one now." He grunted with satisfaction. "Done. We're loose."

"Let's get out of here. Engines on full. Emergency escape maneuver."

"What coordinates?"

"I've got the helm. Let me worry about that."

The engines roared to life. Lila saw a few yellow lights come up on the panel, but that was to be expected when demanding full power from a complete stop. She punched in a flight plan to take them out safely beyond the grip of Grith's gravity.

The angry voice of Se'tali filled the bridge. *"Nightbird,* shut down your engines immediatley. Repeat. Shut down at once. This is illegal activity. You will be boarded and your ship will be impounded. Cease immediately."

The hell with their laws, Lila Artemis thought. There were other laws. for example, the laws of physics, immutable, and specifically, the laws of drive physics. "T'Suimera, cut comms."

Nightbird was moving now, backing away from dock, pulling clear of the two flanking ships to rotate toward the horizon, her snout pointing outward. Too late, Grith Port Police ships were firing up their engines, attempting to intercept.

Lila cut in full power and let their pursuers taste the backblast from *Nightbird*'s passage.

"Savaan is buzzing us," T'Suimera said. "He wants to know what's happening."

"Tell him to pipe down. We're rescuing him."

Inspiration had struck and with it, determination. As *Nightbird* cleared Grith's atmosphere, Lila hit the inter-ship address system to warn Savaan. "Strap yourself in. We're going to have to lose ourselves for a while. Things could get bumpy."

T'Suimera gave her a sidelong glance of disbelief, which, on his scaly ferret-like face, actually made him look winsome. "Captain—"

"That includes you, T'Suimera. Get ready. Counting down."

He made one more attempt. "We haven't calculated any coordinates for drivespace."

"I'll take care of that."

"In-system? Isn't that dangerous?" T'Suimera's expression clearly indicated that he thought she had taken leave of her senses.

"Stop staring, T'Suimera, it's bad manners. Settle down. We'll be fine." She fervently hoped that she was right.

If she plotted the course correctly, they would dive into drivespace and emerge several light-hours distant in five days. Savaan was the expert at stardrive coordinates, but Lila knew that his sense of honor would prevent him from making this escape.

"Captain, sesheyan patrol vessels are approaching."

No time to think. She punched in the coordinates.

"There. Calibrated and ready. Hold on, T'Suimera."

The engines would take them into drivespace for a hundred and twenty-one hours, where they would remain, untouchable. They would emerge five days later at the far edge of the Corrivale system.

The drive engines were beginning to rumble. A beacon lit on the communications board.

"Captain," T'Suimera said. "Diamond Point Port Central is hailing us."

"Ignore them."

Lila strapped herself in. She had never before entered drivespace this close to a planet—or other ships. It was going to be an interesting ride. "Engaging stardrive."

The universe contracted, and color fanned into a blinding spectrum of yellow, orange, red, purple, and the barest hint of blue.

A screech of tortured metal elongated into a series of high jagged notes, and from there to steady pulsations that melted into the very fabric of the air, becoming sensation rather than sound. Time slowed to a crawl. Lila Artemis could count the spaces between each heartbeat.

A sudden shudder passed through the bridge, the vibrations amplifying into a steady nerve-sundering tremor.

Lila held her breath. Was it *Nightbird*? Was she coming apart in drivespace? Would they all be ejected from the dying ship, whirled away to be crushed and torn in the merciless vacuum? Her lungs ached with a slow fire. The tremors slowed, stopped.

"Screens, T'Suimera."

With nothing for the sensors to detect, the viewscreen showed gray snow in every direction. The *Nightbird* rode serenely through a strange unmarked void, alone.

"No damage, Captain. We made it."

Lila could breathe again. She could think and see and feel again. She released her chair restraints, took a deep triumphant breath, and bounced to her feet. They were safely in drivespace.

The screens showed red lights and the boards were flaring as the *Nightbird*'s sensors struggled to scan what couldn't be scanned.

"Shut down all nonessential boards," said Lila. "No use confusing the ship."

T'Suimera fixed her with his gaze. "Captain, begging permission to speak freely."

When have you ever not? she thought. "Granted."

"What have you done?" T'Suimera asked.

"I've bought us time. We're safe in drivespace."

"But in five days we'll make starrise."

"By then," she replied, "I mean to have solved the question of the sesheyans' deaths and clear Savaan."

"We only have a hundred and twenty-one hours."

"If we can't prove it in five days we might as well give up."

"You're confident, then?"

"No. Just desperate."

*   *   *   *   *

Given the unusual physiology of the sesheyans, analyzing what had killed them was a major triumph. Isolating its source was a major—and complicated—problem.

"Did VoidCorp somehow suspect what it couldn't prove—that *Nightbird* was smuggling refugees—and set loose a subtle poison dangerous only to sesheyans?" T'Suimera mused.

"No," Savaan said. "Highly improbable."

"Which is to say that they're not that good?" asked T'Suimera.

"However good they are, we've got to be better," said Lila, "got to outthink whoever—and whatever—could do this." She stared at the bulkheads. "Let's get started. T'Suimera, I'm tearing this pod apart. The hell with Grith laws. Get those corpses out of stasis. I want to analyze everything on them, each piece of clothing that those sesheyans wore. And get their files up. I want to know everything about them there is to know, their favorite foods, what they dreamed about, who they hated."

"That one's easy." T'Suimera's grin looked positively feral. "VoidCorp."

"Besides VoidCorp."

Over the next day and a half, Lila and her crew scanned every object in the pod, every connector, every capacitor. Even Savaan, recovered from his sulk, insisted on participating in the investigation. Finally, after scanning and analyzing every conceivable piece of evidence, they found what had killed the seseyans.

"So," said Savaan, "there's a faint residual energy signature in the pod from a pulsed-radiation beam."

"Sounds like a lanthanide-powered weapon of some sort," T'Suimera said.

"Could that kill them?" Lila asked.

The fraal nodded. "Most certainly, especially in closed quarters. I suspect the weapon was concealed in a boot or a piece of clothing."

"Okay," Lila said, "that answers how, but not why, or who."

Later, frustrated and sleepless, she lay on her bunk running through the questions yet again. Had something been planted on Ka'itei, or did it get in after they were under way? Could those VoidCorp bastards have slipped something in? No, impossible. The pod was sealed and locked, camouflaged. They couldn't have known it was there.

Had the weapon been left behind by previous travelers? This wasn't the first such group that Lila had ferried to freedom. The *Nightbird* was becoming known in certain circles, known to carry people needing help in disappearing.

Lila had neither set out to become a smuggler nor a conductor on an intergalactic underground railway. It had just happened, somehow, by easy stages. It didn't even pay well. Occasionally, it didn't pay at all. Refugees had taken up precious cargo space before T'Suimera had installed the pod hiding place. Now at least the *Nightbird* could carry a saleable cargo in tandem with its hidden passengers.

Late, very late, sleep found her. Her dreams were uneasy and she awoke drenched in sweat.

*   *   *   *   *

At midday, Artemis sat at the wide commons table in the dining room with T'Suimera and Savaan. All of them were bleary from the hours of detail work they had been doing.

"All right," she said. "One more time, what do the passenger manifests show?"

T'Suimera slouched in his seat. "The location of the weapon was in the stitching of Ka'itei's beishen; he was the group leader."

"A defensive weapon that misfired?"

"We can't be certain."

"It wouldn't make any sense otherwise. He was their leader. He assembled the entire group of refugees and contacted the *Nightbird* on their behalf."

"Yes," Savaan said. "He was the catalyst for their voyage. Are you certain that his was the body upon which the weapon was found?"

"See for yourself." T'Suimera pushed the file in the fraal's direction. Savaan read through it slowly, nodding. "Yes. Yes, I see. There's no question. Perhaps then, it was planted on him by one of the others before he died and preset to activate at a certain time? Maybe the murderer placed it on Ka'itei to implicate him, to frame him?"

"Yes," T'Suimera said, "and what if Ka'itei was killed first, and the weapon was then secreted in his clothing?"

"Why?" said Lila. "Did the other refugees know one another? They came from all over space. Did one of them bear a grudge against Ka'itei?"

"He had worked with all of them at one time or another," the fraal said, "and had supervised two of them. Perhaps there was bad blood between them, an old grudge."

"People working together often develop grudges," T'Suimera said with a sharp-toothed grin.

"But he was leading them to freedom," said Lila. "They were dependent on him, dammit. This just doesn't make sense. Why would any of them have wanted to kill him? To kill any of them?"

Again that night, sleep was a fugitive quantity. Lila rotated on her bunk for half an hour before deciding to cut her losses. Yawning, she dragged herself over to her deskscreen and commenced—once again—to review the files on the dead sesheyans.

She made a screen-to-screen comparison of dates and locations, ran searches on VoidCorp connections, and even asked for analyses of family names, looking for clues.

Nothing.

Lila blanked the screen and stared at the matte black field, musing. How could she save Savaan? How could she get free of Diamond Point Spaceport? There had to be a way.

She could just run for it. The Verge was a big place. She could steer clear of Corrivale and still make a living.

It was tempting, but no, she wanted to know what had killed her passengers, and if it had been something peculiar to *Nightbird*. Lila didn't like to cut and run, and she didn't intend to do it now.

She leaned heavily on her elbows, staring at the screen. All right, she thought. We'll do it again, bit by bit.

"Give me Ka'itei's data cache," she told the computer.

The screen chuckled and muttered for a moment. Multiple files came up in quartered-screen display. As Lila gazed from one to another, she noticed, in the far right hand column, a date of five years ago and a place that hadn't registered before.

Catalog. That was the VoidCorp capital in Old Space, wasn't it?

She could have sworn that Ka'itei's data file had placed him elsewhere during those years. Ka'itei had, in fact, been busy working in the Verge, but this file had rearranged the facts. It said that Ka'itei had worked halfway across the galaxy in an administrative position for VoidCorp—in its very capital, for godssake. One of these files was wrong, but which one?

As she read on, she saw a new index key appear over the filenames: DFC. She knew from previous experience that meant Dead Files Cache. This was an old file in Ka'itei's data profile. An old file that contained old information, information that failed to cohere with more recently seen figures and facts, and then Lila knew, knew it in her bones and sinews. The dead file was the right one.

"Oh, you bastard," she whispered. "You lied. You lied, and I''ve caught you!" Oblivious to the hour, she buzzed T'Suimera's cabin. "Get here," she said. "Now."

* * * * *

It was a night of little rest for the crew. By morning, they had learned that Ka'itei had not been what he seemed. However, they still didn't know whether he had been a desperate refugee or a double-agent.

If the latter, why had he waited until their last starrise to kill the other refugees? Why had he committed suicide as well? Nothing added up. Was he victim or perpetrator? Why?

Had his heart belonged to VoidCorp or to the free sesheyans' movement? If he was a murderer, what was his motive?

Savaan struck a dignified pose. "Captain, this has been a noble attempt to save me, but I'm afraid that we must simply face facts. In less than an hour we will come out of drivespace somewhere in Corrivale. No doubt the ship has sustained some minor damage breaking free of the port grapplers that will not become apparent until we're in real space again. There may be commensurate damage to the dock itself for which we must answer. I cannot, in good conscience, put the ship and crew in further jeopardy."

"What are you proposing, Savaan?"

His lips trembled. "That we return to Grith where I will surrender to the authorities."

T'Suimera snorted.

Lila gave the t'sa a disgusted look before turning to the fraal. "Savaan, this isn't the moment to start making noble sacrifices. If you insist on delivering yourself to the sesheyans, I'll have you confined to quarters." She smiled. Survival rations wouldn't have melted in her mouth. "If that doesn't work, I'll throw you in the brig."

The fraal blinked at her, his mask of nobility shattered. "Captain, I—"

"No, Savaan. That's final."

"If I could break into this touching tableau for just a moment," T'Suimera said from where he crouched over a computer console, "I would like to report that I've discovered something about the murder weapon."

Artemis wheeled on her security chief. "Let's hear it"

"The weapon was set to be triggered by the wearer, by Ka'itei. It couldn't have been anyone else."

"So it wasn't planted on him?"

"No. The weapon was implanted too deeply within the fibers of his beishen."

"So it was Ka'itei after all?" Lila felt puzzled and even a bit dismayed. He *was* the murderer. She had to believe it now, but it was a lot to swallow. "Well, we have the murderer, but no motivation, and without a provable motive, the authorities on Grith won't be interested in our speculations."

An alarm began squalling, catching all of them by surprise.

"What the hell?" said Lila.

Savaan peered into his screen and sniffed twice. "Drivespace warning, Captain. We'll be making starfall in twelve minutes."

"Let's get ready, boys."

They scrambled for the bridge. Boards had to be secured, systems immobilized. Anything could happen in the breach between drivespace and real space.

"Counting down," Savaan said. "Ten, nine, eight—"

Lila felt her stomach coil tightly. It could be a rough ride. Coming back into realspace was no light thing. "Everybody brace for transition," she said. "Good luck."

The drive engines began their slow and steady roar. The lights dimmed. Somewhere an alarm wailed. The world went to reds and blues and greens as Lila Artemis sat frozen in her seat, incapable of movement. The light, the very air, twisted and pounded with strange reverberations. Instruments flared.

There was no sense of movement, yet *Nightbird* flew and her crew rode with her, down the throat of time and space to be spat back out into a star-filled place defined by comprehensible measurements, by the amount of time it took to fill the lungs with air, to live a lifetime, to think an entire thought.

Time and space came rushing back with a roar. Screens flashed and flickered as the comm chittered to itself, measuring a palpable reality. Corrivale was a small white spot at the edge of the viewscreen.

The *Nightbird* was back in the noisy universe of sight, sound, and heady sensation. Too much sensation, Lila thought, as a message blared from the main comm board.

"Nightbird! You are under Grith Port Central guns. Do not attempt further movement! Any increased output from your engines will be interpreted as a hostile act. Shut down. Cease and desist immediately. We will take you in tow."

"Captain," T'Suimera said from his station, "there are four fighters approaching. Their inducers are on full-force, and their weapons are charged."

"Our welcoming committee," Lila said. "They certainly found us fast. They must have notified every patrol within three light-years of Grith. Any damage reports, T'Suimera?"

"Number two engine shut down on reentry. We've got red lights on two scanners, hull damage—but no breach—on deck two. Otherwise, we're intact/safe/okay."

"Our deflection inducers?"

"Can operate at full capacity."

"Keep that in reserve. Savaan, acknowledge the message but otherwise make no response."

"They're demanding entry."

"Announce a malfunction of our engine core, making the ship too hazardous to board. Put it on repeat. And on second thought, get those inducers up."

The fraal wore a vexed and frustrated expression. "Captain, would you mind telling me just what you hope to achieve?"

"Stalemate, Savaan. At least temporarily." She unstrapped herself and got out of her chair. "T'Suimera, you have the bridge. If Savaan attempts to turn off the deflection inducer to turn himself in, knock him down and sit on him. I'm going to the stasis chamber. I want to have another look at our friend Ka'itei."

* * * * *

The lights in the stasis chamber bathed the area in an eerie yellow glow. The dead sesheyans lay in their cocoons as if frozen there for all eternity.

Lila triggered the capsule that held Ka'itei. The naked sesheyan corpse held no secrets and she let him be, frozen in stasis, but his clothing—his beishen—now that interested her.

She shook out his personal effects and spread them on the table by the door.

She pried at the clothing for a time, but it had been thoroughly investigated by T'Suimera already. Ka'itei's gailghe yielded nothing. His cloak, although heavily woven in intriguing textures, contained no secrets waiting for her touch to reveal.

Lila massed his clothing together and wondered what to do, where else to search. As she wondered, she fingered the sesheyan's wing ornaments. All rough glitter and thick metal she found them pretty in a barbaric way. She didn't recognize the stones set in the dark metal: blue-black with a bronzy patina.

As she turned the ring, one of the stones popped loose and rolled across the table and off the edge.

Lila caught it just before it hit the floor.

The gem was surprisingly heavy. As she handled it, she felt it vibrate oddly. Holding the stone close and squinting down, she could just make out bands of data running across the face of it, tiny and incomprehensible. By the gods, she thought, it's a data cube disguised as a gemstone.

She clenched it in her fist and ran for the bridge.

"T'Suimera, get this translated." She handed the tiny cube to the t'sa and was rewarded by his startled glance.

He fed it into the comm board. Lights flared and the computer began mumbling to itself. "I don't think our translation program is set up to handle this," he said. "There's some sort of recording here in an obscure Sesheyan dialect. We may only get rough equivalencies."

"That's more than we had a minute ago. Play it."

The translation was slow going, and many words were merely left an untranslated growl.

"Honored family, forgive me. I have been Weyshe the Wanderer, walking in the arms of Cureyfi the Father of Stars. Now I have become Mirraved the Thinker. I must set you free, and now I think that only my death will achieve . . . It is, perhaps, less honorable than I would like, in that I take others, non-clan, with . . . was told to prevent this escape, by whatever means . . . To invalidate this ship as a carrier of other . . . I deeply . . . the deaths and . . . my actions may bring to others. I face death serene in the . . . that I have slipped the bonds of our masters. I cannot . . . on this course. Courage, beloveds. We will hunt together in the shadows of the next world."

As the translation ended, there was silence on the *Nightbird*'s bridge.

The miserable eight-eyed murdering bastard, Lila thought, but why? Why?

She regarded her two senior officers. "Now we have an admission. What we don't have is motive, but this should suffice, at least to remove charges against Savaan and the

rest of us. T'Suimera, transmit this translation directly to
Se'tali's headquarters. Explain to him what we've learned,
then offer to shut down the deflection inducers—if we
have full assurances that hostilities will cease."

* * * * *

Upon reception of their transmission, hostilities did
cease. Lila kept *Nightbird* in bond while Diamond Point
port authorities made inquiries into Ka'itei's background.
The answer was fast in coming and ugly. VoidCorp was
holding his clan members hostage.

"We theorize that the VoidCorp vessel that stopped you
had been alerted to your secret cargo by Ka'itei," said Se'-
tali. "VoidCorp intended to apprehend the refugees and
take your ship into custody, but you had hidden our people
too well. VoidCorp had to let you go, and that in turn left
Ka'itei with impossible choices.

"He couldn't just kill his fellows, nor could he face
VoidCorp with total failure on this mission. His clan members would have paid the price. Possibly the thought of
continuing on in this job, forced to continually betray his
own people, sent him over the edge.

"So he chose suicide, triggered the device that assured
the deaths of all in the pod, and left a false psi-resonance
signature to implicate your crewman. Perhaps that was
intended to trigger your own intensive investigation and
the revelations we discuss now." The sesheyan gave a
deep bow. "Captain, our profound apologies. You are free
to go. May Cureyfi the Father of Stars smile upon your
journeys."

Lila thanked him and saw him off the ship. She had to
admit that the sesheyans had made amends. They had
even provided her with a nice cargo of erfani glass components that would bring a respectable price back in Old
Space.

Amends had been made, yes, but Lila couldn't shake the ghost of the tormented Ka'itei. She felt that *Nightbird* would never be free of him. She would see the sesheyan's image in darkened corridors and imagine his last terrible moments of life over and over.

That he had been driven to his death she had no doubt, but to take the others with him, and to endanger her own ship and crew—who had only wanted to help, after all—bespoke a desperation beyond her comprehension. Suicide had been his only choice.

Lila wanted to weep. The poor damned bastard.

On the heels of that thought came a great weariness. Perhaps, she thought, it would be best to get out of the smuggling business and stick to regular payloads that were safe, uncontroversial, and worth their while. She knew that Savaan certainly wouldn't complain if *Nightbird* stopped smuggling sesheyans.

And yet, she couldn't do it, if for no other reason than that Ka'itei had killed himself on her ship, on her watch. His death had sent a message straight to her heart, four simple letters: *Help.*

How could she ignore that unspoken appeal and look at her reflection in the mirror every morning?

She entered the bridge. The crew was preparing for lift-off. T'Suimera was strapped into his seat, intent on his scanners.

Savaan sat at his station looking smug, a clear sign that he felt relieved and even happy. "So," he said. "I assume that this episode ends our days of running refugees right under VoidCorp's nose?"

Lila's smile could have matched the t'sa's in its savagery. "Not a chance, Savaan. In fact, I'm doubling our runs." She had the satisfaction of seeing the fraal's composure melt into confusion.

"Let's put a recorder camera in the pod," she told T'Suimera, "to avoid future problems, and I want another pod in the other wall. I want larger carrying facilities as soon as possible."

"Yes/aye/affirmative, ma'am."

"Another pod?" Savaan echoed weakly.

Lila was relentless. "At least one more, maybe two, and new shielding. Of course, we'll have to strip-and-search each passenger for his own protection. Put intercoms in each pod. Everybody who rides with me rides safely from here on in.

"Put the word out, T'Suimera. Any sesheyans who want to get to Grith, we'll take 'em."

"We'd better invest in some new armaments," the t'sa said.

"Whatever it costs." Lila threw a strand of long red hair over her shoulder and glared at unseen VoidCorp thugs.

"Whoever wants to go after sesheyans is going to get the *Nightbird*'s guns right up his keester. I'm taking this personally, hear?"

Savaan said nothing, stunned into silence.

Only T'Suimera broke the silence. "Yes, Ma'am/Captain/Lila."

Lila wasn't listening. A sudden chill had crawled up the back of her neck. She spun around in her seat.

A spectral presence stood directly behind her. It had a monstrous appearance: leathery wings, a bulbous head, and eight eyes. It was Ka'itei, and he was smiling.

About the Authors

Robert Silverberg is the author of *Lord Valentine's Castle* and *The Alien Years*, as well as many other titles. A Hugo and Nebula Award winner, he is considered to be a master of science fiction and fantasy literature. His wife, Karen Haber, has written eight novels including *Woman Without a Shadow* and *Star Trek Voyager: Bless the Beasts*. Her short fiction has appeared in Asimov's Science Fiction Magazine, the Magazine of Fantasy and Science Fiction, Science Fiction Age, and many anthologies including *Sandman: Book of Dreams*.

"De Profundiis"

DIANE DUANE

HELM RAGNARSSON sat sweating at *Longshot*'s controls.

Up, he silently urged his ship, more up, up fast! She was already struggling up out of Redcrown's thick gravitational field as fast as she could, and behind him that big blotty shape was still showing on the sensor array. Neither the gravometric sensors or the radar could pick up any detail on it, only mass information that suggested there would be big trouble if it rammed him, and energy information that suggested it didn't need to wait to ram.

They wouldn't fire in this atmosphere would they? Helm wondered. Not even the Corpses would do a thing like that—

Helm had no guarantee of that, so he kept running, gasping against the acceleration while he swore at his losses and at how much this galloping retreat was going to cost him in fuel. He still couldn't believe how much argon had been in that last pocket.

"All shot to hell now," he growled to himself. "Greedy sons of bitches!"

Outside the piloting bubble, nothing was visible but a brownish-red hydrogen-helium atmosphere much contaminated by organic and pre-organic hydrocarbons and

halide-family compounds, under—Helm glanced at the
barometer—some hundred bars of pressure, at this depth.
Thick soup, he thought, with chunks in it.

This high, and at these coordinates, you were likely
enough to encounter chunks falling on you from the rings
above. Redcrown's perpendicular ring system, with its lack
of shepherd moons, was notoriously unstable, so that most
independent gas prospectors tended to avoid this area. But
Helm was not "most indies." He was better equipped than
most of them to deal with this area, which was partly why
he was so annoyed to have *that* underneath him, still
coming up fast.

"What the hell are you? Go away!"

It showed no signs of doing any such thing; it kept
rising fast under him. Helm eased the throttle forward that
last notch, felt the ship shudder as the impulsion drivers
tried to find just a little more thrust . . . then found it. The
gravity was getting a little easier to fight as the pressure in
front of him eased, the bow wave thinning out. The barometer said sixty bars.

Maybe another hundred kilometers or so to clear space.

"Come on, girl! Almost there."

The atmosphere ahead of him was darkening, a good
sign rather than a bad one at this altitude. The sullen glow
of the uppermost cloud layers started to thin and give way
to more directional lighting. It was easing toward twilight
on this side of Redcrown; the cloud off toward Helm's
right was now looking visibly redder, that to his left
browning toward black now.

Forty bars. Just a little farther.

The ship shuddered. The acceleration began to really
kick in as the atmosphere grew less difficult to pierce.

He glanced at the sensor array . . . and blinked. That
massive shape—whatever it had been—was gone, just
gone.

"How can anything move that fast down in that muck?"

Helm mumbled. Nothing could be that big and move that way. "Bloody Corpses. Sons of bitches."

It must be something of VoidCorp's, some new techno-logical monster of theirs.

"Why can't they just leave people alone to make a living?" Because you aren't *people,* said a bitter voice from the back of his mind.

Helm twisted his face into the usual whether-you-feel-like-it-or-not smile as the cloud around him divided into brown-black on one side and red-pale on the other. He threw *Longshot* into full acceleration and arrowed up through the thinning layers.

"This fuel expenditure exceeds preprogrammed spend-ing limits for this month's budget," his computer said.

"Oh, shut up," said Helm.

Not for the first time he regretted allowing his mainte-nance guy to put that damned "Say When" accountancy module into his computer. It was great at monitoring food and fuel budgeting in the normal flow of things, but it had no concept of emergencies—like when you needed to run your tail off, or when you really wanted another black mountain gateau.

Stars began to come out above him, and the overarch-ing secondary ring of Redcrown became visible. Even as he looked warily up at the ring, he saw a chunk of debris come arcing lazily down not ten meters from him, the frag-ment already heating up and leaving a ghostly-glowing trail of ionized monatomic helium behind as it slipped into the upper clouds. Helm would have sworn heartily at this sight on a normal day. Now his angry smile just stretched a little wider as he shot up into clean black space.

Far past the narrow rings, a glitter of light caught Aegis's fire—one of Redcrown's half-dozen metal-lump moons.

Normally, Helm was not overly excited at the prospect of visiting even the best equipped of them. At the moment,

though, anything possessing a dome with a one-bar atmosphere in it looked good. He slapped *Longshot*'s controls
into autodock configuration for the short-term docking
cradles on Nevin, Redcrown's second moon.

He turned around to give the cloudtops of Redcrown
"below" him a long, thoughtful look. Nothing showed
there, just the long, soft somber bands of red and cream
and brown. Like old dried blood they seemed, turning and
sliding silently against one another under the ancient night.

*   *   *   *   *

Nevin was little more than a gigantic iron rock covered
with craters. Long strips had been torn out of its surface,
relics of mining ventures gone sour or abandoned in favor
of richer strikes elsewhere on the moon. It had little in the
way of public facilities—one little ancient domed complex, old and weary and hissing at the seams. On Nevin,
though, he could at least find a place to eat, drink, and
sleep that was bigger than *Longshot*'s main cabin. The
community also housed the one reliable station where
Helm could find some servicing for his ship, though he
always checked the serviced components afterwards, since
mechanics out at this end of the Verge were no more honest
than they were anywhere else.

Here, too, there was some slight relief from the loneliness of his work. A lot of people working Redcrown who
were not with either the Orlamu Theocracy or VoidCorp
touched in at Nevin on a regular basis to stock up on food
or drink or gossip . . . and to complain.

Helm was definitely in a complaining mood, but when
he came out of the station's grungy plastic-paneled corridors, he found precious few people to whom he could
grumble or gripe. Purposefully, but in no particular hurry,
he made his way to the Outside Inn, the favorite drinking
place for the local miners.

It was local morning, not that this would have mattered to the incoming clientele, but Helm would have expected maybe five or ten people in the fake-hardwood splendor of the Outside Inn at any hour of the day. Today, there was only tall, skinny Joss, scrubbing at one end of the bar and wearing his routinely vague yet oddly sweet expression.

Joss looked up, saw Helm coming, and raised his eyebrows until they wound up where his hairline had once been. "Didn't think we'd see you back for another month or so," he said, abandoning the scrubbing cloth to begin rooting around under the bar. "What time is it for you?"

"Afternoon," Helm said. "I thought it was going to be another month or so myself."

"Don't tell me you tanked up early again."

Helm smiled and let him think that.

Joss made a briefly annoyed face. "They've drunk all the waldmeister again," he muttered. He brought out a bottle of something green-amber. "Beer?"

"Fine," Helm said. "Got the hard stuff to go with it?"

"Always." Joss rooted around under the counter again, peering briefly over it at Helm. "Don't know how you're doing it when nine tenths of everybody else is complaining they're not making their nut."

"Native cunning and hard work," Helm said.

Joss made an unimpressed face and straightened up, massaging the small of his back. It was the kind of reaction Helm preferred. Others who knew Helm less well than Joss tended to smile with him when he made such statements, though in a way that suggested they didn't believe him, especially about the cunning. There seemed to be a common understanding that a mutant who had been so physically augmented must have been undersupplied in the brain department.

Sometimes this supposition outraged Helm deeply. Sometimes he was inclined to let it lie, as people who thought he was stupid were likely to make very basic errors in their dealings with him. When he caught them in these errors, he had leverage afterwards. One of those had resulted in the installation of weaponry to Helm's ship that he couldn't have afforded without this convenient cause for blackmail. Either way, he was not about to discuss his methods with most of these people.

Joss was another story. The bartender was one of the few people around here to whom Helm could talk and who did not assume that there was something wrong with Helm's brain because of his shoulder measurements. There was a certain amount of kindred spirit between them as well, for Joss had been a gas miner once—"not with all this fancy equipment you have, oh no!"—a relic of the halcyon days before VoidCorp started coming into the system in a big way, when the Regency government was all you had to deal with, and the Regency wasn't too concerned whether you killed yourself or how often. In those days, you could dive into the orb of Redcrown wherever you liked, and if you came back, no one looked too closely into what you came back with.

"Not like now," Joss said sourly to Helm as he pushed a shot of Bluefall schnapps across the bar and went back to scrubbing the counter. He paused for a second to scratch at a fleck of something stuck to the clear plastic that overlay an extensive collection of old credit chips and coins, then said, "Harry was telling me the Corpses were after him again."

"Wonder if they have some personal problem with him," Helm said. "He been smuggling sesheyans or something?"

Joss shook his head and said, "You didn't see the news on the Grid last night."

"I don't follow it. Costs too much, and all it does is make me depressed."

"Well, this'd depress you all right. VoidCorp and the Theocracy have entered into a joint agreement with the

Regency to limit the operations of independent operators to 'benign areas' in the Redcrown central belts. They're saying they're afraid someone'll have an accident. 'Safety issues' they call it."

Helm snorted. "Yeah, like most of the accidents happening to independents here don't have them at the root in the first place."

"Well, *you* know that and *I* know that, but the Regency doesn't—or doesn't care." Joss snorted, not so much an expression of emotion as of the chronic rhinitis of those who have worked closely with hydrogen and helium for too long. "Concord's making the usual noises about how this limits the independents' civil rights, but who knows whether they're going to get off their bureaucratic butts and do something? Not in time for Harry, anyway. He says he's had enough, he's heading off to some other system. Good luck him finding one where VC isn't controlling the gas mining, though—not this side of the First Worlds."

"What'd they do to him this time?"

"One of those big wandering collectors of theirs came blundering out of a bromine cloud deck and nearly rammed him. 'Radar malfunction,' they said. Not so much as an apology."

Helm finished his drink and pushed the cup back to Joss for a refill. "Typical of them."

"Yeah," Joss said, "well, Harry's had enough. Scared 'im out of a year's growth when he saw that thing coming at him. There wasn't time enough for him to evade, not with everything but the stationkeeping jets on lockdown at that altitude."

"I'd've unlocked the main engines and shown them what a malfunction looked like," Helm growled.

"Yeah, well," Joss said and started scrubbing the counter again, "maybe all of us should start thinking about finding somewhere else to be. No profit in it with the big boys getting together to squeeze us out. While they were still arguing about how to carve the planet up, there was some chance for the indies, but now . . ."

"They're not going to stop arguing that easy," Helm said with a slight smile, "and even if they do, they still can't police an agreement like that. They can't manage whole-world surveillance for a planet this big, not to mention a gas giant. Even if they could, they couldn't enforce their wishes anyway. There are too many of us mining parts of the planet they're not interested in, or where their equipment's too big to handle."

Joss put one eyebrow up and asked, "Spots?"

"Spots," Helm said. "The amount of nobles in the circumspot vortices are too small for them to bother with, balanced against the amount of trouble it takes to get the stuff out. It's just not cost-effective, and the Corpses and the Orlamu, they're bulk dealers, economies-of-scale types." He took a slug of the beer, which was cold, if flavorless. "They don't have the time or patience for 'surgical' mining. I don't see why they don't just leave us alone, but chasing after us is going to be a lot more trouble than it's worth. As soon as they realize that, they'll forget about us and get on with their large-scale stuff. I wouldn't be surprised if this 'agreement' turns out to be some obscure political thing, just someone winning a bout of shin-kicking."

"You might be right," Joss said after another moment spent scraping at the bar. "Spots have been good enough for you, anyway."

"Yup. Found a nice one in the northern hemisphere," Helm said. "There's a standing-wave vortex off to one side of it, keeping things pretty stable. Picked up a nice big load of argon over there not too long ago, eight-five percent pure."

Joss looked surprised at that. "Unusual. You want to watch that, though. Those standing-wave pools can get unstable real quick if the primary gets active without warning."

"Oh, I'm watching the star all right," Helm said, "but Aegis is dead quiet right now—and for the next month, the weather people say. Sunspot minimum. Have you looked at it lately? It's weird, not a blotch on it."

Joss shook his head. "I'm too busy watching my customers," he said and glanced over Helm's head, "and there's one worth watching."

Helm turned. A woman was wandering through the bar, looking for a table that had been recently wiped. Her flawless skin had the chronic tan of someone from Bluefall. She wore the high-piled dark-streaked hair that was this year's fashion and a tightsuit truly deserving of the name. She sat down at a nearby table, while wearing a pout that suggested it would not have been clean enough for her if someone had used a pocket nuke on it.

"Scenic," Helm said approvingly.

"Not that that worries me," Joss whispered. "She shot someone the other night."

Helm considered that. "Really? Did he deserve it?"

Joss looked noncommittal. "Hard to say. Guy sat down to talk to her. Seemed all chummy for a while, then she pushed her chair back all of a sudden and drilled him. He had a knife in his hand, but she was so close that the propellant from her charge pistol half melted the blade—not to mention what the bullet did to the rest of him. Micah had a helluva time cleanin' up the mess."

Helm grunted and downed the last of his beer. What's done was done, and it wasn't his problem.

"Maybe she just meant to disarm him and missed," Joss said and looked thoughtfully over in that direction. "I don't know. If she knew a guy was disarmed . . . might be worth passing the time of day with her, just for the sake of getting friendly."

For a human, maybe, Helm thought. It was not something he would have risked. There were enough women around who, after the fact, would have been glad to exploit the excuse that "the mutant was bothering her" and used it as an opportunity to wipe out one more blot on the universe.

He shrugged. "Let someone else use himself for ballistic testing. This collector Harry saw—did it come at him from underneath?"

Joss thought a moment. "I think so. Yeah, he went on about that for a while."

Helm swallowed, thinking again of that great shape underneath him, that big fat energy reading, swelling with silent threat.

"Been a lot of that kind of thing lately," Joss said, so that Helm looked up in surprise.

"Other people had that happen too?"

Joss nodded. His voice dropped and he said, "Some people think it's something new of the Corpses'."

"Just ships," Helm growled, "collectors."

Joss shook his head. "Something else, something different. Been a secret till now."

"Rumors," Helm said.

"Maybe," said Joss and went to get rid of his scrubbing cloth.

At the same time, Helm thought of how easy it would be to hide things, secret things, down in that brown-black high-pressure muck. He shrugged again and tossed back the schnapps, then started to think about something to eat. Rumors and secrets were nothing to him. He had a living to make.

All the same, he resolved to make sure all his weaponry was ready before he left tomorrow.

* * * * *

The next morning, Helm cast away from Nevin and set a circumpolar course down toward Redcrown again. He was thankful that he had never lost the ability to enjoy looking at the planet, unlike some miners he knew who could barely stand the sight of the thing. It was handsome, though, in the way of any beautiful thing that might nonetheless kill you. The bands blended and moved against one another in trails of little frantic vortices, white with heat and turbulence. These were the great cyclic storms that the miners had nicknamed "Blender," a flat oval squashed like a hurricane turned inside out and spawning eyes or mini-hurricanes at its edges while a huge, slow bloodshot eye-that-was-not-an-eye turned about itself at the heart. All these things could keep Helm looking at them for a long time. They might be ephemeral features as reckoned in the timescale of planetary evolution, but Blender down there in the equatorial band had been there (so the science types said) since before man had gone from the First Worlds into space, possibly longer.

From here there was not too much you had to do to get down to Redcrown to do some mining. It was all downhill into that huge, heavy gravity well. Stopping the fall, controlling it . . . there, as the poet said, was the problem; and getting out again, the eternal difficulty. The status of your engines and attitudinal jets was always on your mind when you began that fall. Otherwise, there might be no climbing back into the safety of vacuum. Helm had checked his jets twice before he left. They were clean.

Now, as he coasted downward, he glanced toward the southern hemisphere. Down there at a great distance he could see the occasional wink of reflected fire—some faraway commdish on the nearly-built Orlamu collector facility near Redcrown's south pole, fleetingly catching Aegis's light. The place was not operational yet, but it would be soon.

Maybe Joss was right, Helm thought. Once that's up and running, and the other one—

He glanced toward the equator. Rotation was carrying it away, but the glitter of sunlight on the complex cubical

structure surrounding the nearly complete VoidCorp collector facility was plain enough. It was even bigger than
the Theocracy site.

How much room is there going to be for independents
then? Helm wondered. They'll get rid of us and then start
in on each other.

VoidCorp was not known for its kindliness to competi-
tors, no matter what treaties might have been signed. They
were masters at covert operations, and this planet's neigh-
borhood would start to become a very unhealthy one for
anyone not directly or indirectly employed by VoidCorp.

Helm shook his head and turned his attention to his console, bringing up the navigation program that handled his
approach to his favorite spot. He never approached it
directly, not seeing any reason to make his intentions obvious. He had mined it three times now, which meant that
this time would probably be his last; he disliked setting too
readable a pattern for anyone who watched, not wanting to
give anyone the idea that this spot was worth fighting over.
Not that I'm not equipped for a fight, he thought.

His face stretched into the grim grin that many people
assumed was its ordinary shape, since it was there so often.
One thing he had learned from childhood, being what he
was—or rather, what he had been made—was that fights
were inevitable, so you had better be prepared for them.
The first fights he'd had, those with his parents, he had
been unequal to. They had the usual unfair advantages that
parents everywhere have over their children: size and
strength, and then later, moral superiority . . . and finally
the shield of good intentions. His rage at his folks had been
such that when he broke away from the family at adoles-
cence, he now rarely thought of them.

The memory of that last big fight suddenly came up,
dimly, stripped by time of much of its venom. The irra-
tionality of it was actually able to make him laugh a little
now. He remembered his voice roaring and breaking as it

roared, "No one ever asked *me* if *I* wanted to be this way!"
It had always infuriated him, his mother and father's automatic assumption that Helm would want to be as they had
become, but more naturally so—stronger, faster, harder.

What they had done to themselves over the course of
their adult lives—the augmentations, the purposeful additions and tailoring to their genetic material—was their own
business. Apparently, it had never occurred to them that by
doing the same to their unborn child, they would put him
over the edge, beyond the pale (wherever the pale had
been, in those days). Forever after people would stare and
point. Other kids his age would sneer. The cry "Mutie,
dirty mutie!" would follow him until he was old enough to
knock down those who yelled it. Afterwards, people still
whispered it and smiled, and even those who did not say
anything aloud would still have that thought in mind every
time they looked at him. That itself was sign enough of his
parents' disconnection from reality—the fake-heroic
sound of the new family name they had taken to signify
their break with "normal" humanity, and the name they
had hung on Helm, which had caused some of his earliest
fights when other kids had pointed out that a helm was
something too hard and thick to get through.

Helm breathed out and studied the cloud decks below
him. This much his parents had left him: a body that was
comfortable anywhere between one and six gravities and
good to somewhere between three and five bars—he had
never tested his upper range in this regard and didn't care
to, since it was the kind of test you might never recover
from. Either way, he was well suited to gas giant work. The
heavy gravity of cloud top mining didn't bother him nearly
as much as the poor squirt "normals" who did a week or
two here and went off complaining about back trouble and
fallen arches and whole-body capillary hemorrhages.

As he brought the ship around the curve of the planet's
north polar region, Helm cocked an eye down at the major

band he was nearing, looking for patches or streaks of a particular silvery-rose paleness. The instruments would pick up the signs eventually, but after some months of doing this work he had learned that good color recognition and a delicate sense of shade could pick up those signs much sooner and with nearly as much accuracy as *Longshot*'s sensors. That silver-rose paleness—like the breast of a rockdove, Joss had told him over a drink—was an infallible indicator of clouds with a lot of water vapor in them. Water vapor in a gas giant's clouds meant lightning. When this phenomenon coincided too closely with areas of high hydrogen content, it was a good idea to be somewhere else . . . some thousands of kilometers somewhere else. One of those two-hundred-kilometer-long cloud-to-cloud thunderbolts could set off a shock wave of white hot plasma that would destroy anything that was too close and permanently derange the sensors of ships caught too close to the attenuated wave crest.

Fortunately, though he saw some of the telltale patches, they weren't too close at the moment. As the planet turned and his descending course brought him around, Helm caught sight of the general location he had been working, the one with the standing wave associated with its eastern side. That wave and its odd hexagonal patch were not visible from here, but a long dark oblong blotch was, and Helm let out a breath of relief as he saw that.

Gradually, the ship, still on auto, arced down toward it. Helm kept an eye on the instruments as he descended. They had cost him a lot, especially the broad-spectrum heat sensors. He had paid extra for a much higher level of sensitivity than usual. The way the clouds' pressures and temperatures varied, a few tenths of a degree either way could mean the difference between finding or missing a big pool of one of the noble gases.

The sensitivity of his instruments also meant he had leisure, while prospecting, to verify for himself what the scientists had been saying for a while, that the heat readings down in the depths of Redcrown were higher than they should be. The scientists were divided over why this was. Some said it was leftover heat from when the gas giant had tried to collapse into a star and failed. Others said there was too much loose heat flying around down there to account for this, and there was some other "independent energy source" not yet accounted for. It didn't matter much to Helm, at least insofar as the extra heat seemed to be steady all over the interior of the planet and did not turn up as hot spots that could cause trouble for him personally.

He reached out and tapped at the console, taking the ship off autopilot and slowing her descent, watching the heat sensors more closely. His main interest in the way the planet's heat behaved was in how the processes producing it affected the upper layers.

Well down inside the clouds, maybe sixty thousand kilometers in, the terrible pressure caused the helium and neon of the planet's atmosphere to begin distilling themselves out in a liquid metallic form like mercury. Down there it rained helium in great long swathes and drifts, and the helium took a lot of neon with it due to the affinity between the two gases. At least that was what the scientists claimed. No one had ever been down that far to tell for sure, but the planet did seem to act that way in terms of heat release and so forth.

The important part of all this for Helm was that deep convection seemed to affect high convection fairly directly. Where there were helium and neon in association down below, he had found there was usually argon high above, in cloud "puddles" underneath the outer cloud decks. There might be radon, too—useful enough for his purposes—but argon was what he was after. It was vital as an assembly component in one of the superchain coolant compounds for stardrive engines, and the industry never

got enough of it. Getting it pure enough to keep it from
driving up the manufacturing costs was a problem . . . but
it sometimes occurred in purities approaching ninety percent in the atmospheres of gas giants. Finding it was the
problem.

Helm had learned how . . . when it was there to be
found. Puddles could vanish without a trace and not reap-
pear for days or even months at a time. The uncomfortable
smile fell off his face as he thought how close he had been
to sucking up that puddle two days ago.

It had just better be there again today, he thought.

He had been at pains not to let Joss or anyone else know
how close to the fiscal margin he had been riding lately.
That puddle two days ago should have put him into the
black for the first time in months. Now, though, Helm was
looking at his fuel consumption curves with nearly as jaun-
diced an eye as his accounting software. If he didn't find
that puddle today, or something else worth enough to cover
his fuel costs for the next dive in, when he next docked at
Nevin, he would be stuck there. Enough would be left in
his credit account to pay for air, but not for docking fees
or fuel to leave.

If you'd stayed with the family, you wouldn't have these
problems, said one of those small carping voices in the
back of his brain. If you'd stayed with the family, you'd be
insane now, said another voice, or in the box for murder.

His father's mute and infuriating righteousness, his
mother's nagging twenty-six hours a day. . . no amount of
financial support was worth that. Of course, they would
have demanded a disproportionately large amount of his
takings. *We're a family business; it's only fair to pool
everything we've got back in. Ships are expensive, fuel is
expensive. . . .*

"Prolongation of this fuel expenditure exceeds preprogrammed spending limits for this month's budget," said
the computer.

"Oh, shut up," Helm muttered more angrily than necessary and slowed the ship's descent to almost nothing. He was almost where he wanted to be anyway.

He coaxed the ship to stationkeeping in the clouds about a hundred kilometers above his hot spot. It was indeed fairly hot, despite being empty—a dark place or "brown barge," a window into the depths that let the heat generated below escape up into nearly clear space. Down under that barge, if things were the same as he had left them, the odd six cycle standing wave whose "children" he had spotted trundling around that band was keeping a peculiar, near-hexagonal splotch in place. About a hundred and fifty to two hundred kilometers above that splotch lay a puddle of argon some fifty kilometers deep. If such a thing persisted, a miner with Helm's condensation and refrigeration equipment could collect thousands of cubic meters of argon, distill it down to a few hundred dekaliters of liquid, and unload it on Nevin for nearly three thousand Concord dollars per load.

The puddle would not persist. If it wasn't down there now or another like it somewhere nearby, Helm would be broke and stuck on that damned lump of metal, and soon enough the port authority would take *Longshot* to pay for docking fees.

Helm hissed softly, then turned his mind back to business. He checked the radar array for any sign of ships within ten thousand kilometers or so, but he saw nothing. He shifted to gravometric sensors and nudged the stationkeeping system so that the ship dropped slowly and carefully into the brown muck.

It always took a few moments for the visual perception of the downward motion to match what his stomach told him. The uppermost cloudtops of Redcrown were thinner than they looked. Shortly the clouds away on either side of him started to thicken, and it began to look as if *Longshot* was dropping down between huge walls of pale pink fog,

the color deepening all the while. The clouds were easily
five hundred kilometers away from him on either side, but
they looked closer, the featureless softness of the cloud
contributing to the illusion.

Down deep in the chasm or lift shaft through which he
was dropping, he could make out a pale patch. Helm
turned to his console and started the process of getting
ready to let down the tube.

It was officially referred to as a gravity-assisted feed,
though the only thing that gravity assisted was the positioning of the intake. It was massively weighted, but even
that was not enough to keep the intake stable against the
buffeting of the atmosphere and the planet's Coriolis
effect. The big sphere at the end of the intake contained not
only the pressure and composition sensors, but also its own
small set of stationkeeping gear that kept the intake positioned where he wanted. In reality this worked less often
than the manufacturer suggested, but it worked better than
going down there and steering it yourself.

Helm smiled slightly at the thought. Once or twice, he
had suggested to Joss that he might be willing to try such
a thing. It had mostly been a joke. Many people assumed
that because his body was tailored for heavy-gravity work,
it was also less resistant to pressure, but that wasn't true.
Helm was comfortable to about twenty-nine hundred mil-
libars without augmentation gear. When he wanted to work
deeper, he needed the same support gear as everyone else,
though everything of his was heavier-duty. Helm's e-suit
had breather gear that could handle either standard air or
one of the superliquids. Helm had modified his to use
mafluon, a hydrocarbon-based compound that shifted back
and forth between liquid and gaseous states on demand,
with extra enzyme "keys" added to the formula so that
oxygen could bond more easily to the receptors in his
blood. A day before one of these jaunts, Helm would begin
adjusting his blood chemistry toward high pressure. This

always gave him a roaring headache, but he did not have to maintain the condition for long.

He couldn't have done so anyway; it would have killed him. That was a thought he usually kept filed where he wouldn't have to look at it. Helm was careful with his physical structure and its safekeeping, that being his livelihood. Deeper motives occasionally played their part.

If this is the only thing that makes me different from them, that makes them hate and fear me, if it's my only advantage over them and also my defense, then I'll take good care of it. It's not entirely rational, but then again, "normal" people were rarely rational when it came to him.

Far down below, about two hundred kilometers down, the structure of the next cloud deck began to reveal itself in streaks and wisps and tatters of rosy cloud, deepening to brick red.

There was his hexagon, a lopsided shape, squashed at one side and dragged out at the other. Along the longest of the squashed sides, the standing wave rested.

He had found it entirely by accident, having seen a little trail of white vortices one morning as he came down to mine another area nearer the pole. It had seemed to be nothing unusual, but the next day they were gone. Sunk without a trace, he had thought.

The brown barge had taken its place. When, out of curiosity, he dipped in to have a look, there were those little vortices, marching away from the far side of the hexagon. The main pool had spawned them, and the vortices had trundled loose from their parent, risen nearly to cloudtop level, and walked all the way around the planet before sinking to rejoin the back side of the hex. What accident of convection had caused this, Helm had no idea, but when he found the argon to be plentiful, he had come back. He sank deeper, getting ready to stop the descent.

It's just looking at things, Helm thought, noticing

things, that makes the difference. He had always been a noticing sort, even as a child.

He still had bizarre memories of early childhood, in which he had been at the bottom of an atmosphere, looking up, seeing clouds above him. The bottoms of them were actually flat, and at the time, this had struck him as a wonder. Not too much later in childhood, after his parents had moved permanently to space, Helm had told other children he met on this station or that one about having been under the clouds, and they had laughed at him and told him he was making it up. Eventually he had come to believe them, until he finally broke away, got out on his own, and stood again on an inhabitable planet's surface. At the time he had been unable to understand why, looking up at that cloudy sky, his eyes burned and swam with wet pain. At the time, he had put it down to the brilliance of the sunlight.

Well, Bluefall's sun was bright enough to make most people cry, but then again, so were the prices down there.

He stopped the descent, shaking his head, wondering what had brought that particular memory up. Childhood on Lirea, it must have been—the last world his family had lived on before going to space. A beach, a genuine ocean, had rolled under those clouds, and Helm had stood there watching the ceaseless roil and shimmer of the water until the conversation of a passing mother and child had distracted him.

"Mommy, why is that boy so big?"

"Hush, dear. Don't stare."

"Why? I want to be big and strong like that!"

"No, you don't, dear. He's . . . " The rest would be whispered, but Helm had come to understand very early what those hushed words were.

He's a mutant. Bad people made him that way on purpose, to not be like normal *people, to be stronger or smarter,* unnaturally . . .

Helm had stared until his mother had appeared from somewhere, taken him by the hand, and said softly, "Come on, sweetheart. They're just jealous because they're not as smart or strong as you're going to be. People get scared when they see people who're stronger than they are who're going to be more successful in life. You just come along and hold your head up and look proud. You're special. You were made to be special. If they can't cope with that, well, that's their problem."

But it wasn't their problem; it was Helm's, and it stayed that way until he left the family. He thought he might be able to handle things right, to blend in . . . but that was an idle dream.

How do you blend in when you're a meter and two-thirds tall but mass nearly two hundred kilograms? All of it in superb physical shape, naturally, but that was no virtue. His form had been programmed into him, and he could eat like a warlion or starve himself for nearly a month, and it would make no difference. Anyway, people were just more discreet about pointing these days, since word had gotten out that Helm always had one more weapon about his person than you did. He had made sure the word got out.

He sighed and put the memories aside, gazing down at the hex. It was lively down there. The turbulence around the area where the standing wave first "broke" had more than once threatened to take his tube off. It didn't look any worse than usual, though, for which he was thankful.

Helm threw the ship into full stationkeeping mode and left her there for several minutes, letting the computer get used to the prevailing winds around her and becoming more adept at predicting eddies and gusts.

The wind speed usually hovered around a hundred meters per second here. This was not one of the horrific equatorial deeps where three hundred meters per second might be considered normal. Even now *Longshot* trembled and rocked as the computer adjusted for gusting, but she did an increasingly good job of holding herself steady and in synch with the structures below her, all of them progressing gradually eastward together.

Finally, the prediction was as good as it was going to get, and the ship steadied down. Helm uncapped the controls for the tube and started it on its way down, instructing the sensors at the sphere end to start feeding him atmospheric information right away. They did. Nothing exciting registered. The atmosphere here consisted of the usual helium-hydrogen mix, some hydrocarbons, and traces of argon and neon.

The argon traces began to increase on the graphic that Helm had instructed to process the data for him. The traces continued to increase slowly. It took nearly ten minutes for the tube to pay out to its full half-kilometer length. Helm could do it faster, but there was always the danger that a gust would pull it free.

Better to be careful, Helm thought. Not that much of a rush anyway. After all, if—

The bar graph jumped sideways—and it jumped much higher than Helm was expecting. He stared at it, suspecting a malfunction, likely enough when the tube wasn't fully deployed.

Eighty-four point six.

Such an argon purity level was abnormally high. Helm tapped the console, not that it did any good. The gauge merely wiggled and then said *eighty-eight point eight.*

Helm stared.

Eighty-nine point three.

Ninety point one.

Another sudden jump, then *ninety-three point two.*

Helm stopped the tube's descent.

Who knows how long this'll last?

The liquifiers in his cargo bay were cycled up and ready. Helm hit the feed control, and the machinery back in the cargo bay started sucking up argon as fast as it could.

The bar graph jumped again.

Ninety-four point eight.

Ninety-six point two.

Ninety-seven point one.

"Gods, it's the mother lode," Helm whispered. He had never seen argon this pure. The assay sensor was now fluttering between ninety-nine point seven and ninety-nine point eight, jittering as if even the machine couldn't believe what it was sensing. Helm certainly couldn't.

He sat still with astonishment as he started doing long division in his head. This big a load of the straight stuff, without the usual refining overheads deducted—

Gods, even the purification people on Nevin couldn't do better than ninety-nine point five, and there was something like—what was it?—a thirty percent per tenth-of-increase bounty for gas that was purer than that.

Helm had scoffed at the size of the bounty often enough, partly because he'd never heard of anyone finding gas cleaner than ninety-nine point three, and partly because such a payout would be cheating the lucky miner who brought it in when balanced against what it cost the middleman to bring "raw" gas up to the purity that the corporate buyers wanted.

The reducers were busy liquifying the gas and storing it. Helm glanced at the gauges. "Thor on a bicycle!" he muttered. The tank was three quarters full of ninety-nine point seven percent pure argon, nearly six thousand liters. At the very worst, this load is going to be worth fifty thousand Concord. At best . . .

Helm sat there shaking his head. From this load alone, he had gone from poor enough to be about to lose *Longshot* to fairly well off. Well, no independent who ran a spaceship was ever really well off. Ships could smell money a light-year off and usually demanded loudly that it be spent on them. Still, he would have enough not to

worry about fuel or food or anything for a good while. If
he could get a second load like this—

Don't be greedy, Helm thought. One like this is weird
enough. Count yourself lucky that you—

The ship's proximity alarms started howling.

Helm swallowed and whipped around in his seat to look
at the sensor array. Something big and spiky was coming
up from underneath, coming fast. He stopped the feed
from the intake and started hammering on the inner lock
controls, shutting down the middle stages of the liquidiza-
tion process, sealing off the pressure gate between the feed
tube and the liquidizers—

Wham!

Far down in the cloud, a confused shape of cylinders
and tubes was coming straight up toward him through the
hexagon, tangled in wisps and churning ribbons of cloud.
Longshot shuddered again, and this time the feed tube tore
away.

"You sons of bitches!" Helm yelled as he watched the
tube snake away down into the depths. It was gone a
second later. Five thousand Concord dollars' worth of collection hardware, gone in a second.

Helm gulped as he saw the big angular shape start drifting up toward him. The thing was massive.

He hit the comms, telling it not to hunt one frequency
but to use them all. That way, there could be no excuses
later that they hadn't heard him.

"VoidCorp vessel! VoidCorp vessel! You have been
involved in a collision, hold your position!"

He'd be damned before he asked them for help, but if
they didn't stop in a moment, he was going to need any
help he could get.

The ship ascended toward him, stately, getting bigger by
the second, not varying its course or speed. It was very
much like that big structure being built way above the
southern cloudtops. The vessel was a mass of cylinders

wound about with tubes and conduits, liquefying coils
sheathed in heat-radiation structures. It was obviously
moving on system drive, but the entire structure was dotted
round about with big attitudinal jets. It was some kind of
mobile collector. The ugly black, red, and gray VoidCorp
logo was blazoned across a large, fairly flat area of the hull.

Probably been drifting around under the clouds for
months, Helm thought as it rose toward him.

"VoidCorp vessel, veer off! Veer off!"

The collector did not change course; they kept coming
straight for him.

How did they rip off my tube? Helm wondered. Maybe
they shot something at me, but there had been no energy
discharge. That meant flechettes or spinbolos or some
other kind of solid projectile, something that wouldn't risk
igniting everything in sight.

The vessel kept coming.

Is this what poor Harry saw? I understand why he
decided to leave!

Helm told the comms console to keep putting out his
last transmission and turned his attention to the console,
hitting the attitudinal jets to push *Longshot* away. She
started to move, doing her best, but it took time to get
going. As his ship started to move sideways with the prevailing wind, the VoidCorp collector veered just a little to
cut him off and match his course.

Helm swore and tried to push his ship in the other direction, but without time to make headway against the wind,
this was almost impossible.

"Boy, I'm gonna be someone's gift to the VoidCorp
publicity people," he muttered. " 'See what we told you?
It's just not safe for independents to work this planet outside of the equatorial belts.' Bastards."

The collector continued rising, swelling beneath him,
hiding the view of the hex, concealing the red-brown view
of the further depths of Redcrown, enlarging to fill his

whole view from one side of the horizon to the other; a big
cylindrical hull coming at him, coming—

Wham!

Longshot shook all over. The system drive console went
black. Helm listened for the hiss that would mean the hull
was broached. Nothing yet, but something had smacked
him hard way in the rear where his drive was. He touched
the console in several places, hammered on it once or
twice, then the attitudinal jets flickered offline. Almost all
controls but weapons and environmental were out as well.

The huge shape below him rolled by, slowly leaving
him some sight of the planet again as it drew off windward,
sinking toward the deeper cloudbank at high speed.

Helm started checking the systems one by one. Very
little was working, and already *Longshot* was starting to
drift downward toward the pale haze of the hexagon.

"If the winds in the middle of that don't get me," he
muttered, "the pressure will."

It was already something like thirty bars outside. His
ship was rated to fifty—not that he was stupid enough to
go down that far—but "that far" wasn't really very far
away now, only a few hundred kilometers further down,
just the far side of the bottom of the hex. And he had no
way to stop himself.

He looked all around for the bastards who had done this
to him, but they were already gone. Hiding, he thought,
waiting for me to go down before they come out again.
Cowards. The sensor array could see them though, off in
the clouds below and to one side of the hex, waiting for
him to plunge on through, probably waiting to see if the
forces of the winds inside it would tear him apart.

We'll see about that, Helm thought as he turned to the
console again. The only attitudinal he had left at anything
like its usual strength was the portside upper, which would
only push him hard, right in the direction of the standing
wave—

Why not? he thought and hit the control. That should confuse them. They'll probably think that the standing wave will do me in.

They were wrong, but they were unlikely to know that . . . whereas Helm knew this wave's habits from long and curious study. The crest of one of the internal waves that kept this hex in place had already rolled by. The next one would not be along for some minutes yet. What probably looked to the Corpses like the most unpredictable and dangerous feature of the hex was actually the quietest . . . for the moment.

While he was there, he would prepare a little present for them.

Helm swung his chair around to the right where the weapons control was, and looked at it with some regret. He had taken a lot of time to build up this array of goodies. A lot of money that could have been spent on more comfortable accommodations or having a good time with the people he met had gone instead into the launchers and other hardware that backed up this console.

"Cowards," he said, "Let's see what you've got."

If he was right about the psychology, the result of what he planned could be very satisfying, and gods only knew he had had enough time to mull over the psychology of human beings.

He keyed open the routine for the cherry bombs. They were useful little toys. Each of them was about the size of a melon, a sphere full of electronics, sensor shielding, and two important moving parts. Each of them was studded with its own collection of small jets. You nominated the positions you wanted them to take up in a given cubic of space and told them when to go off . . . and the results were very impressive.

Helm had thirty of them at the moment, which was probably a lot more than he needed . . . except that now they would all come in very handy. Well, almost all of them. He kept three aboard, because you never could tell,

an old habit. *Never use all your weaponry,* his father had
said, *always save something for later.*

Now then, Helm thought. Time to look even more helpless than we really are. He killed his environmental console, the lights, the last attitudinal propulsor for a moment,
and let himself drift.

Five seconds. Ten. He touched the console.

The cherry bombs made their way out into the darkening pink day, slipped away through wisps of cloud and
were gone.

Helm turned his lights on again, turned them off,
brought up the attitudinal again, and pushed himself once
more toward the "trough" of the standing wave.

There, down low but still some ten kilometers or so
above the thrashing surface of the interior of the hex, Helm
did his best to hold *Longshot* still. The computer was complaining that it wasn't getting decent readouts from the
sensors to steady their descent. Helm let it keep doing this,
declining to correct it by hand.

"Let it have a little drift. A little more. C'mon, girl."

Nothing happened.

You're wasting fuel you could use to get up out of the
atmosphere, part of him thought. This was a vain hope,
and he knew it. Most of his atts were gone already, and
there was no way to push up out of this depth without a
full complement of them.

Still nothing happened out there.

He began, slowly, to drift downward. The atts were
giving up at last.

Come on, he thought. Bullies. Cowards. Come on!

He waited in the silence. It was hard. His entertainment
system was down, so there wasn't even any music to take
his mind off his troubles. Still, he could hear it in the growing darkness, regardless, an old familiar hallucination of
the great quiet. Helm's tastes in music were considered
odd by most of his acquaintances. He liked the somber

stuff that some of them had heard and declared either
oppressive or depressive, but Helm didn't mind. There was
something about the deep voices, the sad sounds, that
occasionally suited his mood. Now he almost thought he
could hear one piece he liked, a choral work, very old,
through the sonorous chords of which you could make out
the refrain of the first line of some old prayer.

*Out of the depths I cry unto you, O Lord; de profundiis
clamorabit Dominus Deus . . .*

Crying would do no good now. Nothing would do any
good. Only one thing was left that mattered.

They came. Out of a cloud about twenty kilometers
away, slowly they came, almost hesitantly, the way a child
approaches something dead to see if it is, really.

Helm watched and waited.

Maybe fifteen kilometers away, now. Helm's ship was
drifting downward and sideways, and it was getting harder
to judge the distance. The shape on the sensor array was
growing, and around it, scattered like many small seeds of
light, were small spherical shapes, points on a grid now
settling into its final configuration.

A few seconds more. Ten kilometers away, certainly no
more.

"Damn, that's a *really* big ship," Helm said, bracing
himself, not sure whether he was going to have a chance
to appreciate what was about to happen. Well, I'm dead
anyway. I know that.

Eight kilometers. Seven. The really big ship, looming,
snapped exactly into the center of the grid on Helm's
sensor array.

"Showtime."

Helm reached out, covered his eyes, and hit the button
on his control panel.

The cherry bombs went off, a helix of fifteen of them
surrounding the VoidCorp collector in a halo of intolerable
fire.

When the first bloom of fire had passed and the shock wave was on its way, Helm opened his eyes and dared to look. The nukes had torn the collector apart into four or five huge chunks and many, many smaller ones. Flakes of fiery metal flew briefly in all directions, and then, gracefully and rather suddenly, began to plunge down as the heavy gravitational field took hold of them. The trails of smoke and burning gas they left behind made a bizarrely handsome pattern in the turbulent atmosphere, like some great flower opening petals of fire that first curled and corkscrewed, then drooped. The biggest pieces, trailing smoke and ionizing gases behind them, plunged down way in front of Helm, drifted silently down into the hex, through it, and were gone.

As the shock wave hit and jarred him, there was a sudden outburst of light down there, some secondary explosion. The hex swallowed it, the light fading down to unbroken paleness again.

Helm imagined their screams. This gave him pleasure for only a few seconds, for now his own would soon be following them. Unless the deep gear—

No, it was useless. He had not planned to work deep today and hadn't tanked up on mafluon before he left. *I couldn't have if I wanted to. I was too damned broke! Damned Corpses!*

Helm was out of time. By the time he had started to acclimate himself, the ship would already be beginning to implode under the pressure. The suit was not equal to the forces that were about to seize him and *Longshot.*

If I live through this . . .

Unlikely, observed one part of his brain.

Yeah, but there must be somebody I could get for this. After all, how did they find me? How did they know I was here? This whole planet, they—

He stopped. Only one person had known exactly where he was coming.

Joss.

"Whoreson bastard!" Helm whispered. Gods knew how long that skinny sonofabitch had been working for them. Anyone who would sell his friends once would sell them twice. Often enough he had heard Joss complaining about the bar's profit margins. Apparently, he had found a way to cushion them a little.

If I live through this, he's going to find that there's one hard bump the cushion isn't going to help him avoid.

He looked at the barometer, which was now climbing fast as he dropped more quickly toward the hex.

If I live through this, Helm thought. *Hah.*

The prevailing wind was pushing him away from the standing wave, away from the hex, helped by an eddy that was pushing him a little north of it as well. Helm reached out to the portion of the console that controlled his system drive, and keyed in the sequence which would begin the process of unlocking it. He had heard stories that suggested the ignition of hydrogen under pressure was far more effective than when it was "light." If bringing his damaged system back online caused any sort of spark along the hull, he would have a chance to test that theory for himself.

One last glance around revealed clouds, too many above him, darkening. Once again, that sight spurred a memory. Clouds above him, beautiful billowing shapes glowing in the clear air, a most abnormal view.

. . . except to a very small child, looking up from the bottom of a blue ocean of air, seeing them sail by.

"All right," he said softly and unlocked the drive. His finger poised above the control for a moment, his hand shaking.

Do it now.

He touched the control.

Nothing.

He touched it again, harder this time. *Drive Failure,*

said the readout.

"Damn," Helm whispered, shocked and gravely disappointed. He had expected to be dead by now.

Soon enough he would be. *Longshot* could not last much longer. The planet was pulling him in, pulling him down. Already the ship was creaking around him, groaning under the strain, and the darkness outside the pilot's bubble was rapidly becoming total. That sound, that darkness, would be the last thing he would hear and see. The bubble would shatter and let in the deadly atmosphere, and much worse, the pressure. He would be crushed before the poisonous fumes had the chance to kill him. Compressed to a small spherical lump, he and the ship would be sucked down into the liquid-metallic morass of Redcrown's innards.

Helm swallowed. There was no chance of rescue. The world was dark brown, fading to black, and full of the sound of groaning, getting louder.

"Damned if I'm going to let the universe dictate when I die," Helm muttered.

He turned his attention to his command console one last time. He was carrying a considerable pile of weaponry still. His engines might not aid him, but there were those last few cherry bombs. Helm opened the safety routines in the computer and began priming them, one after another.

"This action exceeds preprogrammed spending limits for this month's budget," said the computer.

"Oh, shut up," Helm said. Go for broke. He had heard that somewhere a long time ago.

The sensor array began howling at him again.

"Oh, now what!" Helm shouted. "Can't a man die in peace? This isn't fair!" He cast his eyes sidewise to look at the array's display.

Something big was coming up from underneath. He stared, now not so much disbelieving as simply indignant.

"What, you people again?" he shouted. "How many of

you are there? Well, come on," Helm growled, and turned his attention back to the arming routines. "I can take you with me too, maybe. Don't rush, I need another minute or so here."

All the same, he hurried. If he didn't have the bombs set right, when that thing hit him, the nukes wouldn't do any good. Helm busied himself, intent on dying right this time, at least. Third time pays for all.

The sensor array howled in protest. Helm's head finally snapped around as, over the moaning of the ship's suffering framework, the array produced a strange strangled hooting noise, an alarm he had never heard before.

Damned machinery, he thought, count on it to find one more way to fail at a crucial moment. If I were going to live past thirty seconds from now I would hunt down these people's warranty representative and shove this hardware up his—

A bloom of light suddenly covered the array's entire display, and the object was still more than a kilometer below him.

There's nothing that big on this planet, Helm thought in growing astonishment. What the—

Its shape was not normal. It bloomed up out of the cloud underneath him, and now the heat sensor had begun yelling as well, complaining about a localized heat source very close, but too warm for ambient, much too warm—

There was no light to see by out there, and his own lights were gone. That made the faint glow, and the sight of billowing vapor around him, even more bizarre.

What is this, the pressure? Helm wondered, some kind of hallucination? Well, I'm not going to die that way. The bombs are ready.

He reached out—

Thud!

The whole ship shook, not hard, though the noise had been considerable. Shocked, Helm waited again for the

sound of springing seams, of explosive decompression
beginning, the *whoomf* that would be the last sound he
would ever hear, but it did not come.

Whatever had hit him, it had hit him from underneath,
and it was pushing him upwards.

He could see nothing outside, but the barometer was
cycling backwards, entirely too fast.

"What in the—"

Helm swallowed and started to increase the cabin pressure as fast as he could. If he didn't, he was going to have
the bends shortly, on top of everything else. He was scared
to do this too, since it could spring a seam from inside
rather than have one pushed in from outside.

No choice, though, he thought, while the accounting
program started complaining, with reason, about his air
utilization. Repressurizing the ship was using all the
available oxygen. *Longshot* had better have enough power
to get back to Nevin pretty quick.

He turned his attention to the attitudinal jets. One was
still working, the one he had used to get him over by the
standing wave. He reached out to hit the control . . . and
stopped once more, as something pale and vague as a
cloud slipped past the lower edge of the pilot's bubble in
a graceful drift, almost like a fold of billowing fabric.

Helm stared, and his hand dropped back. That was no
cloud. Whatever it was had structure, though it was thin as
gossamer and hard to see against the now-paling background of Redcrown's atmosphere. It wavered like weed
in water, many-fronded and delicate, but consolidating into
a larger, more solid looking part. A tentacle? A limb? Helm
sat there and started to shake as the cloud outside paled,
then started with great suddenness to darken off to one
side.

Cloudtops. Space coming—

He reached out for the control of the remaining attitudinal jet again. A shimmer of darkness went across the

gracefully waving thing that now clung briefly to the outside of the pilot's bubble. Darkness concentrated for a
moment in an irregular patch. This shimmering blot of
shadow deepened to a glossy blackness with something in
it . . . .a hint of light.

An eye. Something was looking at him.

Helm started to feel foolish, sitting there with his mouth
open in astonishment. He closed it, raised his other hand,
and waved "hello."

The dimness went jet black, the light flaring out of it,
then a billow of paleness, like silk on the wind . . . and a
last very sudden burst of acceleration. Something had
kicked Helm up, hard. A moment later he was looking
down at cloudtops. He kicked in the attitudinal immediately, pushing *Longshot* toward the almost invisible spark
of Nevin passing by overhead. He turned and stared down
again at what he could see immediately below him.

Nothing, no silken-curtain billow, no seeing "eye" . . .

Helm turned back to the console and concentrated on
getting himself back to Nevin. He managed to bring the
system drive back online, though only at half power . . .
and it obviously wasn't going to last long. There was going
to be a lot to do when he landed, repairs and unloading his
cargo for starters.

"At least I still have that," he sighed.

Helm immersed himself almost gratefully in damage
assessment and attention to his cabin pressure for the next
hour or so, while Nevin swam closer and he prepared for
docking. Ideally, I ought to stay in here for three or four
hours more to let the blood nitrogen equalize. Let's see
now, six thousand liters at, how much . . . ?

But the thought kept coming back. That thoughtful,
assessing darkness, and all those rumors about big things
appearing out of the deep cloud and vanishing away, here
and gone again. The assumption had always been that
these were some new collector of VoidCorps's. Now,

though, Helm had other ideas.

Did my dropping that collector into that cloud somehow alert whatever was down there, so that it came up to see what was going on?

Nevin's scarred surface was growing beneath him now. Helm looked down and thought about how Joss had passed him one of those rumors. Nice of him, but it's not going to help him now.

Helm got up and went back to the weapons locker for the biggest and nastiest of his charge pistols.

* * * * *

He locked *Longshot* in the docks for medium-term bond. Repairs and unloading could wait. A lot of people saw the short, broad figure making his way purposefully along the corridors and made themselves scarce. Word traveled, apparently. By the time Helm got to Joss's, there was no one in the corridors outside and all the tables there deserted.

He stepped into the Outside Inn and found the night guy, Micah, scrubbing the floor. This was unusual, since it was local day. Helm walked softly up to Micah and said, "Where's Joss?"

Micah looked up and said, "You're late."

"For what?"

"Killing him," Micah said, "assuming that's why you're here, since you're so obviously carrying. They were about to arrest him when someone else got to him first. 'Terminated his contract.' "

Helm stared. "His contract?"

"Joss was a VoidCorp Employee, it seems," said Micah with distaste. "Fed them information on a regular basis, but it seems he fed them some wrong information or something. Nevin private security was about to take him into 'protective custody' yesterday evening. They got word that something was going down, I guess, but they left a little late."

"Who did it?" Helm said.

Micah scrubbed harder and said, "Getting so you can't trust anybody these days. Remember the lady who shot the chummy the other night, the really gorgeous one from Bluefall? That one. Another Corps op, she was. Came in, ordered a drink, chatted with Joss, then drilled him." He shook his head, frowning. "She took herself away in a hurry and hasn't been seen since. This place just isn't safe no more."

Helm blinked at that news. He had a drink, for which Micah for some reason refused to let him pay, and then he made his way back to *Longshot* to get her repairs started and unload his cargo as quickly as possible.

This looks like a good time to leave, Helm thought. Regardless of other associated events, he suspected there was only one way that VoidCorp would view this incident. Some mutant had destroyed one of their ships. His life would be worth very little around here if he didn't leave very soon.

Well, I was planning that anyway, Helm thought. Now, though, there was an additional concern. He wouldn't go anywhere without becoming much better armed than he had been. This last load of argon would make that easy. In the meantime, he would take himself somewhere that the Company was a little less firmly entrenched, somewhere further out in the Verge, and a little quieter. Corrivale, maybe. He would add some more guns to *Longshot*, replenish his cherry bombs, and get someone to rip out that damned accounting program.

It would be a long time before he could look at Redcrown's clouds, or those of any other gas giant, without thinking of pale silk billowing, and darkness that had looked at him, silent, from out of the depths . . .

About the Author

Diane Duane was born in Manhattan in 1952, the Year of the Dragon. She was raised on Long Island in the New York City suburbs. She wrote her first novel when she was eight, illustrating it herself in crayon. After many years, wrote another: *The Door into Fire* published by Dell Books in 1979.

There have been thirty more since then. Five of these were from *New York Times* best-selling *STAR TREK* novels. She wrote a very popular "Wizard" series of young adult fantasies published by Delacorte/Dell. Duane now lives with her husband in County Wicklow in Ireland, along with four cats and several seriously overworked computers. In her spare time, Duane travels (Switzerland being a favorite destination), studies German, dabbles in astronomy, and spends time weeding the garden.

Duane is the author of the first STAR*DRIVE series, the Harbinger Trilogy: *Starrise at Corrivale, Storm at Eldala,* and *Nightfall at Algemron* (available April 2000).

Glossary

Aanghel Empire – The ruling "crime family" of the Corrivale system.

Aegis – A G2 yellow star. The Metropolitan Center of the Verge.

Alaundril – The third moon of Sperous in the Tendril system.

Aleerin – see mechalus.

Algemron – A G class yellow star. Its two inhabited worlds, Alitar and Galvin, are currently at war.

Alitar – The fourth planet of the Algemron system, currently at war with Galvin.

Anacortes – A first world of the Orion League.

arc gun – A weapon that uses a bult-in, low-powered laser to ionize the air between the weapon and its target, then "charging" this ionized trail with a massive electric bolt.

Arist – The third and largest of Platon's moons. Despite its frigid temperatures and thin atmosphere, it is the only habitable world of the Hammer's Star system other than Spes.

Austrin-Ontis Unlimited – A corporate stellar nation that is best known as the strongest arms dealer in the Stellar Ring. Most Austrin-Ontis citizens view themselves as strong individualists with a deep sense of altruism.

Banisese II – A first world in Concord Taurus.

beishen – A type of clothing common among sesheyans made of a loose-fitting coat of leather with long vents through which the sesheyan's wings and tail can extend for flight.

Big Slate – A mountain chain on Alitar. In 2498, this was the site of a major offensive in the ongoing struggle between the Alitarans and the Galvinite occupied forces.

Bluefall – Capital planet of the Aegis system. Ruled by the Regency government.

Borealis Republic – A stellar nation whose citizens are the best educated in known space. Over half of the citizens of the Republic are clones.

Brallis – A second world of the Thuldan Empire near the border of Concord Taurus.

Builder – A segment of fraal society that believes in integration with other species and cultures.

Catalog – VoidCorp's capital planet.

charge weapon - A firearm in which an electric firing pin ignites a chemical explosive into a white-hot plasma propellant, thus expelling a cerametallic slug at extremely high velocity.

chig'tanth – A weren term meaning "battle-rage."

Ch'Nak – The T'sa term for a deity.

Ch'Nalism – The most common t'sa religion. Ch'Nalites believe in a single, all-powerful creator who provides a guardian deity for every sentient creature.

chuurkhna – A deadly melee weapon of ancient weren design. The chuurkhna resembles a huge, four-pronged battle axe with a haft about a-meter-and-a-half long; its blade is large and heavy, intended for chopping rather than thrusting.

Colonial Diocese – The Hatire government on Grith.

Concord – see Galactic Concord.

Concord Administrator – An official of the Galactic Concord, Administrators have the power of judge, jury, and executioner.

Concord Taurus – A Concord Neutrality in Old Space.

corpses – A derogatory term for VoidCorp Employees.

Corrivale - An F2 yellow-white star. Also the name of the system.

Cureyfi the Father of Stars - A sesheyan deity.

cutter – A small, lightly armed military patrol craft.

Cyko riots – A series of muliplanetary riots that rocked the Stellar Ring from 2314-15. Although it is suspected that the "demonstrations" were instigated by the cyktoteks, many sentients with cybernetic implants were involved.

cytoteks – A radical religious cult that views biology as corrupt and technology as pure. Unfortunately, a significant number of the cykoteks have so enhanced their nervous system that it has driven them insane.

deflection inducer – A device that creates belts of gravitational force to deflect physical projectiles and bend beam weapons.

det'sya – A system of ritual tattoos that proclaim a t'sa's clan, profession, and personal tastes.

Diamond Point - The capital of Grith.

Dolthan VI – A gas giant of the Strome system.

drivespace - A dimension in which gravity signals propagate, and into which starships enter through use of the stardrive, thus enabling movement of a ship from one point in space to another in only 121 hours.

Drounli the Provider - A sesheyan deity.

duraplas – Plastic that has been strengthened at the molecular level, often allowing for further modifications such as transparency, malleability, etc.

durasteel - Steel that has been strengthened at the molecular level.

Employee – The official title of all VoidCorp citizens.

erfani glass – A style of glass manufactured on Grith.

e-suit – An environment suit intended to keep the wearer safe from vacuum, extreme temperatures, and radiation.

et ghajh ic – A Fraal term for psychometry.

fliidrun – A meditation ritual practiced among some elements of Aleerin society. The subject is placed in an isolation chamber for four days, whereupon he or she is isolated from all electromagnatic radiation.

Flotsam – The only moon of Jetsam.

fraal – A non-Terran sentient species that was the first to make contact with humanity. Fraal are slender humanoids, many of whom are proficient mindwalkers.

fraal-na kilach – "The People of the Crossing." Those fraal who entered the Sol system thousands of years ago whose descendants eventually established contact with humanity.

gailghe - Goggles worn by sesheyans to protect their sensitive eyes from bright light.

Galactic Concord – The thirteenth stellar nation. Formed by the Treaty of Concord, Concord law and administration rule in the Verge, which is delegated Open Space.

Galactic Standard – The *lingua franca* of known space.

Galsworth Belt – The outermost asteroid belt in the Cambria system.

Galvin – The third planet of the Algemron system, currently at war with Alitar.

gangleleap – A mountain-dwelling herbivore of Tarshad.

Glassmaker – The name given to a long-vanished race or nation of advanced species.

gravity induction - A process whereby a cyclotron accelerates particles to near-light speeds, thereby creating gravitons between the particle and the surrounding mass. This process can be adjusted and redirected, thus allowing the force of gravity to be overcome. Most vehicles in the twenty-sixth century use a gravity induction engines.

Grid – An interstellar computer network.

gridpilot – Anyone proficient in the use of the Grid.

Grith - A moon of Hydrocus and the only habitable world in the Corrivale system.

Hammer's Star – A yellow G5 star. The outermost Concord outpost in the Verge.

Hanover Station – A starport on Penates.

Hatire Community – A theocratic stellar nation founded upon the principles of the Hatire Faith.

Hatire·Faith – A religion based upon the worship of the Cosimir, an alien deity which the Hatire have adopted as their own. Hatire have a passionate dislike for advanced technology, especially the alteration of the human body with cybernetic implants.

Hegel – The second largest continent on Spes.

High Mojave – The only inhabited world of the Mantebron system. Also the site of the best-preserved Glassmaker ruins.

Hurricane – A planet of the Ptolemy system.

Iphus - A planet of the Corrivale system.

Jaeger – Capital planet of the Orion League.

Jetsam – The outermost planet of the Aegis system.

Klimaar vach – A litany of the Vis Jiridiv.

K'san Ch'Nak – The creator of the T'sa religion, Ch'Nalism.

lanth cell – The standard lanthanide battery used to power most small electronic equipment and firearms.

Lightning Nebula – An unexplored region of space beyond Hammer's Star.

Lison – The fourth planet of the Oberon system.

Lilith – The fifth moon of Dolthan.

Lirea – A pristine second world in the outer fringes of Austrin-Ontis Unlimited.

Lucullus – A binary star system in the Verge, infamous for its population of pirates, smugglers, outlaws, and general miscreants.

Lu Harred Kal – A fraal city-ship populated by Wanderers.

Mantebron – An extremely old G2 star near the outer edge of the Verge that is approaching its red dwarf stage.

mass cannon - A cannon that fires a ripple of intense gravity waves, striking its target like a massive physical blow.

mass reactor - The primary power source of a stardrive. The reactor collects, stores, and processes dark matter, thus producing massive amounts of energy.

mechalus – The most common term used for the aleerins, a sentient humanoid species that has achieved an almost flawless symbiotic relationship with biomechanical technology, so much so that all mechalus are actually born with varying cybernetic systems.

Multiplex Cow – The name given to a computer virus that was sent into the Galvinite Grid by a group of Alitarin freedom-fighters.

Naigyun VII – A second world in Starmech Collective whose ecosystem was almost completely destroyed during the Second Galactic War.

Negationists – A splinter group of radical pacifists among the mechalus who believe that the only way to rid themselves of all violent tendencies is to completely abandon the biological aspects of their nature.

Nevin – A moon of Redcrown. The site of extensive mining excavations.

Oberon – A binary star system in the Verge.

Old Space – The heavily populated area of explored space in which the stellar nations are located.

Olympus – Capital city of High Mojave.

Orion League – A heterogeneous stellar nation founded on the principles of freedom and equal rights for all sentients.

Orlamism – A religion based upon the belief that drivespace is true reality or, as the Orlamu call it, "the Divine Unconscious."

Orlamu Theocracy – A theocratic stellar nation founded on the principles of Orlamism.

Outside Inn – A drinking establishment on Nevin.

Penates – An inhabited planet of the Lucullus system populated primarily by pirates and criminals.

Platon – A gas giant of the Hammer's Star system.

Ptolemy – A K class star in the Verge.

Pyritix Corporation – A large corporation based in the Orion League that has expanded its mining and manufacturing operations into a few Verge systems.

Redcrown – A gas giant of the Aegis system.

render rifle – A weapon that projects a graviton beam, which creates destructive tidal attractions within the target's structure.

Revik asteroid belt – The innermost of Hammer Star's two asteroid belts.

Rigunmor Star Consortium – A stellar nation founded on the principles of free trade and profit.

ris – A Weren term for open, formally declared warfare.

Rladh – One of the clans of weren settlers on Spes.

sesheyan – A bipedal sentient species possessing long, bulbous heads, large ears, and eight light-sensitive eyes. Most sesheyans are about 1.7 meters tall and have two leathery wings that span between 2.5 - 4 meters. Sheya, the sesheyan homeworld, has been subjugated by VoidCorp. However, a substantial population of "free sesheyans" live on Grith.

skybike – Also known as a sky cycle, any one or two man vehicle capable of aerial or ground flight through use of a gravity induction engine.

sparks – A derogatory term for the mechalus.

Sperous – The second planet of the Tendril system.

Spes – The innermost planet of the Hammer's Star system with a current population of 300,000 sentients.

Standard – see Galactic Standard.

stardrive – By combining a mass reactor with gravity induction technology, the stardrive engine opens a singularity in space, thus allowing interstellar travel in a mere 121 hours.

starfall – The term used to describe a ship entering drivespace.

starrise – The term used to describe a ship leaving drivespace.

Starmech Collective – A corporate stellar nation famed for its production of high technology.

stellar nation – Any of the thirteen independent nations of the Stellar Ring. They are: Austrin-Ontis Unlimited, the Borealis Republic, the Hatire Community, Insight, Nariac Domain, the Orion League, the Orlamu Theocracy, the Rigunmor Star Consortium, StarMech Collective, the Thuldan Empire, the Union of Soil, VoidCorp, and the Galactic Concord.

Strome – A class M red star in the Verge.

stutter gun – A nonlethal weapon which uses blasts of
compressed air that can render targets unconscious
without causing serious harm.

Tarshad – A first world in the Orion League.

Teminin – A city on Alitar.

Tendril – An F1 blue star.

Thuldan Empire – A militaristic, fiercely patriotic stellar
nation that considers the unity of humanity under the
Thuldan banner its manifest destiny.

Treaty of Concord – The treaty that ended the Second
Galactic War and formed the Galactic Concord.

Verge, the – A frontier region of space originally colonized
by the stellar nations that was cut off from Old
Space during the Second Galactic War.

Vis Jiridiv – A small martial order of philosophers among
the fraal, most prevalent among the Wanderers.

Vis Orishak – A small martial order of philosophers among
the fraal, most prevalent among the Builders.

VoidCorp – A corporate stellar nation. Citizens are referred
to as Employees and all have an assigned number.

warlion – An elite corps of engineered mutants who served
the Thuldan Empire during the Second Galactic War.

Wanderer - 1.) *fraal*: A term used to describe a segment of
    fraal culture that prefers life aboard their wandering
    city-ships rather than settling down to mingle with
    other species. 2.) *sesheyan*: see Weyshe the
    Wanderer.

werewisp – An often aggressive bioelectric creature of High
    Mojave.

Weyshe the Wanderer - A sesheyan diety.

Yellow Pan – An inland sea of Alitar.

ylem – A term applied to theoretical matter that existed
    before the Big Bang.

On the Verge
Roland J. Green

Danger and intrigue explode in the Verge as Arist, a frozen world on the borders of known space, erupts into a war between weren and human colonists. When Concord Marines charge in to prevent the conflict from escalating off-world, but they soon discover that even darker forces are at work on Arist.

Starfall
Edited by Martin H. Greenberg

Contributors include Diane Duane, Kristine Kathryn Rusch, Robert Silverberg and Karen Haber, Dean Wesley Smith, and Michael A. Stackpole. A collection of short stories detailing the adventure, the mystery, and the unending wonder in the Verge!

Zero Point
Richard Baker

Peter Sokolov, a bounty hunter and cybernetic killer for hire, is caught up in a deadly struggle for power and supremacy in the black abyss between the stars.
Available June 1999.

NOVELS

Diane Duane's Harbinger Trilogy

"Duane is tops in the high adventure business..."
—Publishers Weekly

STARRISE AT CORRIVALE
VOLUME ONE

Gabriel Connor is up against it. Expelled from the Concord Marines and exiled in disgrace, the Concord offers him one last chance to redeem himself. All it involves is gambling his life in a vicious game of death.

STORM AT ELDALA
VOLUME TWO

Gabriel and Enda stumble onto dark forces that may destroy a newfound civilization before moving into the worlds of the Verge. Only their deaths seem likely to avert the disaster about to flood into civilized space—until an astonishing revelation from out of the depths of time makes the prospect of survival even more terrible than a clean death.

NIGHTFALL AT ALGEMRON
VOLUME THREE

The stunning conclusion to the Harbinger Trilogy brings Gabriel and Enda to a war-ravaged world whose only hope for salvation may be a discovery out of the depths of time.

Available April 2000

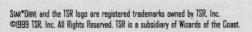

First in the past.
First in the future.

NO LIMITS

The ALTERNITY® roleplaying game is a science fiction experience like no other. The flexible skill-based mechanics handle any science fiction setting with ease. Comprehensive rules deal with high technology, aliens, faster-than-light travel, and all the mainstays of science fiction. Create and adventure in any science fiction setting, from your favorites in television and movies to your own unique worlds.

You can download a **FREE** copy of the ALTERNITY Fast-Play rules, complete with a beginning adventure. See our web site at **www.tsr.com** for more information.

ALTERNITY
Science Fiction Roleplaying Game

Player's Handbook
TSR #02800
ISBN #0-7869-0728-2

Gamemaster Guide
TSR #02801
ISBN #0-7869-0729-0

STAR*DRIVE™ Campaign Setting
TSR #02802
ISBN #0-7869-0738-X

THE FUTURE IS NOW